KILL OR BE KILLED

KILL OR BE KILLED

TEAM SAVAGE™ BOOK ONE

MICHAEL TODD

MICHAEL ANDERLE

A Michael Anderle Production

LMBPN Publishing
PMB 196, 2540 South Maryland Pkwy
Las Vegas, NV 89109

First US edition, October 2019
Version 1.01, March 2021
(Previously published as a part of SAVAGE REBORN)

ebook ISBN: 978-1-64202-497-5
Print ISBN: 978-1-64202-498-2

THE KILL OR BE KILLED TEAM

Thanks to our Beta Readers

John Ashmore, Charles Tillman, Crystal Wren, Kelly O'Donnell, John Ashmore, Nicole Emens, Robert Brooks, and James Caplan

Thanks to our JIT Readers

Diane L. Smith
Dorothy Lloyd
James Caplan
Jeff Eaton
John Ashmore
Kelly O'Donnell
Micky Cocker
Paul Westman
Peter Manis
Robert Brooks

Editor

The Skyhunter Editing Team

DEDICATION

To Family, Friends and
Those Who Love
to Read.
May We All Enjoy Grace
to Live the Life We Are
Called.

CHAPTER ONE

Johnson peered around the corner of the building, keeping most of his body hidden as he made sure the area was clear. He breathed deeply, a calming exercise, and smelled a mixture of tar and rancid water. With the kind of heat this place absorbed during the day, heat-vision was useless. That meant they had to go in using only night vision, which covered the whole place with an eerie green glow. It seemed like they were on another planet.

"It makes you wonder why they don't send us in with suits of armor," Lee muttered into his comms and covered their left flank as the team of ten men moved deeper into the small village.

"This is a covert operation," Johnson hissed through his mic. "Something that nobody but us, our target, and the Lord Almighty can know about. Clanking around in those fucking Ironman suits would get us noticed fast, and this whole thing would blow up—literally and figuratively. And speaking of covert operations, what part of radio silence don't you understand?"

He turned to glare at Lee, who shrugged but kept himself off the comm lines. With the kind of encryption that these things could work with, being overheard was practically impossible. Still, the fact remained that someone might hear them, even on the short-range comms. Even if they didn't hear what was said, they might recognize military-grade encryption if they saw it and the jig would be up.

That said, he wished they had come out there with at least some of the heavy hitters the Army had available these days. Their own suits were far from defenseless, with full helmets that were resistant to gunfire and ceramic plates in the rest of their armor that made it similarly impervious to most handguns. There was even HUD tech in their helmets that usually only came with the full suits of armor. The designers came up with all kinds of hybrids these days.

Which made him wonder why the fuck they hadn't come up with something that allowed them to run these missions using some kind of stealth suit of armor instead of these heavy as fuck ceramic-plate alternatives.

Johnson looked around and noted that no other people were out. Nightfall was essentially an announcement for these people to lie low and wait for the sun to come up again. The small town was stuck in the Middle Ages, although such luxuries as electricity and running water, as well as something as simple as guns, were known and used. It was, however, obvious from the way their roofs were covered with solar panels and the handful of windmills that generated electricity, that they were very sparing in the use of the modern amenities.

He held a hand up and stopped to listen to the silence. It was thick with the threat of hidden danger. He wasn't sure about the rituals these people followed, but the fact that they were all hidden inside their homes was a very good thing since keeping collateral damage low was something of a priority.

At the same time, it could also be very bad. He didn't like how quiet the place was. According to the reports, there was very little night-life there, but there should have been some noise—a pot clanging inside a hidden kitchen, the low murmur of conversation...something.

But the silence was deafening. He didn't even hear the low sawing of crickets in the underbrush. Not that he would, considering that they were paces away from the desert, but hey, at least it would help to hear anything other than their boots.

Something wasn't right. Johnson turned and gestured to Red Three, raised three fingers, and pointed to the top of a nearby building.

Jordi nodded and used a ladder quickly to hike up to the top of the building as the rest of the team moved in. Most of the structures were erected old-style. They were mostly squat, one-story buildings that had access to a rooftop covered with either solar panels or electric matting. Either way, the top of one of the buildings was more than enough to give the marksman a good vantage point over the rest of the village. Even better, he was the squad's long-distance engagement expert and packed a massive fifty-cal sniper rifle.

Jordi pinged him the all-clear. Johnson returned a

checkmark to his HUD and indicated for them to keep moving.

He didn't feel right about this. It was too easy. They were being drawn into the village, which made it all too likely that this was a trap.

Warily, he looked around and kept his rifle ready as he raised his hand. He held up three fingers and then a closed fist, then two fingers and pointed to his left. Three of the men pulled away and returned to their starting location. Two more moved to the left, using the houses as cover. This left him with only three men to help find the target. It was a risky move but damned if he would walk all his men into a trap.

"What is this place?" Lee asked and looked around as he spoke off comms. "And why the fuck would anyone want to hide out here?"

"I'm not sure how you pronounce it in the local language," Johnson said. "But it translates to sandpit. And I think the reason why they want to hide out here is because it's isolated."

The man grunted something and ended the conversation. The four men eased through the village and kept their movements as discreet as they could while they approached one of the houses at the center.

Johnson raised his hand again and his team stopped and looked around. Lights were off both up and down the entire street. It was so dark that his senses tingled. In all his years doing night ops, it was never this dark in any neighborhood in any town or city. There was always some insomniac who counted the hours before the dawn or someone awake, trying to read or get some chores done.

His gaze locked on the houses on either side of the one they headed toward. "Nope," he stated crisply and shook his head. "I'm calling it. We're out of here."

"The house is right there," Lee protested.

"The target's not there," Johnson said. "This is a trap, and we're bugging out." He turned when he heard gunshots from the other side of the village where the remainder of their team had been left behind. They'd heard the communications, all right.

"Insurgents are everywhere," Jordi called over the comms. The boy's voice was low and controlled, but Johnson could hear the panic behind his words. "They were waiting for us just outside the village center. Bug out, squad leader. The east side is covered by bogeys!"

Johnson signaled for his men to move east but to keep to the shadows. He wasn't sure if their movements were being individually tracked or if the enemy had waited for them to get deeper into the village before they attacked. Either way, he would be damned before he left any member of his team behind. He raised his rifle and narrowed his eyes as a group of men converged on the building where Jordi perched.

Johnson snarled, raised his weapon, and opened fire in two tight, three-round bursts. "Red Three, mark the entrance of the building." The thunder of heavy ordinance shattered the night and one of the five combatants dropped with barely a grunt. Another man staggered, sagged against the wall, and clutched his leg. Damn good shooting, Johnson acknowledged and grinned wolfishly. A couple more men fell as the heavy fifty-cal fired and punched through their body armor like it was tissue paper.

"Appreciate the assist, Squad Leader. Bugging out now," Jordi shouted and jumped off the edge of the building to drop smoothly to the ground.

Movement out of the corner of his eye drew Johnson's attention. A group of men emerged from a building in heavy body armor, toting outdated assault rifles. He swung his weapon around and gestured for his men to take cover as he opened fire. Time slowed to a crawl. They were outnumbered and outgunned, but the only thing that mattered to him was to get the rest of his men out.

He scanned the area, tugged a grenade from his pouch, and tossed it through a window of the building the men had exited. Loud shouts issued from inside in the few seconds before the explosion.

"Squad on the perimeter, pull away from the village and give us some cover fire," Johnson snapped into his comms. He indicated for the three men with him to step into the building and clear it as he hid behind one of the walls.

Bullets sprayed around him, but from the haphazard fire spread between him and the three men who entered the building, he could tell that there wasn't much in the way of leadership behind this ambush. They had been prepared to attack, judging by the lack of civilians, but they were still not sure what to do once the trap had closed. He guessed they had assumed that their superior numbers and better positions would enable them to overcome their lack of leadership.

"Roger that, Squad Leader. Stay safe in there," one of the men on the perimeter called. It was a risk to split their forces like this, but those inside the village knew that they wouldn't make it out if someone didn't cover their retreat.

Considering how deep in the black-ops book this operation was, they had nobody to count on but themselves.

"House is clear. Get your ass in here!" Lee called from inside.

Two men peered out of the windows, eliminated a couple of insurgents, and gave Johnson a chance to clear the wall he hid behind before he barreled through the window he'd thrown the grenade through only moments before. Jagged glass dug into his shoulder pads, but he was inside and now behind an interior wall. He moved more out of instinct than anything else. His heart hammered in his chest, which made it difficult to think. The other members of his team assumed defensive positions.

"We need a way out of here, Red Team," Johnson said and tried to keep his voice steady as he reloaded his weapon quickly. His hands trembled but he pushed the weakness aside. He needed to be at the top of his game right now—for his team if not for himself.

Jordi connected his HUD vision to Johnson's. "We see an opening on the west side of the village, Squad Leader."

Johnson now had a good view of the highway that split the village in half. A group of men was crossing it, but there was a slight opening he thought the rest of his team could slip through. "Roger that, Red Three," he said and glanced at his small team. "We need to make it to an opening on the west side of the village. We'll break for it as quickly as we can, and we need to keep on pushing, so don't—"

"Grenade!"

He wasn't sure who made the call, but there was no disputing the fact that one of those little knobby orbs of death had dropped from a hatch at the top of the building. They had been in a hurry and hadn't cleared the roof.

"Shit!" Johnson yelled as the hatch closed again. The three men deeper in the building scrambled to move as far away from the ordnance as possible. Unfortunately, they didn't make it far enough.

Johnson ducked and flinched at the roar of the explosion, which seemed to last longer than it should have. The air smelled of death and the noise-filters in his helmet hadn't kicked in fast enough, which left his ears ringing. He peered into the smoky mess that remained and tried to determine the consequences.

Two of the men hadn't made it away in time. Shrapnel had ripped through not only their armor but their helmets too. The vital signs feeding directly into his helmet had flatlined. They were gone.

There was still one heartbeat, though. Lee lay on the ground. He growled with the effort as he dragged himself to where his assault rifle had landed after it had been torn from his grasp. Johnson knelt beside the man and made a cursory examination—not easy while he struggled to move. He wasn't a doctor, but some training in first aid helped. Lee actually looked like he had avoided the brunt of the explosion with most of his armor intact, except for his right leg. It had almost completely shattered and the lower half of the limb hung on by what looked like the barest of muscle fibers. It didn't bleed that badly, though, which indicated that maybe the wound hadn't severed any arteries. Or maybe the shrapnel was still in there and suppressed the bleeding.

"Fuck!" Johnson exclaimed and put his hands on Lee's

shoulders to force him to a halt. "You need to stay with me, you got that, Red Seven?"

"Need to get to my rifle, sir..." Lee's voice sounded distant like he was half asleep. "Can't...leave any traces behind..."

"Your rifle's done for, Seven. Listen to me and you listen good, because I'll get your dumb ass out of here whether you like it or not," Johnson shouted over the ringing in his ears. "You take this..." He handed the man his own assault rifle and dragged Lee to a spot where he would be out of sight of anyone outside. "You cover that door and make sure nobody shoots me from behind while I clear the roof, do you understand me?"

The injured man looked blankly at him for a moment but after a few seconds, he focused his attention and nodded. He gripped the rifle firmly. Lee was a fine soldier despite being a chatty Cathy at heart. Sometimes, all you needed was to be reminded what your priorities were.

Lee steeled himself, avoided looking at his mangled leg, and aimed the rifle at the door. "Will do, Sarge," he said, his voice shaking gently.

Johnson nodded as he tugged his sidearm from the holster at his hip. He hurried to where the hatch opened to the roof. While he wasn't sure that the small wooden stepladder would take his weight, there really was no other option.

He had almost reached the top when the hatch opened and one of the insurgents peered through the aperture to see if the room had been cleared by the grenade.

Definitely not professional soldiers, Johnson mused as he drew the combat knife coldly from his hip, gripped it in a backhand, and stabbed it into the man's throat. A sudden burst of bright red blood coated the face of his helmet. He twisted the blade and used the movement to hook the man and drag him down through the hatch. His pistol aimed at the opening, he waited until a couple more faces came into view. He pulled the trigger and the almost negligible kick of the pistol punched back into his hand as both faces disappeared in a spray of red. They fell back and shouts erupted on the roof as he hauled himself through the hole.

Three men awaited him. He'd had extensive training for situations like this, and for the first time since the firefight had started, Johnson felt calm and collected. Ice filled his veins, and he knew exactly what he needed to do.

He fired before he'd even fully found his feet. The first man stumbled back as his throat suddenly opened. The hollow-point round tore through his jugular on the way out. Johnson shifted slightly and dropped to his knees when he saw weapons raised toward him. He gripped the pistol in both hands and close to his chest and didn't need to aim when his enemies were this close.

A second man fell, the life in his eyes immediately extinguished when a bullet punched into his forehead. The third tried to turn away. Seeing his comrades eliminated this quickly obviously affected him, and when one lacked training, instincts came to the fore. He wanted to survive but Johnson was ready. A bullet pierced the man's back and severed his spine at his third rib. He dropped and was dead before he hit the ground.

For a moment, Johnson wondered if a swarm of mosquitoes had gotten inside his helmet. A high-pitched whine pushed through his calm and he had to resist the urge to swat at the air around his head. He knew, instinctively, that there were no bugs, but his nerves protested in the aftermath of his killing spree. Three shots, three yards, and under three seconds. Exactly like the rulebook called for.

He looked up and swallowed his bloodlust, and his gaze settled on another man on the roof. He was smaller and leaner and appeared to be a civilian—maybe forced into the situation by the insurgents. The man was on his knees with his hands raised and mumbled something incoherent, clearly begging for his life.

For a second, he was tempted to spare the man. Too many people had died today. Besides, the backlash for killing a civilian in this situation would be beyond massive. Still...

"Sorry, I can't risk it, asshole," Johnson said and raised his weapon. The man clearly didn't speak English, but the intention was clear. He tried to move away but his frantic efforts were too slow. A double-tap through the forehead felled him in his tracks.

A hint of guilt rippled through Johnson as he moved toward the edge of the building, ejected the mag from his pistol, and replaced it with a new one. He would need to set his emotions aside, he knew, or push through them if he wanted to live to regret his actions there today with what was left of his squad.

"Red Three, is the west of the village still open?" he asked and squinted in the direction that seemed to be the best way out. "Red Three?"

He checked the vital signs of the other half of his team.

No response. Either they had all gone offline, all at the same time with technical difficulties, or…

His heart sank and he muttered, "Shit." He stooped to retrieve an assault rifle a dead man had dropped, then peeked over the edge of the building. A fairly large group of men made their way toward the door but, like he had, none thought to check the roof. They would pay for that.

His lips drew back in a rictus snarl as his first shots cut through the massed insurgents. As packed together as they were, the rounds ripped through one and sometimes two men at a time to dispense all kinds of collateral damage.

It wasn't until he had fired the third burst that the men realized that they were being fired at from above and quickly tried to find cover. There wasn't much to be had, though, since the area between the house Johnson was on and the one across the street was almost completely open.

A rout ensued and most of the men didn't even bother to retaliate as he maintained the steady barrage and only stopped when he ran out of ammunition. He drew away from the edge of the building, moved back toward the hatch, and dropped without using the stepladder. A jolt of pain knifed through him when he landed. He scowled at the pieces of shrapnel that jutted from his armor.

"I can't get the rest of the team on comms," Lee gasped as he pushed awkwardly against the wall for support. In all honesty, Johnson was surprised that he hadn't bled out by now. He vaguely recalled something about severed arteries going into spasm on occasion, so if one had been shredded, maybe that was what had kept him alive. Only time would tell whether he would make the inevitably rough trip out.

"Me neither. They haven't responded at all," he replied

and took a moment to collect the dog tags from their fallen comrades. "We'll swing by to see if they're still around. I need you with me on this, all right? I'll carry you out, but you need to stick it out with me. Pass out on my back, and I'll give you time to recover only to kick your ass once we're back on base, got it?"

"Roger that, Sarge." Lee forced a grin that soon became a grimace.

He grinned in response. The man's leg hung by a thread, but he was still game, and Johnson felt a thrill of pride in his team. He was relieved that a man in his crew still believed in him despite the hardship they'd faced tonight. Still, he was well aware of how adrenaline played in these kinds of situations. He kept his thoughts in check and pulled the wounded man onto his back and allowed him to support himself with his arms as best he could.

Johnson let his shoulders do most of the work and held Lee's damaged leg in place with one hand, while the other gripped his sidearm. His heart still hammered furiously against his ribcage, but he moved toward the door despite the sense of doom that had settled over him. The whole village had fallen into an eerie silence again, which made him grind his teeth. He didn't like this kind of quiet. It always meant trouble.

Shouts were exchanged in the distance along with a couple of rogue gunshots, but other than that, the only sound was the wind whipping through the open areas of the village. There were still hostiles around, and he was well aware of the fact that he hadn't been able to take care of all of them. Which begged the question—where the hell were they?

They cleared the building with none of their enemies in sight. He tried not to think of the warm, thick liquid that ran down his body beneath his armor. Obviously, whatever wounds he had sustained continued to bleed. The only thing that blocked the pain was the adrenaline that coursed through his system.

Johnson shook his head and grinned. There was nothing like going for a jog with a man draped over your back to keep the blood and adrenaline flowing. He knew that all the activity simply made it worse. It was a given that he would certainly continue to lose blood, and with the movement and exertion, he would tear his wounds and make them worse. But, if he stayed in place, the chances were he and Lee would both be gunned down. They needed to get back to the evac zone as quickly as possible. All other medical emergencies could wait.

He pushed himself to move as fast as he could with Lee on his back. Johnson hissed and his muscles burned by the time he finally cleared the village. There was no more gunfire and no reports over the comms. The other squad members' vitals were still quiet and the chance that anybody else was alive was remote. He suspected that either their HUDs or his own had sustained damage and he couldn't pick up even the flat-line indicator that would confirm his suspicions.

They reached the desert and moved toward some outlying buildings on the west side. If the enemy dumbasses had any brains, this would be where they waited for Johnson and his squad. There was no sign of them, but there were bodies—in last-stand numbers too, he noted as he scrutinized the area. He raised his pistol when he heard footsteps.

"Don't you dare," Lee growled, but Johnson needed to unload his burden. He dropped his teammate abruptly and Lee cursed and grunted in pain as he landed in a heap. Johnson gripped his pistol with both hands as the three insurgents who searched through the corpses on the ground realized that they had newcomers on their hands.

The armor on the bodies looked familiar—too familiar. Even with the sun having set an hour before, it was hard to miss what his own men had worn into combat. And those men were looting the bodies.

Fuck these guys! He pulled the trigger, faster than they were. As tired as he was and with as much blood as he'd lost, he expected that reaction time would be a toss-up for the victory. At this point, all he could do was take advantage of the fact that the men had been too occupied with looting the weapons and possessions from his dead squad mates to have hands on their weapons.

The insurgents didn't even fire a single shot before bullet holes appeared in their chests and heads as they fell, choking on their own blood. Johnson fired until the nine-round magazine in his pistol was expended. He retrieved the last mag he had for it, slapped it in, and continued to shoot.

Even when he was out of bullets, he wasted a couple of seconds pulling the trigger of his empty weapon.

"Sarge! We need to get out of here," Lee said. His voice had taken on that distant quality again.

"Sure," he responded harshly. "I need to take care of something first."

"Sarge, they're fucking dead! Get it together."

Johnson turned and gritted his teeth. "Just… I need to take care of something."

He could feel the effects of the blood loss take over now. The weakness in his body went beyond fatigued muscles. Those same muscles didn't receive enough oxygen to keep up with the exertions they were forced into and had begun to shut down one by one. But still, he needed to do something first. He staggered toward his fallen comrades.

"Sarge?" Lee asked and propped himself up on his arm to watch as the sergeant quickly collected the dog tags from the men who had been killed. Those little pieces of aluminum that nobody would think to steal had more value to their families than all the money in the world. Of course, the Army would come up with some story about where they were stationed and how they died. Medals would be handed out and funerals would be held as coffins without bodies were delivered back to the States. That was merely how things were done.

Johnson moved toward Lee and tucked all the dog tags into his pouch before he helped the man to stand on his good leg.

"How are you feeling, Red Seven?" he asked as he heaved the man onto his back again.

"Like a fucking twenty-dollar bill, sir," he replied. The man had applied some bandaging to his leg, but there was only so much that could do. He needed surgery. "It looks like one of the motherfuckers tagged you, though."

Johnson glanced down as he moved again. A couple of holes had appeared in his armor and now leaked red. Well, he guessed it was red. With the only light source available to him being a half moon and stars, everything simply looked black.

"We'll make it," he said, moved one foot in front of the other, and actually tried to run. He managed a few steps before he decided that if he fell over, neither of them would get up again. Still, he maintained a good pace—slower than he would have liked, but from the clock on his HUD, they had more than enough time to get back to the evac zone.

It felt like hours. The desert chilled as night deepened and the cold seeped into his bones, although blood loss was possibly to blame for some of it. He grasped Lee with both hands and kept moving, determined to get at least one member of his team out alive even if it killed him.

Hours and more endless hours passed, although it felt like days. He couldn't see the sunrise, but he did feel the heavy rotors of the helo that was sent to pick them up and the chopper's blades that churned the air above his body. Voices babbled and he tightened his grasp on Lee's arm. They wanted to take him. He shook his head in panic, knowing he needed to get the asshole to a hospital. Back to the evac point.

"Sergeant," someone said. "We need to get him some medical attention."

Lee was limp. He'd passed out a while back, but Johnson wasn't quite sure when, though. He struggled to stay on his feet and a pair of arms caught him by the shoulders.

Someone dragged him toward the helicopter. "Get him out of his armor."

"Are you kidding?" a second voice replied. "That stuff is the only thing keeping everything in him from spilling out. We need to get him to a hospital."

The cold faded and so did his shattered senses. It was an unmanageable chore to keep his eyes open. Straps came over him and held him in place as the helicopter took off.

"Save Red Seven," he whispered and shivered with fear at how weak his voice sounded. He wasn't sure if anyone heard him, so he said it again. Well, he thought he did. He couldn't be sure of anything anymore. His eyes closed and he felt his grip on things loosen. He slept.

CHAPTER TWO

He could smell…something. Like bleach, but with a soapy, cinnamon-type hint. The odd combination of smells left him confused—like someone had baked pumpkin pies but put bleach in them. Who would do that?

Serial killers, that's who. Jules loved to watch late-night documentaries on America's most prolific serial killers. She was a moderator on one of those internet forums that talked about them and had told him once that she'd found evidence that H. H. Holmes was actually Jack the Ripper. It made sense that Britain's most famous serial killer was an American, he remembered thinking.

He really needed to call her when he got back stateside. Abigail would want to see him too. He could take her to get tacos and…ice cream? No, she was seven. She didn't like ice cream anymore. She'd told him that the last time.

Johnson opened his eyes and looked cautiously around him. The lights were dimmed, which made it harder to wake up, but sleep wasn't an option anymore. He needed to find the man who ran this base and persuade him to push his visit home to a couple of months early.

"Fuck," he muttered, shook his head, and tried to focus. An IV was plugged into his arm—saline solution and probably morphine too. He looked at his body in a sudden panic. Had he lost his leg? No, that was Lee. Weird. Why… oh, right, surgeries. So many—too many. They should simply release him and send him home.

Well, that explained the smell of bleach, anyway, but it didn't explain the cinnamon. Was it something they used to make the place smell less like death and cleaning products?

The door to his room opened and a young woman stepped inside. She wore pristine white, her black hair cut short to just above her shoulders. A pair of glasses rested low on her nose.

"Good morning, sergeant," she said, and a small, professional smile touched her lips as she moved to the foot of his hospital bed and tapped the tablet there. "I thought I heard some movement in here. It's good to see that you're with us again. We thought we'd lost you back there."

He blinked a few times as he tried to pull his memories into something remotely cohesive. He didn't remember being wheeled in there. Then again, much of his recent memory was too fuzzy to remember clearly.

"Let's start with something simple," she said and drew his attention back to her. "Do you remember your name?"

He nodded and licked his lips. "Sergeant Jeremiah Johnson, 75th Special Forces Group."

"Excellent. Cognitive functions appear to work normally," she said with a smile. He studied her white coat. Weren't doctors supposed to wear their names on their lapels? He craned his neck to see the file that she looked at on the tablet.

Patient 90911. No name. That was less than encouraging. It was one of *those* hospitals. He knew about them, of course—black sites that were created to treat patients who didn't need much in the way of names or identities until they were released.

"How long have I been in this facility?" he asked as he returned his focus to the doctor.

"You've been in my care for the past three days after you were released from surgery," she replied. The smile never left her face. She seemed nervous, he thought, as if she thought she was in the presence of a dangerous animal that could attack her at any moment.

His suspicions about the hospital were confirmed by the way she smoothly sidestepped the question. He leaned back in his bed.

She pulled the blanket down and inspected the bandages that covered his torso. "Tell me if you feel any discomfort, all right?"

Johnson tilted his head to study his wound-riddled torso. There were more holes than he'd expected, including some higher up on his chest. For a moment, he simply stared in amazement when he realized that he had survived despite being turned into a chunk of swiss cheese.

The doctor worked methodically to inspect the bandages and make sure that the stitches all held. She also ran a handful of reflex tests on his knee, a tapping test over his sternum, and a couple more that he was unfamiliar with.

"Do you have any discomfort?" she asked, her expression and tone all efficiency.

"Not really," he replied. "How many surgeries did I have to undergo?"

"From your file, you were subjected to three in total," she replied. "Could you raise your arm for me, please? Right, then left."

He did as he was told. This doctor was apparently comfortable dealing with men and women who had come out of the field from dubious operations around the globe. She was also accustomed to answering questions in ways that didn't provide any unnecessary information, all while being as pleasant and as professional as a doctor could be.

"I have all I need," she said after a few more checks obviously brought no negative results.

"That's nice to know," Johnson replied.

"She wasn't talking to you." Another unfamiliar voice brought his attention to the door of his room as a tall, lean man in his late thirties stepped in. He had light-brown hair and deep-set brown eyes which didn't seem to miss much. Smiling politely, he watched the doctor beat a hasty retreat. "It's good to see you in the land of the living, sergeant."

He nodded. "Is this a debriefing?"

"I'm afraid so," the man said and placed a hard copy of a file that Johnson was sure would be submitted with a horde of redactions on the movable bedside table. "I work with the intelligence unit that ultimately caused your team to be sent into that village, so I thought that it would be appropriate if I did this myself." The man stared into his eyes as if judging how bad his reaction would be.

Johnson felt something cold and angry drop to the bottom of his stomach. It had been bad intel that got his squad killed, for the most part, but it was hard to feel angry when he realized that the man he now spoke to wore a lieutenant colonel's oak leaf. Light birds didn't conduct debriefs. Ever.

He gripped the sheets under him as tightly as he could as his body began to shake with frustration and residual sorrow. But he needed to control himself, he knew that, so he took a deep breath and willed himself to calm.

"Forgive me for saying so, sir, but that was some shitty intel your unit gave us," he said finally and tried to keep his tone as respectful as possible. He wanted to shout and throw things around and lay all the blame on the man standing in front of him. The need was instinctual, even though, as squad leader, he knew the life and death of his comrades lay heavily on his shoulders.

"Agreed, Sergeant," the LC said with a firm nod. "The insurgents expected our attack. They moved your target out and brought in a battalion's worth of men a few hours before you boys set foot in that village. They knew you were coming and waited until it was too late to give you a heads up before you entered. You'd gone dark before we found out about it."

Johnson gritted his teeth and dragged in another deep breath before he nodded. His stomach jolted and for a moment, he felt dizzy and nauseated.

"All your men will be given full military honors," the LC continued. "Although, since the operation was off the books, of course, there won't be any mention of it. A complete blackout was approved. We sent another team to intercept the target while he was in transit to another location and they pulled it off. We believe that they didn't anticipate that we would be willing to bring another team in that quickly."

"That sure showed them," he responded and struggled to keep himself still on his bed. "What happened to Evan Lee? Corporal Evan Lee, the one whom I managed to get out? Is he still in surgery? Will he be all right?"

The LC looked away for a moment. "I'm sorry, Sergeant, I wish I had better news for you. The systemic shock included a nasty infection that made him septic. The surgeons tried their best, but he didn't make it. I'm sorry."

Hot tears welled up and he fought them back savagely. "I don't need your fucking apology."

That was no way to address a superior, but he couldn't help himself. He didn't feel particularly charitable toward the man, despite knowing that he was there because he felt equally as guilty as Johnson did.

"I understand," LC said with a small nod. "I hope you understand that you were declared dead to the world as well."

"What?" he demanded and shoved himself up from the bed. He regretted the precipitous action almost immediately.

"I'm sorry, but it was necessary to keep complete control of the narrative in the Pentagon," LC replied. "That mission was the last that you will run with the US Army, as well as the last time that you will be referred to as Sergeant Jeremiah Johnson, do you understand?"

Johnson breathed deep and tried to harness his thoughts. Of course, this was standard procedure for operations of this kind. They usually didn't have survivors when things went this poorly, but when there were, complete control was necessary. If news of these kinds of casualties reached the wrong Senate committees, it would result in heavy investigations into black operations. That, in turn, meant a shitload of media coverage that could cost operatives still in the field their lives. At least, that was what he was told when he signed up for the covert operations.

"I hope they made my funeral nice, anyway," Johnson said finally.

"It was a beautiful ceremony," the other man replied with a small smile. "Your ex-wife was in attendance, her fiancé, and your daughter. I can't imagine what that must feel like."

"Andy's a good guy." He smiled because that was the truth. "Did you think I would let someone spend so much time with the two people I care the most for in the world without vetting him personally?"

"Right," the man replied and lowered his head. "That said, I think it goes without saying that you can't go back to your old life. None of your friends or family can know that you're alive. You are dead to the world, for all intents and purposes."

"If it goes without saying, why did you say it?" Johnson asked. Rage and respect for rank fought a pitched battle in his heart, and only extreme discipline—and his weakness and discomfort, of course—kept him from rearing up in his bed and placing his hands around the man's throat.

"It needed to be stated," the LC replied. "My superiors

would prefer that all details of what's about to happen be laid out without any room for error, as it were."

"Right." Johnson leaned back in his bed.

The LC closed the file he'd brought in with him and tucked it under his arm. "Arrangements are already being made for transfer into your new life. They should be ready for you to assume your new identity once you've finished your physical therapy. Until then, you should focus on recovery. It's the only way to get through this."

He smirked. "You would know, right?"

"You have no idea," the LC replied with a serious glint in his eye that informed Johnson he had also suffered loss —maybe even extreme loss. The man cleared his throat and said, "Rest well, Sergeant."

He exited the room and closed the door behind him and abruptly, the smell of cinnamon receded to leave only the tang of bleach and rubbing alcohol in its wake. Johnson let his body sag on the bed with a ragged sigh. There wasn't anything that he could look at, so he simply stared at the sheets that covered his battered and broken body. He felt the world close in and the grief in his heart threaten his sanity.

They were gone. His teammates were dead and now, his ex-wife and daughter might as well be too. In addition, his life was in the hands of the same men who had issued false information and gotten every member of his team wiped off the face of the earth.

"Fuck," Johnson griped and dragged in a deep, shaky breath. He closed his eyes as he brushed his hand over his cheeks. Hot, fresh tears trickled down his face. He pulled the sheet up to dab them away.

CHAPTER THREE

Physical therapy was one of the most frustrating experiences in his life. He'd spent almost a full month of his life lying on his back. Recovery from multiple life-saving surgeries always came with a price, and one of the most overlooked was muscular atrophy. His mind and central nervous system knew what it needed to do, but his body needed time to catch up.

It was beyond frustrating. He had been at the top of his physical form when he'd stepped onto that damned helicopter. While he knew that he was lucky to have walked away from that situation alive, there was still a hint of guilt that piled onto all the shitty feelings he experienced when he had to teach his body how to walk again.

Still, despite the struggle, a month and a half were enough to make his body work again. A couple of hours on the treadmill every day had done wonders, and even though the doctors told him that he would have to be eased back into the shape that he'd been in, a part of him would always push, always strive to be good, better, and best. It wasn't even a macho thing. It was simply how he was raised. To stay in the same place all the time—to settle—wasn't what he'd been made for. It was what had driven his wife away. When she'd brought his divorce papers, it had been what had driven him to accept another couple of tours after he'd promised her that he would stay home to help her raise their kid.

A real "type A" personality, he thought with a mental shrug. His own inclination had saved his life more than once, but it had cost him, too. Too many injuries to count, a life on the drift from one engagement to another, and a lost family. Right now, he wished he was more laid-back and could actually settle down to be a dad and a good husband. With a heavy sigh, he shook his head because he knew that like any leopard, he couldn't change his spots, no matter how much he wished differently.

Johnson frowned and stared around the gym. *On top of everything,* he thought with a grimace, *I'm not even Jeremiah Johnson anymore.* He'd decided that he would keep the given name, Jeremiah, since that was his grandfather's name on his mother's side, and he'd loved that man. The old marine had gotten him in the mood to join the armed forces all those years before. It was the family name, Johnson, that would be sacrificed. He still hadn't decided which name he would assume. There weren't many out there that fit with Jeremiah.

He rubbed a starchy white towel over his face, neck, and arms and walked away from the weight room. As he moved, he rolled his shoulders and felt the comfortable burn in his muscles. It was good to be back in the saddle, figuratively speaking. There weren't combat training facilities in the hospital, which was more than a little annoying, but he would get past it. He'd begun basic combat training practices in his room. It wasn't like there was much else to do around there. The whole hospital was an information black spot, with no cell reception and all the Wi-Fi connections encrypted to the point where accessing them was nigh on impossible. And he had tried, although his knowledge of cracking encryption like that was somewhat lacking.

Jeremiah walked into his room, shucked his clothes, and moved into the bathroom. He let the shower run as hot as he could stand it before he stepped into the cubicle. The steaming water, almost to the point of scalding, rushed down over his newly healed scars and he closed his eyes and gritted his teeth against the painfully pleasant experience. It was difficult to identify why this little ritual made him feel...well, a little better. Not much, but these days, he needed to take any good he could get.

He stepped out of the shower and dried himself off quickly before he wrapped the towel around his waist and stepped into the tiny room they'd given him. Old habits had begun to reinstate themselves in his patterns, which showed him that a part of the old him had returned. Sure, the future looked bleak for a man who walked out into the world with a new name and a history of government-sanctioned violence, but it wasn't like there weren't jobs out there for a man of his particular talents.

The thought remained unexplored as he stiffened momentarily before he tilted his head at a jaunty angle and smiled. "You know, if they allowed me a gun in here, I would turn and aim it at you in a very menacing manner right about now."

A tall, lean man in an expensive-looking suit sat in the chair that had been placed in the corner of his room away from all the lights.

"Well, maybe I should consider myself lucky that they don't allow guns in a hospital ward," the visitor said with a small smile as he pushed himself from his seat.

"Something about not trusting your average combat soldier who is hopped up on a cocktail of medications with firearms," Jeremiah said with a smirk and folded his arms. "Call me crazy, but there's a serious lack of trust in these parts."

The man chuckled softly. "I read your psych profiles, Jeremiah…no last name at the moment. Every man who made an analysis of you said that you had an interesting sense of humor. I'm pleased to see it wasn't exaggerated. It gives me a good feeling about the rest of your psych profiles."

"Yeah, there were a lot of them," he admitted. "Those folks always insisted that I needed to be brought in to inspect my feelings after a mission to see if I was ready to get back into the field."

"My guess is that you don't look forward to the profiling that'll be mandatory with your release from this hospital, then?" the man asked. He took a step forward and placed a piece of paper on the bed. Jeremiah moved in closer to pick it up. Release papers, he realized, merely waiting for his signature. He turned to face the man, who had returned to his seat in the corner of the room.

"Who the fuck are you?" he asked and put the paper down.

His visitor wore a small smile. "A potential employer."

"Jeez, your parents must have hated you," Jeremiah said with a chuckle. "I mean, judge not lest ye be judged, but that borders on child abuse."

"What?" the man asked, tilting his head.

"Your name, genius," Jeremiah snapped. "John Doe? Come on, I won't make any deals with someone who isn't up-front with me about who they are and what they want from me. I think I've been around long enough to know a military man when I see one, so why don't you do us both a favor and cut the crap? One pro to another."

The man nodded. "Fair enough. My name is James Anderson. Formerly a full-bird colonel in MARSOC and an operative before that. I've since gone into the private sector. Due to some...hostile circumstances, I find myself in need of a man with your particular talents and disposition."

"I'm not an assassin for hire," he responded. "You can find more than enough of those working in the private sector."

"I know." The other man nodded. "That's actually the point. While I was still with the Pentagon, I oversaw operations run by a company whose people...well, they don't have the morals God gave a goat, and we eat goats."

An odd metaphor, Jeremiah mused, but he didn't comment and simply let the man continue.

Anderson narrowed his eyes as he watched him closely. "Tell me, Jeremiah, what do you know about the Zoo?"

The now former sergeant took a deep breath and tilted his head as he circled the man in front of him. "Officially? It's a military experiment gone bad, with all the pros and cons that come with it. It's called Kudzu by the locals and nicknamed the Zoo. No official word was shared, of course, which means that I 'officially' don't know that the source of the damn jungle that has begun to cover the Sahara Desert is some goop that was found on a meteorite or missile that may or may not have alien origins. Remind me, what is the government's official stance on aliens again?"

Anderson smirked. "The jury is still out on that one."

He nodded. "No worries, I merely want to make sure that our stories match on this one. But I digress. You were talking about a company that I assume has made a metric fuck-ton of cash on the riches to be found in this enigmatic Zoo-place."

"That's a good guess, and through some...less than pleasant means, an acquaintance has recently taken over a majority share of the company in question," his visitor continued. "It's called Pegasus and trust me, these guys are not the kind to take an aggressive takeover lying down, which is why she brought me in. It's also why I need someone like you to watch my back for the duration."

Jeremiah sighed and scratched his jawline. "That seems like the kind of job that doesn't have an end date, especially if you don't want me killing these assholes pre-emptively."

Anderson chuckled. "We want to bring the company down, but it won't be an easy task. The people who run this have connections all through the military, which makes it a very risky, very dangerous job that will take longer than any of us can anticipate. We need muscle on our side."

"And that's where I come in. Your muscle, as it were."

"Look, I'm not usually this kind of guy. I was only retired to the Pentagon because one of the jobs I was on went badly. While they knew I wouldn't be much good in the field after that, they put a lot of money and effort into training me. I was willing to still serve my country when it came down to it, so they sent me to the Zoo to oversee and handle weapons testing that this company, Pegasus, was running.

"At first, things weren't too different than what we were doing at the Zoo. But they used the soldiers they brought in as guinea pigs, dressed them in half-tested suits, and sent them out into dangerous locations to be killed. After a while, they stopped even trying to pretend that it was about testing. They brought stuff out of there—untested—and it was all for profit. And people died for it, good people. Well...not all of them were good people, I guess. Either way, I plan to take them down with my dying breath or all my money, or both. I've hooked up with a team from the Zoo that's committed to helping, but I still need someone on my side to make it happen."

Jeremiah wanted to crack a joke about what else Anderson expected when he got into bed with a corporation. They were filled to the brim with psychopaths who cared a hell of a lot more about quarterly figures than the lives it would cost to get them there. And yet, it didn't seem like the kind of thing someone should joke about. There was too much blood involved to make it a laughing matter.

Well, I might need a few hours to settle into it, but I'm sure I can make a joke about almost anything the world throws my way. I'm simply a little out of practice.

"So," he said finally, suddenly very aware of the fact that he was still dressed in only a towel. "You were in the Zoo, huh? I've heard a lot of rumors coming out of that place. Lots of bad, some good, but very little that's been officially confirmed. The only guys I know for a fact went there always come back with a horde of NDAs to sign and a different look in their eyes. I've been around long enough to know that there are only a couple of places in the world that make that kind of change in a man, and none of them are good. It wasn't like we needed any more of them, but hey, here we are."

Anderson chuckled. "I hear you there. Have you ever been to one of those places?"

He nodded. "Never the Zoo, obviously, but there are places that you can't get out of your head. I can't say where exactly, but there were drugs and a lot of money involved."

"Right." His visitor nodded knowingly.

Jeremiah narrowed his eyes. "Are there bugs in the room?"

The man smiled and reached over to the bedside table where he'd put his hat. He lifted it to reveal a small piece of tech that he'd dug out, presumably from the lamp. "A friend of mine gave me some tools that will make sure nobody is able to listen to what we talk about. Or see, for that matter."

"Still, better safe than sorry," he responded with a smirk because he'd known about the bugs. He'd swept the room a couple of times when they'd moved him there from the ICU, and each time, he'd found at least one that he'd missed. Finally, he'd come to terms with the fact that his every move while in this hospital—and probably afterward —would be watched and recorded for posterity. He wasn't sure why they were doing it, but at this point, it was very, very low on his list of things to care about.

"Right," Anderson said with a chuckle. "Still, I think I trust my friend."

"So, if this interview goes badly, I won't suddenly come down with a nine-millimeter cerebral hemorrhage?" he asked cheerfully.

"Don't worry, nothing happens to you if you say no." His visitor laughed. "I had help locating you and then pulled all kinds of strings to get in here to talk to you. No one wants those at the top to know that I'm here. A dead body in your room would leave too many questions asked by all the wrong people."

"Thanks," he said. "I think."

"How much do you remember of the fighting that got you here?" Anderson asked.

It suddenly felt harder to breathe, and a wave of vertigo swept through him at the sudden question. "It's all buried right now," he said and dropped onto his bed. He took a deep, steadying breath and continued, "I remember most of my team had died. I remember that I didn't really feel the wounds that I ended with until afterward. Other than that, it's all...fuzzy."

Anderson studied him for a moment, and his light-blue eyes softened. Then, he nodded, pulled a phone from his pocket, and opened it to a video he'd already lined up for Jeremiah to watch. It was the recording from his HUD camera during the mission, although it was cut to something that he very vaguely remembered doing. He watched himself scramble up a ladder as a head appeared through a small hatch at the top. A knife was in his hands and he cut the man's throat and dragged him down through the opening. A pistol—not his assault rifle—came up and eliminated a couple more.

He cleared the hatch and shot three more men in an equal number of strikes that made him feel a little pride. There was nothing like showing off the kind of training that had taken him to the top of the food chain to make him feel like he could go ahead and achieve it all over again.

A survivor had dropped to his knees, his hand raised in the air, and he muttered something as he dropped his weapon. Jeremiah felt the same sense of guilt he'd felt that fateful night and bit his lip as the video spooled his actions. "Sorry, can't risk it, asshole," he heard himself say in a hoarse voice, and with two shots, the surrendered man fell.

He knew his actions that night were brutal, but most of his men had already perished and he was damned if he would grovel in disgrace for acting on his aggression. The video came to an end and he bared his teeth in an over-jolly grin. "Damn, the dude has still got it. Ten points for dexterity right there. Did you see that stab? And the three shots? They had the drop on me, every one of them, and I still got them. Three yards, three seconds, three shots."

"You killed an unarmed man who was surrendering," Anderson said. An odd twist of his lips to the right made it difficult for Jeremiah to read the man's thoughts behind the statement. Still, his temper rose.

"They had just dropped a grenade into a room that

killed two of my boys," he snapped. "We were in the middle of a hostile situation where we couldn't leave someone behind to shoot us in the back. We couldn't take prisoners. There was only one tactical choice to make there, Anderson, and you know it as well as me."

"True," his companion agreed with a nod. "But from hearing you describe it and hearing your words in the video, I'd say that you had fun there. Even with all the bullets flying and all the danger that you and your men were in, you enjoyed the challenge of being in a situation where all the rules went out the window and every choice made was the difference between life and death."

Jeremiah looked down and toyed with the fabric of the white towel he wore around his hips. "What can I say? I'm not a man of cultivated tastes, Colonel."

"I'm not a colonel anymore, Jeremiah," Anderson said and leaned forward in his seat. "I'm not even in the military now. But I need to clean up a place that has some wicked and powerful people involved. I don't need a man of cultivated tastes. I can find those all over the damned country and anywhere in the civilized world. In fact, I suspect that there are many cultivated assholes, both male and female, whom I plan to squash like so many roaches. What I need now is the man on that tape." He pointed at the phone Jeremiah had put down. "What I need is a savage, do you understand?"

He looked at the device, picked it up off the bed, and stretched to place it on the bedside table alongside the man's hat. Something inside him needed to click into place when he was in a situation like Anderson described. He'd been in this business long enough to know exactly what was needed for him to go into that dark, furious place in his heart.

"Are these bad guys, Colonel?" he asked.

Anderson opened his mouth to remind the man in front of him yet again that he was no longer a colonel. Then again, he remembered that for people like Jeremiah, you could leave the service, but the service never really left you. In the ex-sergeant's mind—and the minds of those like him—Anderson would always be a colonel, whether he wore the wings or not.

"Loosely defined, yes." He answered the question as honestly as he could. "It could be that they're merely self-absorbed assholes looking out for their own interests irrespective of whether it hurts their fellow man, nation, or the world. I hate to use a phrase from pop-culture, but it fits here. It's about deciding whether you want to take the red pill and learn about shit that will make you question your own beliefs, or the blue pill, where you turn the other way and forget about what's right but get a new name, a new life, and a few hundred thousand to squash your own conscience."

"Well, Colonel, I don't have much in the way of beliefs," Jeremiah said with a small smile. "And…the Matrix—shit. I only watched that twice. Well, three times. Twice in the theater and once on cable. But I suck at remembering which color was which…what did Neo choose again?"

"The red pill."

He nodded. It had been a while since he'd watched that movie. While he hadn't quite liked how preachy it was, he had first seen it when he was in his teenage years and back then, it had been the coolest thing he'd ever seen, bar none.

As a result, it would always pull at the nostalgia strings in his heart.

"Well, I think I'll take that damned red pill, Colonel," he said with a grin and pushed off the bed. Anderson matched his movement to stand and extend his hand to grip Jeremiah's.

"Welcome to the team then, Jeremiah Savage," Anderson said with a smile. "The snacks aren't great, but the money's good enough that you can get some gourmet stuff of your own. Good to have you aboard."

Jeremiah laughed. "Savage. I like that. Did you think that up yourself?"

"Nah, that was my friend's idea. We'll need you onboard before Monday. Finish your therapy as best you can and sign that paper. The day it happens, someone will be here to pick you up and take you where you need to go. Before Monday, you got it?"

He nodded. "I'll get it done."

CHAPTER FOUR

"Jeremiah...Savage, is that correct?"

Jeremiah looked up and stopped toying with the ashtray. He knew for a fact that cigarettes weren't allowed in the hospital wards. The crystal had been cleaned excessively, but there was still a light hint of ash on the outside, and the faintest smell of nicotine on the bottom told him that the ashtray had seen at least some recent use. He replaced it on the table in front of him. He'd never actually imagined that a psychiatrist's office would have a real sofa, but hey, stereotypes had to come from somewhere, right?

"Savage, yeah," he said with a smile. "It's a new name. I'm getting used to it, and I like it. I think I'll keep it."

"Right," the doctor said and tapped lightly on the tablet in his hands. "I'm here to sign off on your release from the hospital. Your physical therapist has said that your improvement after multiple surgeries is...well, impressive. You have made advancements in all your regimens, sometimes exceeding expectations."

Jeremiah smiled. "What can I say? I don't want to hang around hospitals for too long."

"Of course. But the effects of what happened to you have left scars, not only on your body but on your mind."

Rather than reply to the doctor immediately, he studied his right shoulder and the tear on the sleeve of his one good Polo shirt. It had been a long time since he'd actually inspected his own wardrobe and he was dismayed to find that most of his civilian clothing was nothing more than a collection of old rags. Annoyed at the doctor's frank appraisal, he snapped, "I'm afraid that if you're looking to do some shock therapy on me, Doc, I don't think you can shock me any further."

"You'd be wrong about that," he replied. "But that treatment is used only to treat major depressive disorders, mania, or catatonia. Considering that you've shown none of those symptoms, I'm afraid you'll have to rein in your enjoyment of being tied down. Another time, eh?"

Jeremiah chuckled. "I gotta admit, I like you, Doc."

He smiled. "I appreciate the sentiment. Of course, we're not here to talk about me, are we? Would you mind telling me why you feel you should be released from therapy?"

"Other than the fact that I can't stand hospitals and would rather not spend any more time around here than I absolutely have to?" he asked.

"Yes," the doctor replied. "Other than that."

"Well, if I'm perfectly honest, I have a job waiting for me. My potential employers said they want me free to start on Monday. If I don't make it, they'll find someone else."

"So, you have an outside influence driving you to leave therapy before you might actually be ready to leave?" he asked and tilted his head in what might be disapproval.

Jeremiah frowned and wondered if he had walked into some sort of psychological land mine. "Well," he replied. "I've been ready to leave for a while now. I did a lot of physical therapy two or three times a week like everyone else recovering from surgery. The problem was, I didn't actually have anywhere to go, so I simply stayed and attended therapy every day like a madman. Hence the fantastic recovery time."

"And that's a healthy approach, is it?"

"I'd say it is," he said. "Getting better as quickly as possible is a good thing, isn't it?"

"Well, there are a lot of psychological problems that come with that, but you're not here to listen to a long list of psychological disorders men who died fifty years ago came up with," the doctor said and tapped his tablet once more. "We're here to see if you're in a place to continue your therapy…out of this hospital."

"I'm leaving one way or another," Jeremiah said with a small grimace. "So, you can either sign off on me or not. I'm here as a favor to the people who run the hospital since they would rather not be held liable for releasing a potentially unstable former Special Forces operative into the world with a new name and a lot of money."

"Right," the doctor said with a frown. "Which means that I'll be the one left liable if I release you."

"Basically, yes," he said with a grin. "So, are you willing to put your writing on the wall, Doc?"

The man leaned forward. He wasn't sure what it was about Jeremiah that set him on edge. Maybe it was the man's calm as he sat there. Psychiatrists were used to being the smartest person in the room, considering that the people who were sent their way usually came with a boatload of issues—both mental and emotional in nature. But the man who sat across from him, as cool as a cucumber and willing to engage in wordplay, seemed like he was the smarter of the two of them but didn't know it. Plus, he didn't seem to care.

If the truth be told, the doctor didn't like Jeremiah Savage. He didn't like him and didn't know why, which was the most annoying part of it. So, why not let the powers-that-be release Savage into the world and then blame him if everything crashed and burned? This was a dark hospital, a place that would have no name even when it was inevitably shut down, so it wasn't like they would be able to do much to ruin his career if something did happen, right?

He shook his head in annoyance, retrieved a pen off the desk behind him, and peered at the release papers. Most of the doctors who had treated Savage had already signed off on him leaving the premises. All they needed was a psych eval from him.

"I hope you don't make me regret this, Savage." He signed his name quickly and put the pen back on his desk.

"Savage...yeah, I still like the sound of that," he said with a grin, pushed himself off the couch, and picked the piece of paper up off the table. "I appreciate your time, Doc."

Savage made his way out of the room, the release paper clasped tightly in his hand as he stepped out into the hallway. He still had fifteen minutes of the hour he'd been assigned, but he disliked shrinks as much as he disliked hospitals. They made him uncomfortable. There was so much about himself that he wanted to keep hidden, and these guys were trained to look into every nook and cranny a man held deep inside to find precisely those things. The less time he spent under professional scrutiny, the better.

A man waited outside the door for him as he stepped out of the shrink's office. He was in uniform, and from the insignia on his sleeve, he was a corporal—probably stationed around there to make sure that everyone followed the rules and that nobody tried anything dangerous. Savage assumed that there were a lot of folks who could get angry and violent after meeting with their shrink. That made all kinds of sense.

He smiled at the man and nodded. Neither felt the need to make any kind of uncomfortable small talk as they wandered down to the lobby. There weren't that many people around. The hospital was full, but the patients they put in a black site like this made sure that there wouldn't be much use for a revolving door. Well, damned if he would make use of it himself before too long.

A young, attractive nurse manned the front desk and he moved out into the lobby and handed her his papers. She smiled prettily, but there wasn't much in the way of sentiment behind her expression as he placed the rest of the paperwork needed for his release on the counter. Once that was done, he was given a package. He knew what was inside without having to check. A passport, a driver's license, and the paperwork that went into opening a bank account that had a little over two hundred thousand dollars in it. It would have been deposited in increments, matching the pay that he'd received over the past few years, which had gone to his ex-wife and his daughter's college fund.

There was one hell of a bonus included. The Army liked to make sure that the men they allowed to walk free from black ops were well paid for their efforts. That, of course, came with the silent threat of what would happen if they decided to talk, as if the concept of massive political upheaval wasn't enough to keep them in line.

Savage didn't think that he would need the cash right away. Anderson had told him—or rather implied—that there would be a lot of money involved in his work to keep bad people off his boss's back. A white envelope was taped to the top of the military-issued box. He frowned at it and wondered what lurked inside those crisp white folds of paper.

There was a list of things that he needed to do before he could join Anderson and his battle against the evils in Pegasus. Most of his earthly possessions were lost, thanks to the fact that he was dead to the world, and there were more than a few things that he needed to acquire. He had a couple of sets of clothes in the pack that he'd brought with him to the base, but he might as well throw those in the nearest dumpster. Besides a few small keepsakes, he didn't have a damn thing to his name. While he had a decent amount of money, his car had been sold, and he'd lost whatever claim he had on his house after the divorce.

He would make sure that the military ponied up on those losses too, eventually. For now, he merely needed to get himself settled into this brave new world. A military car would arrive soon to take him off base, so he sat on a low, cement bench and opened the letter taped to the lid of the box. The envelope felt over-stuffed, and Savage grinned at a large wad of cash tucked inside a sheet of stationery. He read the note scrawled on the paper from his new boss.

Savage, enclosed is enough cash to set you up with a new wardrobe. Normally, I wouldn't presume, but there are a few items that you will need, and I doubt you'd think of them on your own. First, I want you to buy a good suit. A summer suit, please, with three white dress shirts, black socks, and a good pair of dress shoes. I recommend Stone Brothers on 33rd St. They will know what you need. In addition, please pick up some light khaki slacks, an assortment of short-sleeved Polo shirts, and perhaps a pair or two of sturdy shorts. We will head into the tropics and time is of the essence.

I look forward to meeting up with you soon.

Anderson.

Savage fanned the money and saw that there were five crisp thousand-dollar bills in his hand. *Well, at least my new employer has some cash to spare.* He shook his head and tucked it into his pocket as he sensed someone standing beside him. He immediately recognized the man who wore a suit and tie instead of the uniform Jeremiah had seen him wearing however long ago it had been.

"LC," he said with a smile and stood to take the man's proffered hand. "I would have assumed that you were long gone by now. There's so much more you can do in bases all around the world instead of in some black site hospital in…where are we again?"

"Somewhere in West Virginia," LC said with a chuckle. "Sorry, I can't get any more specific than that. There's a ride coming to pick you up and drop you off where Anderson can help you out, but you'll have a bag over your head for most of the trip. I know that for guys like you, that's barely a handicap, but still, the bosses don't want to make it too easy."

"How about you?" Savage asked and folded his arms when he saw a black SUV pull up close to the hospital. "Where will you go after this?"

"I would feed you some bullshit about how if I told you, I'd have to kill you," the man said, "but if the truth be told, they haven't told me yet. Military Intelligence isn't a clean-cut job, you know. My superiors told me to keep an eye on you and make sure you made it out of the hospital all right. They didn't exactly lay out what I would do afterward."

Savage nodded. "Well, I'm not sure if I needed to be babysat like that, but...I appreciate it."

LC chuckled. "Well, for what it's worth, I've worked with Anderson before. You know, back when he was still a colonel, and a couple of times back when he was an operative in MARSOC too. He's a good person. I'm not saying you should trust him, but he has the best interests of our fellow men in uniform at heart."

The two men shook again. "Go out there and do dark deeds to darker people," LC said with a smile. "And know that there are some of us who'll sleep better knowing about it."

Savage chuckled. "You take care of yourself, LC."

The driver of the SUV stepped out of the car, a black bag in his hands. He handed it to Savage, who stepped into the vehicle and pulled it over his head without protest. He had expected something like this, and while LC seemed to think that he could probably find his way back, there wasn't much in the world that would make him want to return to this place. It was best to simply comply and leave this whole chapter of his life behind him.

LC smiled and watched the SUV pull away down the single road that led away from the facility before he turned and walked back inside. He was curious as to where he would go next. It wasn't like he'd had the time of his life stuck there looking after wounded veterans. It wasn't a terrible job but not the most inspiring either.

Then again, he was curious as to what the newly-minted Jeremiah Savage would do with his old friend Anderson calling the very literal shots.

CHAPTER FIVE

He was allowed to remove the bag a few hours into the trip. The driver understood that neither of them would head back to the damn hospital, so they merely had to do enough to satisfy the letter of the law. Jeremiah wasn't sure what part of the military the man had been in, but damned if they didn't know how to find a whole lot of them to work in the private sector. It was like the government didn't do much to take care of the veterans once they were out of the service or something.

They arrived in a small town as the sun was setting. The lights of a larger city gleamed in the distance. Jeremiah had spent most of his life on the West Coast, so he was somewhat lost as to where he was. LC had said something about West Virginia, but other than that, he simply had no clue where they might be now.

"What city is that?" he asked the driver as they pulled up beside a motel. It was one of those low-slung, concrete-block affairs with an outdated sign picturing a woman in a one-piece swimsuit poised over an aquamarine swimming pool. Beyond the sign, the liver-shaped pool in question was bone dry with a broken diving board that hung precariously over one end.

"Philly," the man said and didn't look at him as he put the SUV into park. "That's where you'll go later, but Anderson wanted you situated and comfortable before you get into the meat of what your situation is. Here..." He handed Jeremiah a small, ancient-looking flip phone and a key with the number twenty-seven on it. Savage stared at the piece of tech.

"What the hell am I supposed to do with this?" he asked.

"That's how he will contact you," the driver said with a small smile. "He's a little paranoid and with good reason. Now, get the fuck out of my car."

"Right." He heaved himself out of the vehicle and into the parking lot. He had barely closed the door behind him before the massive engine roared to life again. The man put the vehicle into drive and it cruised out of the motel's parking lot.

At that moment, Savage felt the phone vibrate in his hand. Whoever had programmed it had apparently done so with as little noise as possible in mind. He could understand their frame of mind, all things considered.

He flipped the device open and pressed the accept call button. It didn't respond to his first touch, which made him growl softly with irritation as he pressed it again, more insistently this time. The screen showed an accepted call. "I'm very happy with my current phone plan, actually, so stop calling," he said as he pressed the piece to his ear.

"I'm sorry?" Anderson's now familiar voice said.

"I'm joking," he said with a chuckle. "How can I help

you, Anderson? And why the hell are we talking through this piece of tech that was ancient ten years ago?"

"Right," the man said. "Sorry. My friend is rather paranoid when it comes to technology. Most modern tracking systems don't work with that flip phone, which will work as a pre-paid burner for you at the moment. While there's nothing illegal happening between us yet, I don't want to be caught on the back foot if something were to go horribly wrong. Are you with me so far?"

Jeremiah shook his head and snorted softly. "You're really not that comfortable with all this cloak and dagger bullshit, are you?"

"Not particularly, no," the former colonel admitted. "But I'm more than willing to overlook that fact so long as we have results. Now, are you at the motel yet?"

He nodded but remembered that Anderson couldn't see him. "Yes, I'm looking for my room now."

"Room twenty-seven has been paid for three weeks in advance. Should you need more time there, the company credit card has already been authorized to pay for any further expenditures," his new boss advised him as he climbed the outside steps of the building that led to what he assumed was his room.

"Nice digs," he said and inspected his surroundings. The place wasn't terrible, but it had obviously been chosen due to the very clandestine nature that most of the patrons preferred. A credit card would have been asked for, but not IDs. He slipped the key into the lock and opened the door. The queen-sized bed looked reasonably clean, although he made a note to never bring a black light in there. He didn't doubt that the whole place would glow like a Jackson Pollock painting.

"There's a safe inside the closet in the room," Anderson said. "Inside, you'll find some fake IDs. I know that the government provided you with something new as well, but I thought you might want to save that to burn on your own, even though Jeremiah Johnson is still dead and won't come back anytime soon."

"That is correct," Savage said with a small grin and opened the closet door. "What's the passcode?"

"It's five-five-five-five," said another voice, one he didn't recognize—a woman's voice with a hint of a Russian accent. "The people you sent didn't bother to change it from the factory-setting code. It's a little worrying but considering that there wasn't much time between the drop and Savage's arrival, it's understandable."

"Hi," he said and typed the four digits quickly into the keypad. The safe beeped and clicked open. "Who the hell are you?"

"Oh," Anderson grunted. "Savage, this is Anja. Anja, Jeremiah Savage."

"Nice to meet...meet you? Is that right?" He peered deeper into the safe.

"Meet works, although I don't think we'll actually meet in person within the foreseeable future," Anja said. "Inside the safe, you'll find a driver's license from Illinois, along with a passport with a matching name and Social, a couple more burner phones should you need to discard the one that you're speaking into right now—or if you feel the need to extend your web of contacts to people you don't trust. Oh, and there's also a selection of non-sequential bills in there that should amount to a little over ten thousand dollars."

Jeremiah nodded and changed the factory passcode on the safe. While the weak software on these things wouldn't deter a skilled hacker, every little measure of safety was welcome. And it wasn't like he could simply carry this shit around with him everywhere he went.

"I'm afraid that we can't be seen to fraternize for a little while," Anderson said as he sealed the safe again. "I'll have too many eyes and ears on me over the next couple of weeks and maybe longer. While I do need you to cover my back, I hope you understand that we'll have to maintain some pretenses. I'd rather we keep you as an unknown quantity among the people you'll work against for as long as possible. We'll use the burner phones for now."

He nodded. "We should probably alternate between them as much as possible to make sure that nobody who might be tracking your lines can pin me down to any one number."

"A reasonable precaution," Anja interjected. He could hear someone talking in the background, but he couldn't hear what they were saying. All he could identify were two voices arguing.

"We have about twenty-four hours before I'll need you to be present at the Pegasus facility," his boss said as Anja cut out of the conversation. "At that point, my benefactor will announce the change of the guard at Pegasus. She'll bust everyone's fucking mind when she takes over and puts me in place. I assume that all sorts of shit will come at me from the board, so you should as well. I'll need you to figure out who is good and who is waiting to see what scraps are left. Do you think you can handle that?"

"I think I can, although I will need something of a vantage point to watch over them and you," Savage said as he dropped onto the bed and tugged his pack closer.

"We'll figure that out when the time comes. Until then, you need to lay low. I imagine that it's been a while since you've had some shore leave, so I suggest that you use these twenty-four hours to get used to being back in the US. Enjoy yourself. Do a little shopping like I detailed earlier in my letter. Relax and try to rest. You may not have time to fully heal once we get started."

"A quick question before I get to enjoy my day of freedom," Jeremiah said as he counted the stacks of bills he'd pulled from the safe. "You are aware that I'm not an actual intelligence operative, right? My training was all about killing people, not discovering their secrets."

"Like I said when we met," Anderson replied, "I don't need you to dig into people's lives. I need you to use your training to find out what will happen at the board meeting —to find anyone who plans to harm us and harm them first. Besides, I assume that you've learned how to infiltrate a hostile environment and collect intel, right?"

Savage nodded. "Well...yeah, I suppose you're right. But I struggle to see how those skills translate into something like a civilized society."

"I have the utmost trust in your abilities," his boss said. "You have all the training you'll need."

Jeremiah grabbed the pad of paper and a pen from the bedside table to take notes. "I'll need access to the building, you know—oh, and access to the security cameras."

"I can get you inside," Anderson assured him. "I have some contacts who work security for the building and can get you an ID badge and entry. Everything else, you'll have to do on your own with help from Anja, who will track communications in and out of the building. We'll need you in place to see who it is that's communicating and get a bead on them immediately. But don't worry about that now, Jeremiah. For today, worry about getting rested and ready for tomorrow, do you understand?"

"I do," he replied. "Catch you on the flip side."

He pressed the button to end the call and continued to make notes of everything he would need for what would come tomorrow. He knew that any fake ID he had wouldn't stand up against a background check—which, as he recalled, was necessary for the purchase of firearms around there. He had worked so long in the military where most of his equipment had simply been fed to him as he needed it. Now, there he was, in need and with nobody to provide.

Jeremiah took a deep breath, set the pen and pad aside, tugged the top three sheets off the pad, and crumpled them in his fist. Admittedly, he was old-school and more than a little paranoid, but he was now in a world of cloak and dagger bullshit, which meant that there was no such thing as too careful.

That said, there really wasn't any law that kept him stuck in this damned building, so he might as well get out there and enjoy his freedom for as long as it lasted.

He tucked a couple of the bills into his pocket along with the white envelope and one of the fake IDs. A few fliers in his apartment gave him an overview of what kind of nightlife entertainment could be found in the area. He would avoid the titty bars since it was Sunday and he didn't want to spend too much of his time pressed up against sweaty, panting assholes.

No. He'd go out for a beer, a steak, some fries, and maybe splurge and get himself a lava cake. He deserved it at this point, right?

First, he needed a rental car, so he called a taxi service and waited impatiently for a bruised-looking yellow sedan to pull up to his door. He got in and watched as Old Yeller made its way onto a side road and turned onto a freeway that took him into the city. It was a fine, cool afternoon, and sunlight glinted off the city's skyscrapers. The taxi stopped in front of a Hertz Rent-A-Car and he paid the driver and exited.

He browsed the parking lot and saw a good-looking, silver Toyota Avalon with all the bells and whistles he could ever need for a night on the town—specifically, a built-in nav system with directions to Stone Brothers on 33rd St. He went inside and used his fake ID to rent the car for forty-eight hours. The transaction complete, he slid behind the wheel, turned the key, and activated the navigation system for directions.

A woman's voice spoke into the JBL speakers. "Stone Brother's Men's Wear, on 33rd and Pike St. Please turn left at the first stoplight," she purred, and Jeremiah grinned in appreciation.

"Sure thing, darlin'," he whispered and moved out into traffic. He turned left and followed the lady's instructions until he entered a lovely, tree-lined boulevard in the center of town. Looking around, he knew he was in the monied part of the city where only the wealthiest clients ever shopped.

Frowning, Jeremiah couldn't help but think that big money often went hand-in-hand with big crime and wondered if this place wasn't too flamboyant for such a secretive operation. Still, he saw normal foot-traffic on the sidewalks, including some plain folks who seemed to be average citizens with little money of their own. Rubberneckers, maybe, cruising the good life. Deciding that it was safe enough, he left the vehicle and walked across the street to Stone Brothers.

Once inside, he gazed about in wonder and realized why there was five thousand dollars in the envelope. Some of the suits on display were twice that much. He wandered toward the back of the store and noticed that the prices decreased the farther back he went. Finally, he stopped and stared at a male mannequin wearing a light-gray suit, white shirt, and deep maroon tie. The price tag read nine hundred and ninety-nine dollars—on sale.

Sheesh, he thought and went to find a sales clerk. Happily, the suit fit fine and needed no alterations, so he bought it, along with three white dress shirts, a couple of ties, some black socks, and a pair of black dress shoes. It came to a grand total of $2,439.67. He gathered the suit and packages and fled for his life.

From there, he went to a nearby Macy's store and selected the rest of his wardrobe—jeans, a pair of Nikes, two pairs of chinos, and an assortment of Polo shirts. Underwear, socks, and a good pair of Ray Bans made the sales clerk smile as he piled everything on the counter. Once he'd paid for the items, he asked the man if it would be all right to change into one of his new outfits before he left the store and the clerk nodded and held onto the sales receipt as proof that he didn't steal the new duds.

Finally, Jeremiah stepped outside into the falling dusk and studied himself in the building's windows. He smirked. *Well, if it ain't Richie Rich, live and in person!*

Finally, his stomach growled a protest and he worked out that he had enough cash left to buy a really great steak and an even better beer. Hell, forget the lava cake. Maybe he'd have enough to get himself a crème brûlée—or whatever the high and mighties called it.

CHAPTER SIX

Jeremiah spent the remainder of his time off goofing around, eating too much, and taking long naps. On the following afternoon, he was called to a garage on the south end of the city and met up with a team of nine other men. He looked around as he stepped out of his rental car and grimaced when the men cracked insider jokes. Jeremiah hated insider jokes. Well, he hated them when he wasn't a part of them, but at this point, there wasn't much to decipher. They discussed one of the men who'd had a blow job from a stripper hired for his bachelor party. Someone had taken pictures and the wife found out about it.

Jeremiah couldn't determine from their jokes whether the wife was merely giving him the silent treatment or if the situation had actually escalated to a pending divorce. They stopped short of making jokes about what was actually happening and kept the jokes to whether the stripper's work was worth the trouble he now faced.

It was a typical scenario—friends giving other friends a

hard time. He was used to it, except that he had once been on the receiving end of it from his friends. It surprised him to realize that he missed the comradery, the kind that came with having people around you who were more than happy to watch your back and make sure that nothing bad happened to you.

They all piled into a large black van and waited silently as the big Mercedes made its way to a tall, brick office building.

"Hey, new guy!" one of the men snapped as Jeremiah peeled away from the group. "You stick close and you listen up. I don't like repeating myself about all the stuff that needs to be taken care of before our big shots get here and ignore us for a couple of hours, got it?"

He nodded. "Roger that."

"Roger…come on, man. You're not in the army anymore." One of the others laughed and they moved as a group to one of the service entrances. The jokes continued for a few more minutes when they entered the building, but once they reached the part that was full of actual employees, they quieted. Their attitudes reflected the professionalism that might inspire confidence in the people they protected.

"We need people to cover the elevators on every floor," the man in charge instructed as the group of ten men continued through the building. "We're only here to supplement the security they already have, so follow the lead of the folks that we'll work with. They know the building and the escape plans should an emergency come up. Stay on your toes but don't look nervous, and never,

ever stand alone at your station. That's how dumbasses get themselves killed—or worse, fired."

"It sounds like someone needs to reevaluate their priorities there, boss," another of the men chuckled. "What, is your ex draining you dry for alimony?"

"None of your damn business, Krovski," the leader snapped. "Where the fuck is the new guy?"

"He said something about having a nervous stomach and ducked out to find a bathroom," one of the others piped up from the back.

"Shit, we don't have time for this," he muttered and squinted down the hallway. "Okay, if any of you see him, send him my way. I'll man the command post in the basement. The rest of you have your assignments. Stick to them and don't get lost. I swear, if that dumbass gets in trouble, I won't bail him out. He'll have to get himself out of the fryer. I don't care that he's new at this."

The group moved away and stopped to chat as they waited for a service elevator to make its way down to the sub-basement to take them up to wherever it was that they were going. Jeremiah didn't have time to keep track of them as he pulled off the uniform that they'd given him and slipped into the locker rooms. At the moment, they were all but deserted with only a handful of men talking in corners.

He quickly picked the lock on the one that he had been given the number to and donned the employee's clothes. The man apparently worked at the front desk, which meant that the uniform—a suit and tie—would make the operative invisible to the eyes of those who might look for him.

He hated ties—or cheap ties like this one, at least. The way that they constricted around his neck made him uncomfortable. Still, he was willing to put up with it so long as he could get the job done. Anderson still hadn't told him where he could go to oversee the meeting that was supposed to start in… He checked his watch to make sure. Fifteen minutes.

"Fuck," he mumbled and tugged at his tie. Maybe nobody would notice if he left it a little looser than was fashionable. People didn't look at simple employees too closely, right?

He was making his way out of the locker room when a man in a matching suit and tie came in.

"Hey, buddy, let me fix that tie for you," the youngish-looking man said as he stepped in closer than Jeremiah was comfortable with and tightened the tie until it literally squeezed his Adam's apple.

"There ya go, bud," he said cheerfully. "Say, I don't recognize you. Are you new around here?"

"You could say that," he replied and tried to relax as he felt the tension in his shoulders tighten against the confining suit. "They transferred me from the other building downtown."

"No shit," the man replied. "Anyway, my shift just ended, but we should meet up sometime and get a drink. The Eagles are playing this weekend."

"I don't really follow football," he said with a grin. "Look, my shift's about to start."

"Hey, don't let me hold you back," he said with a chuckle. "Have fun out there, tiger."

Bud? Tiger? Who was he, a caricature of a sitcom character from the eighties? Jeremiah shook his head and headed out into the hallway in a jog as he checked his watch. He was running late. Where would Anderson send him? More importantly, how would the man contact him?

He reached the elevator, which opened as he came up to it. A pair of the security men he'd arrived with stepped out and almost bowled him over. They didn't bother looking back to apologize as they made their way past and talked about their smoke break.

Well, at least the uniform did, in fact, make him all but invisible to the people around there. He smirked and stepped inside to press the button for the tenth floor. Anderson had told him that the uniform would work since it was what most of the employees in the office level would wear or was at least similar enough that he wouldn't be noticed. He stepped out of the elevator and followed the map that he'd committed to memory before coming in. He'd had to ask Anderson for it, and damned if it wasn't worth the trouble. Navigating these halls without some sort of frame of reference would have been a nightmare.

"Mr...um...Savage? Saváge?" Someone said from behind him. He whipped around, not sure if he should be alarmed that someone used his real name, but when he realized that it was one of the interns, he relaxed. Damned if this whole infiltration thing was so much more stressful when he didn't have a gun in hand.

"Savage is fine, I'm not French," Jeremiah said with a chuckle.

"Is it an office joke or something?" the teenager asked and looked a little confused.

He opened his mouth to answer but wasn't sure what

the right thing to say would be. And he didn't want it advertised that someone called Savage actually prowled the building. "Did you need something, kid?"

"Uh…yeah, I have a package here for you," the young man said and lifted a manila envelope from a trolley behind him. Jeremiah signed for it, took the envelope, and waited for him to move away before he opened it. He was confused for a second as a tiny, pink earbud fell into his palm, but the confusion dissipated as a small piece of paper dropped out with words printed on it.

Put it in your ear. *Now!*

"Huh." He grunted and toyed with the little piece of tech before he pressed it gently into his ear.

"Okay, can you hear me, big guy?" The Russian voice was familiar. Anja, was it?

"Big guy?" he asked and kept his voice low. There were still people around, and he didn't want to attract attention by appearing to talk to himself. From what he remembered from the quick lessons he'd had with intelligence officers, the idea was to always be as unnoticeable as possible.

"Yes, I can't really call you Savage," Anja said into his head. "I mean, I've tried, but I always laugh. Who the hell calls themselves that? Willingly? I'd understand if it was a family name, but from what I heard from Anderson, you actually chose it. Seriously, who would do that?"

"Well, me, for starters," he retorted. "And it was supposed to be a joke. When he pitched his recruitment thing to me, he said that he needed a savage on his side. He then called me Jeremiah Savage, as a joke, and it sounded like fun. So, I kept it."

"Bozhe moi," Anja laughed. "Your name is Jeremiah Savage? Did you actually try to not give yourself a chance?"

"Well, Jeremiah was my real name before I changed it, and I thought I'd keep it," Jeremiah said. He didn't like how he had become defensive about his name.

"Oh…" Anja grunted. "Well, I won't call you either of those names. Can I call you Jay? Or Jer?"

"That's a negative on both," he said firmly. "Now that my name is out of the way, would you mind doing… Wait, you're the one who's supposed to tell me where I have to go from here. I'm flying blind and the meeting will start in under five minutes."

"Only if I get to call you Jer," Anja insisted. He ground his teeth. From what he could tell about the woman, she wouldn't have decided to imperil their mission simply because she wanted to give him a nickname, which meant that she behaved like this because she knew that he was close to where he needed to be.

"Absolutely fucking not. But in the interest of putting this argument off until we actually have time for this kind of banter, I don't think there's any way that I could reach out and smack you over the back of your head from here if you were to call me by any nickname you want."

"Good point," she said, and he could almost hear the grin of triumph in her voice. "Well, if you feel like eavesdropping on the meeting that will start in the next three minutes, I suggest you make a hard right…Jer."

"Fuck, I already regret this," Jeremiah protested. He turned right down what appeared to be an almost abandoned hallway. The whole place looked like it had been closed for renovations from the sight of the exposed wiring in the walls, but there weren't any signs that told him he shouldn't be there, so he continued.

"Okay, there aren't any cameras in that area of the building, but it should be the seventh door on your left," Anja said, and her voice had taken a more serious tone. He counted them quickly, pulled the door open, and winced as it creaked on its hinges. There wasn't anybody around to notice, though, so after a few seconds of listening for a reaction, he slipped into the room and closed the door behind him.

What he saw was odd. It was hard to really pin a description on a room that was about five feet by five feet, with the entire left side of the room covered in monitors. As he stepped inside, they turned on to display a wide variety of camera feeds from all around the damned building. He dropped onto the office chair provided at the screens.

"I assume that this whole thing is more your area of expertise than mine," he said as he scowled at the mouse and keyboard in front of him. "Which begs the question of why I'm here if you're more than capable of running this whole operation from the comfort of your desk?"

"Oh, that's easy." She brought the cameras from a conference room up on the screens directly in front of him. "I'm not close enough to be any help if Anderson suddenly needs backup. Plus, from what I saw in those videos, you are way better at punching people until they die than I am."

"Right." He leaned back in his seat. A horde of questions had already risen in his mind regarding precisely who this woman was. He knew a thing or two about computers, and he thought that he would be able to hold his own against the average Wi-Fi connection, but what this woman was currently doing was impressive. He had no doubt that she had accessed what he had to assume were secure camera feeds from wherever the fuck it was that she sat comfortably in her office.

Hell, it was downright scary. He'd never left much of a digital footprint before, and he seriously considered never doing so ever again. Knowing that there was someone out there who could actually track him down from anywhere on the globe and know as much about him as he knew about himself was enough to make a man wonder if the comfort was worth the loss in privacy.

For a lot of people, it wasn't much of a debate. They loved their luxuries and didn't mind the loss of privacy so long as it didn't intrude too deeply into their habitual laziness.

"The meeting's starting so you might want to focus," Anja said and drew his attention back to the screens. "I can see these people and process the data, but you're supposed to be the one who reads the people in there to assess the danger levels and act on it. Just saying."

"How did you know I was distracted?" he asked and leaned forward to prop his elbows on the desk in front of him. "I thought you said there weren't any cameras in this part of the building."

"Well, there weren't any in the hallway." He could hear the grin in her voice. "This is one of the older monitoring stations that was shut down for repairs and they never came back to it, even though they left the camera feeds and connection open. They needed to have someone watch the watchmen, as it were, so they put cameras inside the security rooms too. They only activate them when they're in use, so I had to do some electronic calisthenics to bring this feed online while not alerting anyone that this room is in use. Ain't no thing, as you Americans say."

"I can honestly say that I've never said that," he said with a soft chuckle. "And wait a second—why the hell would you want to keep an eye on me, anyway?"

"Well, I don't want it to sound like Anderson doesn't trust you or anything," Anja said.

"But he still wants someone to keep an eye on me to make sure I don't do anything stupid. Right," he said with a nod. "I get that. Oh, and by the way, I love that fucking movie."

"How good was Rorschach in that movie?" she asked.

"So good that I've actually used some of his lines out in the field." He grinned at the memories. "'I'm not stuck in here with you. You're all stuck in here with me' is a favorite. You'd be surprised at how relevant it becomes out in the field. Of course, you can say it out there, but you can't expect it to have the desired effect on people who don't speak English."

"Right," Anja said with a chuckle. "You know, I think we're getting off track here again. The meeting has already started."

"I'm following it, don't worry." Savage propped his head on his hands as he studied the screens closely. "I can multitask. Don't worry about that."

"That's not what I'm worried about. Do you see anything?"

He shook his head, knowing she could see it. There

were a couple of men standing up, and while there was an audio feed from the cameras, he mostly studied their body language. It had been a skill that he'd had from a young age and had developed with the help of some of his mentors from boot camp onwards. They told him that it wasn't a skill you could acquire. You had to have it, and only then could you hone it.

Right now, he wasn't sure about that. As he looked at the men who stood and delivered pre-prepared speeches welcoming a new member to the board and saw the mixture of boredom and annoyance in their faces, it seemed almost too obvious. Like they tried to let the newcomer know that she wasn't welcome.

The woman herself looked perfectly comfortable as she took her seat at the head of the conference table. She looked calm and collected, and yet there was something about her that seemed poised and on edge. It was as if she expected a fight and the dirty glares and false platitudes fed her anticipation. This was Anderson's benefactor, of that he had no doubt.

She looked young—almost too young to be in a place like this with so many veterans of the business game. Jeremiah didn't know enough about the woman to be able to pass judgment on her age, but it did make him wonder if she was a little out of her league in this situation.

Which was why Anderson was there, he mused. And it was also why he had been brought into this mess of corporate politics.

CHAPTER SEVEN

"So, who is this woman?" Jeremiah asked and stretched as most of the speeches came to an end, which opened the opportunity for her to finally make one of her own. It wasn't so much a meeting, he realized, as an introduction. She looked like she would take up a position of some authority over the men and women present, and while they didn't seem too happy about it, they appeared more than willing to let her have her say before they joined forces to depose her.

"Her name is Dr. Courtney Monroe," Anja explained. "I've actually met her. She's nice. A little intense, but nice. Anyway, she spent almost two years going in and out of the Zoo and was one of the first people to actually work inside the jungle. It made her…something of a legend."

"A doctor, huh?" He leaned in closer as she gathered her papers. Despite all appearances, she did look a little nervous at this point. It was perhaps a hint of glossophobia in her past that had been dealt with but still left a mark on her that itched every time she was called upon to speak in front of a large group of people. "Tell me something, Anja, have you ever been in the Zoo?"

There was a pause on the line as Monroe started her speech and addressed and thanked the various members of the board for their time.

"I went into that fucking jungle once," Anja finally said and a tense, uncomfortable tone entered her voice. "I didn't much care for the place. How about you?"'

"I've never been, I'm afraid," he said. "Although 'didn't much care for it' does seem to be the consensus among the people who went in there. Those that I met, anyway. But that raises a fascinating question. If the Zoo is such a terrifying place to be, what would drive someone without any prior combat experience—I'm assuming, anyway—to keep going in there for almost two years? Because if it's a death wish, I have to say that didn't work for her."

"I don't know, honestly," Anja said, and her chuckle sounded mirthless. "I've actually met a couple of people who are of a similar mind. I mean, they don't really enjoy going in there, but when they get back, they always look... refreshed. You know, the way that a person looks when they've returned from the gym?"

"Huh." He grunted. It was a common feeling—an adrenaline high was what his shrinks told him it was, one that made everything else feel like it was grey and lifeless by comparison. He knew that it was something screwed up in his brain, and while it was a common side effect of being crazy enough to charge into a war zone willingly, it was still interesting. In the back of his mind, he'd always assumed that there would be some kind of line that he would feel hesitant to cross. Now, though, he knew about a place that was even more dangerous than anywhere he'd ever gone before. A part of him wanted to at least try it out to see if it was as bad as everyone made it out to be.

That had to be something wrong with the wiring in his brain. He was aware that the human brain was more complex than that, but still.

"Thank you all so much for your warm welcome," Monroe said and let her gaze travel over the board members. "I could not imagine this company being run without the minds that brought it all together, and you should know that I fully intend to respect your decisions in the company so far. Honoring the spirit that built the house, as it were."

Oh, God, this wouldn't go well. There would be changes, and all she did was rub the fact that she now held the power to change the company in their faces. With the kind of mindset that was required to be in this business—the kind of ego that these people had to have—they definitely wouldn't take it lying down.

The question remained as to whether she did any of this on purpose or not.

"However, the embarrassments that Pegasus has suffered over the involvement in a variety of...unsavory ventures both inside the Zoo and out have left us open to outside attack," Monroe continued and leaned forward on the table in front of her. The more he watched her, the more he decided that everything she did was rehearsed and very, very deliberate.

What the hell was she doing? Was she trying to poke a hornet's nest?

"For precisely that reason, I've found that we need someone of experience on this board," she stated. "Someone who's overseen Pegasus holdings in and near the Zoo for the past few months and knows a thing or two about what we'll deal with in the following months of government investigation and audits. Please join me to welcome the new CEO of Pegasus' holdings in the continental US, James Anderson, a former colonel with the United States Marine Corps."

The shock of what she had said was enough to make the obligatory clapping broken and disjointed. Jeremiah watched as the corporate coyotes, amidst looks of shock and anger, jostled one another into a pack. He studied them with narrowed eyes. A few men rose from their seats, their papers in hand as if they had a whole horde of questions that they wanted to ask before Anderson was given his moment to speak. Some of them talked over each other. The audio coverage from the camera feeds made it difficult to make out even one voice, but so many climbing all over each other like Amazonian fire ants meant that all he could hear amounted to white noise.

But he didn't need to hear what they said. Their lips all seemed to converge on the word outrage enough to let him know that they were upset about bringing someone new and comparatively unknown into the fold, and in such a lofty position too.

No, what he was more interested in were the people who didn't have all kinds of outrage to express. Those who were taken by surprise by this move weren't the people he had been brought in to deal with. His mind was on those who had anticipated it and had already planned their next moves—five or six steps at a time. They were the ones who had the planning capacity to overthrow, for lack of a better term, someone who had forced herself into a ruling position on their board.

At the moment, there was only one man on his mind. He sat at the far end of the table and tapped on his phone despite the noise and ruckus around him. The executive was tall and lean and sported what could easily be described as the most expensive suit in the room, as well as the slickest portrayal of a silver fox that Jeremiah had ever seen. He wore a pair of glasses and seemed to have no interest in what happened around him whatsoever.

"Who's that guy?" he asked and pointed at the screen.

"I...can't see who you're pointing at, Jer," Anja pointed out.

"The guy with silver hair and an expensive suit sitting there with not a care in the world," he replied and tapped insistently at the screen in front of him.

"Oh, that's Evan Carlson, MBA out of Harvard. His father actually founded Pegasus back in 1941," Anja said. "Huh, look at that," she murmured. "Evan was actually the CEO in charge of operations in the continental US until three weeks ago, when he resigned the position and left it vacant. I assume for Anderson to fill?"

"Does that smell like a trap to you?" he asked.

"I...yes?" she replied.

"Well, yes, it is a trap. He intentionally left a vacuum for

Monroe to fill, which tells me that there's something tied to that position that he wants Anderson to take the fall for," he continued. "Do you think you can get a bead on what he's typing on his phone? Who he's talking to and why he's doing it during a power shift in his company?"

Anja went silent for a few moments and Savage assumed that she was typing away at her computer, hacking or…whatever it was that people like her did.

"Hey, Jer, I don't think I'll be able to break his encryption in time," she said when she finally came back online. "There's some serious coding involved. Like, military-grade shit. I can intercept what he sends to break later, but that's basically it. If you were able to clone his phone, though, I would have all the time in the world to handle it with no pressure from any security systems."

"Okay," Savage said. "How would you go about cloning his phone?"

"I need you to get that little piece of tech in your ear within fifteen meters of him," Anja explained. "With the signal that his phone gives off, I should be able to get my hands on a cloneable signal."

"Right," he said and nodded. "And how would we go about that, again?"

"Well, you need to get in close to him. How else do you think, genius?" She sounded exasperated.

"Honestly, I wondered if you would have been able to mail him the earpiece in a similar way to how you got it to me," he said with a shrug before he pushed himself from his chair and made his way toward the door.

"Come on, Jer, I had Anderson help me with that," she protested as he stepped out of the security room. All the lights went out behind him as he set off toward the elevators. The meeting was happening five floors up. If he could get there and not make anyone suspicious, getting within fifteen meters of the man would be a cakewalk.

"Hey, Jer?" Anja pinged his earpiece softly as he reached the elevators.

"What?" he muttered from the side of his mouth as others waited for the elevator alongside him.

"There's a small hiccup in the plan, but you should probably know that Carlson has exited the meeting prematurely," Anja said. "People were shocked, some were offended, and a couple needed smelling salts, but the fact remains that your target is on his way up to the fucking roof."

"Shit." His familiarization with the building's plans told him that the elevators only took people up to the eighteenth floor. There was a private elevator that pushed all the way up to the nineteenth, which was the penthouse, and stairs led from there up to the roof. Those stairs weren't accessible from any of the floors between the fifteenth and the eighteenth, as those levels had separate fire escape options.

"Fuck," he muttered softly and moved away from the elevators. "I'll have to have to climb ten fucking stories of building, won't I?"

"Considering that our friend has access to the private elevator, you might want to make that climb a sprint," she suggested. "You don't know how long he'll be up there, and you certainly don't want him to know that someone is tailing him. Right?"

"Correct," Jeremiah said. He'd already slipped into the

stairwell and proceeded to ascend at a sprint. As good as his therapy had been, he doubted that there was much his doctor could have done to prepare him for something like this. Even if he had been at the peak of physical health, he would have found rushing up ten flights of stairs an exhausting prospect.

And there he was, at less than his peak of physical health, sprinting up the stairs. He would be lucky if he didn't pass out at the top once his body had time to settle.

Fucking stairs.

He gripped the railings to help him after the first three flights, and after the fifth, he realized that his speed had greatly decreased. He had barely reached the eighteenth floor when Anja pinged his comm again.

"If you to tell me that there is more bad news waiting for me up there," he panted, "I will hunt you down in whatever fucking hole you're hiding in and kill you myself."

"Well, you might want to hold off on that," she replied and clearly didn't believe that he would follow through on his threat. "Four men are standing guard at the top of that staircase. They don't look armed, but they do look bulky, and they have radios on them."

"Shit," Savage hissed through clenched teeth. "Is there any way I can get to our target without engaging them?"

"That's a negative," she replied. "He's on the other side of the building, so unless you feel that we have the time to break into the penthouse office, I don't think so."

"Goddamnit," he said, probably too loudly, but he couldn't hear any reaction from above him.

He pulled his jacket off, hung it on the railing halfway up to the nineteenth floor, and yanked his tie off. He was about to hang it as well since it felt like it was soaked in sweat, but he quickly thought better of it and wound the pale red tie around his right fist.

"Is that a plan that I see hatching in that brain of yours, Jer?" Anja asked.

"I think so." He smiled despite the uncomfortable burning in his muscles. "I merely have to pray to whatever gods might listen that it's a good plan, or all this bullshit will be blown right to hell."

The tie bound around his hand gave him a little padding, and he kept the long, skinny end gripped in his left hand as he resumed his ascent of the last of the steps. He no longer rushed. At this point, if they heard him, the jig would be up, and they were all royally fucked. He had one chance to get this right.

Well, it was a good thing that they had brought in a savage, right?

"Will you still kill me for telling you the bad news?" she asked as he reached the nineteenth floor. He could hear conversation from the level above him.

He didn't think he could deliver on that promise. For one thing, he still had no idea where she was in the world. She could have been hiding out in the middle of the Amazon or all the way back in Russia, for all he knew. Considering that he had a job to do there, he doubted that he would be able to deliver on his promise of impending violence.

"Well, wait a second, and it might all be a moot point anyway," he whispered as he tried to make out the precise positions of the four men who stood in front of the door. "I'm about to attack four well-trained goons who have the height advantage and possible weapons, while the only weapon that I have is…" He looked at his hands. "A butt-fucking ugly tie."

"I believe in you?" Anja said.

"Shut up," he retorted.

CHAPTER EIGHT

The operative hugged the walls as he prepared himself for the last flight of stairs. He had recovered his breath, even if the sweating wouldn't go away in time. Well, tough, he would simply have to play into that. He gripped the tie tighter in his hands and drew in a deep breath.

Four men. He could hear them talking, and from the sound of their voices, he could more or less place them on the steps. One stood near the door. Two more stood on the same step, three down from the door to the roof, with the fourth seated five steps below that. From the sounds, Jeremiah assumed that the man was probably playing something on his phone.

He needed to come up with a game plan. While he was well aware that any plan that he came up with would go to shit the moment the first punch was thrown, he still needed to have an idea of what he intended to do. He needed to create a mental picture of his progression through the four men, something that would give him the best chance to get through them before Carlson decided to come down.

Also, he wanted to avoid them having any kind of contact with anyone outside. He knew these kinds of people well enough. If he showed up with a gun or some other kind of weapon, they would go for their radios first. As it was, if he attacked them by surprise, their first reaction would be to help their comrades before they reported it.

That was how it needed to happen. He couldn't afford to have a veritable army of security coming down on his head at this point. He didn't doubt that he would bash heads and trade bullets with these motherfuckers eventually, but he did want to keep it restricted to a time where he actually had some bullets to give back.

"Are you ready?" Anja asked through the earpiece.

"Are you sure you can't block their radio transmissions?" he asked and tried to keep his voice as low as possible.

"I can run some interference, but I can't guarantee that nothing will get through," she replied. He nodded, concerned that the men on the stairs would hear him if he said anything more. She would run that interference. It was up to him to make sure that it wasn't necessary.

"Do you actually have a plan?" she asked. He knew that she could see him. The stairs had cameras that were all connected to the central security system. He assumed that she would have a way to make sure that there was no evidence of him in the building, but he still needed to get in and out with the information they needed.

He gripped the tie in his hands, took a deep breath, and

reached in deep for that cold, violent part of himself as he started up the steps. All attempts at stealth had been discarded as he stormed up the last flight of stairs and circled into view of the four men that guarded the door.

A quick assessment of the situation confirmed what he already knew. The man playing on his phone tucked the device into his pocket and took another step down. The others looked relaxed enough, but Savage could see the radios hanging from their hips. They didn't look like they had any other weapons on them—no holsters on their belts or tucked under their suits. They could have been packing something tucked into their pants, but he doubted it.

Still, there was no sense in playing too fast or too loose.

"What are you doing here?" the man on the lowest stair asked and scowled at Savage. "This is a restricted area."

"Dude, I work here," he said and assumed a more submissive posture to hide the tie wrapped around his hand. "I always come up here for a smoke break. What the hell are you guys doing here?"

He noted a hint of confusion among the four men. They were all new and weren't aware of which locations in or on the building were restricted to staff members. Their status as new members of security plus the confidence that he projected made them hesitant, which allowed Savage to take another couple of steps up the stairs without raising their alarm levels.

"Look, man," the man at the top said and tried to be reasonable. "We were told to keep this place clear of all foot traffic, no exceptions. Can't you find yourself another place to smoke this one time?"

"Come on, man, I hiked all the way up here from the

twelfth floor," he whined and ascended another step. "It's one cigarette and I'll be gone. I don't even need to get out of sight of the door. I only have fifteen minutes off."

He breathed deeply as he watched the man closest to him take another step down to stop him with a hand on his shoulder. He knew it was meant as a friendly gesture, to comfort him over the thought that he would have to hike all the way down and probably give up his smoke break.

Jeremiah honestly felt bad about what he was about to do to these men. They were honest, working-class citizens, some of whom were veterans. Brothers.

That said, he knew what he had to do, and they were in his way.

He reacted quickly at the same moment that the man's hand touched his shoulder. The tie anchored by his hand worked as a leverage point and he slid it around his opponent's wrist and twisted it savagely. With a soft grunt of surprise, the man's body was yanked around by the manipulation of his arm and shoulder and his head smacked into the railing to his left. The soft crunch was masked by the ringing sound from the brass railing.

Savage gripped the back of the man's head and hammered it into the railing one more time for good measure.

The clock was ticking. Surprise would turn to annoyance and then into rage as the men saw their comrade take two hits like that. He had less than two seconds before he would have three men to deal with at one time.

He bounded up the three steps between himself and the two men who had begun to descend. The one closest to him leaned in to power a heavy haymaker at him. He used both hands and the tie between to hook the man's wrist, drag it to the side, and throw him off balance.

One of the problems with having his hands bound in the same length of cloth was that he didn't have much range in his striking ability. This forced him to replace momentum with balance to power his strikes.

On the bright side, he could bring a lot more speed to bear.

He came in close and hammered a series of three hard punches to his opponent's stomach, aimed at the solar plexus. The air rushed from the guard's lungs as he doubled over and tried to catch his breath. The operative didn't give him the opportunity. As he twisted his body, his elbow hammered into the man's temple. He crumpled without a sound.

Savage shifted as a fist collided with the side of his torso and grunted softly when he felt a stab of pain from his ribs. There wasn't any cracking sound, so he could safely assume that nothing had broken with the impact, but it still hurt like a motherfucker. Which made it far more satisfying when his body spun out of instinct and his elbow lashed out to strike the man on the side of the head hard enough to make his elbow ache.

The third guard lost his balance, and if the elbow hadn't knocked him unconscious, the tumble down the stairs would have.

That left only one more. Who the hell said that plans were bad for a fight like this? Well, he was fairly sure that nobody in history had said that, but he could still feel a hint of pride in his work.

The fourth and last man standing looked at him and the

realization that he might actually now face someone who was more than he could handle finally dawned on him. Based on that knowledge, he made the smartest move—one that had eluded the three men who hadn't been quite as astute.

He reached for the radio at his hip.

"No, no, no," Savage snarled as he bounded up the final few steps to the top and reached him as he raised the device to his head. It was old-school like most security systems were.

The operative looped the tie around the guard's wrist and pulled it tight. He twisted and yanked hard and the man growled and cried out in pain. A gentle crack from his hand indicated that something had broken, and Savage hauled hard to drag his target closer to him.

The radio fell, clattered down the steps, and shattered on the way. That was one problem solved, at least. He wondered if the people around there would invest a little more intelligently and give their security personnel earpieces after today. Then again, they were all hired from a third party, so he sincerely doubted it. Pegasus would most likely hire a company that equipped their people better, though.

The man roared in pain and swung a hook at Savage's head, which he ducked to avoid. He dragged the man's trapped hand down and the rest of him followed, and he brought his right elbow up into his adversary's torso with as much power as he could muster. It wasn't much, but in the end, the security officer's momentum as he fell forward added the impetus needed. Ribs crunched and his lungs expelled his breath in a rush as he flailed and tried to pull himself in closer to avoid any further hits like that. It was a good tactic but one that required being on the losing end of the fight in the first place—and it was one the operative had trained for. You had to train to win. Everyone knew that.

Savage brushed his adversary's good hand aside, shook him off, and released the broken wrist from the tie. In almost the same motion, he twisted on his back foot to hammer a hook behind the man's ear. The guard's eyes remained open, but they glazed over and gave him enough time to loop the tie around his neck and drag him toward the railing. With a grunt of exertion, he pushed him over.

A hint of guilt touched Jeremiah as the man dropped to the lower floor. He didn't want to kill anyone there, but everything in his training had told him to push the beating to the extreme and really release his inner beast—the one he kept hidden from everyone, even Julia. He always maintained a tight hold on it and didn't want to get used to feeling the rush that came when he handed out violence with utmost prejudice.

It was only a floor down. The guard gasped for breath as he came to again. He would have a concussion and a broken rib, and Jeremiah had to assume there were some other broken bones from the fall. But he would live. He'd seen softer people walk off with less.

Still, it was still a shitty feeling. He didn't like it, but it was supposed to be what made him human or something like that. It was supposed to be a good thing, too.

He gritted his teeth. If he had time, he would make sure that someone brought medical help to make sure that they were all breathing. They would be able to sue their employers for their on-the-job injuries, which would pay for their medical costs and give them a good amount of money on top of that. They might retire in relative comfort on that kind of money. Any company that wanted to keep hiring people would pay out without too much fuss.

It wouldn't make up for the injuries, but in situations like this, you had to look for the silver linings. Otherwise, the world was simply the worst kind of mess with very few redeeming qualities. He unwound his hands from the tie and gripped the railing until he was sure they had stopped shaking.

"Are you all right?" Anja asked. She sounded more subdued over the little earpiece than she'd been the last time.

He could understand why.

"Yeah," he replied and dragged in a deep breath. "I need to let the adrenaline wash away."

"Don't take this the wrong way, but you're kind of scary," she said as he moved toward the door. "That was an inventive way to get rid of four guys. I only hope they're all right."

"Me too," Jeremiah admitted. "Me too."

He eased out onto the roof and stayed low enough that he wouldn't be sky-lined. The sun was still out, even though it was well on its way to sinking toward the horizon. It hadn't moved enough to splash the sky with colors, but he could feel a chill as the temperature changed.

It occurred to him again that he needed to get his hands on a gun—or some kind of weapon, at least. He felt naked without anything to fight back with except for what was now a blood-stained tie.

"You're in range of his phone," Anja announced, and he immediately stopped. "I'm starting the cloning now."

Savage nodded and dropped into a crouch. This wasn't his show anymore, it was hers. Any information that would come from this whole shindig would be a result of what she was able to get from his phone, which made him the muscle and her the brains.

It wasn't like he hadn't done it before. He breathed deeply and released the tension in his shoulders, his jaw, and his hands. Right now, he needed to be relaxed. The exertions of the day had begun to tell on him. He still wasn't at his peak, he realized, and that needed to change. His position as the muscle of the organization required him to actually function as the muscle. He rubbed his ribs and grimaced at a spike of pain as he did so. His wrists and arms ached too, and his knuckles had swelled, even though he had wrapped them.

Yep, he definitely needed to up his game if he wanted to fulfill his purpose in this organization.

"I'm done with the cloning," the hacker said. "And it looks like our boy is headed back to the door, so if you feel like making an escape, now's the time."

Savage nodded, unsure if she could see him do it. He hadn't seen any cameras on the roof, but he had some lasting paranoia about what satellites could see, thanks to some underrated spy films involving Gene Hackman—as well as who might be using them.

He peeled away from his cover and moved as quickly and quietly as he could toward the door. There was no doubt that he could beat Carlson there, especially since he could detect the very noticeable odor of nicotine. The man had taken advantage of his time up there to sneak a quick smoke in, which told the operative that the man was a little less settled about what was happening than one might think.

In a few moments, he made it to the door and pulled it gently closed before he jogged down to the stairwell. He paused for a moment to check that all the men were still down and alive. It took only a couple of seconds to gather their radios, just to be safe, and he threw them down the steps to break as he continued his descent.

"Could you alert someone to the fact that there are four men in the stairwell who are in need of medical assistance?" Jeremiah asked as he retrieved his jacket and pulled it on.

"Already done," Anja said. "So long as you're out of there in the next few minutes, our boys over there should make a full recovery. Do you think they'd be able to identify you to anyone who might ask?"

"I doubt it," he said and increased his pace. He would have to get rid of the tie somewhere else. Obviously, he couldn't return it to the locker that he'd taken it from. "In the heat of the moment, they won't remember much of what they saw. They'll recall the fact that I wore a uniform and maybe my hair color and basic features, but not much else. Especially with the concussions that some of them have, they won't be reliable witnesses and probably wouldn't recognize me if they encountered me on the street. Here's where I cross my fingers that they'll make a full recovery."

"Cross your fingers?" Anja asked.

"Oh…it's like…knocking on wood?" he said as he reached the fifteenth floor.

"Americans are weird," Anja muttered.

"No argument there." He gave himself a quick once-over to make sure that nothing about his appearance would draw any attention. Other than the light sheen of sweat that covered his body, nothing seemed out of place. He had to hope that it wouldn't be a problem because if medical professionals scoured the stairwell, he couldn't be found. With a deep breath, he pushed the door open and closed it carefully before he stepped back into the offices that he'd left behind.

Nothing looked different. People worked at laptops or talked on phones, held meetings, and conducted the businesses that were a part of their everyday lives. He made his best attempt to look normal as he moved to the elevator.

"You're looking up what knock on wood and crossed fingers are, aren't you?" he said quietly out the side of his mouth as the elevator arrived—thankfully, empty.

"Yes," she admitted. "But that's not the point. I'm working on wiping any footage of your having been in the building. Considering the kind of crap security that these guys have protecting their local servers, it shouldn't be too difficult."

"I think they outsource all their security in this building," Jeremiah observed as the elevator opened to the basement. He walked back toward the lockers and made sure to maintain an even pace, the kind that people did when they had finished a long day of work and didn't want to be rushed yet were still in a hurry to get home.

"That's the thing," Anja said. "From my experience with

these assholes, they've had everything locked up tighter than a baroness' jewels. Yet a couple of weeks ago, everyone was moved off-site, and they brought in a bunch of cut-rate outsiders to handle it."

"Did Carlson actually work with those guys I tussled with upstairs?" he asked as he stepped into the still-abandoned locker rooms.

"Yes, those were his personal boys," she said softly.

"You're not watching me change, right?" Savage asked as he yanked off the uniform that he'd sweated in.

"Sorry, Jer, no cameras in the lockers," she responded and almost sounded disappointed. "So you're not worried about all these changes that happened in the company just as Ceecee is taking control of it?"

"Ceecee?" he asked as he dressed in normal clothes.

"Courtney," she replied. "As in, Monroe. As in your boss' boss. I need to lay all this out for her. She might be walking into a trap with this whole company."

"She's undoubtedly walking into a trap," Savage replied. "But that's no reason not to spring the trap in question. She wants to know what it is that Carlson has planned. Now that she knows to be careful, it's less likely that he'll be able to take her by surprise."

"And if he does anyway?" Anja asked.

"Well, that's where I come in, right?" he replied with a small grin as he moved out of the locker rooms, now dressed in a pair of jeans and a bowling shirt. It hadn't been necessary to change out of the heavy shoes that he'd come in wearing.

"Right. All the footage of you in the building is erased. I also went ahead and helped the folks in the security company that hired you to lose the paperwork that they had on you. There's now no official trace of you having been in the building, and more importantly, nothing connecting you to anyone else there either."

"A good day all around."

"Although I would suggest that you leave the building as quickly as possible," Anja warned him. "I received a notification from Carlson's phone. He found the guys from your little fist party upstairs and has called someone, and it's not the medical services."

"What an asshole," he said with a grin, but he increased his pace to a jog toward the exit. "Not as big an asshole as the guy who left them in that state in the first place, but still."

CHAPTER NINE

Jeremiah sat in a Denny's restaurant and stared at nothing as the day's events spooled in his head. His ribs ached and his wrist felt as if it were sprained, at least.

"Sir?"

He blinked and dragged his gaze from its million-mile stare to the young woman who stood beside him. She wore a waitress' uniform and carried a pot of what was hopefully freshly brewed coffee. Although she was small, she had the look of someone who carried herself and others through the sheer force of her good mood. She also seemed to be the kind of person who didn't mind being that kind of person.

"I'm sorry, I must have zoned out," he said and managed a sheepish smile. "What were you saying?"

"Well, I asked if you needed a top-up," she replied with a smile that seemed both natural and practiced. "And when you didn't answer, I asked if you felt all right. And that's when you came back to us."

Jeremiah chuckled. "I could do with a top-up, yeah."

She smiled again and poured the steaming black stuff into his mug. "Are you having a rough day?"

He shook his head. "Not rough. Merely long. Well, maybe a little rough, but I've had rougher."

"So have we all, mister," she replied and despite the humor in her tone, he somehow believed she meant it. "It don't take away from the toughness, though. I hope your day gets better."

"Thanks," he replied and sipped the brew appreciatively. He had mostly demolished the steak and was halfway through the fries. Actually, he even toyed with the idea of eating the salad. This was supposed to be a cheat day, after all, but he didn't feel very hungry at the moment. It was common in soldiers right after combat. The adrenaline wore off and they developed jitters in their hands and experienced a loss of appetite and drowsiness. He knew the effects of it almost too well, and it never stopped sucking balls.

Jeremiah selected one of the fries, dipped it in ketchup, and took a bite. It tasted like ash, tomatoes, and sugar, with a hint of potato mixed in. Potatoes didn't have much of a taste, anyway.

He threw the unfinished fry down on his plate and sighed. This was what he hated. He detested the whole downer feeling that he experienced every time he went into combat. At a rough guess, it was most likely his body acclimating to the heightened state of focus and prowess that came with an overdose of adrenaline pumping through his veins. When it faded, something that felt very much like a hangover inevitably took its place.

After a deep breath, he finished his coffee and left half of the fries and the salad for someone else to finish or throw out, as people did around there. He had to furtively check the other diners to see what the acceptable tip amount was, and he tipped precisely that, no more and no less. There was no need to make anyone any more aware of him than they already were.

It was funny, he supposed. Jeremiah Johnson was dead, and from that point onward, he needed to act the part. He would have to be a ghost, whether he liked it or not.

The thought rattled around in his head as he made his way out of the diner and pulled his jacket on. This shit wasn't acceptable. He had a new life, wasn't paying alimony anymore, and had a lot of money to fall back on and many skills that would be in high demand if he wanted to market them. He was free and clear if he wanted to be.

And yet...something about this whole situation didn't appeal to him. What was he supposed to do with his life now? For so long, it had been all about serving his country first, getting his boys in and out of their hardcore missions alive and well—for the most part—and then helping to raise his baby girl into troublesome adulthood.

Before the divorce, his priorities had been a little different. He had spent more time at home, taken his daughter to school, and...hell, was she still going to soccer practice?

After he and Jules had parted ways, she had told him that he could be as involved as he liked. Over the first few months, he'd tried, he really had. Then, she started dating Andy, and Mr. I'm-a-lawyer-and-I-have-regular-hours was actually a decent person and genuinely cared for both Jules and Abigail.

No, Jeremiah didn't hate Andy, and for the life of him, he couldn't understand why. But as it turned out, he was the jealous type, and watching the love of his life fall in love with another man had made him regress into the kind of person the US government had invested millions into making him be. He'd picked up another tour and gotten the hell out of Dodge. While he'd made it back a couple of times for Abigail's bigger moments, other than that, he'd avoided going home.

Abby seemed to understand. He hated that, but she was happy when he visited, sad when he had to leave, and never once tried to play the guilt card to push him away or bring him closer. She simply wasn't the manipulative type. As it turned out, Andy was a good influence on her life. That rat bastard.

He pulled the Toyota up to his dingy motel room and stared at the aquamarine-colored door. "Fuck," he growled as he reached the door of his room and patted his jacket for his keys. "I need to get laid."

"Well, I don't think I can help you with that," Anja said through the earpiece. "Although I can direct you to some of the best places where you can find someone who takes cash and doesn't ask questions on short notice."

"Yeah, that would be great," he said with a chuckle. "I don't think I'm in any kind of shape to get laid, though."

"How *are* you feeling?" she asked and sounded a little less playful than she had all day. "You doled out a real beating, but I can't imagine that you didn't take some punishment yourself."

Jeremiah sighed as he moved into his room, locked the

door behind him, and removed his jacket. He groaned softly and probed his side tentatively.

"Bruised ribs," he said and hauled his shirt off to inspect the place where one of the men had actually landed a punch. He winced as he leaned to the side and grimaced at the dark-purple bruising that definitely explained the pain. "My arm and wrist are a little sore, my knuckles are bruised, and my muscles feel like shit. Fuck, I'm out of shape."

"You seemed in shape to me. Just saying," she said.

"Well, comparatively speaking," he replied as he bound his ribs with some tape. He winced at the immediate pain that came from it but sighed as the anesthetic in the tape took immediate effect. He was finally a little more comfortable. "Wait, you can see me?"

"Of course not," she said with a chuckle. "But I do have footage from the fight. And the sprinting up the stairs. And seriously, I hang around people who stay in combat shape all the time, and I don't think any of them could keep up with what you did."

"Well, yeah, obviously," Jeremiah said with a chuckle. "They pick the best and brightest to join the 75th, and it only gets harder from there. All respect to the Marines that they probably have scouring that Zoo place—and if I'm honest, they probably have more balls than I do by running around there, but..."

"What?" Anja asked as his voice trailed off.

"I...army guys make it a habit to trash everyone who isn't army," Jeremiah said with a chuckle. "I mean, that's the same with most of the branches. They trash everyone who isn't them, but there's always respect between the boys in the service. We all put our lives on the line for our country. Except I'm not one of the boys anymore. I'm a dead man, and all my ties to any of my service died with me."

She didn't reply.

"Sorry," he said and dragged in a deep breath. "I'm bringing the mood down. I…kind of…uh, have to be alone right now."

"No worries," she said quickly. "Take the earpiece out of your ear and it'll disconnect you."

"Thanks for all your help today, Anja," he said softly. "I couldn't have done it without you."

"Duh," she said with a chuckle. "Rest well, Jer. You have a long day tomorrow. I need a couple of hours to decrypt all this junk from Carlson's phone anyway."

He made no answer and instead, removed the earpiece and placed it on the bedside table. Having someone in the fight with him was all that he could really ask for, but he still felt like shit.

While he still had the energy, he applied the same tape that he'd put around his ribs to his knuckles and growled softly as it squeezed and felt more painful than the ribs had. Once the pain subsided, he lay back on the bed and closed his eyes. Despite the drowsiness, he still felt wired. It seemed very clear that he wouldn't drift off to sleep, despite the lateness of the hour. He had taken a shower, had a decent meal, and now, he was supposed to sleep the adrenaline hangover off.

It was the coffee. He shouldn't have drunk the damned coffee.

Irritated, Jeremiah rolled over to the side of the bed and picked up the burner that he'd left on the table beside it. He flipped it open and took a moment to familiarize himself with the controls of the cheap, old device.

He found the numeric pad, and after a few seconds of internal debate, he entered a telephone number. One of the downsides of having a memory as good as his was the knowledge that he would never be able to forget the number that he'd made himself delete from all his phones and all his databases. Of course, he didn't actually have those phones anymore, so it was a moot point.

The phone rang and he pressed it to his ear. The call was across the country, so he was sure that it would bite deeply into the prepaid minutes on this phone. That was fine, of course. He didn't need to make any other calls, so it wasn't like the minutes would be missed. It was only a way for Anderson to contact him when he needed something.

Jeremiah stared as the phone continued to ring, and as he waited, he began to question whether or not this was a good idea. The more he thought about it, the more he realized that it was terrible.

At the eighth ring, the dial faded at the press of a button on the other side.

"Hello?" A woman's voice answered. He opened his mouth, but he couldn't bring himself to say anything. Jules had been to his funeral. She'd met with all his old army buddies who were there to tell her what a hero he'd been and that his memory would live on. Abigail needed to have her normal life with Andy as her dad. Sure, she would feel sad that he was gone, but there was already someone there to take his place. He'd already been obsolete, and they both knew it. There wasn't much to say that would change that. He was a relic from a life that she'd already left behind.

Him calling in a moment of stupidity wouldn't change anything. It wouldn't make anything better. It would only complicate her life—and his. There was no way that would all end without pain for everyone involved, including him.

"Hello?" she said and sounded frustrated. "Look, I can hear you breathing, asshole, so don't think that I won't pass this number on to the cops. I don't need this kind of harassment."

Thankfully, he knew her well enough to feel confident that she wouldn't follow up on that threat. She'd simply vent her frustration and ignore it for now—as long as he wasn't stupid enough to pull the same trick more than once. Even twice was once too many. For sure, she'd call out the cavalry if he made another dumbass attempt to hear her voice.

Still, a few more seconds passed before he could actually bring himself to press the button that cut the connection. Warm tears trickled down his cheeks as he placed the phone on the bed. The device slipped from his numb fingers.

Jeremiah Johnson was dead. He wouldn't come back, and he wouldn't reconnect with his family. Jules wouldn't see him across a crowded room and jump into his arms. Abigail wouldn't come over and hug him and be happy that Mommy and Daddy were together again. That simply wasn't how the world worked. He needed to get that information through his thick skull. There was no coming back from the dead for him. Not today, not tomorrow, and not ever.

He lay back on his bed and stared at the ceiling. The tears fell for a short while, but after a few minutes, they stopped and something that definitely resembled peace filled his mind. Closing that door in his life for good, while painful, was something that he hadn't looked forward to doing at all. He knew that it needed to be done, even if he had courted the idea that he could somehow slide away from the inevitable.

That didn't mean that it might not happen one day. He could always circle back in a couple of years in the future and meet his daughter, have a coffee, and maybe crack some joke about actually being a zombie—provided he survived that long. Considering the day that he'd had, it wasn't a given that he would be around for a few more years. Things would only get worse from here on in.

No. He shook his head firmly and had a mental conversation with himself. Jeremiah Johnson would be a dead man from this point forward. There was no daughter, no ex-wife, no detestably likable new boyfriend—or fiancé, rather. Jeremiah Johnson was dead.

Jeremiah Savage was who remained, and he wouldn't live in the past or be chained by futile longings that would only bring more pain to everyone concerned. He had a job to do, one that would save the lives of the men and women whom he cared for. He could do that in the guy's honor.

His muscles gradually relaxed as he looked at the ceiling. Releasing that part of him felt...pleasant. Like he no longer carried a heavy load and he could actually start to live his life. From here on out, he could live free from all entanglements and from everything that had held him back before.

He closed his eyes, and this time, coffee or no coffee, he drifted off without any effort. It had been a long day.

CHAPTER TEN

His eyes flickered open. Whatever bright something that glared into them remained persistent and, for the life of him, wouldn't fucking go away. He blinked a few times and rolled in the bed as he wondered if he'd closed the blinds in his room. No...

He blinked a few times and finally realized what had woken him. The blinds were pulled, which meant that the tiny blot of light that came through and ruined his sleep pushed through the cracks in the shades. Which, he reasoned morosely, was only to be expected from a place like this. Running cheap was basically their business motto. That, and ID's weren't necessary for check-in.

Something buzzed in his room—something loud and obnoxious, which made it impossible for him to go back to sleep. He still felt like he needed a couple more hours, but it obviously wouldn't happen.

The buzzing thing was the phone he'd put on the night-stand. The one he'd called Jules with. He scowled at it and wondered for a moment if she had redialed. All the complications that would come with that were notably cringe-worthy, but he quickly put that thought aside. It wasn't the likely answer.

More than likely, though, was that it was his employers wanting to get in touch with him to talk about what had happened the day before. The men had been found and there was probably an ongoing investigation, but the fact that no flashing red and blue lights were outside to help ruin his sleep along with the sunlight meant that Anja had done a good job of covering his tracks.

He picked the phone up as it started to ring again and groaned softly as he pressed the receive call button. "What?" he demanded into the receiver as he dragged himself up from the bed.

"What?" Anja's very familiar style of sass and Russian accent sounded way too chirpy for this early in the morning. "Yeah, that's nice. What, is that I've called you for the past fifteen fucking minutes. Why don't you answer your damned phone? Or phones, I should say?"

Well, this wasn't a promising start to the day. He drew in a deep breath and tried not to get defensive. It helped to remind himself that he did not need to go on the attack. Self-control was necessary these days, he mused as he scratched the stubble that had made a home on his cheek.

"I'm sorry. I didn't sleep well," he said. "What's up?"

"I'm still decrypting the stuff from Carlson's phone," she replied, and he could hear her typing into a computer through their connection. "There's a lot of stuff to work through. I've already sent everything that I have to Courtney and Anderson and given them a heads-up about what Carlson might be up to."

"Do you know what he's doing?" he asked and grimaced at the crumpled clothes that he hadn't bothered to remove before he went to sleep. At least he had some new duds to change into. The thought made him feel marginally better. He knew that very soon, he would head out to hunt or kill or acquire intel—wherever it was that Anja would send him next.

"I don't have a perfect bead on it yet," she said quickly. "But it seems that after everything happened three weeks ago, he's been doing damage control. A lot of people were fired and then rehired by another shell corporation that was tied to Pegasus, but again, not after three weeks ago. He's pulling everything that he's been doing in Pegasus away. There's a lot of work that he put into the company that I think he wants to continue, and he's putting the continuation of the work above actually getting back at Courtney and Anderson. It would seem that they're not really a priority at the moment."

"And that's a bad thing?" Jeremiah asked, moved to the closet, and examined the new clothes inside. The tags were still on them, and he chose a pair of chinos and a pale blue Polo shirt. Knowing he would be there for another two and a half weeks or so, he looked high and low for an iron in case he needed to launder what little he had. He was fresh out of luck, though, and scowled as a single word came to mind. *Unacceptable!* It was the military man in him, of course. Steel-edged creases had been drilled into him for years, and it wasn't something you simply walked away from. Not willingly, anyway.

"Do you think he means to pursue what happened to his men yesterday or get back at us in some way?" he asked.

"Well, not really," Anja replied, still tapping at her computer. "It means that while getting back at our people is on his list of priorities, it's pretty damn low. It also means that since we don't have to be on the defensive, we can actually go on the offensive. There's still a lot that we don't know about this man. He could have plans on top of plans that could end up hurting our benefactors anyway."

"I have to imagine that after yesterday, our man knows that he has someone on his tail and will eventually want payback for his injured men, right?" Jeremiah asked. He had pulled his new pants on and now stood staring at himself in the mirror. His body sported a lot of fresh scars, but many of them were hidden behind the tats that covered the flesh of his right side. He was inordinately proud of his ink. Much of it was military and some of it was taken from snapshots of his ex-wife and daughter, intertwined with vines of ivy and the serpentine tail of a fighting dragon. Anja's words interrupted his thoughts.

"That's the thing," Anja replied. "After he found the men you left behind, he didn't try to call any emergency services or anything. I have audio on the call from the cameras, but I only have one side. He was calling someone to tell them to step up the schedule, and that he needed the facility empty before the weekend."

"Were you able to track the call and find out where this facility is?" He hurried into the bathroom to brush his teeth, twisted the water faucet, and winced as his wrist twinged in outrage. As he hissed through his teeth, he decided to stop lolling around like a lazy piece of shit and buff up smartly before his hard-earned strength abandoned him completely when he needed it the most.

"No and yes, respectively," Anja said. "Tracking the call was a little complicated, considering that it was routed through a lot of redundant VPNs and the call cut off before I could get around to finding the source. But I did see that the IRS was notified about a massive chunk of funds pushed into a small Pegasus facility in North Carolina. There are a lot of payments into that place, but they were always very well-covered. It seems like he doesn't care much about covering his tracks anymore."

"Or maybe Carlson is trying to use the IRS to depose Monroe and Anderson," Savage replied. "Or both. There's no reason he couldn't be using the one stone, two birds tactic. I can't imagine that he doesn't have something like that in mind."

"Right," Anja said. "Anyway, Mr. Carlson has chartered a company jet to head to North Carolina to look over Pegasus' business interests in the area. Apparently, that's where the company sent most of their research—you know, enough big locations to keep all the goop research away from the civilians."

"The what research?" Savage asked.

"Oh…nothing, never mind," she replied, evading the question quickly. "Courtney had to approve the chartering since there's no reason why one of the senior members of the board shouldn't go out to check on how all the research is coming along. That said, she and Anderson don't trust him as far they can throw him, as Americans say, so they want you to head to the location as well and keep an eye on him."

"You keep using American idioms, but you constantly reinforce that it's what the 'Americans' say," he said with a chuckle. "If I didn't know better, I'd say that it's what you say too. Don't Russians have your own idiots to translate?"

"Our *idioms* don't really work in English," Anja said but didn't sound quite sure, like she'd never actually tried it. "They don't translate well from language to language. It requires too much knowledge of the culture. Kind of a linguistic form of an inside joke."

"Right. I've always hated inside jokes, ya know," he said. "So, is it wise that I'm the one tracking Carlson down? Won't he recognize me from the dust-up yesterday? One of his goons could have given him a description."

"Well, he never ran into you personally," Anja reminded him. "And the men whom you worked over are still in the hospital. He made no effort to speak to them on site or at the hospital. Anyway, like you said, they wouldn't have recalled much as it happened so quickly. It looks like they'll make a full recovery, but I can keep an eye on them if you'd like."

"That's not necessary," he said.

"Well, the records and security feeds have all been wiped," she confirmed. "It was a rush job, so the people combing through the servers will know that they were wiped, but they won't ever be able to reverse-track me. I'm good like that. Still, they know that there's someone working in the shadows against them. You'll need to be a touch more careful from this point forward. Anyway, you should be in the clear."

"Roger that," he said with a nod. He had been rushed into some situations that he would have preferred to avoid back there, so he wouldn't argue against the obvious. "Wait a second, *should* be in the clear?"

"It's the best I can do," Anja said. "I have a plane ticket lined up to get you to Charlotte, but you'll have to rent a car and drive to the location. Your plane leaves in...three hours, so you might want to hurry and get packed, and I'll text the details to your phone. Oh, and try and keep your earpiece on."

"I'll take that under advisement." He grinned as he pressed the button to end the call, opened the bathroom door, and tossed the phone onto the bed. Three hours. He had time for a quick shower, a shave, and packing before he called a taxi to get him to the airport once he dropped the rental off. It was unlikely that he would need his passport, but it was like Anja had said when he first moved into the room. It wasn't like the safe would actually stop anyone from coming after him, so he would need to keep everything he owned close. Now that was he was on the radar of the people he was going up against, he didn't want to leave anything behind for them to use against him.

He stepped into the shower and turned the water as hot as he could stand it. The familiar sting rushed over his body as he lathered himself hastily in soap and shampoo and washed it all away. He took a moment to inspect his wounds, new and old, to make sure that nothing had broken or ruptured during the night. He could still feel pain in his side, and there were additional colors behind his already colorful tattoos. His newer wounds ached more than usual, but not so much that he entertained the idea of visiting a doctor. That was a luxury that his inherent caution rejected.

Walk it off! he mused with a sardonic smirk. *Rub dirt on it and the pain will go away.* That was what the drill instructors always said, but right now, that phrase seemed like the story of his life.

He stepped out of the shower and wrapped a towel around his waist. Then, he shaved, combed his hair, and decided he needed a new haircut. Not high and tight like before, but short and possibly even stylish. He chuckled and murmured, "I'm not a military man now, so I might as well knock 'em dead with my fine good looks."

Thankfully, he remembered to pull the price tags off before he dressed quickly, so he didn't look like Minnie Pearl. He filled his duffle with everything he owned. It was spacious and everything fit perfectly, even the new suit and dress shoes he'd purchased. He called for a taxi and walked to the front desk to return his key.

"Philadelphia International Airport, here I come," he muttered, pressed the earpiece into his ear, shouldered his bag, and headed toward the motel's front door.

Anja heard him end the connection and leaned back in her seat. It creaked softly as she leaned back as far as the seat would go before it flipped and she fell on her back. Any other employee would request a replacement with something that wouldn't fall over and didn't make annoying noises every time you sat down, got up, or leaned back. But the soft noises were comforting to her.

It felt worn, something that she had a measure of power over. Home was where the heart was, and to her, the heart came from the way that the A-key was already worn on her keyboard, the way the chair creaked, and the scratches on the floor from rolling her chair around instead of getting up and walking.

This was home. There were all kinds of psychological implications that came with what she did in this room, and she did spend a couple of quiet nights researching that. She had even talked with a few psychiatrists whom she was able to track down over the dark web. Most of them seemed to agree that it was a subconscious effort on her part to make a foreign location feel more like home. It made sense, and she didn't think that it was really a bad thing. A part of her simply wanted to be reminded of a home that she was forced to leave.

And she was actually okay with that.

She gripped the sides of her chair and her eyes scrutinized the screen in front of her. While she had erased the video files from the cameras in the building, she had copied one of them for herself. Well, most of them, actually. The bulk of the footage was simply Savage lurking around the building and trying not to get caught.

There were some small tidbits that she was interested in keeping, though. A part of her wondered if she was drawn to it because she wanted to think that this was all some action movie that happened too far away for her to actually worry about. And yet the way that he had dropped away from the action and immediately worried about the men he'd all but annihilated was something that she hadn't seen in the videos of him in action.

Anja remembered those. She'd watched them and pushed them away. Seeing someone stepping into a kill or be killed state of mind was...unsettling. She'd watched him knife and gun his way through assailants, some of them unarmed because he couldn't risk taking prisoners or leaving potential enemies behind. He'd made that decision in a split second and punctuated it with a one-liner…and then had long conversations with the man. To actually see someone who could switch from one to the other without so much as a blink was definitely unsettling.

"Hey, Anja, are you coming?" someone asked from the door. She glanced up from the screen. Madigan stood in the doorway. She looked sweaty like she had just come from a workout.

"Coming…where?" Anja asked, tilting her head.

"Sal wanted to have a meeting to get an update on everything that's happening in the States," the other woman said and stepped into the room. "He's getting Courtney, Anderson, and Robinson on a group call to include everyone on this. We need to have everyone on the same page, and that includes you. Especially since you're the one holding most of the information we need."

"Right," she said. "Before we go, could you take a look at this for me?"

Madigan moved closer to the screen and narrowed her eyes as the video flipped to a man coming up a flight of stairs to greet a group of four men, a tie wound round his hands.

"Woah." She chuckled and fanned imaginary heat away from her body in a theatric flourish. "That's one good-looking man, right?" She immediately fell quiet as he looped the tie around another's wrist. In silence, she folded her arms over her chest and watched the footage to the finish. It didn't take longer than fifteen seconds and when it came to an end, she replayed it without comment. They watched the segment four times, and neither woman spoke throughout.

"Where did you get this?" Madigan asked with a slight frown. "Is that the guy Anderson hired to be his muscle? The one we all saw the video of?"

"Yeah. Shooting a surrendering man kind of sticks with you," Anja replied and tapped to pause their fifth replay. "What do you think? I haven't seen that kind of technique with any of the people around here before, not even you."

"Well, there are special training regimens that you can take in the military," Madigan said with a shake of her head. "The way that he closes like that, using a tie to wrap around his wrists to keep from injuring himself which in turn allows him to hit harder and more often? That seems like our boy had some training in urban warfare. It's something that they get from the Israeli Mossad or the Brazilian Special Police Operations Battalion."

"Huh," Anja grunted. "You don't usually think special police operations when you think Brazil, do you?"

"I know, right?" Madigan chuckled ruefully. "Anyway, the US government doesn't like to advertise it, since we're supposed to have the biggest and best powerhouse of military might in the world. But they do, on occasion, pick some of the best and brightest to have some unregistered extracurricular training. It looks like our boy here made the cut. Anderson probably knew about that when he suggested bringing him on. He's uniquely qualified."

The Russian nodded. "They told me he was one of the best. I thought that what I saw in the video was only an act of war, you know?"

"Yeah, some people can simply flip that switch," she

said, and an odd, haunted look slid through her eyes. "Come on, Sal's still waiting, and you need to bring everyone up to speed."

Anja nodded, leaned in, and closed the video player. "Yeah, I'll be right in."

CHAPTER ELEVEN

Carlson sighed and shifted to a more comfortable position. *This city will be the death of me!* He absolutely knew it. The sports fans, in particular, were dreadful to deal with. Considering that he was from Boston, there wasn't much that would change that. People in Boston hated people in Philly almost as much as they hated people from New York. That was essentially drilled into their DNA, so there wasn't much anybody could do about it. It probably had something to do with the original colonies back in the Revolution days.

He suppressed his irritation and plucked a glass from the limo's bar. From the heft, it was made of crystal—for the most part. Even though he was forced to hire everything from a third party these days, he always made sure that anything that catered specifically to him was top-of-the-line. Which meant that the amber liquid in the decanter with a similar amount of crystal in the making had to be at least thirty-year-old scotch as he'd personally requested. He poured five fingers of the liquid into his glass, replaced the decanter, and took a moment to inhale the rich aroma before taking a sip. It burned in the most delicious manner all the way down his throat, which prompted him to take in a deep breath and inspect it again.

There were problems. He wasn't sure what they were exactly, but he knew they were there. He'd read into Courtney's particularly troublesome history after Covington had been spectacularly outplayed by the woman. It was impressive. There weren't many trained soldiers who survived that long in the Zoo, much less specialists, and she had been in it from the beginning. He'd read some therapy session the woman had attended in which she'd complained about having to live in the shadow of her academically accomplished father. There was also the fact that he'd been the one to get her working on the goop project in the first place, but there was something about her that...well, that scared him.

Of course, she had to go. There were problems that she couldn't even begin to comprehend which started with where the goop came from in the first place. Allowing her into the project would end badly, he knew it. Something was in the works—some kind of serious trouble. It was on the horizon, but everyone was too concerned with their attempt to get their share of the loot to see it. Not Carlson, though. He saw the bigger picture.

That didn't mean he couldn't respect the woman he was up against as a real competitor, as well as her teammates. The rest of her squad were still in the Zoo. Anderson, who had been squeamish about what Carlson and Pegasus had done there had been brought in as the inside man. And now, somebody else had joined her team. Or somebodies.

He still wasn't sure. The video footage had predictably turned up squat, which meant that they had someone with technical skills on their side. Honestly, how did four men end up in the hospital without so much as a peep to the men and women on the other side of the security team's radios? That worried him.

If he didn't know any better, he would have thought that Courtney had pulled it off. She had, after all, taken care of the goons whom Covington had sent after her with impressive skill. He'd read that report too—and it made for some fun reading—and yet he knew that she wouldn't risk herself by taking this on personally. He was also aware of the fact that she hadn't left the conference room for the duration of the meeting.

Someone had come up the stairs and taken out his security team, one that he'd picked personally for his own protection. He or she had made it all the way to the rooftop where he was alone and vulnerable, with no eyes watching, and simply left.

That didn't make sense. If they had him out in the open like that and didn't take the shot, it meant that he wasn't the target. They were after something else and considering that they were gone by the time he'd discovered his team in the stairwell, it could only mean that they had probably acquired what they came for.

Carlson shook his head. He couldn't wrap his head around the fact that medical personnel were already on the scene before he'd even made the call. Why would someone who had beaten his people up like that bother to make sure they received medical attention?

It didn't add up. The only way that it made sense, to his

mind, was if they were somehow unaffiliated with Anderson or Monroe. Which was possible, he was willing to admit, even if it was unlikely. Who would want to come after him? No, that was a metaphorical can of worms that he wasn't willing to crack open just yet. He'd save it for the congressional hearing.

He stepped out of the limo as it came to a halt and didn't bother to wait for the driver to open the door for him. Never let it be said that he was a lazy fuck who couldn't get his own hands dirty. He smiled at the pleasantly confused expression on the driver's face, pulled a fifty-dollar bill from his pocket, and slipped it to the man in a smooth handshake.

"Thank you, sir." The driver tipped his hat with a soft chuckle and slipped the bill into his jacket pocket.

"No, thank *you*." Carlson felt the midday sun begin to bake through the black silk suit he wore. "You made some excellent time. I'll be sure to mention that to your boss."

He didn't wait for a response but proceeded across the open tarmac to the private jet that already taxied toward him. He hadn't liked submitting this travel to the new powers that be, but he still needed to kiss the ring, no matter what else he was supposed to do.

A man in a suit and sunglasses carried what looked like an Uzi under his jacket and waited at the door of the jet. After the recent developments, he simply couldn't be too cavalier with his own security. The guard spoke quickly into a wrist-mounted radio as the executive climbed the steps into the cabin, where a pretty, young blonde stewardess waited for him. She smiled and guided him to one of the seats.

"We'll take off momentarily, Mr. Carlson," she said with a smile. "Can I get you anything to drink?"

"I'll have a scotch on the rocks, darling, thank you." He forced a charming smile as he buckled into his seat.

"Of course," she responded crisply and walked away as the plane moved across the runway again. A few seconds later, she placed a glass with an amber liquid swirled over three ice cubes in front of him.

"Our chef will prepare your lunch once we're in the air, Mr. Carlson," she said. "Until then, we ask that you please remain in your seat and observe the fasten seatbelt and no smoking sign. Please enjoy your flight."

Carlson nodded and leaned back in the plush, leather seat as the plane gradually accelerated. While he wasn't particularly fond of flying, doing so in luxury could assuage any bad feelings. He simply couldn't imagine what the people who had to fly coach went through.

"I hate flying coach," Jeremiah muttered and tried to stretch his legs as he made his way with the rest of the passengers toward the baggage claim. It hadn't been that long a trip, but the flight had been overbooked, which meant that he had been crammed like a sardine into a giant flying tube of aluminum for a few hours. Honestly, that would not improve anybody's mood, even on a good day. A bruised rib and issues with closed spaces on top of that made him a very unhappy customer when he finally stepped off the flight.

Which meant that he didn't give a solitary flying fuck

about who might be concerned about him talking to himself. Well, he wasn't really talking to himself, but he didn't see the need to share that he had a Russian woman talking to him through an earpiece. People were paranoid enough about flying in this day and age. It was best to simply let them think that he was crazy.

"Well, I would have tried to get some first-class tickets, but they were all out," Anja replied.

"Really?" he asked.

"No, genius," she snapped. "Having someone like you show up as a first-class passenger on the flight list with money from Pegasus would raise all kinds of red flags—the kind we don't need raised. Nobody questions a couple of hundred bucks lost from the budget, especially if it's quickly replaced. And that's all it costs for a quick flight to Charleston, which is what you needed. Now, all you need to do is rent a car and get your ass over to where Carlson is getting his corporate kiss-ass on."

It was a pain in the butt, but he'd requested the longer route. Irrespective of what happened down the line, he needed to be sure that no one could tie him directly to Carlson or even his location. Under the radar sometimes meant the painful delays.

"Which one of my IDs should I use to rent it?" he asked and already knew that he would pay cash for it. He pushed through the crowd and hovered impatiently at the baggage claim. It would have been much quicker and easier to simply use a carry-on, but that wasn't an option with a mobile life. He had no real base, and his entire life—literally—was in that damn duffle. Finally, the baggage came through and he snatched his off the conveyor belt and pushed through the crowd once more. He tried to walk slowly, but every instinct told him to keep moving and get the hell out of there.

"You look like you're about to have an aneurysm while having a colonoscopy," Anja snarked. "Why do you look so uncomfortable? You're on the way to get the job done. You're doing what you do best, right? There's no need to be all…uptight about it."

"It's not that," Jeremiah said and kept his voice low as he looked around. Airports had all the cameras that someone like Anja would want, but it left him feeling a little uncomfortable. He didn't like knowing how easy it was for her to get around the kind of security that was supposed to protect these places.

"What is it, then?" she asked. "Come on, your ass is all clenched, your face is twisted… You're making me nervous, Jer."

"I'm sorry to hear that," he said with a hint of sarcasm. "I feel…naked."

"You could do with getting naked," she replied immediately, almost as if she'd waited for the opportunity. "Preferably with someone else. Guy or gal. I don't judge."

"That's really not what I meant," he snapped. "I'm sure there would be TSA agents crawling up of my ass for saying this, but I need some weapons. Something. Knives, guns, anything. I like to think that I'm a good match for any Kevin-imitating sonofabitch, but in the end, there's only so much I can do with the little I can get my hands on. There's a limit to the number of bones I can break with sticks and stones."

"I think I can help you with that," she replied. "Kevin? Who's Kevin?"

"Come on, you have all the references down pat, but you don't know about *Home Alone* and the tiniest epitome of bad-assitude called Kevin McCallister?" he asked and managed to sound horrified. "Anyway, if I have to track Carlson everywhere I go, I'll need something to defend myself with. I guess I could probably pick a hunting rifle up in the nearest Walmart, but they still require a background check and I don't think that either of my IDs can stand up to that kind of scrutiny. I know there are always ways around all that, but my contacts either think I'm dead or are on the other side of the fucking world."

Anja sighed softly into his ear. He scowled and tried not to snap at her and insist that she stop doing that. While he didn't much care to have the people in his ear respond like that, he could tolerate it if they didn't behave like they knew they had a very captive audience.

"What?" he demanded finally.

"Well, I have some contacts in the area," she replied. "They aren't really the most respectable folks, or the most trustworthy, but they won't ask for IDs. And they do think that I'm a force to be reckoned with, so there is a small deterrence factor that you can count on. It's not much, but I think it should be enough. I'll get in touch with them to see if they're packing and are willing to take on a new customer."

"Deterrence, eh?" Savage asked, a little intrigued despite his ill humor. "My, my, Anja, are you secretly a powerhouse?"

"Nothing secret about it, Jer," she said with gay assurance. "Sure, not all of us can beat security goons up on a flight of stairs, but there are other ways to make people fear you. Knowing as much as I do about the people I encounter makes them think of me as something of a modern-day deity. They usually forget that I'm only a girl behind a keyboard."

"Right," he acknowledged with a sigh and decided not to get into what she might be able to find out about him if she put her mind to it. "Well, I do appreciate that. In the meanwhile..." He looked around him and tried to follow the signs that were placed specifically to help navigate the hellhole that was the Charleston airport.

It took him a few minutes and a great deal of patience to get a feel for how the place was laid out before he finally located the car-rental agencies. As things stood, he realized that he would definitely need to keep his presence there as quiet as possible. When he was asked to present a driver's license and credit card to rent the car, he gave them the cards that were associated with the name that Anderson had given him.

When given an option of which vehicle to hire, he knew he couldn't go for anything flashy or large. While he needed to be mobile, he also needed to be inconspicuous, which in turn meant that he needed something American.

A Ford Taurus was his final selection. It was a ten-year-old model but still in reasonable shape, although some of the red paint peeled away from an obviously puttied dent on the left fender. Still, he'd deliberately chosen the smaller rental company over the big names so could hardly expect the latest models. Discretion, at this point, was the order of the day.

"There's a reason why people in my line of business like to use rental cars over actually buying something, you know," Jeremiah said as he strolled through the parking lot until he reached the car that matched the keys he was given at the desk.

"And what business is that?" Anja asked. She sounded a little more curious than he would have given her credit for.

"Killing people in a clandestine manner," he answered matter-of-factly. "People rent cars all around the world. People need killing all around the world too."

"And you've been all around the world?" she asked. "Killing people?"

"On Uncle Sam's dime," he said bluntly. "Where do you think I got all these skills that have us working together? Anyway, the reason why people like me prefer rental cars instead of driving our own is simple. Every time you're finished with one of these cars, you turn it in, and they have to clean it. It doesn't mean they always do, of course, but if you mess the inside of the car up enough, they have to go at it with all the cleaning ingredients they can find."

"Which conveniently wipes away any trace of the fact that you were in the car in the first place," Anja replied, and he could hear a soft creak of what he assumed was a chair. He could picture her as she leaned back in her office. "That's actually smart."

"That, added to the fact that there's a fake name and social in the registry of the rental company and you have yourself a vehicle that nobody could ever trace back to you." He slipped in behind the wheel.

"How did you learn all this?" she asked as he started the vehicle and eased slowly out of the parking garage. "I mean, I doubt there's a textbook for international assassins somewhere. And I can't imagine that you learned about this through experience."

"Well, a little of both, if I'm honest. There are tricks you can pick up from people who have done it a lot longer than you have, which counts as a textbook, I guess. And the rest, you simply learn from common sense and trial and error. Or, in the case of a business where you don't get to survive most of your mistakes, the errors of others. You know what they say, right? Success is earned by learning from the mistakes of others."

"And would you say that you're successful?" she asked as he pulled the Taurus onto the street and joined the traffic.

"Beware an old man in a profession where men usually die young," Jeremiah said with a small smile.

"Aren't you full of folksy wisdom today?" She laughed, and it lent a light quality to her that was almost appealing.

"What can I say?" His smile disappeared and his expression sobered. "I get maudlin when talking about my past. You should know that about old soldiers."

CHAPTER TWELVE

He didn't much care for the location he was in. Anja had given him an update about what Carlson was up to before she went dark herself. Her vanishing act had irritated him for a moment before he reminded himself that she had a life as well. She needed to eat and sleep like the rest of the human race, and he didn't need to be there for that. He was lucky that she was around as much as she was.

Carlson was, apparently, playing the part of the company man. He shook hands, gave pay raises, and generally convinced people to like him. All things considered, Jeremiah could understand why the man wanted people to have a good impression of him. He wanted control of his company back, and that wouldn't happen if he didn't have the support of the people in it.

From the way people seemed to react to his presence, his efforts were working. While he didn't actually say it outright, from what the Russian was able to pick up, he had planted the seeds of doubt in the new leadership. He knew that something would go wrong soon, and he knew that someone would have to be around to pick up the pieces when the shit hit the proverbial fan. And that person, without a doubt, would be Carlson.

Jeremiah had been driving for most of the afternoon, and he didn't really mind it. Some people were bored after hours and hours spent in the car, but for him, sitting in a car allowed him to simply stew in his own thoughts. He had learned from a young age that it was important to learn how to enjoy your own company, and he had taken that advice. He'd hung out with himself with some tunes on the radio and a good supply of junk food that could be found at the various stops on the road between Charleston and his destination. He made sure to drop as much trash in the car as possible so that when he returned the car, they would be forced to deep-clean it thoroughly.

Although his military training went deep as far as tidiness went, he didn't mind making a colossal mess in the vehicle. He shrugged as he tossed a half-full bag of Doritos onto the rear floor. He told himself that everyone on earth had an inner pigpen, and it wasn't often that they were able to let it loose without consequences.

He pulled the car to a halt at a small gas station outside Raleigh, the lights of which he could see glittering in the distance. Since that was where Carlson was schmoozing with the executives of Pegasus, he wouldn't have to drive for a couple more hours into the night to reach it. Anja would undoubtedly keep Anderson and Monroe informed about the man's movements, which meant that they knew what he was doing and were apparently more than happy to simply allow him to keep doing it.

Of course, Jeremiah would have felt more comfortable if he had an inkling of what their master plan was, but at the moment, he didn't really need to know. His job was to keep tabs on Carlson, discover what his plan was, and make it as difficult to accomplish as possible. He was a regular wrecking ball.

Or would be, once he got his hands on some weapons. Hopefully, Anja's friends would be able to help him with that, but in case they weren't in an agreeable mood, he didn't want to leave himself without a way out. He needed to plan ahead for essentially anything. It wasn't like anyone else would do it for him.

He stepped out of the car and caught the fragrance of magnolia blossoms and the faint tang of gasoline in the warm evening breeze. After a cursory glance around the area, he closed the car door and locked it, leaving the duffle bag behind but bringing the cash that would be required for this. He wasn't there for gas or snacks, so he circled to the back of the station. Anja's directions indicated that the path would lead to what looked like a warehouse and he had to admit, that was exactly what he found.

Train tracks still existed in front of the long, low building that hadn't been used in at least a century, and the warehouse next to them would have been where the goods were unloaded. He wasn't sure what would have justified a shop this big. Who knew? Maybe, considering where he was, the big building had once housed bales of cotton or even tobacco.

That said, the place wasn't quite as deserted as some might believe. A man stood outside the front doors. He was big, tall, and dark-skinned, and from the bulge that showed under his heavy leather jacket, he was also heavily armed and very likely expecting trouble.

He evidently saw that possible trouble approaching in the form of an unknown stranger by way of the gas station. The jacket fell away to reveal a semi-automatic, sawed-off shotgun. The large weapon rose smoothly and aimed at Jeremiah as he moved closer.

"You're lost, dickwad," the man said belligerently and gestured with the weapon before he resumed his aim. "Get back in your piece of crap car and drive away."

"I'll have you know that the Ford Taurus is an American icon, my friend," he said. "It's right up there with the Mustang, the Camaro, and other such classics. Just because it doesn't make the same sexy grunts doesn't mean that it doesn't have a strong history in American culture. Oh, and it's not actually my piece of crap car."

"Whatever, man," he growled. "Get the fuck out of here."

"I would if I could, Popeye, but unfortunately, I'm here on business," he said with an easy smile and made no effort to back down as the man stepped closer.

"Are you a cop?" he demanded, and the thick voice grew more menacing.

"And if I was, would that be any kind of deterrent against killing me?" Savage tilted his head in silent challenge. "I'm asking for a friend—well, an acquaintance. I don't really like him."

"Not fucking likely," the thug replied and shifted the shotgun closer.

"Well, it's a good thing I'm not a cop then." He raised his hands. "I'll let my friend-slash-acquaintance know. He'll be crushed. Anyway, I actually am here on business, both for myself and your boss. You can tell him that Artemis sent me."

The man looked rather nonplussed by his response. He kept the shotgun trained on him, but there was a hint of hesitation in the guard's eyes as he leaned in closer and pulled a radio from his pocket.

"Yo, Max, are you expecting anyone from someone named Artemis?" he asked.

"Why are you holding them up, Dee?" a man's voice crackled from the other side of the connection. "Send them the fuck in."

"It's only the one guy, though," Dee replied.

"Then send him the fuck in," Max ordered.

"I guess I'm going in," Jeremiah said with a smile. "Should I bring something out for you to drink? Maybe a snack?"

"Fuck you," Dee growled, but he shoved the shotgun under his jacket once more and turned away. Savage grinned and moved past the huge, muscular man and into the warehouse. Most of it looked like it had been left to fall into disrepair, but one small section had been cleaned and equipped with lights and furniture. A small generator in the corner provided electricity and, from the look of the tech that was set up, also an internet connection. This place was completely off the grid, at least from what he could see, but had everything someone might need to keep a criminal enterprise running without garnering the attention of the local law enforcement.

One of the men working there drew away from the group and walked toward him. He was tall, wore a Bulls jersey, and looked like he had actually played basketball in his day. Well, not that Savage would really know. He wasn't a fan of that sport, but still.

"Artemis sent you?" the man asked and extended a hand, which he took and shook firmly.

"That would be me," he replied with a smile. "You must be Max."

"That's right. And who are you?"

"I was told that names and IDs wouldn't be necessary for this transaction," he responded and folded his arms.

"I like to know who I'm dealing with," the other man replied. "I mean, a word from Artemis does go a long way, but I don't like strangers walking around with my weapons, you understand?"

"Jack," he said with a forced smile. "Jack T. Ripper. Do you need a social with that?"

"You know I can simply have my boys kill you and find out from the license in your wallet, right?" Max asked.

"Yep, I'm well aware of that. Are you aware of the fact that should your boys make that move, you won't survive long enough to be privy to the details that they find out about me? So, if you're done with the dick-measuring, can we maybe get back to business?"

"Sure," he said after a couple of seconds. "If you'll follow me?"

They moved to the back of the operation and a table that held a collection of revolvers and hunting rifles.

"Consider these classic beauties," the man said with a smile.

"No." Savage shook his head firmly. "If I wanted cheap and legal, I'd go to Walmart, not you. Stop trying to unload your old stock and show me the good stuff. Come on, I have five grand in small, untraceable bills burning holes in my pocket."

"Five grand, huh?" Max moved farther back. A blanket hung over the wall, and when he pulled it back, Savage saw a wide selection of pistols, rifles, and shotguns. "Five grand gets you enough to arm a small army. Nothing automatic, though. The ATF cracks down on dealers that push that military shit a lot harder than the small timers like me."

"If it was shit, the military wouldn't use it," Savage said with a small grin. "But I don't need to arm a small army. I do need enough to kill a small army, though. Something to keep in mind."

He removed a shotgun—semi-automatic and sawed off like the one Dee had outside—and a Glock 17 from the wall, as well as a small yet sturdy rifle with a scope.

"I don't suppose you guys have any knives in stock, do you?" he asked once he had finished inspecting the merchandise. It was used, likely stolen from police stock or something like that, but it would more than do in a pinch. He wasn't sure why it was that Max didn't mind selling his best stock to a friend of Anja's, but he wasn't afraid to press the issue if needed. Versatility was everything in this business, and he needed as much of it as he could get.

"Our stock is limited," the man admitted, but he withdrew a small case from under the table and opened it to reveal a selection of military knives of varying lengths and origins. "But I think you'll be satisfied with what we have."

He wasn't wrong. Most were some variation of the Kabar, which Savage quickly passed on as his eyes found what looked like an eight-inch variation of the KM2000. He picked it up immediately, ignored the rest, and took a moment to inspect the steel and the edge before he added it to the pile he'd already selected.

"All that, plus as much ammo as I can afford with what's left of my money." He took the cash from his pocket and placed it on the table. Max picked it up, smiled, and handed it to one of his men who quickly put it through a counter. A few seconds later, the man nodded.

"For five thousand, three hundred, and twenty-five dollars," Max said and turned to face him. "I think we can add enough ammo for you to kill an army and a bag for you to carry it in, free of charge."

"Can you make it a duffel bag?" he asked. "I love duffel bags."

"Duffel bag, coming right up," the man said and chuckled darkly. "You know, not many people I know are as trusting as you are."

"I'm not trusting, not really." He tilted his head as he watched the men load the weapons in a large bag. "You know that this weaponry here isn't for me, it's for Artemis, and whatever she's holding over your head is enough for you to do business with someone whom you don't know. That kind of trust needs to be reciprocated."

Max glanced quickly at him with a smirk. "That's some solid thinking. I wouldn't expect it from someone like you."

"Someone like me?" Savage asked.

"Military. You can cover it up all you want, but truth be told, I could tell you were fresh out of the service from a mile away. Nothing smells quite like the military bullshit. Were you Army?"

"Rangers," he said.

"Which makes me wonder how a man newly out the service like you finds himself working for someone like Artemis." The men had all but completed the load up and the duffle bag bulged almost to bursting. "How does a man like you get tangled up with someone like that?"

"I could ask you the same question, Max," Jeremiah responded and took the bag that was handed to him. He paused to adjust the strap and used both hands to drag it over his shoulder. "But I think the answer from the both of us will be spookily similar."

"None of your beeswax, it's personal?" Max asked and grinned.

"Like I said, spooky." He shrugged and returned the grin. "Now, if I manage to kill that army and avoid it killing me, I think that there is definitely business that could be done between us in the future. What do you say about that, Max?"

The man shrugged. "So long as you don't mind paying in cash and up front like you did here, I see nothing but benefits for everyone involved."

"Look at that. We have something of a like mind. Take it easy, Max."

The two men shook hands and Savage headed casually toward the door. He couldn't help but feel that he would be shot in the back with every step on his way to the exit, and he didn't doubt that there were at least three weapons aimed at the back of his head in case he decided he wanted his money back and planned to use their weapons to get it.

But, if nothing else, he was a man of his word. In this respect, anyway. He knew that the likelihood of him needing weapons in the future was high, and should that day come, he wanted to make sure that he parted ways with everyone on the best possible footing. People didn't like to be violent for violence's own sake, even among criminals. If you wanted to do business and were willing to pay without any trouble, they were more than happy to help. It was a lawless kind of capitalism.

When he reached the door, he saw Dee waiting, his shotgun out of the jacket and aimed at him. Savage took a moment to read the man in front of him before he pressed forward. It was a show of force. A reminder that turning any of the weapons against Max and his crew would be a losing proposition. He didn't mind. Most times, he picked his battles, and pointless testosterone measurements were the kind of thing that he simply couldn't be bothered with.

He stepped around Dee and turned to face him as he walked away.

"Now I have a shotgun," he said and grinned cheekily. "Ho ho ho!"

The man didn't answer and used the hand that didn't hold the shotgun to flip him off. Jeremiah chuckled and turned away to stroll back to his car at an easy pace. He knew that the vehicle, as well as all his possessions, would be there when he got back. It wasn't a stretch to assume that it was known in this area that people who parked in the gas station were doing business with Max, and the man would take offense at anyone who wanted to get in the way of that.

He opened the trunk of the car, dropped the duffle bag in beside his original one, and paused. Even if he didn't intend to use the weapons he'd just bought against the people he'd purchased them from, he still didn't want to walk around unarmed for any longer than was necessary. Quickly, he pulled the Glock out of the bag, found the rounds for it, and filled the mag hastily.

There were a couple of extra ones included with the sale. These enabled him to fill two more and slip them into his pockets before he zipped everything up, shut the trunk, and walked to the driver's seat. He put the pistol in the glove compartment where it would be easily accessible before he started the car and pulled back onto the highway.

Yes, he could definitely say that he felt more comfortable. Of course, if any cop pulled him over and decided to search his trunk, he would be in violation of too many laws to count. So many that the officer would possibly consider letting him go due to the sheer amount of paperwork that would ensue from trying to bring him in. That said, he wasn't overly worried. It wasn't like he would spend too much time in the heavily policed sections of the city, anyway.

CHAPTER THIRTEEN

"Hey, Jer," Anja's voice spoke suddenly and very surprisingly in his ear. "How did it go with Max?"

His reaction wasn't his optimum or his fastest. He had felt jittery as he started to draw closer to the city. There were more patrol cars in the area than he'd expected, and while he was one of the best when it came to portraying a cool and calm demeanor to any who might observe him, he sure as hell didn't feel calm in that moment. His grip on the wheel weakened for a second as his right hand moved instinctively to the pistol in his glove compartment.

"God fucking dammit, Anja," he retorted acidly. "You can't show up unannounced in a guy's ear. Just…clear your throat or something before you pop up like that."

"And good morning to you too, Jer-Bear," she said. Her tone clearly indicated a grin even though he couldn't see her. "I slept well, thanks for asking. How about you?"

"It's still early evening around here and you know that," he pointed out gruffly. "But how did you sleep?"

"It was short but sweet." She yawned expressively in his ear. "How did it go with Max? Did he give you any trouble? You know, I really think you should have waited until I was back to help cover your actions with him. He's kind of jittery around new players, so it might have been best if you had—"

"It went fine," Jeremiah interjected and shook his head. "We bonded over our mutual knowledge of you. We even had friendship bracelets made. Although his man Dee didn't seem to like me much. He constantly waved a shotgun in my face to try to intimidate me."

"Wait—Dee is the guy who stands at the front?" Anja asked. "Big—and I mean huge—and sports a custom shotgun?"

"That's the one," he agreed. "He's clearly watched *Die Hard*, though, so he can't be all bad."

"*Die Hard?*" She sounded genuinely confused.

"Oh, you *have* to be fucking kidding me." For a moment, he felt genuinely annoyed. "You haven't watched *Home Alone* or *Die Hard?* I know what we'll do if we ever meet face to face. We'll have a movie marathon. I'll educate you in all the American culture that you've missed. I almost feel bad for you. It's like never having seen the Mona Lisa or heard any of Beethoven's music."

"You're comparing an action movie to timeless art classics?" she asked.

"Okay, I wouldn't really consider *Home Alone* to be an action movie so much as a comedy, but yeah, I'll stand by that comparison," he confirmed.

"You know that I was talking about *Die Hard*," she snarked and actually sounded annoyed herself. "Do you mind if we get back to business now? How did it go with Max? Did you get everything you needed?"

"I'm now walking into any operation in this area heavily armed and raring to go," he said and eased his car off the highway as he saw the sign for a motel a couple of miles down a side road. It seemed exactly the kind of place he was looking for.

"Fantastic." Anja clearly sounded proud of her work.

"You should know that I blew all my cash on this purchase," he said. "And while I could probably sneak these babies across state lines as long as I'm not pulled over and searched, I won't be able to get them onto a plane. And I can't actually take a rental car across the country, either."

"Well, you might want to think about buying a car for your own use, you know," she replied. "I know you like having a car that someone else has to clean, but the fact remains that you'll have to be self-sufficient at some point. You might as well start now."

"Well, with all these work-related purchases that you guys have me making, you have to know that I'll keep all the receipts and look forward to having them refunded in full." The motel came into view and he slowed.

"You do know that all the purchases you've made thus far over your time with Pegasus were made with money we gave you, right?" Anja reminded him.

"Well, yeah, but it's the principle of the matter." Jeremiah turned slowly into the motel's parking lot. The place looked well-lit, and the absence of trucks and the scattering of cars in the lot told him what kind of place this was.

"You should get your own car in the morning," she

insisted as he put the rental into park. "You can turn the rental car in. There should be a drop-off point in the city."

He let the moment of silence hang as he yanked the parking brake and stepped out of his car to open the trunk.

"And yes, of course I'll wire you some money." It seemed like she was only talking to end the awkward silence that had ensued. "It should reach you tomorrow morning. Let me know which room you get in the motel."

"Oh, come on," he said with a grin as he hauled both bags out of the car. He fumbled briefly to hook the one with the weapons over his shoulder and held the other in his left hand as his right hand closed the trunk and locked the car. Walking awkwardly with the weight, he made his way to the front desk. "I thought you would be able to track me through the cameras or something like that."

"I could hunt the feeds that come from some no-tell outside the city, but how about, instead of that, you simply tell me which room you're in and save us both some time?" Anja asked. "I have a job and a life to get to that doesn't involve you, you know."

"Yeah, yeah, I know. Jeez." He chuckled dryly. "I was only teasing, sorry. Do you think you should go ahead and get yourself a morning coffee?"

"Yeah, I'll get right on that." Her voice lost its snippy quality as he stepped up to the front desk, which was manned by a younger man who looked like he was more intent on watching something on his phone than taking care of his station.

Then again, he couldn't really blame the kid. The place was all but deserted at this time of the night, and if he didn't have anything else to do, he could keep on watching whatever it was that had him so absorbed. Hopefully, it wasn't porn, although given his age, it most likely was.

"Hi," he said and suppressed a smile when the kid scrambled to put his phone away and stand behind the desk. "I'll need a bed for a couple of nights. I'll pay in cash, if that's okay? Oh, and how long does the complimentary continental breakfast last?"

The young man looked at him and his mouth gaped in bewilderment for a few seconds, which made Jeremiah wonder if he wasn't high on something. "I'm sorry, sir, I don't think we offer—"

"Yeah, I know. I was joking, kid, don't sweat it." He shook his head. "Oh, and I'd appreciate it if you could lose the name on the registry form."

The clerk smirked and selected a key from the stacks behind him. "It's nice to have you with us, Mr. Smith."

With the check-in completed, Jeremiah sauntered toward his room, which thankfully had the afternoon sun rather than the morning sun blazing through the windows. He growled in irritation and rolled his aching shoulder as he reached the door and pulled it open. His bruised rib ached far worse, if the truth be told, but he'd deal with that once he was settled.

This place was cheaper than the one where he'd stayed in Philly, but at this point, they all simply looked the same to him. He didn't even bother to put anything in the safe yet as he locked the door behind him. Right now, he needed a nice long shower and some sleep before he applied himself to the task of hunting Carlson and tracking the man's every move. He wasn't sure if intel gathering was part of what Anderson and Monroe had hired him for, but if not, he could always say that it was for his own good. He didn't like to walk blindly into any situation.

"Nice digs," Anja said, and sarcasm seemed to ooze over the earpiece. Before he could even wonder how she could tell, she answered his unasked question. "I've accessed the motel's site. They seem to cater almost exclusively to nameless trystees. If you stay there for a couple of nights, you'll probably be their longest-staying customer in the past decade or so."

"Yeah," Savage growled. "I honestly don't think that any guy has it in him to last a couple of days. Besides, when you come to a place that charges by the hour, stamina probably isn't what you have in mind when you rent a room here."

"You're gross," she retorted and groaned.

"Yep, I'm a terrible person all around," he agreed. "While it's nice to work for someone who can actually foot the bill that comes with all this intelligence work for a change, I really wish that I had an ID that would allow me into a hotel that doesn't have all the Pay Per View porn channels laminated."

"And that's my cue to cut this conversation short," she said and laughed. "Have a good rest, Jer. I hope you sleep well."

"Thanks, that makes two of us. If you need me, call me on one of the phones. I might answer but then again, I might not. That's simply how mysterious I am."

"That's not funny."

"I know, I'm tired."

"Is that the title of your sex tape?" she asked.

"Now who's gross?" Savage asked ruefully. "Anyway, I'll catch you on the flip side."

"You do that."

He removed the bud and placed it carefully on the bedside table. He wasn't sure how he felt about having something that he would put inside himself touching the surface. In all honesty, he had serious doubts about how well it had been cleaned but there was no real alternative. He was exhausted at this point. All he wanted was a shower, some food, and sleep. That was all that mattered right now and damned if he didn't intend to get it.

As he settled in, he realized that he hadn't been kidding about working for someone with money now. The US government was known to pinch pennies anywhere that it could, and the fact that they always fought with weapons that were made by the lowest bidder hadn't escaped his notice. There were almost always problems with the equipment they carried. It had reached the point where they had to assume that something would go wrong—something like Murphy's Law, but with military equipment.

Now that he worked for someone who could afford proper equipment, maybe he could convince them to spring for quality stuff that he didn't have to buy second-hand from a two-bit arms dealer outside of the capital of North Carolina. Sure, he wouldn't discuss it with them outright, but it was something he could possibly look forward to. Assuming, of course, that he survived this fight and was called upon to fight another.

He pulled his clothes off, moved into the bathroom, and turned the light on. It was surprisingly pristine, he realized, which made him wonder exactly what had happened in the bathroom with the previous occupant that necessitated that it be cleaned to a much higher standard than the rest of the hotel.

Then, he decided that he really didn't want to know.

CHAPTER FOURTEEN

Carlson didn't like this town. Admittedly, this was where most of the larger weapons developers situated their labs since the testing laws in this state were significantly laxer than they were in the rest of the country. That, sadly, still didn't alter the fact that there was far too much of a small-town vibe to the capital. Most of the restaurants—even the higher-end ones—all had something they called a "She-Crab" Bisque. Honestly, it seemed like the kind of thing he would try when he was drunk, hungry, and rocking some low standards. At any other time, he would prefer his crab to be served in a ceviche, paired with some white wine, and followed by a medium-rare steak.

Regrettably, he had to play the politician around there, and honestly, when it came down to it, he didn't mind. These people were impossibly easy to please. He simply made sure they realized that the man who used to run the company had come down there to ensure that everyone who had been in the company for a while received raises and had their grievances heard. This detail guaranteed that they would agree to help him rather than the faceless woman and military man who had forced their way in.

He would never be caught dead trashing his new bosses, but he didn't need to. It really was a simple matter of hinting at their ineptitude before the rain of IRS inquiries and congressional hearings began to make the company's stock plummet. They would clamor for someone to save them from their woes, and now that he had a couple of scapegoats to feed to anyone who came looking for guilt, he could walk away from all of this like it was a bad dream.

That said, he wasn't only there for the politics of it. While he did need these people on his side when push came to shove, he also needed to oversee the way his people covered his tracks. They needed to be reminded that it was *their* tracks that they covered, too. He needed to remind them that all the money they'd made over the past decade or so of prosperity had a paper trail that would point a finger at them as much as it would at him. All the research had to be pushed to new locations that *he* had control over, not Dr. Monroe. Most important, that locale needed to be far, far away from the people who tried to break him.

Carlson took another sip from his fifth scotch of the day and paused before he swallowed. It wasn't even mid-afternoon yet. He needed to get a grip on his drinking if he wanted to trust his own judgment in all this. Shaking his head, he muttered, "I'm not an alcoholic." He was fully aware that he'd had the same discussion countless times with a wide variety of people, ranging from ex-wives and friends to business partners. "I merely need to take the edge off."

He wasn't wrong. At any other time, he only drank socially. He'd take a sip of champagne for a toast and order water for the rest of the evening. True, he had suffered from drinking problems in the past, but a couple of months of therapy had helped him kick the worst parts of the habit. These only resurfaced in times of great stress like the past few months had been.

Crap, had it only been months? It felt like years.

"On to your next appointment, sir?"

The executive looked up from the almost obsessive twirling of his glass and saw his driver looking at him. He recognized the man's face. It was one of his men, a hardened combat veteran a few years out of the service and who now made more money than he ever had while wearing a uniform.

Well, he still wore a uniform, if you could call a mid-range suit, sunglasses, and a sub-machine gun a uniform. Carlson could. He liked to think that there was something a good deal more terrifying about a faceless horde of men in suits than a man in military dress. Men in the military weren't supposed to instill fear in the people they encountered. Not the kind of fear that came with a suit, at least. The shock of civility mixed with the barbarity of violence was so much more powerful, he mused.

"Call in the teams," he said and rubbed his temple as he took a sip from his glass. "We'll head out to the compound. No more delays. We need this shit done now."

He had been in this town for the past three days, and all the assurances that the compound would be evacuated before the weekend had been dashed after a call he'd received from one of the managers of the location. He'd told him that there was still a lot that had to be done, and they wouldn't be finished with it by closing time on Friday. And considering that most of the people who worked on site kept regular hours, that meant that anything that wasn't done would have to be finished on Monday.

And that was simply un-fucking-acceptable. He needed everything around there to be wrapped up in a pretty little bow before he returned to Philly and Dr. Monroe's conditions for his surrender. Anything that hadn't been resolved before then would be a vulnerability. He was not a man who dealt in vulnerabilities—unless, of course, they belonged to his opponents. In which case, he thought with a hard smile, they were useful.

With this in mind, he headed out to the damned location and hoped that his presence would help to streamline the process. As a last resort, he could probably authorize overtime to make sure that the people stayed for as long as it took. That was what he would have to do if it came down to it, but he would rather keep all trace of what was happening there off the books. There would be a huge influx of cash for the IRS to track down, of course, but that was intentional and could be traced back to Monroe, not him. An overtime authorization would point a finger directly at his chest.

No, he would prefer it if he could tell people to keep working until the job was done without any questions asked regarding exactly what the hell he was doing in North Carolina.

"Step on it, Linus," Carlson said, knocked back the remaining scotch in a single gulp, and refilled the glass without even thinking. He was a functioning alcoholic, at worst. Nothing he couldn't handle.

"So, do you have any idea what they're actually doing in there?" Savage asked and plucked his shirt irritably away from his chest. It was warm, although fall had already officially begun, and trees had started to change colors. Ads for Halloween mingled with Thanksgiving and even Christmas. But still, the weather remained unseasonably warm. Not unbearably so, but enough to be uncomfortable. He lay out in the middle of what looked like nowhere but was actually some seven hundred yards from a facility with fences, a significant number of armed guards, and considerable movement. No logos were displayed on the side of the windowless building.

"Well, the building is owned by Pegasus," Anja said and actually sounded interested. "And a good chunk of money went into a lot of high-end security and transport. Carlson pinched pennies back in the central building by hiring second-rate companies to run security and IT, but he didn't spare any kind of expense here. Yggdrasil SSY was appointed to provide the armored car services, and they brought in a hell of a lot of muscle. Obviously, someone wants to make sure that whatever they're moving out of that place gets out without anyone trying to mess with it."

"Yeah," he agreed and squinted into his binoculars. "These guys are all armed to the teeth. There are some hints of power armor in the stuff they're wearing. Nothing compared to what the military uses these days, but still similar."

"Do you think you could take them out?" she asked.

"Take them out? What, like...kill them, take them out? I could if I had a team of fifteen men, equally armed to the teeth, and a couple of weeks to plan an operation. All of which we lack from what I've been able to see."

"Yep." She sounded almost disappointed. "Just you in there by your lonesome. I would have thought it was how people like you preferred to work. Lone-wolf types who only work alone and don't take no partners."

Savage couldn't help but smirk. It was funny how she seemed to be able to drop her Russian accent to take on the stereotypical gruff loner voice. He still wasn't sure where that particular stereotype had come from, but it really didn't matter. So many people these days made assumptions about what kind of guy he was supposed to be, all without even bothering to ask what kind of guy he actually was.

People liked to throw the lone wolf idea around when it came to military men and somehow forgot that men and women in the service were all drilled and trained to work best when they were in a group. Military tactics were all about coordination and precision in groups, with each individual cog performing what they were brought in to do with the utmost professionalism. That was what made military operations a success. Lone wolf characters wouldn't make it past boot camp, but there was no real need to clarify the situation for Anja.

What was interesting was how well-coordinated the men on the ground were. He knew that they couldn't anticipate that anyone would come in to try to identify what they were moving, but they were all ready, anyway. Head comms would make it more difficult than the last time, as well as the fact that they always moved in groups of two, three, or more men to cover the perimeter. The precision and alertness as they watched the armored cars arrive and leave told Savage that security had truly been stepped up.

Anderson and Monroe would want to know this as well as where all the shit was being moved to, but at the moment, there wasn't any point in trying to stop the process. There was only one road leading in and out of the facility as far as he could see. If anyone could actively trail them, it would be Anja. She had mentioned that she had access to a satellite, so maybe she could use it to track them?

He couldn't actually recall when she'd dropped that nugget of useful information. It had been at some time over the past couple of days of watching and studying Carlson's every movement while in Raleigh. He'd monitored the man through the various hotels he'd visited, Pegasus' headquarters at the location, and a group of high-end restaurants.

They said that the age of actually physically following someone to keep track of their movements was at an end, which possibly explained why Jeremiah couldn't identify a single time that he'd been made. The men who drove him around simply didn't think to check to make sure that nobody was following them.

Obviously, he'd done his part to stay off the radar too. He'd parked the first rental in a shady corner of the motel parking lot and rented a second vehicle to use in his surveillance work. Not only that, he'd deliberately selected a car that was almost more invisible than a Taurus. The Prius was the kind of car that people seemed to actively ignore in these parts. From the number of them in the lot of the rental car agency, he had to assume that they were a popular choice around there. That boded well for him too.

He hadn't had much training in actually following people in traffic, but the rule of thumb from a quick search on the web had told him that alternating your distance was more important than keeping it. People noticed patterns better than they noticed randomness, one site had noted.

It was fun, learning on the job like this. Of course, all that had been canceled when Anja noted a sudden change to Carlson's calendar that indicated that he would pay the facility a visit in person. While they had kept tabs on what moved in and out before, the fact that the man himself would make a physical appearance at the location was important. If he planned to tie Monroe and Anderson to the place, it was the least that they could do to tie him to it as well—if only for the kind of leverage they would need.

Jeremiah blinked and realized that Anja had been talking the whole time that he'd been lost in thought. She seemed like the kind of woman who would be shy and not say much more than a couple of sentences if he met her in person. That notwithstanding, she made up for it by talking his solitary ear off since they weren't actually standing face-to-face.

"Do you have an ETA on when Carlson will arrive here?" he asked when he sensed a lull in the barrage of words that she tossed his way. She might have even simply inhaled to keep going, but after his question, she paused to quickly check her computer.

"I have his limo service leaving the company building fifteen minutes ago," she said after a quick pause. "The GPS indicates that they are heading your way. I guess we have to wait to see if it's actually Carlson himself and not him throwing up more red herrings. And speaking of which, how come you didn't pick up some of the binoculars in the shop that had a Bluetooth connection that would let me see what you're looking at?"

He sighed. "Well, they didn't have anything like that in the store," he lied.

As it turned out, his prevarication was a futile gesture in the end. "I found the store's online outlet. Everything's online these days, Jer, and I found that they have one of those in the store, waiting for pickup."

"I have no idea what you're talking about," he lied again and grinned as he peeked through the pair he had again.

"You didn't want me to see what you're looking at, right?" Anja accused. "You're not ogling the asses of the lady guards in there, are you? Need I remind you that we're on company time here?"

"Firstly, I'm not hourly, so that's not how all this works," he retorted. "Secondly, they didn't have anything of the kind when I went in there. Besides, you were the one who told me to be frugal with the spending from this point forward."

"Well, yes, but there are certain things you can splurge on, you know."

Before she could say anything else, though, he cut in. "It looks like we have a convoy moving in." He squinted for better focus. "Not armored cars. A couple of SUVs sandwiching a limo. I'd say that's our boy."

"Yep, the GPS tells me he should be in eyeshot," she agreed. "Let's hope that Carlson is in the car."

Jeremiah nodded and abandoned the binoculars to use the sight of the rifle he'd bought from Max. The scope on it wasn't as powerful as the binoculars, but it was a lot more target-focused. Unfortunately, the windows were tinted to an illegal degree, which made it difficult to actually see who was in the vehicles.

"There's movement from the compound, though," he said as he returned to his binoculars. "It looks like they're expecting the convoy."

"Did they radio ahead?" she asked.

"How should I know?"

"I wasn't talking to you," she hissed back.

"Were you talking to yourself? You do know that they say that talking to yourself is the first sign of early-onset dementia, right?"

"Come on, man," Anja said softly. "It's in my family. I don't need to worry about that shit right now."

"Oh, fuck, sorry. I didn't know," he said softly. He'd been told that he had a morbid sense of humor sometimes, and most of those times, he simply leaned into the skid, as the term went, and accepted it. But there was a time and a place for humor like that, and he'd misjudged the situation.

"Don't worry about it." She sounded apologetic herself. "How could you know?"

"Still, though, I shouldn't have been that flippant about it..." His voice trailed off as the convoy entered the facility. The gate closed quickly behind them, and a group of guards exited the SUVs. The ten men wore uniforms that were painfully distinct from what the men already on site wore, which was interesting. An idea began to hatch in his mind, one that required Carlson to actually make an appearance.

The ten new arrivals did a quick security sweep that collided with the men and women of the original teams who were doing exactly the same thing. A quick argument ensued as two of what looked like the men in charge clashed over who would have jurisdiction over the site before they parted ways. Neither seemed to have had a clear victory.

At that moment, a man stepped out of the limo. He demanded attention with perfectly cut salt-and-pepper hair and an expensive suit. His demeanor was confident as he looked around before he retrieved a pair of sunglasses from his coat and put them on.

"Silver Fox alert," Savage said with a small smile. "It looks like our target is in the area. Carlson is making a personal appearance here, folks!"

"Who are you talking to?" Anja asked.

"Well, I was imitating a sports broadcaster."

"You seem like you have had a lot of practice," she said playfully. "In front of the mirror?"

"Maybe," he conceded. "But we have bigger issues to deal with. I think I need to get into the facility myself."

"How is that supposed to happen?" she demanded. "We were able to get you in and out of the Pegasus building back in Philly due to the fact that your bosses have some pull in how those buildings are run. You have no such advantage here."

"Have some faith, Anja." His grin broadened as his plan settled in comfortably.

CHAPTER FIFTEEN

By the time the convoy that he'd put together converged on the facility, Carlson felt more than a little buzzed. The place had been one of Pegasus' longest-running operations and had opened before he'd even assumed control of the company. It had made sense to move most of their goop testing there when it became clear that they would get the bulk of the government contracts for it. All things considered, this was the end of an era, in one way or another. Even when he retook the reins of the company, he doubted that he would be allowed to reopen the lab.

Then again, even if he could reopen it, the facility would probably not see the same kind of work that it had before. There was a lot of history embedded in the walls, and it was sad that things had come to an end like this.

He could feel the whiskey starting to affect him as they parked in front of the facility. It had, he admitted to himself, been a questionable choice on his part to put the partition up to keep the driver out of his decision to continue drinking. Three-quarters of the rich liquid was gone. He was no lightweight and had been known as something of a party boy, even after he'd married and taken control of a Fortune Five Hundred company, but these days, it was difficult to find drinking partners. Some of his old buddies were in rival companies and couldn't be seen with him. Some were out of reach, living comfortable lives in countries that didn't have extradition treaties. A couple were in jail. There were risks involved in the lives they lived.

Regrettably, he had begun to slide into that part of life when he lost more friends than he made. That was a fucking depressing thought—and one hell of a good reason to keep on drinking, as far as he was concerned. There was always a good reason if one simply looked for it.

He waited for the driver to come around to his door this time and allowed the man to pull it open. With extra care, he stepped out and thankfully didn't have to lean on the side of the car as he pulled a pair of sunglasses out of his jacket pocket, flipped them open with one hand, and put them on smoothly. It was a practiced move that was meant to show that he wasn't as drunk as people might think he was if they got in close enough to smell his breath or see his bloodshot eyes.

Speaking of, he would probably need to talk to someone about getting a breath mint. He would light up a breathalyzer test like a Christmas tree. While a mint wouldn't help with that particular problem, it would certainly play better with the employees if they didn't know that their boss' boss three or four times removed got himself hammered while on the job.

These people didn't know that they would all lose their employment with the company, and him showing up sloshed would only hint at bad things that would happen in the future. Even if the reason why he drank wasn't necessarily a sad one. Not a particularly happy one either, but hey, who was counting?

"Sir, are you ready for the site inspection?" one of the men asked him. They all looked like they were dressed for combat. Carlson could appreciate that, considering the new elements that had been introduced. What was the term? The fly in the ointment. The wrench in the works.

"Mr. Carlson will be ready to inspect the facility when he says so, and not before," his head of security Mr. Stevens remarked. The executive narrowed his eyes and stared at the two men who seemed to be locked in a silent yet very real battle of wills. He mused that if both these men were as drunk as he was, they would be throwing punches.

It really was comforting that not everyone was as unprofessional as he was.

"I think I'd like to have a quick view of the facility, first, to make sure that everything's up to code," Carlson said and drew in a deep breath. If anyone would notice his condition, it would be scientists, so he might as well start with them and get it over with. Besides, he was interested only in what they attempted to accomplish. Nothing mattered except meeting the deadline.

He took a moment to gather his balance before he moved around the car. While he wasn't sure what he would do to cover for himself during his inspection, he would think of something. Maybe those pills the doctor had given him. He still had those, right?

The driver saw him check his pockets and moved quickly back into the limo. Carlson watched as the two men in charge of the security on location argued once again over how the viewing would proceed.

Well, maybe they weren't as professional as he would have liked.

The driver stepped out of the car. He held a small white pill in one hand and a glass of water in the other and handed both to Carlson. Without comment, he stood between his boss and the two arguing security men as the executive popped the pill down the hatch and chased it with some water. It would be a little while before it kicked in, but it would have to do.

"A mint, sir?" the man asked and handed him a small container.

"Thank you, Linus." The driver tapped a couple of the little white tablets out. Linus was the one who had been with him the longest. The exact nature of his training had never been explained, but he had seen the man handle some tough situations with ease and precision. That fact alone told Carlson that whatever training it had been, it was not something to scoff at.

And the man had something that was even more valuable than the ability to break people in two, drive like someone who had just robbed a bank, and to always have something up his sleeve that would help with whatever maladies Carlson experienced. That was loyalty. The man had been with him for the better part of a decade and a half and had never faltered in his duty. He was being well-paid for it, of course, but so were the people who had failed him in the past.

The executive could feel the pill already starting to take effect. The buzz in his brain slowly faded. He knew that he had a killer headache coming on, but that was par for the course. Linus would have something for that, too, when they began the return trip to the hotel.

Hopefully, he could put all this bullshit behind him and turn his attention once more to reclaiming his company from those assholes.

"If the two of you are done arguing," he said, and straightened his suit. "I think we have a facility to inspect, don't you, Mr. Stevens?"

"Oh," Stevens grunted and turned away from his argument with the man in combat armor. He cleared his throat. "Of course, sir. If you would just—"

"Follow me, right this way, sir," his opponent cut in.

These two men needed to get a hotel room and work all this angst out, Carlson mused and shook his head. Seriously.

"I don't give a fuck who I follow," he snapped, and his tone of voice immediately sucked the testosterone out of the air. The fact remained that neither of them was the one in charge of this shindig.

"Of course, sir," the man in armor said and turned without further comment to guide them toward the building. As per his original request, all markings of who it belonged to were erased. The only people who knew that the facility belonged to Pegasus were the ones who handled the paperwork, and not even them, sometimes.

God, that pill was working miracles, Carlson thought. He would have to ask Linus what it was when they were alone.

"And you got this information how, again?" Savage asked in a hushed whisper as he moved through the tall grass.

"I followed the paperwork," Anja replied and sounded much calmer than he felt. "Continue in that direction, and you should reach the junction."

During the days leading up to this moment, he had taken the time to buy some equipment that he might need should push come to shove. The one purchase he definitely didn't regret was the heavy clothes. Anyone else in his position would have gone for a ghillie suit, but he didn't have the time to crawl secretly closer and closer to the facility over a couple of long days in the sun. He had never done that himself, although from what he knew of the few truly skilled snipers he'd met in his time, they had been men and women of incredible focus and patience and had ice water running in their veins.

Thankfully, the Russian had filled him in on the details as he'd shuffled in closer. Three hundred yards could be covered fairly quickly when he didn't have to worry about outside security. A place like this didn't rate the kind of security that usually came with government testing facilities. It made sense since what the government wanted these third-party companies to do was lower the cost of the testing they needed.

The price was usually accommodated by lowering security standards. In this case, it was replaced with the remoteness of this location and the fact that there wasn't much in evidence that could identify it as a testing facility. For all anyone knew, it was a place that tested lipstick on bunnies. Anyone who broke into the place would find themselves up against some angry people with guns, and that would usually be sufficient to scare them off.

If it didn't...well, it was an isolated place with a lot of open space in which to bury the bodies.

"Fuck," Savage grumbled under his breath.

"What?" Anja asked and sounded distracted.

"I'm really glad I don't believe in ghosts right about now," he admitted. He'd reached the fence surrounding the facility and started to circle around it.

"Well, thanks for that very random piece of information. Do you anticipate that ghosts might be a problem if you did believe in them?"

"I'm merely wondering how many bodies have been buried out here," he explained as he finally reached the junction that she had mentioned.

"What do you mean?"

"Nothing, really," he responded. "But I would imagine that these people don't really turn any intruders over to the police. So the real question is how many people would be stupid enough to break into a place like this."

He paused beside a massive upheaval of dirt that had clearly been removed from a hole under the fifteen-foot fence.

"I wish to amend my previous statement." He dropped quickly into the hole that came up to his waist and allowed him to slip through the gap under the fence without any difficulty. It even amused him that he didn't need to do much more than bend over at the waist. "What the hell kind of paperwork would tell you about the work of the world's largest and most industrious dog?"

"They planned to restructure the sewer system in the facility. About six months ago, the paperwork went through for the construction of the new sewer line and it got clogged in the local bureaucracy until about a month ago when it was authorized."

"You'd think that companies like Pegasus would be able to jump to the front of the line," Savage commented, now safely inside the facility's fence.

"Come on, you've worked with the government." Her chuckle was definitely derisive. "You know better than that. Six months is the front of the line."

"Fair enough." He sighed. "How did you know that it wouldn't be covered up by now?"

"Well, all construction work was put on hold when Carlson sent out the alert that the place would close down," she explained. "There wasn't any paperwork to hire people to fill the hole in, and since the people working in this place aren't exactly the most ambitious of creatures, I assumed it would still be open."

"You assumed?" he mused with a smirk. "You gambled the success of this mission on an assumption?"

"It worked, didn't it?" She sounded suddenly defensive.

"Hey, I'm not criticizing," Savage whispered as he eased closer to the front of the facility. "It was an informed guess and a good gamble that paid off, so that's the end of the discussion."

"Well, that conveniently moves us on to the next problem," Anja continued. "All I can do is get you inside the fence. There isn't any paper trail that will magic you a way into the building proper."

"You have your magic, I have mine." He took a deep

breath as he hugged the walls. He couldn't see any cameras in place, which meant that they really hadn't put too much money into the outside security on site. It didn't matter, though, since he couldn't walk through walls.

"Are we going through with this magic metaphor?" Anja asked. "Because I think I like it. I do all my stuff from afar, and that makes me a spellcaster, while you're a battle magic sort of guy. You like to get all hands-on. What do you think, Jer? Jer?"

He didn't answer because it really wasn't an option. Voices drifted closer—a pair of them, two men walking at a leisurely pace. There were other voices too, but they were further away and sounded fairly heated like an argument was in progress.

If he could have talked, he would have disagreed. Like anyone with a hint of sense, he had to say that he didn't particularly enjoy getting up close and personal. But still, he was pretty damn good at it.

Savage slid back behind the wall as the men moved even closer. He drew the knife he'd bought from Max out of its sheath and tucked it into his jacket. While he wasn't sure what he would do, he knew that he needed it to be quick and precise. He doubted that he would have the chance he'd had in the Pegasus building in Philly.

"Like, I knew she was doing the open relationship before we started dating, you know?" one of the men said as they circled toward where he had been forced to drop back. "And she keeps saying that everything's great and why change it if it's going so well? I don't want to say it, but it's not really going well for me, you know?"

"She's not acknowledging your feelings, Ray," the

second guard said, patted the man's shoulder, and shook his head. "You need to talk to her about this, and if she's not willing to put up some kind of commitment for you, you need to let her go."

Jeremiah almost felt bad for what he was about to do. He could understand that the guy had some girl problems and he didn't really want to do anything to make it worse. But he was there to do a job, and he could only hope that the guy ending up in the hospital would buy him some kind of sympathy from the woman he had trouble with. Honestly, he'd never really seen the kind of open relationship that the man described. He had heard of them and it actually worked, from what he'd been told.

It didn't mean it wasn't complicated, though, and he was about to put a whole heap of complication on top of that. Work troubles tended to spill out into relationships.

He remained close to the wall as he advanced on the men. The fact that they moved from where the sun was shining on the building and into the shade would hopefully give him enough time as their eyes adjusted to close the distance.

Anja wasn't the only one who gambled in this. He could only hope that his had as good a payoff as hers.

The men's eyes flickered to the side as he sprinted toward them, but their eyes were drawn to where he had been a half second before. It gave him time. Not all the time in the world, but in these situations, seconds might as well be decades.

The man on his right—the one having girl troubles—was the first one he closed on. He didn't have a kill on his mind, but he needed the fight to be finished quickly so used the momentum of his advance to crack the handle of the knife on the man's skull. His eyes immediately went blank as he slumped. Savage was already on the move and spun before the first man had even fully fallen. He dropped to his knees as the other man tried to track his movements.

Dammit, what was his name again? The first guy just said it a few seconds ago? Ray? He wasn't sure why it mattered, but it did for some reason.

Savage used the power provided by his spin and drop to ram the blunt end of the knife as hard as he could on the inside of Ray's knee. He could feel the crack and pop that told him of a possible tear in the ligaments as he pushed up from his kneeling position and hammered his gloved fist under the man's jaw. The pain of the impact flared up his arm, but the damage done to Ray was much, much worse. The man's head snapped back as his knees immediately buckled and his eyes rolled to show the whites. He caught the unconscious man by the collar and dragged him and then his friend into the shade cast by the building.

"Sorry about this, guys." He made a quick guess as to which man wore what was closest to his size and selected the lovelorn unfortunate as his best match. There wasn't time to strip the man down, but thankfully, his own dark pants and boots were similar enough to pass a quick inspection. All he needed was the blue coat and Kevlar vest that the man wore.

"You really should talk to your girl about committing more to you," Jeremiah said softly once he had finished donning the uniform and dragged the two men over to the hole under the fence. "I'm not saying that open relationships are easy, but if you can pull it off, they can be rewarding. So talk to her, and maybe get to know the other guys she's dating. If you can be friends with them, all the better."

Savage paused once he'd dumped Ray into the hole first, followed quickly by the other man. "You might want to see a concussion doctor first, though. Just my opinion."

He inspected the radios and IDs that he'd retrieved from both men. Again, a quick judgment call was needed, but in this case, he actually looked a lot more like Ray—brown hair, green eyes, and rugged features. The man actually had a nicer jawline than he did, but nobody would peer too closely at the two-by-two picture that he pinned on his chest. He retained one of the radios and smashed the second. No need to have either one of them wake up and call for help at the worst possible time. Ray also had a pack of cigarettes and a lighter in his coat pocket, which he kept. There was no telling when those could be useful.

"Let me guess...you want someone to be alerted that these boys are down too?" Anja asked in his headset.

"How did you know?" he asked and adjusted the jacket. As it turned out, the lovelorn dude had broader shoulders than he did himself. It would be a little uncomfortable, but he would simply have to manage.

Savage circled toward the group that lingered near the vehicles. They were engaged in what appeared to be a battle of wills between a couple of the men who looked like they were in charge and wanted to be more in charge than their opponent. They yelled and generally attracted the attention of the others, which was why he was able to slip into their ranks.

The weakest part of any security system would always

be the human element. When would people actually understand that?

Well, he really hoped it wasn't soon. Otherwise, his part in this sordid business of cloak and daggers would rapidly come to a very ignoble end.

Carlson stepped in quickly to remind everyone that he was actually the man in charge. He pulled the reins on the two and briskly told them to get moving. Just in time, too, as Savage didn't want to hang around in one place for too long and risk being made. He moved toward the door leading into the facility as the others fell in behind the leaders. It was necessary to stay in formation and remain a nameless, faceless part of the horde. Anderson was right. He did have some theoretical training in how to do this.

His experience called for other skills, though. The kind that had taken care of the two men who had loaned him their uniforms and radios.

Savage grabbed the door quickly and held it open as the executive passed him.

The man didn't even glance at him and looked like he was on that magical bridge between being drunk and being hungover. Savage wondered how much of a scene he would have to make before the man realized that he wasn't part of his security detail. The men who were actually guarding him were in a similar situation. They appeared to be more focused on the job than who they were working with.

"Thank you," Carlson grunted, removed his glasses, and stepped inside. The operative was right behind him.

CHAPTER SIXTEEN

The research facility was run-down and surprisingly shabby. The pale-blue walls had faded, and dirty handprints and assorted stains marred every surface. The linoleum, which might once have been glossy with industrial wax was scored with deep, black grooves and scuff marks. A glance inside some of the glassed-in offices revealed piles of paperwork and garbage strewn about as if in the aftermath of a storm.

For now, there wasn't much Savage could do except follow the rest of the procession as they moved deeper into the facility. He couldn't break away from them like he had at the Pegasus building. Unlike his previous mission, his sole focus now was to stay close to Carlson and make him feel superior and secure in the thought that no one would try to take him down in a building like this.

Well, he was there to do precisely that, if indirectly, but the man didn't know that. For all he knew, Jeremiah was merely one of the new guys. His scheming and plotting notwithstanding, the executive seemed to trust his inner circle despite not knowing a thing about them. It wasn't a terribly clever trait, but it was one he could exploit.

Carlson looked like he was recovering from his earlier condition fairly quickly. He didn't say much as the man in charge of securing what was carried in and out of the facility explained the process to him.

"It's not easy to move an entire scientific testing facility," one of the team explained. "I was here for about five days, talking to the people who run this place as they complained about the problems that arise when you move tests in progress. As it turns out, jostling a collection of Petri dishes in an armored car isn't good for the percentages or something."

That man has to be stripped of the armor he's wearing, Savage decided. He recognized it from some of the military installations he'd been in. There were power functions to the armor that allowed the people wearing it to carry heavier weapons and take heavier fire. Of course, they weren't as good as the full suits they had started to roll out for the grunts in the Marine Corps. And no, he didn't begrudge soldiers some way to keep themselves alive in the field of battle, but that wasn't the point.

The point was that if the big man in armor noticed that he wasn't a part of the original security team, there wasn't much that he could do to defend himself. He could handle men in Kevlar, especially with a knife. But that man's suit wouldn't give him any opportunities like that. Worse, a punch from one of those bad boys would dent his face in ways that didn't buff out.

Oh, well, closed-casket funerals are all the rage these days, he thought with a small sneer.

"I don't care about a few ruined tests," Carlson said and rubbed his temples with obvious irritation. "These people work for me, and I'm sure they won't mind if their work is pushed back a couple of weeks so long as the funding checks continue to come in."

"If you don't mind me asking, sir," the man inquired and looked sheepish. "Why are you moving all this out of here?"

"I do mind," he grumbled. "But considering that I'm happy with how you've managed to get the move back on track, you should know that a few weeks' delay in the deadline of these tests is a small price to pay. The people who have taken over the company are the kind of buzzkills who don't see the big picture. They'll bring everything to a stop for months or maybe years and...you'd believe me if I told you that I was doing this to save the world, right?"

"Sir, with all due respect," the man in armor said, and Savage could see a small smile on his face. "For three hundred large for two month's work, I'll believe whatever the fuck you want me to believe."

"I normally don't approve of that kind of language used by my employees," Carlson said with a small smile. "But I am paying you a small fortune for your opinion. And I'm not some prude who gets all up in arms about language."

"I'm glad to hear that."

Wasn't this a happy circle jerk, Savage mused. They continued deeper and deeper into the dingy facility. Most of the place was abandoned, but there were a handful of labs still in operation. Some of the men and women in white coats seemed to be in a hurry, and from the looks of things, they were forced to work around the clock and with minimal supplies.

He couldn't help but wonder what it was they were doing that was so important. Saving the world? Was the man that egomaniacal, or did he really think that what he did there was saving the world?

Of course, there was always the possibility that he was merely a lying prick, but that wasn't as much of a problem. He didn't really care whether they could stop global fucking warming at this point. His task was simply to stop him.

At the same time, he didn't trust his own moral compass that much. He knew he had a couple of screws loose in his head. But then, there were guys like Anderson. Men who really had an idea of what people were supposed to fight for, and Jeremiah, while he lacked that, knew how to identify someone whose ideas he could trust. He also knew how to spot the kind of men who sounded like they knew right from wrong but were more than willing to do wrong. These were simply pricks who knew all the secret codewords to make people follow them.

Carlson was one of those. Sometimes, they learned the tricks but sometimes, they were born with them. They lacked the earnestness that came with men like Anderson. They sure as hell could fake it, though.

The executive and his security chief continued to talk and walk. Savage knew he needed to get away. The two men had resumed their useless chatter about how they were saving the world, and as distracted as they were, he decided he couldn't stand around watching it. He wasn't sure his gag reflex could take it.

As they circled a corner, he waited until he was in the back of the line and broke away from the group. This place was fucking massive, and if he was ever going to find something that would help their cause, he needed to do it on his own. He had a feeling that the planned tour wouldn't cover any of the really interesting places.

"So, how was the tour?" Anja asked once he was alone. He stood in front of a men's lavatory and could smell the sharp odor of urine.

"Can you see me?" he asked and looked around. A couple of cameras and sensors were clearly visible.

"Well, the security in the facility is all run on a closed circuit and not connected to the internet," she said but her chuckle sounded smug. "I needed physical access."

"Hi, there," he grumbled under his breath. "My name's Physical Access. I've heard all the jokes. You don't need to make it worse. My parents really hated me, and that's all you need to know."

"It's still better than Jeremiah Savage if you ask me," she mused aloud.

"Nobody asked you, Russian hacker-lady," he retorted.

"I heard that," she hissed.

"Well, I did say it aloud," he reminded her. "So, now that you're patched into the camera feeds, do you have any idea of what I'm looking for? Do I need to find a server room or something? Hard drives?"

"Oh, please," Anja sneered. "They have the whole place under a web of wireless connections. I couldn't get in from outside, but now that we're inside, this whole damn place is my playground. I copied all the files they have online. They might be moving everything out, but they still keep files on what kinds of tests they're running. If I'm honest, I don't understand a word of what they're talking about, but then, I don't have to."

"Let me guess," Savage said with a sigh. "It's need to know, and I don't need to know?"

"Do you really want to know what Anderson and Monroe are doing?" she asked.

"Not particularly." He chuckled. "Then again, I don't like being kept out of the loop. The last time that happened, my people died, and I'm still angry about that. If people start dying because Anderson and Monroe think they know more about the situation than someone with boots on the ground, you can tell them that the savage they wanted is the savage they'll get."

"Oh, is that a threat?" she asked. Her voice was dead serious now, and he could practically see her suddenly sit straight and rigid in her chair.

"It's a promise, actually," he replied, and his voice gained an extra edge of chill. "But if you'd like to pass it on as a threat, I don't mind."

The Russian was silent for a few moments. "How do you do that?" she asked, her voice a little softer. "Get your voice all mean and menacing like that? It's a neat trick to have up your sleeve, you know."

"I know. But there's no secret. You simply really have to mean it. Do I actually have to do anything, or should I stick around until you have everything you need?"

"I need you to keep the connection for thirty seconds," she said and laughed. "Come on, you should know that's not how all this works, right? I've already copied everything I'll get from their digital files. You need to look around and see if you can find some hard copies that you can whisk away. Oh, and maybe see if there's any trace of where they're sending everything. I haven't been able to find anything on my end."

"Sure," he said softly as he wound his way slowly through mostly empty halls. "Wait—back on the Pegasus building, on the roof, where was all this alacrity then?"

"I needed to crack the encryption, that's all. Once it was done, a couple of seconds, tops. Seriously, what is it about the speed of connections these days that you don't understand?"

"The core concept, I think." Savage kept his voice low and moved cautiously. He could hear people talking. "Too many TV shows. You know, I've heard that they rot your brain."

"Shut up." She sounded amused like she tried to be serious but actually enjoyed herself a little too much. "There are some scientists ahead of you, packing up a lab. Apparently, the stuff is a little too delicate for the rough hands of the security boys. If there's anything to be learned, it's from them."

"Look at you, being all helpful," he murmured. He couldn't say any more as he approached the group of men and woman in crisp white lab coats. Unfortunately, it was the only thing that looked crisp about these people. They looked like they had been run ragged.

His training told him to find a weak link. The people who conducted experiments in a facility like this would be secretive, so he wouldn't be able to learn anything from them. He needed to find someone who was capable enough to know about what was going on but didn't care enough about it to keep quiet.

There were a few extra steps to that, but those escaped him at the moment. He needed to play it by ear. After a casual survey of the group, he identified his target, a younger-looking woman who labeled the vials the rest of the scientists were packing up. She didn't have the stuffy professor look of the man who pretended to read notes while looking at his phone, but since she was in charge of labeling and not packing, she would at least be knowledgeable of what was happening on location.

"Hey, how's everything going around here?" Jeremiah asked casually and tucked his hands in his pockets as he assumed the look of a bored security guard.

"We've been here for the past fifteen hours trying to get everything wrapped up before the weekend," the woman said and didn't bother to look up from her work. "How do you think we're doing?" She did, indeed, look exhausted and her voice dripped sarcasm.

He tilted his head and his gaze slid across the stacked packages. The writing on the labels was a series of numbers and letters. They looked like some sort of algorithm, he decided. Maybe an obscure filing system but with vials instead of files?

"I thought the bigwigs were paying overtime for this," he ventured.

"Yeah, well, they said they needed it done before the weekend, and you're crazy if you think I'll hand my life's work over to the bozos handling the transport," she replied and finally turned from her work to peer at him from behind a thick pair of glasses. "Some offense intended."

"Some taken," he replied with an easy grin. As scientists went, she wasn't quite what the stereotype demanded.

While yes, she had to be legally blind without those glasses of hers and there was a ragged look to her features, she looked normal with her thick brown hair wound in a bun over her head. He should have known better than to trust in stereotypes.

Her hard look at him softened marginally. She sighed and shook her head, then rubbed her eyes under her glasses.

"I'm sorry," she said and shrugged apologetically. "It's been a long month and a half, and I'm stressed because it's finally over. Soon, anyway. Hi, I'm Dr. Jessica Coleman, one of the...well, I *was* one of the senior researchers around here. I'm not sure how long that'll last, though."

"What do you mean?" Savage asked and blinked when he realized that the woman had actually extended her hand and offered her name as a form of a polite greeting. "I'm sorry...Raymond Burrows. I was just moved here since Mr. Carlson came to oversee the last day of moving himself. Well, he thinks it'll be the last day, but who knows at this point, right?"

"Right." Coleman shook her head dismissively. "I mean, we want to have everything done here so we can actually continue with our work. There's nothing we want more, but at the same time, all the stuff we've worked on here—in some cases, for years—could be ruined if improperly stored. Worse, you dumbasses won't let any of our people ride along in your damn armored cars, which means we have to anticipate that anything you might do will fuck things up and prepare for that. It's been stressful."

"I don't think there's anything more stressful than having to anticipate the actions or lack thereof of stupid people." He deliberately injected a note of sympathy into his tone. "And that's coming from one of the aforementioned dumbasses. Although, in my defense, we don't actually work for the same company. They manage all the moving. We only handle the personal protection."

"Oh, right," Coleman replied with a nod. "You know, they never actually gave us a reason for why we're moving, Yeah, they simply up and told us that the facility would close, fed us a bullshit line about how the funding was drying up in this region and if we wanted to continue to receive grants for our work, we would have to move to a more accessible location. Which would make sense if we worked in some charitable organization, but this is a company-run lab."

"Hey, you know as much as I do," he responded with an offhand shrug. Well, he wasn't Savage anymore. He was this Raymond fellow and probably liked surfing and taking long walks on the beach when he wasn't writing poems or playing a ukulele or something.

"I doubt it," Coleman replied dryly. "What we're transporting here is volatile, so unless Mr. Carlson has put in for the paperwork to move it across state lines, we'll still be in North Carolina. That, along with the fact that the stuff needs to be kept secured... Seriously, this Zoo crap is a frigging nightmare."

"The Zoo, huh? I've actually spent some time in the area and even made a couple of trips inside the jungle. That considered, your stuff might be in better hands than you think."

"But I thought you weren't going to transport anything?" Coleman asked with a smirk as she tugged something out of her pocket. "But I need to get to work. These vials won't pack themselves. That said, you should give me a call. We can grab a drink and you can tell me more about the safe hands my life's work is in."

"Fair enough." Savage grinned broadly, took the card, and noted that the number inscribed on it was a personal number. "I think I might do that when we both don't have our bosses riding us like rented mules."

"I look forward to it," she said, and he moved casually away. He'd learned everything that he could from this place, and what he needed to do was get the hell out before one of the men he'd left incapacitated woke up and tried to call for help.

CHAPTER SEVENTEEN

Despite the heavy lockdown over the facility, Jeremiah found that getting around the site wasn't that difficult. With his badge and the vest, people assumed two critical things—that he was security and that he had work to get to that didn't involve any of them. It seemed that people had an odd view of what security was supposed to be and tended to fill the lack of facts with fiction. It worked in his favor, and he all but had a free run of the facility as he worked his way back the way he'd come.

Anja was suspiciously quiet for the duration. He assumed that she had better things to do than butt in on the part of the job that actually was his specialty and would only intrude when she no longer had anything more important to do.

She was a pro like that, he thought.

He reached the door that he'd entered through. Most of the men in armor had moved away, probably since their job was on the other side of the facility where all the stuff was being moved out. Most of Carlson's security had gone into the building with him. The driver eyed him from inside the car, but the man didn't move when he pulled Ray's cigarettes from his coat pocket, tapped one out, and lit it.

It had been a while. He'd quit a few years before soon after the divorce when he'd gone through packs each day to deal with the stress of it. He'd quit cold-turkey when he signed up for another tour of duty and hadn't touched one since. But damn, if it didn't burn so good all the way down to his lungs.

He noted that the driver had now turned his attention away. He was cleaning something, but he couldn't see what it was through the tinted windows. It was probably booze glasses for his boss to use on the drive home. The whole concept of having your own personal driver was such a foreign thing to him. Then again, if he ever was rich, maybe he'd understand it.

That probably wouldn't happen, though. The thought didn't faze him at all.

Jeremiah wandered aimlessly and assumed the pace of someone who was merely taking a smoke break before they had to get back to work. It was a pace that he was only too familiar with. He sighed and drew in a deep breath as he meandered toward the hole in the fence. Once he was out of sight of the car, he picked up the pace, ducked into the hole, and took a moment to leave the things that he'd taken from the men. They were still unconscious. It couldn't have been more than fifteen minutes, but they would still have some troubles when they woke up. If they woke up.

"Are you there, Anja?" he asked once he was clear of the

fence and hiked back to where he'd left his rifle and equipment.

"Yes," she replied. "I'm passing the information you got from the doctor on to our overlords that the new facilities are still in the state. They're processing."

"It's not good news." His muscles burned pleasantly as he upped his pace to a jog. He was out of sight of the facility and headed deeper into the forest that surrounded the building.

"It's not bad news either," she said. "Sure, North Carolina is a big place where a lot of things can be hidden, but it's a lot smaller than the continental US."

"Carlson has handled stuff from the Zoo ever since there was stuff to handle," he said, and his lungs started to burn as he forced himself to go up a hill at a full sprint. "At least, that's what I've read about the man. If Anderson and Monroe think that he hasn't figured out how to transport Zoo materials—which is what we've now established they're transporting—we might not be on the winning side of this."

"What are you thinking?" Anja asked. "You sound like you're thinking of switching sides. You know I'd have to tell Courtney and Anderson about that, right?"

"Perish the thought." Jeremiah panted for breath as he reached the spot where he'd left his gear. He took a moment and leaned on his knees to recover. When he spoke again, his voice was low and calm and spoke each word in a monotone. "I know people like Carlson. Assholes who think that the world is owed to them because it was written on the silver spoons that were found in their rectum after their pre-planned C-Section. They know how to manipulate people and always think they're doing the right thing, no matter what. So no, I don't want to switch sides. But as much as I hate that asshole, we definitely won't gain anything by underestimating him."

He worked swiftly to take the rifle apart and packed the pieces and everything else in his trusty duffel bag. Anja was quiet for a few seconds, and he began to feel bad. He didn't like sounding preachy, and he knew that it sounded like he was talking down to her. It was stupid, but the day hadn't quite gone the way he'd wanted. He wasn't sure what he'd wanted for the day. It had been planned as only a surveillance operation, so why did he feel so unfulfilled?

"Look," he said finally as the silence continued and he finished his packing. "That wasn't how I meant to say it. I don't want to sound condescending. You probably know more about this whole thing than I do anyway."

"You're right, though," she said but still sounded a little miffed. "We have to leave the underestimating to Carlson and not make the mistake of thinking that we're above all that ourselves. And your apology is accepted."

He smirked, more relieved than he'd expected. "Thanks for that."

"By the way, have you ever actually been in the Zoo, or was that something you fed our lady friend to make her like you?" He could hear the now familiar creak of her chair in the background.

"The doctor seemed to be fascinated by anything and everything that came from the Zoo," he replied, taking his time now as he headed toward the back road where he'd left the rented car. "I assumed that her interests would expand to the people who went in to grab the stuff that she ran tests on. As it turned out, it worked like a charm. I have her on the hook. She gave me a card with her personal number. I think I might give her a call. Do you think I could actually get lucky with a doctor?"

Anja chuckled. "Well, I think she might normally have higher standards than a jock like you, but you do have an in with all that talk of going into the Zoo. But, by the way, do you actually have any stories about what happens in the Zoo to be able to sell it? She will want to hear about your trips inside and if you don't indulge her, she might think that you're full of it."

"Well, I am, but she doesn't need to know that. And while there are stories aplenty that I could pull off this ZooTube site that I've seen advertised online, I think that someone as obsessed with the Zoo as our doctor friend is would be able to see right through that."

"So, did you have a plan B?" she asked as he reached the car, pulled the trunk open, and placed the duffel bag inside. "Or do you think that you could simply come up with something on the fly and hope it works? Or maybe you thought about plying the poor girl with alcohol and charm? Or maybe, just maybe, I could help fill that gap in your knowledge."

Jeremiah tilted his head as he pulled the door to the Prius open and slid inside. The mess was now close to unbearable, and he knew that it was almost time to turn the vehicle in. They had a branch in the city that would take it off his hands and give it a good strong clean on top of that.

"Do you really think I should pick up a car of my own?"

he asked as he started the vehicle and put it into drive. He eased slowly back onto the road.

"Well, if your job requires you to be mobile, you should always have a car, but never *in your own name*," Anja replied. "You know that. Cars are too easy to track these days, so you'd need to create an alias or something and register it to them. That way, if it's involved in something that goes wrong, you can always say it was stolen."

"I know, but I don't mean for the job," he replied as he accelerated. "I mean…I have to start a life here now. I lost my home, my car, my life, everything. All my friends think I'm dead, and I think…well, I need to start somewhere so I might as well start with a car. What kind of car do you think I should go with?"

She went silent for a few seconds. Not that he minded. He enjoyed the silence and watched lazily as the sun began to set in the distance.

"Are we really doing this?" she asked. "Do you really think that we should have a normal conversation? We're not friends, you know."

"I don't have any friends," he said softly and kept his eyes fixed on the road. He tightened his grip on the steering wheel until his knuckles turned white. "You're the most human contact I've had since I've started my new life. You're the closest thing I have to a friend these days. It may not seem that important to you, but it is to me. Feel free not to indulge me, but I'll keep on asking."

The Russian sighed softly over their connection. "Well, it depends on what you're looking for in a car," she said. "I don't actually know much about them, so my selections have always leaned toward user-friendly and reliable so I wouldn't have to take it into the shop too much."

"God, you sound like you've been driving one of those electric cars," he said. "It's not so much the cars. I've driven one around and it was reasonably...okay. Nothing really replaces the thrum of a powerful engine in my opinion, but still. It's the people who drive it around that are the problem. They think they're saving the environment but ignore the fact that to produce all those cars, you need batteries, and the by-products of making those is as bad as all the fun stuff that comes out of regular cars. They're cheap and easy to run and come with all kinds of fun gadgets, and that's why you want the car. Don't try to sell me on marketing bullshit."

"Wow," she said with a laugh. "How long have you been holding that one in?"

"Too long, believe me." He laughed. Andy had an electric car, so maybe his feelings regarding them were conflicted. "How do you feel about muscle cars?"

"It depends," Anja said. "Are we talking classic or modern?"

Carlson rubbed his temples in what even he now recognized as a habitual gesture and tried to pull himself back into the kind of mind frame he needed to be in. He hadn't been the same since Andressa had died. The dumb bitch had tried to go into the Zoo herself, and while he normally would have admired that kind of resolve, idiocy was not something he would tolerate in the people who worked for him. Not ever.

And now, she was dead, and he hadn't had anyone to take his frustration out on. Other than himself, of course. But the grieving process had to come to an end. He needed to come back to reality. All his wallowing had ended with more problems than they'd had before.

His head of security stepped out of the building. From the look on his face, good news wouldn't be on the menu. Carlson had started to feel guilty about not remembering the man's name. It all worked out in the end, though. He would be sacked the minute they were finished in this fucking place.

"All the security feeds were wiped," he said, speaking in a low voice. "I hoped that we could track the intruder's path through the building by which ones were wiped, but everything was scrambled beyond recognition. I don't think we'll get anything off them for a while."

"Did he take anything?" the executive asked. "Was any of our material here compromised?"

"Nothing physical was taken, no," he replied and kept his eyes lowered as if he sensed Carlson's building anger. "The servers were completely wiped, though. We intended to do that anyway, but the IT people haven't arrived on site yet so it's safe to assume that it wasn't them. And, of course, that it was the same people who broke in."

Carlson scowled. While it was good news that the person hadn't taken anything, he wasn't sure how much data had been stored on the servers. Any data falling into the hands of his enemies was too much. He shook his head.

The two men who had been disabled were wheeled out

and into an ambulance. The driver and paramedics had been thoroughly vetted before they'd been allowed to take a look at them. Both guards were severely concussed, and one sported a knee injury that he wouldn't walk off in a hurry. It hadn't been their fault. A man who had been able to take down four of his private guards wouldn't pause for two. They would, of course, sue Pegasus for damages, and he was sure that the bleeding hearts would pay out.

"Get out there and get me something that I can use," Carlson snarled at the man, who almost fell over his own feet to comply. The driver, dressed in a tuxedo and a bow tie, stepped beside him.

"Did you get a good look at him?" Carlson asked.

"I saw him when he stepped out the building," Linus replied. "I didn't get a good look at him, but I did think that it was a little odd that someone in your retinue had broken away. He tried to cover it up as a smoking break. I almost believed him until the alarm went up. Brown hair, green eyes, average height and build..." He paused and shook his head. "I can't think of anything else, really. He was remarkably ordinary-looking. I don't think I'd even recognize him if I walked past him on the street."

"Shit. We can't keep waiting for him to show up. Somehow, we need to find a way to bring him in. Draw him in on our own terms and take him out that way."

"You don't want him taken alive, then?" Linus asked.

"You've seen what he's capable of," he retorted as the two of them walked back toward the limo. "Does he seem like the kind of person who would give up useful information if we were to get our hands on him?"

The ambulance drove away and left the entrance clear

for them to leave. The people had continued to work and from the looks of things, were almost finished with the packing. They would be there until deep into the night, but they would get the job done. One way or another. And there wasn't anything that he could do from this point forward other than let them do their jobs.

Linus opened the limo door for him and once he was inside, shut it and stepped into the driver's seat.

"No," the driver replied. "I don't think he will in the slightest."

"There you have it, then." Carlson shook his head disgustedly as the car pulled out onto the road and smoothly picked up speed. "Kill him with the others. We need to clean this city up once and for all."

CHAPTER EIGHTEEN

Jeremiah pulled in alongside the pub that he'd punched into the navigator in his car and glanced around quickly to make sure he was in the right place. He tended to avoid Irish pubs, although he didn't hold them in active dislike. They simply weren't his kind of scene. He could get behind English pubs which generally had a more subdued environment and a homier look. He even liked the occasional sports bar when he felt raucous.

This place appeared to be reasonably quiet and more upscale than what he was accustomed to. He couldn't believe he had fallen for this trick—to actually call Jessica Coleman for a date with the express purpose of pumping the good doctor for information. It was a sleazy move and he knew it, but at least he could offer her a pleasant evening while he sucked her brain for corporate secrets like some kind of mind vampire.

"You look uncomfortable, Jer," Anja said. She sounded like she enjoyed seeing him in that awkward kind of situation. "Do you think you should get a drink to calm your nerves? How long has it been since you've been on a proper date, anyway?"

"Would you be surprised if I said that it's been years?" he asked. "Wait, no, of course you wouldn't be shocked. You've probably dug into my life so deep that you know me better than I know myself right about now."

"Yeah, take that tone," she responded with a laugh. "And no. I can do my research as much as anybody else, but when it comes down to people I have to interact with on a daily basis, I try not to pry. You never know when you might find something that has been hidden deep for a reason, after all."

Jeremiah nodded, knowing that she could see him from the camera across the street. He knew a thing or two about what she was talking about. Probably not to the extent that she did, of course, and he also knew there was a story hidden in there somewhere that would explain why she felt the way she did. But that was a story for another time. They had bonded over the past couple of days, and the more he got to know her, the more he grew to like her.

He doubted that anything he might find out would change that, but why take the chance?

"So, what were you able to dig up on our Dr. Jessica Coleman?" he asked as he crossed the road to the bar.

"Well, for one thing, she's already there," Anja replied. "And she started the party early, from the looks of her drink tab."

"That, or she's as nervous as I am," he said. "I'm play-acting to get something that I need, and I'm good at that. Well, decent enough. I'm okay."

"Way to feel confident there, tiger." Anja chuckled.

"My point being that as far as she's concerned, this is a real date," he continued and didn't bother to respond to her barb. "She has a reason to be nervous. What else do you know about her?"

"Ah..." The hacker paused—to pull something up on her screen, he assumed. "Well, she got her PhD from Johns Hopkins. Actually, she got her bachelor's and master's there too, all three with a full ride. Her parents are locals and both alums, and she lived with them until she finished her PhD at twenty-five. She's had offers to work all around the country—and all around the world—but it doesn't seem like our girl likes straying too far from home.

"Her income is a comfortable six figures a year and while she's taken vacation days, she hasn't ever gone on any kind of vacation. Her life is her work. She lives three blocks away and comes to this bar, and this bar only. She has friends, mostly academics like herself, as well as a couple of boyfriends—mostly academics too with the exception of a biker bad boy a couple of years ago. I think she needed to break free from her trend of brainy paramours."

"And time," he said as he paused outside the entrance. "Is there anything that you don't know about her at this point?"

"I don't know her mother's shoe size," Anja said. "And that wasn't for lack of trying, but she doesn't do much shoe shopping. It's annoying, really."

"Well, you're terrifying, and I have to go in." He brushed his hands over his leather jacket. "How do I look?"

"That depends. Do you have your story right?"

"Raymond Burrows, born in Seattle, two brothers, one

died." He recited what he'd committed to memory. "Joined the army after being caught on a couple of B-and-Es back in his teenage years and a judge offered him the choice of serving for the military or serving jail-time. He picked the Army, served his first tour in Iraq and the second all over the place, with the last few months in the Zoo before a couple of runs got him enough money to be honorably discharged at the same rank as he entered, Buck Private. He had a problem with authority. A friend got him a job in a security company. He's quiet, no wife, no kids that he knows about, and stays away from social media."

"And all the rest I've covered for you if our gal decides to do some research of her own," she said. "Nice job memorizing all that, by the way."

"I have a great memory," he said. "It's one of the perks of being me, blondie."

"I'm not blonde," the hacker protested.

"Worth a shot." He steeled himself and stepped into the bar. Dance music played loudly, which meant that he had definitely walked into happy hour. It was a common tactic for bars. Mondays and Tuesdays tended to have a lot less traffic than the weekends, which meant they would inevitably lower prices to almost cost price to encourage people to come in. From the crowd that already gathered, he could only surmise that it was working.

That said, it wasn't long before he found the woman he was looking for seated in a corner booth. She saw him a second later, raised her hand, and waved him over.

"Don't *you* clean up well?" she asked, stood, and offered her hand. "Nice to see you out of the uniform and in civilian clothes. Come on. I'm a regular here, so they keep this booth for me."

He took it and grinned cheekily as he raised her hand to his lips and kissed the back of it. "Well, I have to say, you look a lot better than you did when we first met. I have to imagine that having the stress of the move out of the way should let you relax more."

"A lot more," Jessica agreed. "I'm not supposed to tell anyone this, but they handed out pink slips to all the project managers over the weekend. I got mine in the mail this morning and was happy to see the very hefty severance package they gave me. It's not exactly retirement money, but still."

Jeremiah chuckled and slid into the seat across from her. "Well, I have to say, you've taken being fired with a lot more positivity than anybody else might. You actually seem like you're relieved."

"I liked my work with Pegasus, I really did," she responded with a smile. "I couldn't stand the bosses, though. They were judgmental and demanding, for one thing. And most of the time, they didn't understand the science of what they wanted, but they wanted it anyway. I've had job offers for the past few hours. Many companies want what Pegasus has and are willing to pay through the nose for it, but I don't think corporate research is really what I want anymore. I haven't made my mind up yet, but I've considered a job teaching rather than another Pegasus-type scenario."

"Really?" He regarded her with open curiosity as a waitress came over to their table. "Where would you want to teach?"

"I'll have another Daquiri, please," she said to the woman and he wondered if she had a reason to avoid his question aside from the obvious presence of a third party. "And he'll have…" She turned to him and waited for him to complete the order.

"I'll start with a boilermaker," he said with a smile. The waitress nodded and headed back to the bar. They had their drinks on the table in less than a minute later.

"To answer your question…" Jessica sipped her drink through the straw. "I wanted to go back to Johns Hopkins. It's my alma mater, and I've missed the place. I still have a lot of friends there."

"Huh." He nodded casually and picked up the shot glass to pour the contents into the beer pint. "I don't think I could ever see myself as a teacher. Honestly, imparting wisdom isn't my thing. Don't get me wrong, I respect the hell out of the people who can, but I don't think I have the patience for it."

She shrugged. "Well, it's not for everybody, but I think I could do it. And if it turns out I'm wrong, they have a significant number of promising research positions at the university. As an Ivy League School, they never lack for funding—or for interesting topics to research. True, they'll be about six months behind what I did for Pegasus, but that'll be part of the challenge."

Jeremiah smiled. She was passionate, but that was what made most people in her line of work do what they did. It was the passion that enabled them to dedicate their lives to the advancement of mankind. There were consequences to that single-mindedness, though—like not even noticing that someone who wasn't a security guard but had posed as a security guard now sat and enjoyed drinks with her. It was that kind of head-in-the-clouds thinking that changed science to science fiction or nuclear power into atomic bombs. And DNA research into Jurassic Park.

It wasn't a bad thing, but the fact that there were people like Carlson out there—people willing to take advantage of their curiosity—made them a danger to the world, whether they knew it or not.

He sipped his drink and savored the mix of the beer's bitter taste and the smooth burn of the whiskey. It made for an interesting libation and was one of his favorites. Thankfully, it was also the kind that buzzed without shoving him too deep in his cups.

"I'm sorry," he said and shook his head. "I know I'm not exactly the best company. It's not like we have that much in common, right?"

Jessica shrugged. "Look, I haven't been on a proper date in forever. I'm buzzed and plan to be more so as the night goes on. I've dated all kinds of men in my time, one of whom actually went on to win a Nobel Prize in biology."

"Way to make a guy feel insecure," he said, and his chuckle suggested that he wasn't insecure at all.

"Well, you should know that the geniuses I've dated in the past all had their personal neuroses and complications. Usually, those made it impossible to be around them while they were sober," she pointed out. "Sometimes, I need someone who isn't from my little world. A man who's simple. Some offense meant."

He smirked. "Some taken."

His gaze flickered to the entrance of the bar where people constantly came and went. Happy hours were created to exploit the high turnover scenario. People arrived and left again without too much of a break in the flow, and yet a couple of men stood out. He studied them unobtrusively, his instincts keen. Their jeans hung low but not enough to cover the high laces of combat boots. Despite the increased heat inside, they kept their jackets on —heavy and dragging with more weight than the leather they wore.

"Did I lose you?" Jessica asked.

Jeremiah turned his attention back to the woman he was supposed to focus on with a smile. "Sorry, I thought I saw someone I recognized. Wait, so you said your research in Johns Hopkins would be months behind what Pegasus has. What does that mean?"

"Well, a third-party security company wouldn't know much about it, but Pegasus actually has a lot of military connections." Jessica leaned in, already a little drunk judging by the way she had to hold onto the table to keep from planting her face on it. "I'm not supposed to know that, of course, but you hear things."

He raised an eyebrow encouragingly, and she almost giggled before she lowered her tone. "Things like what happens in the Zoo, and the fact that Pegasus somehow gets their hands on specimens that are only revealed to everyone else months later. It's hard not to notice it when you have the inside track, you know? Well, of course you do. You were in the Zoo, right?"

That had come a little out of left field, he noted. It was a probe on her part, which told him that she didn't entirely trust him. Also, perhaps, that she had wanted to get him drunk in order to find any chinks in his armor. She'd also made the rookie mistake of reaching the drunk goal herself way before he did.

"Exactly like we practiced," Anja whispered softly in his earpiece.

He still wanted to hear the story of how she knew so much about what happened in the Zoo, but right now, he would simply leave himself in her hands. If Jessica was to really believe him, he needed to nail this.

"Well, I was only in there for a couple of trips." He focused his gaze on his beer and channeled some residual shame from his last operation into his performance. "I don't think I really have what it takes to be a regular in there. There are some who survive and even thrive. I wasn't one of those, and I doubt I ever will be. My first trip wasn't that eventful—in and out to get some of those Pita plants. I was really surprised by how beautiful the place was. It was like walking on an alien planet right here on Earth. I don't know how else to describe it."

She nodded and leaned in closer. Like a trout on the hook, Savage mused. All he had to do was ease her in.

"It was the second time that—" He rasped in a deep breath, closed his eyes, and drew on the impotent rage he felt at losing all the men on his squad. His hands gripped the side of the table and he clenched his jaw.

"We went in there on another trip to get more of the plants," he continued, careful to pitch his tone high enough that she could hear him over the music but not much more. "The first few days went by without incident. Then, there was this...massive thing—like a T-Rex, I suppose, although I know that sounds bizarre—right there with a blood-curdling roar.

"But we were a team of six, all dressed in the best armor the military could buy, and we managed to kill the damn thing…but barely. When we killed it, though, something in the Zoo changed. It was as if everything in the jungle suddenly wanted to kill us all. We only had a couple of seconds until all these monsters attacked in waves to avenge the death of the Rex. Things got blurry after that, like we were stuck in a repeat of shooting at waves and waves of monsters of all shapes and kinds. Every last one of them attacked wildly like they didn't care about their own lives.

"Reload and start firing again. Fighting and fighting with no end in sight. It was afternoon when we started, but it was morning by the time we got out. Another team had come over and joined us. We were bolstered by their numbers, but we still lost about half our people. It's weird." He chuckled. "For the life of me, the whole thing is a blur, but thinking about going back…"

He let his voice trail off, drew in a deep breath, and took a long sip from his drink. For a second, he wasn't sure if his performance had convinced her, but when he put his glass down, she put her hand on his.

"I'm so sorry you went through that," Jessica said and squeezed his hand gently. "People don't understand how everything in the Zoo doesn't play by the rules of the world. Even our testing seems to be all over the place. There's a set of rules in there, and we've scratched at the surface, but nothing along the lines of what we've seen before.

"I worked to test the goop they got out of the Zoo a couple of weeks ago. When it interacts with something human, it has the reaction that most people desire—it prolongs life and makes them younger, stronger, faster, and more virile. That's why people buy it. Put it in with animal DNA, though, and there are all kinds of different reactions. I won't go into it now, but there's a different reaction between species. It's difficult to put into words."

Jeremiah nodded. She was really passionate about this stuff, he realized. Again, that wasn't a bad thing, but the fact that she worked for someone like Carlson said that she needed to get a grip on her curiosity. She didn't strike him as being the shady type, but she was vulnerable. Self-control was necessary if only to ensure that the benefits weren't reaped by the wrong people. Or that she didn't unwittingly participate in human torture or the nefarious scheme behind some evil science experiment.

He breathed deeply and prepared to resume the conversation, but his gaze flickered back to the men he'd noticed before. They hadn't moved. While they weren't close enough to hear the conversation between him and the doctor, they were obviously waiting for something. He simply wasn't sure what. There was a possibility that someone had recognized him, of course, but he doubted that.

Concern prickled behind his calm. He needed to get away. Right now, he needed to be able to talk to Anja in private.

"I'm sorry," he said and cringed inwardly at how abrupt it sounded. "I need a second to go to the bathroom. I'll be right back."

"Of course." Jessica nodded. She looked a little embarrassed like she felt bad for drawing out what had to be bad memories. If they actually had been his, he wouldn't have felt too much empathy with her feelings. But considering that he was the liar in this case, he couldn't help but feel bad for the situation he'd put her in.

He pushed up from his seat, gulped the last of his drink, and replaced the empty glass on the table before he turned and headed toward the bathroom. He put a little effort into the show and staggered every third step to make it seem that he was drunker than he really was. He wouldn't try to oversell it, though, as he hadn't been there long enough to make fully drunk even remotely plausible.

It was possible that he was a little tipsy. That was something that could happen after you'd downed a full pint of beer and a shot of whiskey on an empty stomach. He moved closer to the bar and confirmed that the men eyed him every step of the way. Savage coughed and slid his hand over the bar top as he glanced casually around to check that the men maintained their surveillance. The bartender, rushing to fill orders, placed one of the empty plastic bottles of soda on the counter. When he turned away, Jeremiah calmly picked it and held it casually at his side.

Instinct told him that he should prepare for a fight. He needed it to be both fast and quiet. Obviously, he didn't want his date to realize that they had been followed there, but the question remained—were they there for him, or for her?

The way the two men slid from their seats to follow him told him that it was the former. They were there for him, and they weren't there to watch. Which begged the question of how they knew who he was. The limo driver at the compound had seen him, of course. While it had only been a glimpse, that would be enough for a smart man. And Carlson seemed like the kind of man to make sure that the people in charge of his safety were the best of the best.

That was…worrying.

"What are you doing, Jer?" Anja asked. She had her eyes on the security feed, and she could tell that he now moved toward the bathroom and held a bottle in his hand.

"Something drastic," he whispered under his breath.

CHAPTER NINETEEN

"I'm serious, Jer, if you need my help, let me know," the Russian said as he stepped into the men's room.

"There are two men here to kill me—and possibly our good doctor, as well," Savage replied. He kept his voice low as he moved through the bathroom. Dozens of small decisions needed to be made, all in a couple of seconds, and everything had to be performed to perfection. If not, he definitely wouldn't walk out of that bathroom. He had a weapon of his own this time, but he wouldn't be able to initiate a battle that only he knew was starting. He didn't have the element of surprise. Two trained killers were about to follow him in there, and he needed to be ready for them.

One of the two bathroom stalls was occupied, which meant that nothing could happen while a customer was in there. His would-be assassins knew that as well. The simple fact, though, was that it gave him a little more time.

The operative stepped into the second stall, placed the bottle on the back of the toilet, and looked around. Thankfully, it was still early enough in the night that the toilet paper hadn't been exhausted by drunk patrons, which gave him precisely what he needed. He sat on the closed seat and quickly yanked out as much of the paper as he could before he stuffed it into the bottle. It was slow work—and immensely stressful when every second counted.

The bathroom door opened. His fingers trembled in a familiar tension response and his heart thudded at a mile an hour. He knew his body had begun to prepare itself for action in the way that only it knew how. While he knew it was necessary, he also knew that he needed to keep himself under control. It wasn't easy, even under the best of circumstances, to stuff toilet paper through the narrow hole of a soda bottle. Perversely, it seemed so much more difficult now that his fingers were jittery from the sheer volume of adrenaline that pumped through his body.

He needed to remain calm and composed. To simply burst out and attack anything and anyone that crossed his path wouldn't achieve what he wanted, and it sure as fuck wouldn't end well for him. This was a situation that demanded skill and precision, not mindless violence.

The door of the stall beside his opened and the blissfully ignorant man stepped out. He'd no doubt head back to the bar to join his friends, unaware of the kind of violence he had barely escaped. Savage wanted to keep the collateral damage to a minimum. And while Carlson was known for his disregard for the body count left by his actions, he couldn't kill indiscriminately either. Even the ex-CEO made some effort to disguise his killings and cover his well-heeled tracks.

Mum was the proverbial word in this game. Savage's

time had been cut down to however long his newest non-acquaintance took to wash his hands.

It wasn't that long, he realized after only a few seconds. The man was probably drunk enough that his hygiene wasn't very high on his list of priorities. After a quick splash and dash, the man left the bathroom in what sounded like a hurry.

His time was up.

"I don't have eyes in there, Jer," Anja said and sounded genuinely concerned. "Anything you do will have to be on your own."

That reality hadn't really entered his thought process. It wasn't like he hadn't lived his whole life that way. Well, that wasn't entirely fair. Most of his operations had been carried out after months of planning and arduous hours of research by people who would never receive any medals or recognition for their efforts. Once they had done their part, he charged in, killed people, and hauled others out, whether they wanted it or not. Of course, he wasn't given medals or recognition for his efforts either, so they were all essentially in the same boat there.

At least the people who ran the intel didn't have to deal with the actual battle and risk life and limb. And, of course, when the mission went bad, they also didn't have to die or fake their death to ensure that none of the paperwork on a black op ever reached the Pentagon, much less any elected officials. The kind of rules that black ops played by would unleash a host of indictments on any number of people. And those people were usually the kind who weren't indicted, which made for dangerous repercussions.

Oddly enough, he wasn't even mad about that. There

were people out in the world whom you simply didn't touch, and Savage knew well who were and who weren't off limits. The fact that he had been left alive and given money and the opportunity to disappear wasn't something he would forget. He didn't exactly forgive those assholes for ruining his life, but he was well aware that he had nothing to gain and everything to lose if he clashed with them.

He refocused on the tissue-filled bottle and knew it was as full as it would get. Satisfied, he adjusted his right shoelace so one side was left with a much longer section before he drew his knife and cut a piece off. Old habits died hard, and he still used the extra-length round nylon braided ones and probably always would. They were a godsend in an emergency, and he still had enough to still tie his boot.

Max had supplied an extended barrel for his pistol, and for some reason, today was the day he'd chosen to fit it. He jammed the barrel into the bottle. It was a tight fit, but it needed to be to accomplish his purpose. With deft movements, he slipped one end of the shoelace through the trigger guard, wound both around the neck—one from each side—and made sure to secure them as tightly as he could. He gripped the pistol and its new, improvised suppressor and slid it into his jacket pocket before he stood, rolled his neck and shook his hands, and stepped out of the bathroom stall.

He gritted his teeth and his stomach lurched sharply when his gaze settled on the two men waiting for him. They stood far apart, and both had their hands on their weapons, prepared for the possibility that he might decide to come out shooting. The distance between them ensured that even if Savage hit one of them, the other would be out of angle for a clear shot on his part and could easily gun him down. Why they had waited for him to step out of the stall was what stirred his curiosity.

Then again, they wouldn't want any trace of the violence that was about to ensue to remain once they'd left. They were ready for a shootout if they were forced into one, but there were better, simpler ways to eliminate someone like him in a public area that didn't leave bullet holes and shell casings all over the damned place.

Savage realized that they now waited for him to make a move. If he wanted to regain the element of surprise, he needed to be quicker on the draw than they would be. And he needed them to be relaxed about his preparedness in the situation.

He inhaled slowly and forced out a burp as he leaned against the side of the stall. With a soft, inane laugh, he moved to the sinks and made sure to add a slight stagger to his step. Again, he wouldn't attempt to indicate that he was fully drunk, only enough to make them think that their opponent in this fight wasn't at his full capacity.

His gaze tracked their movements in the mirror as he turned the tap on and let the water run until it was icy before he dipped his hands into the flow.

"There's no need to make this messy," one of the men said and stepped in closer behind him. Savage noted that the bathroom door had already been locked. Nobody would be able to enter or interfere.

"Make wha' messy?" he asked and carefully added a hint of a slur to his intonation as he dried his hands. "I…didn't make a mess in there, I swear. I aimed and everything. And I put the toilet seat down too. I don't know why since this is the men's room but it seemed like the right thing to do."

The two men exchanged a glance, and the one farther back shrugged. The suggestion of confusion between them told him they didn't actually know who he was. In their minds, he was merely a threat that needed to be handled—which meant that he wasn't the actual target.

Fuck.

The closer man withdrew what appeared to be a piano wire from inside his coat. In doing so, his hand moved away from the firearm. Savage adopted a bewildered expression but watched the man in the mirror as he moved closer and eventually blocked his comrade's line of fire when he raised his hands to draw the garotte up and over his target's head.

Using the guise of discarding the paper towel allowed him to drift his left hand under his coat. He raised the pistol in almost the same motion and used his image in the mirror to aim. It was a point-blank shot, of course, but he only had one attempt.

A look of surprise contorted the man's face when he felt the elongated, bottle-barrel of his pistol shove into his ribs at the same moment that he tightened the wire around his quarry's neck. It tightened and loosened almost immediately as the man hesitated and tried to decide if he was better off using the garotte or if he needed his gun.

He didn't have the time to choose.

Savage pulled the trigger and the garotte tugged for a second as a bullet punched into his assailant. The sound was still loud but not enough to penetrate the dance music that played outside. Besides, it didn't sound like a gunshot —more a soft pop like a bang snap. His attacker released the garotte, his eyes fixed in a look of shock and surprise as he stumbled back a step.

His partner wasted a second before he realized what had happened. That was all Savage needed as he spun, ready to confront his second assailant. It proved to be a second or two, considering that the man's own long suppressor had to clear the holster too, which provided time for the operative to grasp the now dead man firmly around his neck with his free hand.

He circled, the movement slow and awkward as he held the dead weight of the first assassin between himself and his opponent as a shield. Hopefully, the blood from the bullet hole in the man's chest wouldn't be a problem—how the hell would he explain leaving the bathroom soaked in blood to his date? Anxious to end it now, he shoved his weapon under the first man's arm and squeezed the trigger. The weapon snapped with the same dull pop and a bullet hole appeared in one of the doors beside the target.

Damn. Maybe the drink had affected him a little more than he realized. It should have been a simple, contained kill at close quarters. Or maybe, a part of his brain analyzed around his adrenaline, he'd lost his edge after all that time in the hospital—and his human shield wasn't lightweight, either, so the dead arm slowed and restricted his movement. Either way, there was no time to evaluate it.

The assassin's gun was clear and now aimed at Savage. The corpse jerked when a slug pounded into it. Thankfully, he hadn't tried to take another shot, or his aim would have been thrown even wider. His human shield already had two holes in him and the chance that he would be on the receiving end of the third was high. The first shot had probably been one of impulse. His adversary would definitely fire again. He was good enough and they were close enough that he would find his target through his partner and didn't have to hesitate. The man was dead already, and there was no need to even attempt to shoot around his body.

The meat shield had lost his usefulness. Well, most of it, anyway. Savage had only one more shot before the bottle disintegrated. It already looked ragged from the two shots he had already fired. It wouldn't survive a third. A tactic spilled into his mind, and before it had even crystallized, he pushed into motion.

He shoved the dead man toward his partner and ducked, keeping both hands on his pistol. This was it—the deciding moment—and he couldn't afford another miss.

As the assailant tried to dodge his falling comrade, Savage raised his weapon and pulled the trigger. Another, louder pop reverberated in the small area as the bottle was shredded by a third bullet. Thankfully, he wouldn't need a fourth. The man's knee exploded in white and red and his face contorted suddenly. His leg collapsed and he fell with a shriek of pain. Savage lurched closer to grab the hand with the gun and wrestle the weapon loose.

The assassin held on and he had to deliver a hard jab to the man's nose before he finally released the pistol. Both of the wounded man's hands now clutched his leg and he shook his head as if in an attempt to grasp what had happened. He paled even further when the aluminum suppressor pressed against his temple.

"I think you and me should have a little chat, don't you?" Savage snarled and added sufficient pressure to his grip on the weapon to keep the man on the floor.

"I'm not telling you shit," his adversary snarled and spat at his feet.

"Let's not make promises that we'll regret, asswipe," he retorted. A small grin settled on his lips as the gun moved away from the man's temple and jammed against his good knee. "Did you play sports? You look like you were a high-school quarterback—you have that strong jaw structure some people might consider attractive. That means all the girls liked you and all the boys wanted to be like you, which means they always gave you the ball to toss around. Yeah, I'd say you were a quarterback, wouldn't you say?"

The man shook his head and made no response.

"Yeah, you look like you played QB," he continued with a nod. "An injury made sure that no college would touch you, though, so you signed up to serve your country. If there's anything the chicks like more than a man in a gridiron helmet, it's a man in uniform. But my man, if you think people won't hire you after a torn ACL took you out for the season, wait until you see the kind of money they offer a guy who needs to walk around with a cane."

His captive looked firmly at him. There was a suggestion of terror in his eyes as he imagined what his life would be like with both his knees gone, but it wasn't enough to make him talk. Savage gritted his teeth and shook his head.

"Sorry, pal," he muttered, raised the pistol to the man's forehead, and pulled the trigger.

"What?" Anja asked. She'd been silent for a while, obviously leaving him to get on with what he had to do. "I thought you would make him talk. Why did you kill him?"

"Firstly, we don't have the time to make someone talk," Savage said in a low voice. "Secondly, torture doesn't work. The fear of pain is the only thing that will render reliable information. Once you enter the pain itself, you have to reach the person's pain threshold to make them talk. At that point, any information you acquire is suspect because the person might simply spew what his interrogators want to hear only to make it all stop."

She didn't respond, and he didn't need her to. He searched the dead man and located a small radio connection wired to the man's arm and ear. Quickly, he tugged it clear, tucked his own pistol into his pocket, and kept the .45 Colt in his hand as he attached the radio system to himself.

"We've secured the girl in the van," another man's voice said through the connection. "Have you handled the guy inside? Don't waste time in trying to move him out. You can leave him in the stall and they'll only figure out that he's dead in the morning."

"Well, that's not nice," Savage grumbled and moved clear of the man. He dropped beside the first assassin and tugged the garotte from his lifeless fingers. You never knew when you needed to dispose of someone quickly, and if worse came to worst, a garrote worked far better than a tie. He retrieved the man's weapon as well. On some level, he felt rather like a scavenger, but at this point in his life, it was kill or be killed. He knew which of the two he'd prefer.

"Tell me something, Anja," he said as he finished looting the two men's corpses. "Jessica said that the rest of the scientists involved in that facility all got their pink slips. How many of them are still alive?"

Her keyboard tapped rapidly as she ran searches. He assumed that she at least had the names of the people she was looking for, considering that she had been able to capture all the digital information from the facility.

"Shit," the hacker said softly. "Seven researchers were fired and given hefty severance packages. All have been found dead in their homes. Accidents all around, apparently, except for one that was an overdose suicide. How did you know?"

"Because they plan to do the same thing to our friend Dr. Coleman," he replied and stepped out of the bathroom.

CHAPTER TWENTY

Savage made sure to lock the bathroom door as he made his way out and shoved the key into his pocket to dispose of somewhere else. The longer he could keep the two dead men in there a secret, the better. He didn't really have the time to deal with police on top of the people who had apparently kidnapped the doctor.

"Anja, did you see anything happen?" he asked as he entered the bar. The loud music still pounded, and despite the fact that he couldn't have been gone for longer than five minutes, the place looked far rowdier than when he'd left it.

"I'm sorry. I was trying to keep your ass alive and didn't think to check on the doctor," she protested over the comm.

"I don't care what you were doing before." He deliberately kept his tone as calm and collected as he could. She did need to focus but it wouldn't help if he antagonized her. Despite the fact that he felt some responsibility for the danger Dr. Coleman was in at the moment, he also knew that she was the best opportunity for them to discover what Carlson was up to.

"The cameras in the building have terrible angles," Anja said. "They mostly cover the entrances and exits, with nothing shown inside except for the hallway to the bathrooms, so I can't make out when—" She paused, and he pushed through the drunken groups of people that were clearly celebrating something. He couldn't figure out what and didn't care enough to investigate.

"When what, Anja?" he asked and surveyed the area with careful focus. The men on the radio he'd stolen seemed impatient and now debated whether they should send someone in to see if their team needed help, or if they should merely leave with their prize. There seemed to be some argument as to whether Savage was even a target.

"They took her out the back," the hacker said and sounded calmer. The girl had a talent for gathering herself quickly in hot situations, and he had to admire that about her. "I can't see very well, but it looks like they have a panel van out there. Three guys were with her, and I would put money on there being a fourth out there to drive. Be careful, Savage."

It was the first time that she used his fake name without sounding like she made fun of him. He would have to bring up the fact that it was a sign of maturity on her part, but there were more important things to worry about right then. Important things like rescuing the good doctor. It didn't sound like they actually wanted to kill her on location, but he doubted that they would be too picky when he descended on them like a wave. A big, angry, annoyed wave with two suppressed pistols he had looted from their dead comrades.

He spun and moved to the back entrance. The weapons nestled in his coat pocket and he drew one as he stepped outside. It was dark already, and the alley he entered made it even darker. Two buildings, one of which was the bar that he'd just exited from, closed in around him and provided barely enough room for vehicles to move in either for delivery or to empty the containers of garbage that could be found along the side of it.

Thankfully, no additional vehicles or trash trucks were in the vicinity. A hasty glance in either direction confirmed only a small panel van with closed doors flanked by a couple of men. Both guards turned to look at him, but in the darkness, they weren't able to make out who it was. He needed to get in closer. In an attempt to avoid suspicion, he held the stolen weapon so it would be visible, and he hoped it would be enough to make them hesitate, thinking he was one of them, rather than fire at him. It was his only chance—and Jessica's only chance, as well.

"Hey, did you take care of him?" one of the two asked and tilted his head with suspicion as he stepped forward. The guard squinted as Savage's face was outlined by the light coming from inside. It wasn't something he'd planned but damned if he would waste this kind of opportunity.

The man's mouth dropped open and his hand had already moved to a weapon inside his jacket when Savage raised his pistol. The suppressor caught most of the sound and made the subsonic rounds that the team used in their clips sound much like a car door closing. The heavy .45 kicked back into his hand. The suppressor weighed the barrel of the pistol down so the kick had minimal impact on the bullet's trajectory. The target fell back a step and clutched his throat as a hole appeared. A stream of red squeezed between his fingers.

He fired again without a pause, the pistol gripped smoothly in both hands and settled closer to his chest as he delivered another slug to his target to eliminate him.

"What the fuck?" the second guard shouted and sprinted to the other side of the van. While Savage couldn't see anything inside, he could safely guess that the remaining men—most likely two out of Anja's count of four—guarded the doctor. He didn't mind. That would give him time to dispose of this last dumbass on the outside, so he had no problem waiting for them to come out. One idiot at a time made good odds.

He dropped prostrate as the man circled the vehicle. Imprudently, the kidnapper had chosen to move slowly and carefully instead of making himself a fast-moving target. Savage now lay on his side and aimed the pistol at the legs that were visible from his prone position. He pulled the trigger and the weapon kicked a split second before the man's right shin exploded and he fell with a cry of pain. By the way the blood spurted, it was obvious, even in the shadowed lighting, that the slug had hit an artery. The wounded man cursed and tried to staunch the blood that flowed fast and hard. He would be unconscious from blood loss in fifteen seconds or so, and dead in less than a minute.

Savage didn't have the time to wait, though. His target seemed torn between his wound and the need to return fire, and his indecision cost him dearly. His gun slipped from his hand and he sagged, then toppled. A low moan confirmed that he was still alive, so the operative pulled the trigger again. A spray of blood and brains erupted from the other side of his head and the body twitched one final time.

He dragged in a deep breath.

"What's going on out there?" someone asked over the radio. "Come on. Someone needs to talk to me. And no, this isn't fucking funny, you dumbasses."

With his mind refocused, Savage pushed from the ground and removed the magazine from the pistol. He had two rounds left. That was why he didn't like these Colt guns. No matter how much the world had advanced, they still produced these admittedly sturdy but outdated weapons with only seven rounds in the magazine and one in the chamber. The assassin had fired once in the bathroom, and his subsequent shots left him with only two more.

Not enough, he thought and shook his head, tucked the weapon in his pocket, and removed the full one. That still had eight rounds ready to go, and while he would have preferred to have more at this point, he'd have to work with what he had.

Savage gripped the handle of the door. He knew they would expect someone hostile to pull it open. The moment he tugged at the handle, he'd face a hail of bullets and there was no way he could survive that. He needed a better plan than a direct attack. They had made all the other deaths seem accidental or self-inflicted, so it was unlikely that they would actually shoot Jessica. He thought for a moment and decided he would have all kinds of warning if they tried to get away.

Impulsively, he dropped to his knees with the idea that he could crawl under the van itself and take his shots from there. He discarded the rough plan as quickly as it had formed. Unlike them, he couldn't afford to shoot wildly into the van for fear that he'd wound or kill the woman he was trying to save. He paused once again.

"What are you doing? What are you waiting for?" Anja asked. She could see him from the camera that had an angle on the van. It wasn't ideal, but she still had an idea of what was happening.

He couldn't reply as he didn't want to reveal anything to the men inside. Instead, he wanted them nervous and trigger-happy. Ignorance left them without any smart moves.

"Savage, the longer you wait, the higher the chance will be that they'll kill Dr. Coleman," the hacker said firmly. "You can't let them do that."

She was right, and he was well aware of that, but he still needed to think and hopefully, give them time to make the wrong move.

He shook his head and let her see him do that as he leaned closer to the van. They no longer spoke into the radio, and he wanted to see if he could hear what they were saying. It was hard to hear anything over the rhythm his heart hammered in his chest, but he thought that he identified the scrape of boots over the bottom of the van's bed. He remembered his training on angles and eased back until he had his shoulder pressed against the corner of the van.

His breathing settled as he listened for movement once again.

The handle of the back door clicked, gripped from the inside, and he knelt hastily as the door unbolted and swung open. He managed to duck under it and gritted his teeth as he flattened himself on the cold ground. The play had delivered him another gamble. If he didn't get a shot off in the first second, he was a dead man.

Thankfully, he had a shot.

His target hadn't even seen him when Savage squeezed the trigger. The bullet thwacked in under his jaw to spray blood and brains across the roof of the vehicle. The man toppled forward as the operative pushed upward. It was a mistake he quickly regretted as the second man sat far back with Jessica held in front of him and aimed his weapon at the door. Savage barely had time to duck before three shots rocketed past him. A sting on his right cheek confirmed a flesh wound, and as he hit the pavement, a droplet of blood fell onto his hand. He gritted his teeth. He wouldn't have the luxury of even a single shot at the man because he couldn't afford to hit Coleman.

An idea burgeoned and he took a deep breath, calmed himself, and resisted the urge to simply barrel in there with guns blazing. Instead, he gripped the dead man's forearm and eased the hand up until it crested the edge of the vehicle's floor. The man fired immediately, and the hand jolted as bullets punctured it at least twice. Savage counted the shots.

One, two, three, four, five—all fired in quick succession with the carelessness of a man who didn't actually know what he was doing. That knowledge was comforting.

And God bless John Browning, he thought, as he hauled himself into the van's bed. The kidnapper pulled the trigger again. Savage blinked and wondered for a second if he was wrong. He was beyond relieved when the gun clicked empty. The man fumbled around the alarmingly limp Coleman, obviously in an effort to find a magazine to replace the empty one. Stupidly, he hadn't bothered to eject it either.

Savage almost felt bad that he had to eliminate someone this bad at his job. Almost, but not quite, because inept or not, he was still party to kidnapping and a planned murder.

He stepped in closer and hammered the pistol grip into the man's face to open a cut on his cheekbone. The blow distracted his target and he dragged him clear of the doctor before he aimed and squeezed the trigger a couple of times. Two holes blossomed red in his head as he fell without so much as a gasp.

With the kidnappers all eliminated, he needed to make sure that Coleman was still alive.

He fell on his knees beside her and frowned. Her eyes were shut, and she hadn't reacted at all to the commotion. He feared the worst for a second and fumbled for a pulse on her neck. It took a moment, but he exhaled with relief. There it was, slow but strong. She was sleeping.

Who the hell fell asleep during a kidnapping?

"Jer?" Anja asked in his headset. "Jer, are you there? I swear, if someone doesn't start talking right fucking now—"

"I'm here, don't worry," Savage said. "All the kidnappers are down, and Dr. Coleman is passed out. I can't see any—

oh, shit." The reason for his curse was a small vial of medication beside the sleeping woman. It was still half full, but a used syringe laid on the ground nearby.

"Anja, I found what looks like medication and a syringe." He paused and peered closer to see the label. "Ketamine."

"Was our girl injected with it?"

"It looks like it." He eased into a seated position beside Coleman and patted her cheek gently. After a few taps, her eyes opened. There wasn't much in the way of pupillary response, but she recognized him.

"Who's Anja?" she asked and her voice slurred.

"Nobody you need to be concerned about, honey," he said with a smile and pressed his finger to her neck again. Her pulse had picked up, but not by much.

The drug made sense if you wanted to calm someone down for long enough to get them out of a crowded location and transport them somewhere. It also meant they could be controlled until they were killed in a way that would look like some sort of accident, so it would work. He'd never actually used it himself before—or even had it used on him—but then again, there was a lot involved in this sordid business that he didn't know much about.

"Will she be okay?" the Russian asked.

"I think so," he replied. "She'll be a little groggy for a while."

"What will you do with her? It's not like you can take her to the hospital."

"Why not?" he asked.

"Well, not only would you leave her exposed in a place where there are all kinds of ways for her to 'die by accident,'" she pointed out, and he didn't have to see her to know there were air-quotes involved. "But you'll also reveal yourself to any cop who might come asking questions. And I don't need to tell you that's a bad idea."

"Well, apparently you do," Savage mumbled softly. He didn't want to be seen carrying a clearly groggy woman away from a bar. At the same time, he also knew that he wouldn't drive out of there in a van that he didn't know. He took the time to search through the dead man's possessions but found as little as he had on the others. No wallet, no cash, no ID, and no phones. Their only possessions were the guns and the radio system.

"Fucking hell," he muttered and shifted his position to one knee, dragged one of her arms over his shoulder, and heaved her up on it as he stood. He maintained a firm grip on her while he held his weapon in his other hand, just in case they ran into any other members of the kidnap team neither he nor Anja was aware of.

He didn't think that would happen, but at this point, he really couldn't afford to make any assumptions. Jessica murmured a groggy protest as he half-carried her down from the van and moved as quickly and as subtly as he could toward where he'd parked his car.

His breathing was a little more ragged by the time he managed to manhandle her into the car and buckle her into the front seat. She looked like she had a hard time keeping her head up. To anyone who didn't know the context, the assumption would be that she was drunk and needed to be taken home.

"Is there anything I should be alarmed about?" Savage

asked as he jogged to the driver's seat, slid in, and started the car quickly before he buckled himself in.

"No one has called the police to report a guy carrying a girl to his car, no," Anja said. "I'll keep you updated on that front. Do you have any idea where you'll take her?"

"The motel is as good a place as any," he said as he eased the car onto the road. "I trash their no-questions policy all the time, but damned if it isn't exactly what we need right now."

"Just have it on the record that I don't approve of you bringing in a doctor who was working for the people we're up against only a weekend ago," she said, her tone clipped.

"Noted," he responded. "Although it should be mentioned that they did fire her. And then try to kill her. So maybe she doesn't feel that great about them right now."

"Fair enough." The hacker chuckled. "Drive safe now."

CHAPTER TWENTY-ONE

Coleman couldn't feel her tongue. That was the first thought that came to her mind as she drifted slowly back into consciousness. It was much like the way her arm fell asleep when she lay on it for too long. The question was, though, how the hell did one's tongue fall asleep?

The question vexed her to the point where she knew she wouldn't be able to sleep at all, and she opened her eyes to stare at the ceiling. Her eyebrows furrowed into an uncertain frown. The room was dark enough that she didn't need much time for her eyes to adjust. She stared at a very unfamiliar ceiling.

How drunk had she been last night? Had she really gone home with someone and spent the night? That was so unlike her. Then again, she had been fired from a job she had excelled at for the better part of the last decade, so she really was in uncharted territory at this point.

Except that she didn't remember anything from the night before, either. The truth was that she wasn't ever inclined to drink until she was blackout drunk. Which meant that either she had suddenly lived life on the wild side, or something iffy had happened to her while in the bar.

She pushed herself up onto her hands and inspected the room. Light filtered through the shades, which confirmed that it was already the morning after, but she definitely wasn't home. From the cheap TV and idyllic cottage art on the walls, it looked like she was in a motel room.

The fact that she still wore her clothes was a good sign, she supposed, and inspected them to make sure they weren't torn or damaged. They revealed nothing alarming. She did feel a little sore, but not in the places one would expect after—no, she couldn't even bring herself to think it.

Jessica jumped when she heard a noise behind her. She turned as the bathroom door opened and a man stepped out. He looked vaguely familiar, but it took her a few seconds to put a name to the face.

"Raymond...damn it, what was your last name?" she asked and inclined her head in concentration. "What am I doing here? How did I get here?"

"It doesn't really matter," the man said. "I'm glad to see you're awake, though."

She opened her mouth, not really sure what to make of his response. It didn't really matter? What didn't really matter? He took advantage of her silence to walk over to a duffel bag on the floor and pick up a small pen flashlight before he approached the bed.

"What doesn't really matter?" she finally managed to ask as he sat beside her. "I asked you three questions."

"And it's the same answer to all three," he replied with a

small smile. He wasn't a bad-looking man although not particularly handsome. While there was nothing striking about his eyes or bone structure, something about the way that he carried himself was different. He didn't look like the nervous man she had met the day before, and he definitely didn't look like the man she had met at the facility.

"What the fuck is that even supposed to mean?" she asked.

"Hold still," was his only response as he leaned closer and placed a finger on her right eye to keep it open as he flashed the light into it. He did this first to the right one, then the left.

"Not many date rapists actually bother to make sure their victims are okay after the assault, you know," Jessica grumbled as he moved away from the bed, apparently satisfied with the results of his inspection. "I assume you're new to this stuff."

"I didn't drug you," the man—whom she was now sure wasn't named Raymond—said with a smirk. "And I didn't rape you. You know that."

"And how the fuck would I know that, precisely?" she asked and leaned forward on the bed.

He opened his mouth but appeared to have come up blank as he stared ahead at the wall he now walked toward. "I actually have no idea. I merely assumed that women knew. You'd be sore and achy in all the wrong places. Something like that."

It was a better answer than she'd expected, and to be honest, he appeared to know about as much as she did. Thankfully, she'd never really had to deal with anything quite so traumatic as that. Still, from the snippets of memory that seemed to filter back to her, she had a feeling that she had a whole other set of traumas to deal with. She didn't know if she felt relieved or not.

"So, what did you mean when you said that the answers to my three very pertinent questions didn't really matter?" Jessica asked once he'd replaced the flashlight in the bag. "Your name isn't actually Raymond Burrows, is it?"

"Nope." He shook his head and took a seat on one of the chairs a few paces away from the bed. If nothing else, he appeared to be willing to give her some space to process everything.

"Can I ask you what your real name is?" She shifted to the edge of the bed and swung her legs over the edge.

"You can call me Jeremiah," he said and nodded as if he'd made his mind up about something. "That is my real first name, but I won't give you my real last name. I hope you understand."

"I don't," she snapped, pushed off the bed, and walked over to him. She thought that standing over him would give her some kind of presence, something that would make her feel more empowered. But, as she came close, all he did was blink calmly at her, and she found that she had assumed in error.

"What do you want to know?" he asked and leaned back in his seat to regard her placidly.

"Am I being held captive here?" Jessica asked. She returned to the bed and sat. The situation simply didn't feel quite right—like someone had messed with the controls and she still needed to fix their blunders.

"Nope," Jeremiah responded curtly. "You can leave this room and go on home whenever you want."

"And what makes you think that I won't do precisely that?" she demanded. "For all I know, you kidnapped me and brought me here. You may not be a rapist, but that doesn't make you a good guy. And I know your face. And your first name. I could call the cops."

"You absolutely could," he agreed with a gentle nod.

"So, what makes you think that I won't?" By now, she felt more than a little frustrated by his lack of reaction to her raised tone. Most people got defensive or shut down. Jeremiah, on the other hand, merely acted like he got yelled at for a living and knew that the best way to deflate someone who was losing their temper was to be calm in response.

She already knew that she would hate the fact that he would be right all the time. It was one of those premonitions.

"Because your other memories from last night should come back soon," he replied, his voice calm and almost monotone. "I'm not sure how they managed it, but they did get you out of the bar and into the van before they injected you with Ketamine."

Jessica did remember. It was fuzzy and incomplete, but it came back in random snatches like movie stills. Two men had approached her when she moved to the bar to order drinks. She felt bad for upsetting Raymond—Jeremiah, rather—when she'd pushed him to share a traumatic experience and she wanted to make it up to him. Halfway to the counter, a couple of men had bumped into her. When she tried to move away, they nudged her again and between them, edged her toward the back of the bar. She was about to tell them to fuck off when she saw they were armed and both guns were aimed at her.

The rest was a little easier to remember—the mind-shredding terror and the way her heart thundered in her chest as they turned and walked her out of the bar. One of the men muttered quietly that if she screamed, they would put a bullet in her back—in a place that would kill her but would take a while. She hadn't made a peep as they dragged her into an alley, where a white van had waited. Two men waited inside, and the others pushed her in.

All kinds of terrifying scenarios had played out. Would they rape her? Pinned face down on the dirty floor of the van, she had waited for them to rip her clothing off. Her breath had caught around the lump of fear in her throat, but they made no effort to continue the awaited assault. Instead, something like a bee sting bit into her upper leg. Within seconds, everything became fuzzier and fuzzier. She remembered looking at Raymond with a vague feeling of rage and—

No, not Raymond.

"Who were those men?" she asked quietly as Jeremiah had remained silent while she processed her memories. He seemed to know a thing or two about what she'd gone through and didn't want to press her too hard.

"I'm not sure." His voice was still calm, soothing, and soft as he spoke to her. There was something disarming about his honesty. "If I had to guess, though, I would say that they worked for your former employers, Pegasus—or, at least, the former CEO, Carlson. He cleaned up shop over the weekend. Of the seven lead scientists who worked in the facility that was shut down, five are dead—oh, six out of seven, now. Thanks, Anja."

"What…what happened to the last one?" she asked as tears welled in her eyes. Jessica knew many of her fellow scientists and although she didn't much like some of them, three were her best friends in the whole world. She felt like the ground had opened up to swallow her whole. Worse, she somehow felt a little jealous of this Anja person. She wanted to ask who they were, but she couldn't get it past the lump that had suddenly appeared in her throat.

"She's sitting in a motel room, talking to some asshole about how she survived an assassination attempt," Jeremiah replied, but his calmness was no longer soothing. The tears spilled, hot and beyond her control, and dripped down her cheeks as a hard, ugly sob forced itself from her throat. Her vision wavered and the room seemed to recede as the sobs came harder and faster and she collapsed on the bed.

He moved to the side of the bed and sat. She tensed, but he seemed to know that she wasn't in the mood to be hugged and only placed a hand on her shoulder and gave it a gentle squeeze.

CHAPTER TWENTY-TWO

It took Jessica longer than she would have liked before she finally managed to calm herself. Surprisingly, he had remained with her for the duration despite that he was probably uncomfortable with the sight of a crying woman. All she'd wanted was for him to give her the time to process it.

From what she'd seen, he was definitely unaware of that, but he made the good choice to not crowd her while he remained somewhere close in case she needed him.

She wasn't sure how long she had spent in bed, how long she had been asleep, or what time it was. All she really knew was that it was morning, and she still felt sore from the day before. She wasn't sure how long that would last. She had taken a couple of anesthesiology classes for extra credits when she'd studied for her masters, but she didn't remember much of anything about them, much less the effects that usually came after.

No, she did remember. After surgery, people tended to feel sore due to what their bodies had gone through. All things considered, she had been handled roughly, even after she'd been rescued like the world's lamest damsel in distress. No matter how gentle it had been, she had been buffeted without being able to protect herself from it, which was why she felt sore.

Jessica had come to terms with the fact that someone out there wanted her dead, but she didn't understand why. She pushed from the bed as Jeremiah finally stood and walked toward the minibar. He pulled a couple of small bottles of vodka from the compartment.

"I don't know about you, but I need a drink," he said and dropped a couple of ice cubes from the bucket into a glass. "Might I interest you in some self-medication?"

"Isn't that considered a no-no after being injected with surgery juice?" she asked.

"Well, you were halfway trashed when they injected you with it in the first place," he replied with a shrug. "Anyway, cheers." He poured two of the bottles into the glass and swished it in his hand for a moment before he took a sip. His face twisted as the burn traced down his throat.

"This stuff sucks balls," he lamented and shook his head. "Of all the things to skimp on in a motel room."

Jessica chuckled. He narrowed his eyes at her as he took another sip.

"What's so funny?"

"Nothing." The disclaimer didn't work as she still stifled laughter behind her hand. "I think it's hilarious how we're in a situation where both our lives are in serious danger and all you have to complain about is the alcohol."

Jeremiah smirked. "Yeah, well, I've been in situations like these before. Enough times to be able to go with the flow and complain about the smaller, more important things in life."

She smiled, moved quickly, and joined him at the minibar. She didn't bother with the ice and instead, poured herself one of the tiny bottles of vodka and sipped cautiously. He was right. It was terrible. She could still taste the fermenting potatoes. On the upside, she could taste the alcohol too.

"So, I guess you're not working for that security company," she said as she sat on the bed once more while he reclaimed the chair he'd used. "And you say you've been in dangerous situations before, so I have to assume you're not an insurance adjuster."

"I was in the military for most of my adult life," he admitted with a smile.

"So, all that stuff about being in the Zoo—"

"Bullshit." He sipped and made another sour face. "You seemed to have a fascination with the place, so I had a birdie on my shoulder feed me a couple of stories from other people's experiences. It seemed to work well. I think you would have told me everything I wanted to know after that line. Some offense intended."

Jessica laughed. "God, I was pathetic last night. I had just been fired from the only job I've had for the past decade or so, and I tried to cope with that with some—what did you call it?—self-medication. And a date with a man whom I thought was interesting and different from the men that I usually go out with."

"In your defense, the way the night went wasn't your fault," Jeremiah replied and drained his glass of the terrible vodka. "I played the role of the lying asshole—although, in my defense, I did it for...well, I suppose they call it corporate espionage purposes. Then, I had to save you from other assholes who wanted to kill you. In that case, I'd say that you aren't to blame for anything that happened last night. You were vulnerable and taken advantage of. Not in that way, but you know what I mean."

"Would it really shock you if I told you that doesn't make me feel any better?" She leaned back on the bed and placed her empty glass on the covers that she'd slept on top of the night before. She didn't feel particularly rested, but she wouldn't fall asleep now.

"The truth isn't there to make you feel better," he said softly as he toyed with his glass. "But yeah, I get it. Just because it's not directly your fault, it won't keep you from feeling guilty. And the fact that you know you shouldn't feel that way only makes things worse."

"You sound like you've been through something like this before." Jessica kept her gaze fixed on the ceiling. "Is that a part of your history in the military?"

"I was a part of a black ops unit in the US Army." His voice was low and level. "One of the missions we were sent on went bad. The other members of my team ended up dead thanks to some bad intel we were fed. I managed to carry one of them out, but I was wounded too, and when I woke up, I was told that he died on the operating table. I was in command of that squad, and the fact that I should blame some intel officer sitting in an office in Langley, Virginia, doesn't take away from the fact that what happened out there was my fault. Nothing will change that in my mind. So yeah, I've been through something like that before."

"Way to show me up," Jessica said and chuckled as she shifted to lean on her hands. "Is that another one of your Zoo stories?"

"I wish." Jeremiah shook his head with real regret. "After what happened, people in high places—places so high you'd think they wouldn't mind the occasional hit of pot—decided they wanted me gone. They had to make sure that I never ever talked about what happened there again. Of course, they could have simply 'erased' me. Instead, they gave me a new name, a chunk of money, and proceeded to tell my family, friends, and loved ones that I'd died overseas. Seriously, they had the fucking funeral while I was in physical therapy. No more lies. I don't want to put up with them anymore."

She leaned forward and fixed him with a look that was part irritation and part empathy. In all her time processing, she had forgotten that there were other people suffering out there too.

"You still shouldn't have lied to me," she said softly.

"If you want an apology, you won't get one," he said, and his voice took on a colder note than she'd heard from him before. "I stand by what I did like I stand by the reasons for it—as well as the fact that I saved your damn life. At the same time, I don't expect you to forgive me for what I did either. But if you want me to feel remorse, I'll tell you right now that it's a long wait for a train that won't come because you're standing on a track that was abandoned since the 1870s."

"What?" Jessica asked, her expression now simply confused.

"I get the most creative with my insults when I'm angry," he explained and shook his head.

She nodded. "If you don't feel any guilt, why are you angry in the first place?"

He opened his mouth to respond but stopped before he said anything. She wondered if she had won an argument with him before she realized that he was actually listening. Obviously, she couldn't hear anything, but he tilted his head and his eyes went out of focus in the same way that most people reacted when they wanted to focus more on what they heard than what they saw. That told her he was intent on something she wasn't party to.

"What?" she asked, but he raised his forefinger at her in silence. He didn't reach for the weapon—which she now realized bulged under his shirt—but whatever it was that he heard seemed to worry him.

"I know they're all dead," he stated.

"Who is all dead?" Jessica asked, and he rolled his eyes.

"Is there any way for you to include her in this conversation?" Jeremiah asked. "I really don't want to play translator between you and her— Yes, I know she's an unknown element, but in this case, considering that she's one of the prospective victims… Oh, fine, I'll make sure she doesn't leave my sight. And I won't tell her your name."

"I already know her name is Anja," she interjected into what was, to her, a one-sided conversation.

"Shit," he protested. "Well, even I don't know your last name, so how the fuck am I supposed to tell her that… Okay, fine… What, she still has her phone? Can't people track her through it?"

Immediately, she glanced around the room. She'd

somehow assumed that she'd lost her phone in the tussle, but as it now vibrated in her pocket, apparently not. A little startled, she retrieved it and scowled at the blocked number indicator on the display. There really was no way to determine who or where the call came from. She pressed accept and put the phone to her ear.

"Good, now I can talk to both of you at the same time," Anja said softly. "For starters, I blocked any signals coming or going from your phone the moment that it connected to the motel's wi-fi. Which, by the way, could only happen if you'd been there before and had connected to it already. Is there something you want to tell us about, Jessica?"

"We're not here to pass judgment or make people feel bad for past choices," Jeremiah said, although he did give her an odd look. Not judgment, per se, but a question that she knew he would address later. Not that she would answer any questions, of course.

"Anyway, the connection should be secure for now, although I wouldn't trust that," the hacker continued. "I would still suggest that the two of you check out after this call and find a new place to stay. Oh, and get rid of that phone."

"I still have five months on my plan," Jessica complained.

"Well, I checked on your provider and they have you insured for a new phone should it be lost or stolen, you loyal customer you," Anja responded with a cheeky chuckle.

"And about the whole check out together thing?" Jessica asked. "Shouldn't I head home? You know, to allay suspicion or let people know that I'm not actually a threat or anything like that?"

"That would be nice, yes, in a perfect world. But I assume Jer has told you about the deaths of the researchers who worked for Pegasus around there." The hacker sounded a little angry. "They've still put some effort in to make them look like accidents or natural causes, but a couple of them have been home invasions. That makes me think that the order is out that the priority is to make everyone dead first and be careful about it later. They all happened last night. Carlson must have a ton of resources to back him in this."

"Well, the man did run a government-funded research lab," Jeremiah mused aloud. "He has to have connections in the private security business who wouldn't mind taking care of some in-house cleaning for him."

"Private security?" Jessica asked.

"Companies that hire mercenaries from all around the world and pay them to basically be government-sanctioned hitmen," he explained in a tone that told her that she should know all this by now. "Okay, so let's run the numbers. Were there any other hits last night I don't know about? He would have brought everyone he could in if he was in a hurry. Oh, and how come the police haven't made the connection between the dead people and Pegasus?"

"In order?" Anja said. "The number of people who died last night was six. Of course, we don't know yet if there are others that happened before. I've only run the checks on the scientists themselves, not support staff. I don't know how many people he would need for that many hits at the same time."

"They wouldn't want to have teams doing more than one job in a single night." He pushed out of the chair. "That much pressure leads to mistakes. So, six teams, including the one that went after Jessica last night. I'd say about three to six members per team. Fireteams are how these people usually operate. That means...between eighteen and thirty-six men on call. Fuck."

"And regarding your second question," the Russian said once he stopped talking. "Most of the murders happened in different counties, so different police forces are involved. Plus, most of them didn't look like murders. And finally, the fact that their documentation was worded to make their connection to Pegasus as tenuous as possible, it'll be a while before the local PDs catch wind of what's happening."

"Ten bucks says that if anything was left behind, it'll be left to incriminate Anderson and Monroe," Jeremiah said with a chuckle.

"No bet," she responded smartly.

"Who are Anderson and Monroe?" Jessica asked.

"Our benevolent overlords," he said with a grin. "Also known as the people paying the bills. My bills, anyway. Do you know where Carlson is at the moment? I think it's time that he and I had a little chat. I'm talking to you now, Anja."

"Well, he chartered a company plane to fly him to Philadelphia on Saturday morning, but he never arrived. I'd say that our friend Carlson has a bad case of micromanage-itis, and he wanted to make sure that the house cleaning was done before he heads back to deal with our...what did you call them, benevolent overlords? Is that how you really think of them right now?"

Jeremiah narrowed his eyes. "Am I wrong in assuming that you told them about this, and they told you to fill me in? Or in assuming that you've already told them everything that happened last night and are now simply waiting for their orders on our next move?"

"Well, in my defense, I'm only doing this as a favor to a friend," Anja replied.

"Well, my benevolent overlords, then." He shook his head to help him refocus. "But back on track, I assume Monroe and Anderson didn't okay me having a heart to heart with Carlson, or you would have told me where he is by now instead of telling me where he isn't."

"Well, yes." Anja laughed. "But I'm sure they'll agree with you. A chat with Carlson is in order. Too many people are dying, and we need to make sure that this all stops now."

"In the meantime, I need to make sure that Dr. Coleman is alive and well, yes?"

"That is correct," Anja replied softly. "Good luck and be safe, Savage."

He nodded and the connection on Jessica's phone cut.

"Did she call you a savage?" she asked as he moved over to her.

"That's a loaded question," he responded as he extended his hand and suddenly spoke in an Austrian accent. "Your phone, give it to me."

"What will you do with it?" she asked.

"Break it and flush it down the toilet." He shrugged off

her instinctive protests. "The best and quickest way to get rid of technology is to waterlog it. Everyone knows this."

"Fine." Jessica rolled her eyes and slapped her phone into his hand. "And why would you say that it was a loaded question?"

"Because the answer is both yes and no at the same time —a remarkably resounding no, actually." Jeremiah took the phone and strode to the bathroom. After a few moments, the toilet flushed but she ignored it. There really was no reason to bother with it. All her data was saved to a cloud, anyway, so she would be able to access it again. She felt bad, knowing that her parents would call and try to contact her over what was happening. The best decision in this situation seemed to elude her. She honestly didn't know if she should involve them—even if only to tell them to be careful—or leave them entirely in the dark.

Once he exited the bathroom, she stepped inside and stared at herself in the mirror. She hardly recognized the woman who gazed back at her. Her neat, shoulder-length hair was tousled, and her pretty green eyes were bruised—probably more from shock and the heavy anesthesia than from anything else, she decided. Still, those same eyes were haunted by what had happened. Inner scars remained from the loss of her long-time job, the men's attack and attempted kidnapping, and the sudden deaths of her fellow researchers.

Plus, she couldn't shake the realization of how complicated her life had become and would continue to be going forward—if she survived that long. Only a week before, she'd been merely another researcher studying mind-blowing materials. The mind-blowing part was true but other than that, she had been nothing more than one of the faceless hordes that worked on deciphering the secrets smuggled from the Zoo. Now, she was on the run, her life saved by some almost-handsome but definitely messed-up military goon. How fucked up was that?

She shook her head as she left the bathroom and asked Savage, "Will you explain why Anja called you a savage?"

"The short of it is that, after that whole thing about my life that I told you about, I was given the offer to choose my own name," he replied with a smile. "I kept my real first name but drew a blank when it came to the last. My boss said I might need to be savage when it came to this job. I liked it and decided to keep it."

"Well, most people have their parents to blame for terrible name choices," Jessica said with a smirk, but she frowned and looked around. "Where are my glasses?"

"Your glasses are in your purse, where I put them." He tipped his chin at the purse sitting on a chair in the corner of the room." Then, he continued, "I thought I'd blamed myself for enough already, so I might as well have fun with my own name choice." He grinned to take the seriousness out of the words. "Get ready, okay? Anja said that people might have tracked your phone to locate you. I wouldn't put it above Carlson to already have someone doing a survey of our location before they send one of the fireteams in to kill us. I want to make sure that nobody knows we're gone until it's too late."

"What will you do?" She stood hastily to collect her bag.

He cocked an eyebrow at her. "Be a savage, of course."

"Thanks, Anja, I'll be in touch," Courtney said and ended the call as she looked over the conference table at Anderson and Robinson, her business manager and assistant, both of whom worked hard to handle all the paperwork that was required to change the name on the front of a company.

Well, technically, the lawyers handled the paperwork. Anderson and Robinson examined it to make sure it was in order before she signed it.

"How is our Russian friend?" Anderson asked and glanced up from his work. He looked tired. And damn, Courtney felt tired too. She'd spent more time in this conference room than at the apartment the company had set up for her in Philly. She even had a beautiful corner office that she'd only been into a couple of times. Since all her time was spent down there, working with other people was a lot simpler than having to call them up to her version of Olympus.

Of course, she thought with a frustrated sigh, how long it remained hers depended on how the rest of their work went.

She almost envied Savage the freedom he'd been given. In his case, paperwork was something to be avoided since it led to a trail. Up there in the clouds, everything needed a paper trail. That was one of the costs of being legit, she acknowledged.

"She tells me that most of the scientists involved in the research are already dead," Courtney said softly. "Savage is keeping the one he contacted alive for the moment, but things don't look good for any others he might have on his list. Jeremiah wants to talk to Carlson himself and make him call his dogs off, but we can't bet on how successful that will be."

"Savage getting to Carlson, or trying to convince Carlson to stop whatever it is that he's doing?" Anderson asked. He set his papers down and rubbed his eyes. They already looked red and tender, but he was a man of focus and purpose. She doubted that she could drag him from the conference room.

"Either?" Robinson interjected. "I don't doubt Savage's competence here. I'm only stating the obvious. We know about Carlson's connections and about the number of people in high places who are invested in him staying in control of Pegasus. Savage is good, but he's up against an army."

The older man drew a deep breath before he focused on Courtney. "He's not wrong. Savage has a lot of people to go through to reach Carlson—and that's assuming he isn't above doing what every other person in the world would do if someone came after him, which is to call the cops. If he confronts Carlson, it could spell disaster for all of us, including him."

"What are our options?" she asked and leaned her head wearily against the padded backrest.

"Well, Savage has gathered all the intelligence he can," Anderson said. "He has a witness to what Pegasus did in the facility—someone who survived an assassination attempt."

"The first step to make sure survivors can't hurt you is to discredit them," Robinson said and looked around when the two stared at him for a moment. "What? I read spy novels. Tom Clancy is kind of my jam."

"Right," the other man said. "Then again, he's not wrong. Dr. Coleman needs to give us actionable intelligence. We won't be able to take any of this to court if it comes down to it."

She nodded. "I'll tell Anja to let Savage know that he should probably run an in-depth with Dr. Coleman about what she did at that facility and where everything was moved to. Carlson has planned for this for a while, it seems, but there has to be a crack in his armor. Something we can use against him."

"And while we don't want Savage to actually engage Carlson personally, you might want to think about getting information from him," the ex-colonel said with a shrug. "Our target is still in a hotel in Charlotte, which is about as vulnerable as he'll get. Savage actually has a better chance to find intel there than in the fortress Carlson has here in Philly."

Courtney nodded. "Good point. I'll pass it along."

Exhaustion weighed on her nerves, but she pushed herself to reach for her phone. As it turned out, taking Pegasus down from the inside was a difficult, dangerous process—one that had already stirred far more hazards than she'd anticipated.

Of course, the Zoo was full of monstrosities, but this was something else. It was equally as devious, if less inventive in the use of evolution to create death and destruction. She was out of her depth.

This wasn't the first time she found herself wishing she could return to the Zoo, and she doubted that it would be the last. Still, she would sleep for a week when this was all over.

CHAPTER TWENTY-THREE

As jobs went, this was about as easy as they came, Harry Bolden thought.

He wasn't sure who footed the bill for this particular job, or even if they wouldn't turn and try to bite him in the ass when push came to shove. No, actually, he anticipated it. Nobody showed up with a blank check—or, in this case, a wad of small bills—and told him that all they wanted was a little surveillance on a motel without having something devious in mind. That simply wasn't how this whole thing worked.

What he could tell was that the people who hired him were in a hurry and were rich. He doubted that they would allow him to walk away from all this, but he wasn't the kind of person to turn cash down when offered. That said, he was most certainly the kind of person who would walk away with their money if he smelled something fishy.

Harry had little in the way of military training and only five years on the local police force before he'd been pushed out for early retirement for being too much trouble for his bosses. What he did have, though, was a solid dose of street smarts. He knew when a deal was about to go sour, and he knew when to walk away. That was how he'd survived three years in Vice and lived to tell the tale.

And he'd done it without turning dirty, either. Or, at least, not as dirty as others. The pricks who wanted him out had done so because they weren't as clean as he was. When some low-level officer made them look bad, they couldn't allow that to stand. *Fuck those guys! Right in the down-unders.* The thought was vaguely satisfying even if he couldn't see it fulfilled anytime soon.

Five grand was what they'd paid him up front. It wasn't the kind of money a man could live on, but it was enough to get him out of the city and set up elsewhere, where he could access the retirement fund that waited for him in San Mateo. He'd been clean when it came to things like running protection scams or appropriating drugs for personal distribution—the big stuff that inevitably hurt others.

But that didn't mean that he was above dipping into the stashes of the dealers he'd busted. It was money that would, at best, sit in evidence for half a century before it was burned. Besides that, other cops would probably take it if he hadn't. He had merely got his nose wet—looked out for himself in case someone tried to fuck him over.

And, lo and behold, he'd been fucked and fucked bad. He was stuck in the state while he waited for the depositions on the case that he'd worked on to finish so that he could give his testimony and leave. If the truth be told, the assholes he would testify against would probably cut fifteen different deals and walk away without having served a day in jail. Given that, he needed to be out of the state by the time they focused on the little matter of vengeance. Hell, out of the country would be even better.

Those Colombian bastards really didn't go about vengeance halfway.

If this chunk of scratch was all he needed to set his plans in motion, he wouldn't thumb his nose at it. The guys who expected him to sit around to testify would assume that Batista's men had found him and left him in places where people didn't find bodies. There were swamps in the south of the state that did that for them.

All this had led him there to a small motel just outside Charlotte where he waited for two people to step out into the sunlight so he could identify them and call the people with the money. They knew their quarry was there, they said, and merely needed to confirm which room they were in. For that, they needed someone unaffiliated to do the legwork.

That was him. Unaffiliated legwork specialist. Bolden was under no illusions as to what would happen to these people when they were found. He didn't much care, either.

They'd given him two pictures. One resembled an employee badge photo of a young woman with dark brown hair, thick glasses, and a serious expression. From the lab coat, he identified her as a doctor or something like that. The second picture was vaguer. It wasn't a photo, for one thing. It was an artist's rendition of what the man looked like and obviously drawn based on someone else's memory. There wasn't anything notable about it at all. He merely looked like an average man with dark hair and a trim build. Bolden knew he could walk past this man on the street and wouldn't recognize him. What it narrowed down to, he acknowledged, was that any man who left the motel with the more recognizable woman in the photo would be the target.

The sleuth had been parked outside the motel all morning. He'd snacked on the cheap delicacies he'd brought for the stakeout and now suffered when the sun started to bake his car. Even with the windows closed and the air conditioner on, there was only so much that could be done. He would be a ham by the time this was over.

"Why don't you come out?" Bolden asked in a low hiss. "I thought these places charged by the hour."

He leaned in closer to his window as he finished the beef jerky he'd brought with him. That might have been a bad choice because, while he'd brought drinks to wash it down with, he didn't look forward to having to use the empty bottles. He wasn't above it and had done it before, but a part of him wanted to put it off for as long as possible. Hopefully until after these assholes decided that they needed a breath of fresh air.

One of the doors opened, and he almost pressed his cheek into the window of his car as he tried to make out who it was. He'd brought all the standard surveillance equipment that was usually needed for jobs like these, but someone who sat in a car and peered at a motel through binoculars tended to attract all the wrong kinds of attention. The kinds he wasn't willing to attract to himself at the moment. If, God forbid, he needed to spend the night out there, that was when he would use his binoculars.

A man stepped out of the room. From across the street, he seemed fairly ordinary in a Polo shirt, jeans, and sneakers. His short brown hair, average build, and average height provided no notable features that would make him stand out. Bolden couldn't be sure if this was the man in the sketch, all things considered. He was also reluctant to use the camera that rested beside him on the seat—that was as obvious as the binoculars—but the specifics had been clear. They needed a photo, so he focused his camera, made sure to zoom in, and caught a couple of frames of the man's face as he locked the motel room door and strolled toward the stairs.

If this was his man, why did he bother to lock the door? Unless the woman in question was a hostage of some sort and he held her there against her will? That scenario wasn't half as crazy as the fifty others he'd thought up during his boring stakeout. If this was a hostage situation, it would explain the willingness to part with cash to get him on the job. It would also explain why these people had so much cash readily available too, he mused and leaned in closer once again.

The man left the motel and crossed the street toward one of the cars parked in the same car park where Bolden was parked. He stepped into the vehicle, started it, and accelerated. Well, if he was his man, there wasn't much he could do about it now. The investigator turned his attention to the motel.

How would he survive any more time without any jerky? He knew he'd gone through his stash too quickly. Maybe the establishment had vending machines where he could get his fix without having to leave his post.

His attention was quickly drawn back to the present when a car stopped behind him. It was the same one the man had gotten into, and alarm bells clanged in his head. They intensified when his quarry stepped out of his car, a gun in his hand, and moved quickly toward Bolden.

Instinctively, he stretched his hand to the glove compartment where he kept his Beretta. He barely had his hands wrapped around the cool grip of the weapon before he was showered with glass pellets. The man had broken the window, and hands latched onto his collar. For a medium-sized man, his assailant was as strong as hell and smoothly and effortlessly dragged Bolden through the window, thrust his back into the car parked alongside, and dropped him unceremoniously.

The sleuth realized that he still had his weapon in hand. He aimed at the man who loomed over him and yanked forcefully on the trigger.

It clicked and he tried again with the same result. He scowled at the weapon. Had it chosen right now to jam? Of all times? Well, he guessed that any time a gun jammed was the worst time that it could happen, but this was really fucking up there.

"Safety's on, dumbass," his attacker pointed out and wrenched the pistol from his grip. It didn't take much effort, and the man hammered the butt of it quickly into Bolden's nose.

"Oh…fuck, what did you do that for?" he asked and clutched his face as blood leaked between his fingers.

"I have anger issues," the man said with a small grin. He tucked the Beretta into his belt before he aimed what looked like a Glock at his head. "I could see you from the window of the room. You're not very subtle, which tells me that you aren't the same caliber of the people

I've dealt with over the past couple of days. Please tell me that you're only here looking to ogle some motherfucker cheating on his wife. I'd like to think that I warrant better goons than you. It's an ego thing, you understand."

"Yeah...the dude's cheating on his wife." Bolden seized the out with relief. "The wife wants a divorce and needs leverage to make sure she can retire in the luxury that she deserves and all that."

"I wish I could believe you," his adversary said with a sigh, yanked the car door open, and disappeared inside for a couple of seconds. The thought that he might be able to escape crossed the investigator's mind. Or maybe fight back...but he doubted it. He liked to think his instincts were something he could rely on, and every instinct in his body told him not to fuck with the man who had made him, destroyed his car window, and maybe damaged his face in ways that only a plastic surgeon would be able to fix.

Don't fuck with the guy with a gun. The more he considered it, the more he thought it sound advice.

"See, I really hoped that you weren't lying, but this is some damning evidence," his erstwhile quarry said from inside the car before he stepped out. The two pictures that Bolden had been given were in his hand. "Shit, is that really what I look like? I mean, I get the whole...rugged thing, but I always thought I at least had some flattering cheekbones or something."

"Sorry, you just don't have it," he grumbled through his broken and bleeding nose. "I'm sure you make up for it in other ways. A sparkling sense of humor, maybe? Or you simply have a big dick that lets the ladies ignore your less than striking features."

"I wouldn't want to make you feel inadequate, dumbass," the man said with a grin as he pocketed the camera as well as the images. "Besides, it seems like you and I have better things to talk about anyhow. Get up. I don't want to drag you but I fucking will if I have to."

Bolden nodded and shoved up from the ground with the aid of his captor, who hauled at his collar. Maybe the asshole assumed that he tried to stall when he took so long and overlooked the fact that he'd just broken his fucking nose.

He half-walked and was half-dragged across the street toward the motel room the man had exited only a few minutes earlier. There were no cameras in the establishment, obviously, not even at the entrance, where a disinterested young woman tended the front desk while she watched daytime television. Nobody was there to back him up. Even if he had someone, his aversion to using modern phones due to his status as wanted by murderous psychopaths high on cocaine meant that nobody would know where to find him if they knew he was in trouble.

The car was a rental, Bolden remembered as the man shoved him up the steps. He would have to pay for the broken window. That, or it would be charged to the credit card he'd left behind. That would suck. His credit history was bad enough as it was. Maybe disappearing wasn't such a bad idea.

The door unlocked with a click and the woman from the picture opened it. The two of them entered and she closed and locked it behind them. He was tossed onto the bed as his captor drew the Beretta from his belt, checked it a couple of times, and dropped it on a table before he trained the Glock on him.

"You'll want to talk right about now," the gunman said in a cold voice that sent chills down Bolden's spine. The very real possibility that he wouldn't walk out of there alive slid in behind the shiver.

"Savage, you can't kill him," the woman said and looked panicked. She clearly wasn't as well-trained as her comrade, and she looked like she was about to puke.

"This room is paid-up for the next two weeks, and the staff are under very strict instructions not to clean it," Savage—which, apparently, was his real name—said in that same cool voice. He might as well have been talking about the weather given his tone.

"That's why I don't think you should kill him!" The woman took a step closer. She seemed to have a rapport with the man, and he seemed to listen to her, although he kept the gun aimed with quiet intent. Their interaction meant she probably wasn't a hostage. Too bad.

"Well, if he talks and makes himself helpful, I won't have to," Savage said, and his smile wasn't at all encouraging. "Now, would you mind if I conduct this little investigation? You can stay in the bathroom for the duration if you don't want to watch."

"Fuck you," the woman said and rolled her eyes. Bolden smirked.

"What are you smiling about, Peeping Tom?" Savage asked and took a step closer to the bed. "Do you have something to tell me about who hired you to be on the lookout for us here in the motel? Why you're...well, what looks like a private dick instead of the pros we've dealt with so far? No offense."

"Private dick?" he asked. "Nobody talks like that anymore."

"I talk like that anymore, smartass," the other man snapped. "And if you keep deflecting, I'll find other parts of you to break that aren't as easily fixed as your nose, got it?"

He nodded. "Look, I'm a businessman. Not a particularly good one, I admit, but I don't have any loyalty to the guys who are paying me beyond the fact that they are paying me. Now, you can torture me to your heart's content, but nothing will make me talk. At least, not anything that will be quick enough. You obviously want to get away from these guys, and they already know what motel you're staying at. That means you need to get out of here as quickly as possible. Am I wrong?"

Savage tilted his head and regarded him with a blank expression. "Keep talking."

"Right," Bolden tried to talk as quickly as his mind moved. "Again, I don't have any loyalty to these guys, but they've paid me, and you haven't. Tell me we can make a deal here. Add some incentive, and everyone walks away happy, you know?"

The gunman narrowed his eyes. "What kind of incentive are we talking here?"

He shrugged. "How much do you have?"

The man looked like he was thinking it over. He had a quick mind too and apparently agreed with the concept that they both needed to get out of the place as quickly as possible. Options were limited. He strode over to a duffel bag in the corner of the room, shoved some items aside, and returned with a wad of small bills.

"There's about twenty-eight hundred bucks in there—all small bills, all nonsequential," he explained.

"What do you know?" Bolden grinned and took the money, careful not to stain the bills with his blood. "The perfect amount. What do you two want to know?"

"Who hired you?" Savage asked quickly.

"Some guy in a suit," he answered truthfully. "He didn't give me his name, not even a card. He gave me cash money and a number to call once I could confirm that the two of you were in the motel and which room you were in. The man was a local hire, like me, but he said his employer was in something of a rush. I didn't ask for any explanations, and I didn't get any. He gave me the pictures and the motel address."

"This all happened last night?"

"I'm something of a night owl," he replied with a shrug. "And I put the word out in town to call me any time of the day or night and that I take cash only. No checks. A guy has got to have standards, right?"

"Right." Savage smirked. "How did the guy contact you?"

"In person, at my bar," Bolden said. "It's where I do business since I can't exactly have an office."

"Here's what I need you to do—what's your name again?"

"Harry Bolden," he replied quickly and almost forgot that he hadn't brought any ID and that he probably should have lied about his own name. Oh, well, the horse was already out of the gate on that one.

"Bolden, here's what I want you to do." Savage sat beside him on the bed, the pistol still aimed at his head. "I need you to call that number. Tell the people you were proactive and took me and my friend here captive. Tell them you saw this as a way to make extra money, and you want them to pay double what they offered before, plus expenses. The guy broke the window of your car when you took him down, after all. Name a place and a time and have them go there to meet you."

"Look, Savage, you look like you're a real smart guy," Bolden retorted with a nervous chuckle. "A right, bright fucking penny. Twenty-eight hundred is enough to make me talk with a gun to my head, no doubt about that. But if you actually think that I'll be involved in a sting for that, you're not as smart as I thought you were."

The man smiled. "Who the fuck said you would be involved in a sting? No, you'll make the call, take the money and, I assume, get the fuck out of Dodge. You were hired by some incredibly dangerous people who have access to unlimited guns and murderers who have killed people all weekend. I'm here to make the killing stop, understand?"

Bolden nodded. Well, things had started to look up now. He might make it out of this room alive after all.

Savage pulled out the phone that had been in the investigator's pocket. Bolden made a face. He didn't even recall the man taking it. Then again, he had been a little distracted on the walk over to the room.

"Make the call, dumbfuck. And you'd better fucking sell it."

Jeremiah couldn't help an eye roll as Jessica stepped out of the changing room, dressed in a sundress with floral patterns. He had to remind himself that according to Carlson's plans, she was supposed to be dead. That meant she couldn't go back to her house and collect the clothes she still had there because someone was likely to be on the lookout to finish the job.

The problem was that he didn't like the fact that he had to come along for the shopping trip.

"Fucking hell, Jer, could you be any more of a cliché?" Anja asked through his earpiece. "I can see how bored you look from five different camera angles."

He glanced around irritably. Shopping malls these days did have beefed-up security—electronically speaking, anyway—since the men who were supposed to actually enforce it looked like they were about five years away from retirement and couldn't outpace a Zamboni.

Jessica strolled over to him and smiled prettily as she spun to show off her new shoes as well as the dress.

"What do you think?" she asked and tilted her head to look at him from under her lashes. She had acted oddly for the duration of the shopping trip, and he couldn't really get a bead on what she was thinking.

He rubbed cautiously at his chin. "The colors are subtle and tasteful, but they don't really match your hair."

She paused and raised her eyebrows. "Really?"

Jeremiah shrugged. "I'm joking. I don't know anything about fashion. You do look fantastic, though."

"Agreed." Anja sounded like she was grinning. "It's

subtle and understated, which is exactly what we're going for here."

"Anja says you look fantastic too," he told his companion, and she beamed.

"That's great! Now we only need to get our hands on some jewelry, and we'll be ready to go."

"Goddamnit," he grumbled under his breath as she moved to the cashiers to pay for her new clothes.

"Haven't you ever had to infiltrate a hostile location using disguises?" the hacker asked.

"Well, yeah, but people hold men to a much lower standard." He shook his head in heartfelt exasperation.

"Fucking double standards." Anja tsked at him. "But remember that we have about three hours before Carlson's goons will show up to look for Bolden's car."

"We'll be done by then." He chuckled as the cashier raised an eyebrow at being paid in cash instead of with plastic. Anja had needed to wire them extra additional funds to spend on this little venture, and Jessica went through it quickly. He wasn't sure how much all this was supposed to cost, but from the price tags he'd seen, they wouldn't have much left over.

"That's assuming Jessica doesn't get lost in the jewelry stores." The Russian chuckled softly.

He couldn't help but grin in response despite his desire to be done with it.

CHAPTER TWENTY-FOUR

"Are you sure we should have let him go?" Jessica asked.

Jeremiah looked up from cleaning his pistol and made a face. "We couldn't keep him here. And as much as I hate to admit it, you were right. We couldn't kill him. But I took his phone, so he doesn't have any choice but to get out of town before Carlson's goons try to track him down for lying to them. Well, unless we prove to be too much work and they forget about the random PI they picked up to case the motel since the rest of their teams were too busy killing your coworkers. I'm sorry about that, by the way."

"Don't be." She shook her head, her expression surprisingly calm. "It's not your fault. Besides, only three of them were actually friends. The others...well, it seemed to me that most of them either pushed me around or tried to go after my job. It was nerve-wracking, actually. I'm sad they were killed but they weren't close to me."

"Right." He could understand the concept behind what she said although he'd never experienced it himself, not with any of the men he'd gone into the field with. You had to trust the people who would watch your back, which was why he'd never thought that he would be able to fit into a company that hired people based on their skills and never once questioned their moralities. After the divorce, he'd had a couple of offers from various companies that would have readily paid top dollar for a man of his skills. But, aside from the fact that he had something against mercenaries in general, these were men whom he would have to trust with his life. And, simply put, he didn't.

Which was why he'd signed up for a couple more tours. It didn't pay quite as well—by two or three zeroes, realistically—but he knew he would go into the field with people whom he genuinely trusted.

And now, he was out there alone. While there was probably a lesson to be learned in that, he didn't get it.

"Anja arranged for us to stay somewhere else now that this place is blown," Savage said as he quickly and mechanically put his weapon back together. "You should probably head out there, check the place out, and set up, then wait for me to get back. Stay safe, don't make any calls, and don't try to contact anyone, not even for food. Raid the minibar. She said that there would be a minibar."

"Wait, if I go there alone, where will you go?" Jessica demanded and suddenly looked annoyed and a little scared.

"I need to take Bolden's car to the drop-off spot." He felt rather annoyed as he thought he'd made this part of the plan clear to her. "They know the rental car he used, so if anything else shows up, they won't take the bait."

"Well, yes, but how will you get out of there? Will you

steal someone's car? How will that work if you're in a hurry?"

"Are you suggesting that you come along?" He looked incredulously at her.

"Who else do you have on your side?" she asked simply.

Jeremiah took in a deep breath. He wanted to respond, but he couldn't come up with an answer. While his plan did work best with two people, having an untrained person in the field alongside him was merely asking for all the wrong kinds of trouble. Then again, having a second pair of eyes on this would be helpful. Besides, she was the only one who knew what he was looking for, and he really didn't want another voice in his head to muddle things while he ran an operation.

It would be best to keep her out in the open.

"Fine," Savage said and sighed. "But you follow my lead at all times, obey my instructions, and don't act on something without clearing it with me first. We can't risk having the entire Charlotte PD drop down on our heads."

"I understand." She smiled, and he scowled in response.

"This is how I die," he mumbled and shoved a full magazine into his pistol. "Acquiescing to the requests of people who don't know the risks and then rushing in to save them."

"What was that?" Jessica turned to look at him.

"Nothing," he lied. He really wished he could have fitted one of the suppressors from the 1911s onto his Glock. It wasn't possible, of course, not without some major modifications that he didn't have time for. That, unfortunately, meant that if he ended up in a gunfight, it would be very loud and very public.

He really hoped the knife and garrote in his jacket would do the trick.

"Get ready to go, Doc," he said. "We need to be out of here before Carlson's boys decide they want to call Bolden's bluff."

"Are you ready for this?" Jeremiah asked and checked his weapons again. He would have preferred that the situation be covered by someone who knew what to look for and could warn him if someone was on their way to kill him.

Well, he had Anja, but that didn't really count. She watched from the other side of the world—he assumed so, anyway—and was restricted by the view through cameras. He wasn't sure if he liked that scenario more or less. On the one hand, she did have the kind of eagle's eye view that none of his previous operators had held, but he wasn't sure if he trusted her instincts. Like it or not, he would charge directly into the teeth of it and she wouldn't.

"Don't you think I should have a gun for this?" Jessica asked. "I feel a little naked without some kind of weapon. People will shoot at us, so don't you think I should be able to shoot back?"

"Come on, newbie." He chuckled. "You don't know the first thing about guns, do you? I don't have the time to teach you either. You could shoot me or an innocent bystander instead of the people we actually need to shoot. Besides, if this goes the way it's supposed to, there won't be any shooting at all."

"How do you know that I don't know the first thing

about guns?" she demanded. "I could know something about guns. My dad could have taken me to a gun range. He could be a hunter or something."

"Your parents are anti-gun activists and very vocal about the topic on all social media," Jeremiah replied with a grin. "Your dad wouldn't have given you a gun even if it meant saving your life, much less your mom."

"How did you know that?" Jessica asked.

He grinned and tapped his right ear. "Anja sends her regards. And, by the way, why am I the only one who can hear you again? Couldn't you have bought her one of these earpieces too? Something to get her in the loop? I hate having to play translator between you and her."

"Come on, I managed to get you this very expensive, very rare technological marvel while you were in a building that Courtney and Anderson were in the process of taking ownership of," Anja said. "Do you think I would trust something like this to…oh, I don't know, a bicycle courier?"

Savage sighed and shook his head.

"I think it's annoying that I'm the one left out of the loop in these conversations too." His companion folded her arms over her chest. "What if we're in danger and I need to hear something but you're too busy fighting off the bad guys by yourself to tell me about it?"

"Actually, I think it's better that I'm the only one to receive intel from Anja in a combat situation." He stretched against the seat of the car. "You're my responsibility to keep safe, which means you'll need to follow my instructions. Anja relays the information to me, and I process it and pass it on to you."

"Would you like a side of testosterone with that?" Jessica snarked.

"This has nothing to do with testosterone," Savage retorted and twisted to look at her. "You asked to be here instead of back at the motel. Against my better judgment, I agreed, but only on the promise that you would follow my lead."

"If you think back, I never actually promised anything," she said with a cheeky smirk. "I merely said that I understood."

"Look..." He took a deep breath and held it for a moment before he spoke. "I'll go into the field, where there's a very real chance that we'll face people who are determined to kill us. This isn't a game, which means that if I go into the field with you, I need to know that you'll watch my back the way that I'll watch yours. In your case, that means to follow the instructions that will make sure that I spend as little time keeping you out of the line of fire as possible. If you don't think you can do that, I think I'll call this operation off. We'll head back to the motel, leave this plan, and devise a new one."

"I was only joking, come on," Jessica protested.

"You don't get to joke," Jeremiah said but chuckled to keep it light. "I get to joke because I know about the situation we're getting into, and I know when we have the time for wisecracks and when we have to be serious. Now is the time to be serious."

"While we sit in the car and wait for something to happen?"

"Yeah, well, I need you to be alert and make this a learning experience. For me, I need to make sure you survive to be able to learn. I can do that and still hone my razor-sharp wit. Can you continue to learn while you do the same?"

"I guess we'll see, won't we?" Jessica peered out the windshield, a little jittery. "How sure are you that anybody will actually show up for this little party of yours?"

They were currently parked in an office parking garage close to a major hospital. The building housed a fancy motel in addition to the office suites. Hopefully, Carlson's men would focus on the parking garage across town where he'd left the other vehicle. While it was logical for the somewhat inept PI to specify a location where his apparent hostages weren't stashed, it was very likely that the other team had no intention to simply roll over and cough up any more than they already had. Hopefully, the ploy would keep the mercenaries occupied while they attended to the real business of the operation.

"I don't think Bolden sold it very well, so I think anybody who does look for him will pay the motel a visit first," Savage said. "Once they realize we're not there and he isn't either, they will move on his car, which will lead them to where we want them. Or they'll realize that it's a trap and back away, and we'll have to find another way to lure Carlson out into the open. It's tricky, all this spy business, but someone has to do it."

"And what if Carlson is merely waiting for us to make a move on him?" she asked. "What if this is his trap and not ours?"

"Well, there's only one way to make the hunter come out, and that would be to inspect the trap that was sprung, wouldn't it? Either way, we get what we want—which is

Carlson out in the open, where he hates to be. That's the weakness of people who like to live in the shadows. They hate any kind of spotlight."

"And what if our friend resists the spotlight?" She wiggled in her seat and pulled the lever that lowered the back a little to make it more comfortable. "What if he makes things difficult?"

"That's what the guns are for," he replied, drew in a deep breath, and closed his eyes as he tried to focus. This was his time to crawl into that little dark place inside him where he could make hard decisions based on tactical necessity and not worry about the moral problems that might arise along the way. It was a Darwinian principle deep within that he needed to live by—kill or be killed. Other people lived safer lives and didn't need that darkness, but he wasn't them. He needed to be that other person right now.

And, more interestingly, he wanted to be that person too.

"It looks like someone's taken the bait," Anja said into his earpiece. "I have eyes on almost a dozen people converging on Bolden's car.

"It's go-time." Savage opened his eyes. The hammering in his chest had calmed to a steady, smooth, rhythmic thump. Adrenaline pumped through his body with every pulse, but it wasn't a jittery feeling. Despite the heat of the heightened rush of anticipation—or perhaps because of it —ice settled in his veins.

He stepped out of the car and scrutinized the underground parking lot. His senses scanned the area to make sure that nobody approached. Out of habit, he touched the

Glock tucked into his belt to make sure it was there. His first choice would always be the knife and the garrote, but it was nice to know that he had something he could fall back on if things went sideways.

"Carlson left his room in the penthouse and took most of his posse with him," the hacker said. "You're clear to go all the way up."

Savage nodded, confident that Anja could see him as he and Jessica sauntered toward the entrance of the hotel where Carlson was staying. The sun was setting and painted the sky with all kinds of brilliant colors and the chill breeze started to cool the city down for the night.

"Good luck," the hacker said.

CHAPTER TWENTY-FIVE

Anja leaned back in her seat and sighed as she watched the screens in front of her. She worked methodically to select the various camera feeds that would provide everything she needed to know. As tempting as it was, she acknowledged that when the lives of two people who depended on her were on the line, it probably wasn't the best time to try out a new algorithm. Which really was a pity because she was certain that it would help her to sift through the veritable mountain of data that flooded into her servers to find what would help her.

There were good and bad things about modern hotels like the one Carlson had chosen. On the bright side, they had top-of-the-line everything when it came to cybersecurity. They had cameras on every floor and in every public room, as well as sensors that told them who was where at any given time. Anyone could walk into the hotel and not be tagged, but anyone who wanted to get past the lobby would have to receive an ID badge that would allow the security teams who ran the place to make sure that nothing hinky happened.

Millions upon millions had been spent on places like these since they attracted a very particular kind of clientele. The kind that wanted the best of the best all the time and didn't want to worry about their lives or privacy being threatened.

Top-of-the-line security, best of the best. Ironically, it was the kind that Anja and her various friends across the globe had a very instrumental part in building, and each one had left their own particular kind of signature on their work. Those signatures worked as back doors should they ever need to get past those security systems. Thankfully, the one at this particular hotel was on an open, if secure, feed back to the hotel's headquarters in New York, which allowed Anja all the access that she needed. And more, unfortunately.

She had no interest in watching old billionaires cheat on their trophy wives with even younger women, and she certainly had no interest in all the back-door deals that were made. Well, there was an interest, sure, but it wasn't exactly her priority, which meant that she had to save everything to sift through later. She needed to keep an eye on Savage and Coleman's progress through the hotel.

It hadn't been difficult to assign them their own ID badges—nothing physical of course, but the computers running the hotel didn't need anything physical to keep from triggering alarms. They searched for RFID chips of some kind that were usually given to them by the hotel's receptionists, and when a guest already had one, there was no need to ask them for another confirmation. Savage and Coleman would get into the hotel's lobby and even the elevators without any trouble.

The real difficulty, of course, would be to get to the penthouse suite that was currently occupied by Carlson.

While the security in the rest of the building was mostly run on automatic with security personnel only alerted should someone trigger something, the security in the penthouse was watched by nine specialists who worked in eight-hour shifts, three at a time. They remained on constant alert to ensure that nothing out of the ordinary happened on the upper floor of the hotel.

Anja could trick the computer, and nobody would be the wiser, but she couldn't trick people who scrutinized every camera feed like their lives depended on it. It was more than a little annoying. She wondered if this was the kind of security they provided for all their guests, or if it was something Carlson had demanded. Either way, it was an obstacle she needed to find a way around.

Savage and Coleman were already heading out of the parking garage and toward the elevators. He had changed out of his jeans and Polo shirt and now wore the suit he'd purchased a couple of days earlier. Anja studied his figure with new interest. *Man, Savage sure does clean up nice.* She'd also told Jessica to look the part and she definitely did so in a long, flowing summer dress. Expensive shoes and jewelry accented the simple lavender garment, all acquired during a hasty and very last-minute shopping trip specifically for the occasion. The Russian had needed to wire them more cash, but the benefits were difficult to deny. Subtlety and taste were what separated the rich from the wannabes. Maybe people would see wealth and high-class in Savage. Or maybe they would home in on his intimidating nature and think he was possibly the younger woman's bodyguard.

Or maybe folks would assume they were lovers, Anja thought with a grin as she leaned back in her chair which responded with its familiar satisfying creak. Without looking, she fumbled for a few chips from a bowl on the table beside her and chewed slowly as she watched them move through the hotel. Despite his dangerous looks, Savage definitely sold the look of someone who belonged there.

"What are you doing?" someone said from the door of the server room. She glanced up as Amanda walked in. The woman looked like she'd been working on the armored suits all day and needed a break. Anja wouldn't deny her one there. It was pleasant, air-conditioned, and had an entertaining show already in progress on the three screens in front of her.

She liked Amanda. The tough mechanic with a heart of gold and an affinity for firearms had become a very unlikely friend in these troubling times. "I'm watching Savage and the scientist break into the hotel, one step at a time." The hacker grinned and rolled her chair back to give her companion a better view. "Do you want to watch?"

Amanda shrugged. "Sure, why not?" She took a couple of chips from the bowl and leaned back against the table.

"How does it do that?" she asked. "It switches over from one camera to the other so you can follow their movements through the hotel. Wouldn't you normally have to do that manually?"

"Sure, in the nineties, perhaps." The Russian chuckled. "This is a modern age, and I have all kinds of modern toys at my disposal. I piggybacked into the security feeds that run through that hotel, and I have one screen that scans the hotel for any of the men marked as security for Carlson. You can do that in a high-end hotel like that without too much trouble, but they still have to be registered at the front desk as guests. On screen number two, I keep track of all the security alerts. I have it on a delayed feed to the actual security team, which lets me kill any inopportune alerts that might be sent their way. It won't be permanent, of course, but it will give our people a heads-up should something go bad."

"Right." The armorer nodded but still looked a little confused. "And how are you able to keep track of Savage and the good doctor through the hotel like that?"

"That's the genius part," Anja said and grinned happily. "I have the hotel alerted to their presence, but not in a way that would actually...you know, alert people. It lets me use the alert system to keep track of them without having to search through the literally hundreds of feeds that come from the hotel."

"That is pretty genius. Did you have Connie help you with the setup?"

"I didn't need our super-AI on this. I helped to write this security system as part of my thesis for graduation. Our professor gave us all A's, of course, but he put his name on the code and sold it for millions of dollars. He has since retired from his job as a professor and set himself up with a little mansion in Scotland. This is my petty revenge. The asshole's name will be tarnished forever, and very rich people will find him to demand a refund."

"It's not that petty," Amanda said with a chortle of real amusement.

"Well, it is for me," the hacker shot back with a mock-serious look on her face. "And now you know what will happen to you if you ever betray me. Keep that in mind, Gutierrez."

"Will do, Anja," Amanda grumbled but shook her head with mock disapproval. "So long as you only use your powers for good. And try to remember that I was always nice to you when you take over the world."

"It will be taken into account."

"Hello, Anja?" a voice said from the computer. "Are we clear to head on up to the penthouse or what? Or should we wait out here all day?"

"Shit." she dragged herself closer to the screen and put her headset back on. "Uh…no, you are not cleared to proceed into the penthouse. Sorry, I'm still working on getting past the security people who watch it like hawks."

"Are you really?" her companion asked with a grin.

"Shut up."

"What?" Savage asked.

"I'm not talking to you," Anja snapped.

"Well, you'd better fucking start." He used that ice-cold voice of his. She hated how he managed to sound menacing despite being over ten thousand kilometers away.

"I'm working on getting their security feeds on a loop," she replied and hated that she sounded rushed. "It's a little difficult to do when these guys are paid six digits a year to do nothing but stare at a screen and hope something bad happens."

"Do you have an approach vector for us?" True to form, he sounded like he already had a plan.

"Yes, the service elevator," she said quickly. "It gives you direct access to the penthouse without needing a key. Only select people are allowed to use it since only select people have the passcode for it. The only thing is, there's a camera there too, and someone watches that at all hours of the day."

"And is anyone watching the way into the room where these peeping toms are situated right now?" Savage looked at the camera in the hallway where he and Coleman currently waited.

"No." She had a bad feeling about where his mind process would lead. More importantly, she hated the fact that he'd stumbled onto the simplest solution to her problem before she had.

Her apparent failure irked her, but she encouraged herself with the reminder that for her, violence was always a last resort. That made her a good person, right?

"And what floor are these watchers on?" Jeremiah asked.

"Fifteenth floor," Anja grumbled.

"Back to the elevators." He took Coleman's arm and walked her in the direction from which they'd come as fast as her new shoes would allow. Less than a minute later, they sauntered through the hallways of the fifteenth floor and followed the map of the place he'd asked her to send him to memorize. He reached the service entrance and opened the door that had been left unlocked.

Amanda stepped closer to the screen that followed the duo and narrowed her eyes. "Is this the Savage guy people have been talking about? He has the look of a man with violence on his mind, but he doesn't really look like much.

So maybe he's handsome enough, especially in the suit, but he's not very big, or tall, or strong-looking." She sounded disappointed.

"They never are," the hacker replied softly. "The door to the security room should be unlocked."

"Thank you." He motioned for Jessica to stay where she was as he moved to the door. With measured movements, he drew the gun from his pocket and the knife from his jacket and held both like he intended to use them in ways they definitely weren't intended to be used. Anja frowned as she considered this, then decided that pistols could be used as clubs. It wasn't unheard of.

He opened the door to the room and her feed switched automatically to the one inside. Three men spun to face the entry, surprised to have someone visiting their little room. It was rather cramped with so many screens, computers, and three people besides.

"Hey, I'm from IT," Savage said with a charming smile. "I was sent to inspect...something."

That absolutely wouldn't cut it, and he knew that. She wondered if his purpose was to play for time, which would allow him to get in close enough to the three-man team that had now all stood. They saw the weapons in his hands and froze for an instant as they absorbed the reality of the situation.

Savage reacted quickly. He smacked the butt of his knife into the closest man's skull. His target dropped quickly and quietly, probably concussed and very likely with a cracked skull. Anja couldn't tell from her perspective. She needed to move on since the operative had already done so. The remaining men tried to back away and draw the pistols holstered on their hips. He attacked in a blur of motion that delivered a flurry of blows with both his firearm and the haft of the knife. His onslaught first caught the man on the right on the jaw. The one on the left met the knife blow in the gut with a grunt. It doubled him over and the attacker brought his knee up hard into the man's nose. He fell back but clutched his face, down but not out although it might take a few seconds for him to regroup.

His colleague stumbled forward, groggy, and flailed in an attempt to gain a grip on his assailant. The motions were futile, and his eyes bulged as he stumbled back when Savage's knee connected painfully with his groin.

"Ouch," Amanda said, and she looked like she had actually enjoyed watching the fight. "Maybe a little more than meets the eye, this one. Marine?"

"Army, from what I gathered," Anja replied as the operative dispatched the final man into an early naptime.

"Ugh, douchebag." The armorer shook her head.

"Okay, Savage, if you're done beating three guys up, you might want to get rid of the security footage." The Russian chuckled as he looked around at the screens. "Here's what you need to do—"

She paused when she realized that he wasn't listening to her. He yanked the computers out of their sockets and removed the hard drives and motherboards by hand. Methodically, he proceeded to drop them and crush them beneath his dress shoes.

"Was that what you had in mind?" Savage asked when he finally stepped over the unconscious men and the remains of their computers. He took the time to relieve them of their phones, radios, and weapons before he left the room.

"I wanted to do something a little subtler, but yeah, that was the quickest way to make sure no sign of your presence in the hotel remains." She focused and shook off the feeling of dread that had reared its head when she saw someone manhandle a computer so roughly. "Let me guess —you want me to alert the medical services about the poor bastards you crushed with your big man-hands?"

"Nope, nothing like that." He dropped the items he'd taken outside the door before he removed both the key and handle from the inside with a rough tug. He looked hurried, like they were running out of time. She wasn't sure what he knew, but by this point, she had learned to trust his instincts. He locked the door and left the key in the lock. "We need to reach that room and be in and out before anyone realizes what happened. That means these guys will have to survive without any medical attention until we're out of the hotel. Now, which way to the service elevator?"

"To your left." Anja leaned back in her seat and was immediately comforted by the creak. It wasn't as satisfying now as it had been ten minutes before, though.

"Do you have any idea of what we're looking for?" he asked as the elevator doors pinged and he and Coleman stepped inside. She could hear the woman arguing in the background and her saying something about how they couldn't leave the men there. He attempted to wave her protests aside.

"Well, Carlson would need to keep all the transfer paperwork of what he took out of the Pegasus facility on hand," the hacker said softly. "Any transfer like that would have to be authorized by the board of directors of the company and go through a government inspection. That would be to make sure that nothing hazardous was transferred without the proper authorization, as well as to ensure that it is currently stored in the proper containment. To get around that, most people like Carlson would file these papers with the proper authorities but grease palms to make sure that any judge in charge shuffles it to the bottom of the pile. You only need to have an application in place in order to actually do all this."

"But Carlson would need to have the paperwork on him or close to him in case questions are asked," Savage replied with a nod of understanding. "Since he's still in possession of all the transferred items, he needs to make sure he would be cleared if Monroe or Anderson start an inquiry on the facility."

"Right," she confirmed. "You have to find the papers and get a location of precisely where the items were transferred to. Once we have both and with the application paperwork out of his hands, Carlson opens himself to a government investigation. That, hopefully, would allow his entire network of lies to unravel. And considering that he handled government contracts, that will be huge. He'll see jail time in the rich-guy prisons they have in Florida, which will then give Courtney and Anderson free rein to eliminate Pegasus."

"And fun times will be had by all." His sarcasm carried no amusement. It was a good plan, there was no denying that, but things were so rarely left that clean for them to work with. It was a pain and there would be a lot of obstacles still to face, but Anja felt the difficulty that remained would be one they could live with. All they needed were those application papers.

Savage and Jessica stepped into the penthouse. She looked somewhat awed by the sheer luxury of the apartment, but he remained more focused and hurried toward the bedroom of the suite in search of the safe.

"What am I supposed to do?" she asked.

"Look around for anything that might tell you about where they transferred all your research," he responded. "I assume that the number of facilities that can actually safely store stuff like that is fairly limited and that you'd know about most of them, so look around. See if you can find receipts or something that might give you an idea of where they are."

"You're giving me busywork to get me out of your way, aren't you?" she challenged.

"This search will come to an abrupt end if Carlson decides to return to his room. If I were in the business of wasting man-hours rather than doing what we have to do, I would have left you tied up in our new motel room," he snarled in response. "Now start looking!"

She jumped at his tone and scanned the apartment in bewilderment. In all fairness, there was a lot of space to search and they had no idea where to start. He worked methodically through the main bedroom and finally located a safe tucked under the bed.

"Anja, do you have any idea how to crack this thing?" he asked and looked around as if he expected to see her.

"Uh...yeah, hold on." The hacker moved quickly to her third screen, minimized the alert notifications, and opened a search bar. She knew which safes the hotel had fitted in all their rooms three years before, just as she knew that there was always a way to revert the safe to factory settings if a guest forgot to do so themselves and left the door locked. It took seconds to find the process on the company's site after she'd sifted through a weak firewall and she immediately walked Savage through the process. It was fairly simple, with a simple ten-digit code that he had to input while he pressed the reset button continuously. In a few seconds, the safe clicked open.

"Have I told you that you're something of a superhero?" Savage asked as he retrieved a thick binder of papers from within.

"No, and you could stand to tell me a couple more times to make sure I heard it," Anja said with a small smile and returned her attention to the camera feeds.

"Doc, did you find anything yet?" Jeremiah asked. He didn't intend to look through the documents now. Time was of the essence, and he could only assume that he had what he'd come for and leave. The clock ticked loudly in his head.

"Nothing yet," she said. "There are a couple of pictures with local dignitaries in the trash, but that's basically it." She walked into the room and glanced around a little helplessly.

"Take them anyway," he said. "Our time's up here. Anja,

let me know when the service elevators are clear to use again."

"Will do," the Russian confirmed. She entered a couple of commands into her keyboard and called up the relevant camera.

Her heart immediately lurched into her throat as she realized that the elevator now contained seven men, all heavily armed. Without a doubt, all were headed up to the penthouse—and, in fact, were scant seconds away from their destination.

"Savage, you have a problem," she said once she'd found her voice.

CHAPTER TWENTY-SIX

"Problem?" Savage asked as he tucked the folder of papers under his arm and hurried toward the elevator. "What kind of problem?"

He froze when he heard the doors open a second before they came into view of it. His instincts clicked in and he had already reached for the gun tucked into his belt as the doors peeled apart to reveal the seven men who stood inside. All were armed with sub-machine guns and definitely seemed more than ready for a fight.

"That kind of problem," he quipped and shoved Jessica into the living room of the apartment they'd just exited. His Glock was already clear of his belt and his fingers closed around the weapon smoothly to aim it at the men, who seemed almost as surprised to see him as he was to see them.

"Shit!" one of the team shouted as the operative pulled the trigger. The noise was deafening. The weapon kicked back into his hand as it always did, and three slugs rocketed into the cramped elevator before the occupants could get out and into proper cover. One of the bullets flew high, the second winged one of the targets on the left in the shoulder, and the third drilled into another man's head, which snapped back, and a red hole appeared in his forehead. A spray of blood and brains stained the wall behind him.

The body fell noisily, but Savage knew his window of surprise was over. Pure instinct powered him back into the living room and into cover of his own as the air behind him erupted in a hail of gunfire a second after he'd left it. It was loud and chaotic, but he suddenly found himself in a place of peace. He could do this and had trained to do it for his entire life. If they intended to try to stop him, he would simply have to stop them first.

"It's that fucking driver at the compound," he muttered belligerently as he crawled to where Jessica currently sheltered. "I knew there was something off about that guy. He made me way too quickly. It takes one to know one, they always say, and in this case, they're fucking right."

"What driver?" she asked and winced and covered her ears as another volley of gunfire roared in the other room. "What the hell are you talking about?"

"This is my fucking fault," Anja said through the earpiece. "I put the algorithm to only notify me for security people, but I never thought to put it in for drivers. I don't know how Carlson knew about the loophole—or if he even did—but I should have kept a watch on the elevator. This is on me."

"The both of you, shut up!" Jeremiah yelled over the ringing in his ears. "Anja, this is not the time for a fucking pity party. You find me a way out of this fucking penthouse right now, damn it!"

"On it," she snapped.

"As for you." Savage rounded on Jessica. He still shouted but only to keep his voice loud since he couldn't hear much of anything over the sound of gunfire in the penthouse. "You need to get into the bedroom, get under the bed, and cover your head with your arms. Do you understand? Nod!"

She nodded like he told her to. There was a tone in his voice that immediately cut through the panic that threatened to rush through her body. She certainly didn't feel calm, but she now had a definite purpose. Something she could direct her attention to so that she didn't succumb to the desperate need to scream her head off.

"I'll cover you, but you need to be quick, all right?" He looked unnaturally calm—far calmer than Jessica felt as she watched all hell break loose in the room. The men remained protected and covered for one another with precise barrages that allowed them to move in closer without putting any of them in danger. Soon, the wall that formed a barrier against their bullets wouldn't be enough.

"When I say move, you move. Got it?" Savage said and she nodded again before she eased toward the wall. The bedroom was across the open door through which the men would enter, and that would leave her vulnerable to their fire for a second. She paused and prepared herself. Savage's arm dropped onto her shoulder and she realized how close she was to the doorway.

"Move—now!" he roared and thrust out from cover with his pistol ready. She wondered if he had anything to shoot at or if he simply covered for her as she scrambled across the aperture, keeping herself low as she made the most of the distraction he provided. One of their attackers was caught out in the open and immediately dropped when two slugs plowed into his torso. She didn't have the time to see if he was dead or if he perhaps wore some kind of body armor, but after what felt like the longest second of her life, she was clear of the door.

"Bedroom. Go now!" Jeremiah commanded and shoved the file into her hands with enough force to make her stumble for a couple of steps. Thankfully, they were steps in the right direction, and she pushed into a sprint toward the bedroom.

She caught movement out of the corner of her eye and realized a second too late that the massive windows that she'd so admired for their fantastic view of the city also provided the gunmen an unexpected advantage. The corner of the building created an L-shaped apartment. The windows in both the living room and bedroom were comprised of massive plate-glass panes—enough to give the shooters a clear view of her through the empty outside space.

One of them had noted it, seen her flight, and raised his weapon. She screamed as the glass showered around her when the slugs shattered the transparent barrier. It wasn't an easy shot, she realized, not with two heavily reinforced windows between her and them and a fair amount of wind between. Somehow, though, the man behind the gun didn't mind that he had to spray and pray that one of the bullets would find her. She sprawled full length on the plush carpet and examined herself frantically. Aside from a couple of cuts and abrasion from the glass, she was thankfully intact.

"Fuck!" Savage bellowed over the intermittent gunfire. She looked back to check that he was all right. He did the same and held her gaze for a moment, his expression grim. "Stay down and crawl to the bedroom! Keep going. You're doing great."

She wasn't sure how she knew that he really didn't mean the compliment. Still, she didn't have time to wonder what he was up to. He spun back to the corner, his pistol gripped in both hands, and immediately opened fire. She heard no screams of pain or thuds, which told her clearly that things weren't exactly going their way.

Why had she done this? Why had she been stupid enough to think that she could actually be a part of this? Admittedly, Savage would have still been stuck in this situation, but he wouldn't have had to bother with keeping her safe. He could have simply barreled through them and not even had to kill everyone to get free and clear. All he had to do was reach a public place and they wouldn't be able to continue their attack.

From the lobby, he could probably escape and vanish like Batman or some stupid spy in those stupid thrillers she loved reading. Jessica breathed deep and looked around once she reached the bedroom. He still held his ground and quickly changed the magazine in his pistol before he resumed his barrage. The hammering her eardrums took as each of the unsuppressed shots exploded through them made her want to curl up, cover her ears, and pretend this was all nothing more than a bad dream.

She could do that...once she reached the bed. Focused

again, she remained on her stomach and shuffled as quickly as she could while she ignored the fact that the cuts on her arms and legs left a trail on the carpet behind her.

What the hell did she know about spycraft? She shouldn't have come. What did she know about breaking and entering? He had let her come because she had insisted. And, stupidly, she'd done that because she had some insane romantic thought that she could actually be useful. The reality was that she was in the way, though, and had to be saved over and over again. She didn't belong there. Someone like her would be far more useful in a lab somewhere—or maybe helping their benevolent overlords, as Savage had called them, to track down where all the lab materials had been taken. Somewhere safe, in other words.

Somewhere that didn't put her in a room being shot at and more of a burden than a help.

She continued to crawl and forced herself to keep moving even while the battle inched closer. Finally, she reached the bed—a massive, king-sized monstrosity that could have held fifteen people. There was more than enough room for her to hide under it, she realized, and eased herself into the space. On closer inspection, she noticed that the framing was all some kind of metal—maybe steel, maybe bronze—but hopefully something that would protect her from a hail of bullets that might make it through to the bedroom.

He was a quick thinker, that Jeremiah Savage. A bit of an asshole and someone who was annoyingly cool under fire, but he knew how to come up with solutions on the fly.

Jessica reached the dead center of the bed, give or take. She didn't want to move anymore so she curled up and covered her ears as the gun battle continued. While she couldn't tell if Savage was all right, at this point, part of her fought the need to curl up and stay there until it was all over. She wanted to be useful. It wouldn't be now since she didn't have a weapon of her own, but she could keep the file safe. That was her job. And if there was an opening that she could pull out of thin air, she would take it.

CHAPTER TWENTY-SEVEN

The practiced motions of a man who had been through this a hundred times before, and would likely do so again if he survived, could actually be felt. Muscle memories were the kind that never really went away. It was where the term "like riding a bike" came from. Sometimes, the things you learned simply came to you automatically. He no longer even had to think about it. Drop the empty mag, pull the new one from his pocket, and slap it in, and the slide would slip forward automatically to chamber a round. It all happened in less than a second before he resumed fire.

There was a problem, of course. He'd only brought three magazines, and this was his last. Savage knew that planning for the worst-case scenarios was always the worst way to go about this kind of operation. He'd told himself that bringing more—like maybe the shotgun he'd bought from Max—would only be useful when the mission had already gone so pear-shaped that it didn't really matter.

Well, things were definitely pear-shaped now, and they

fucking mattered, and he really wished he'd brought something with more firepower than a Glock. He had nothing against it, but as of that moment, he merely tried to stay alive as bullets peppered across the wall he currently used for cover. He was really relieved that they hadn't skimped and had used actual concrete instead of simply drywall. Then again, most buildings still needed actual walls, so maybe it wasn't only luck.

He adjusted his grip on the pistol and whipped around the corner again as he tried to locate the position of the enemy. There had been seven of them at the beginning. One was wounded and two more were dead. He'd made sure of that. They didn't wear any kind of body armor, thankfully. Then again, neither did he. He still had the other four to deal with, and a finite number of bullets with which to do so. Seventeen, to be exact.

Two of the men were exposed and moved in search of cover as they approached the door. Savage held his weapon steady and took his first shot. One dropped and clutched his throat and the second spun as the bullet caught him in the arm.

In that precise moment, the operative realized that he'd made a mistake—to put it bluntly, a big tactical boo-boo. He froze as one of the men emerged from cover. The attacker was too close for it to have been a coincidence. How had these guys decided which of them would die or be wounded so one would have the chance to get in close to their quarry?

The logic behind it was more than a little weird, he thought as the man launched himself forward, faster than he could turn his weapon on him. The aggressor didn't bother to slow and, instead, lowered his head and careened his shoulder into Savage's midsection in a powerful and painful tackle.

If this had been a football game, flags would have flown. Roughing the passer. Fifteen-yard penalty. First down. He really needed to watch the game again.

As they landed in a violent tangle of limbs, a twinge of pain skittered from his still recovering ribs as they were put under pressure again. The blow drove the breath out of him, and he struggled to bring his weapon to bear on the man who now lay on top of him. The whole damn adventure would enable the other dumbasses to close the distance as well, but that couldn't really be the problem he had to focus on right away.

He realized that while he attempted to ready his Glock, his adversary did the same with his sub-machine gun. The weapon was a Mini-Uzi, by the looks of it, but with the modifications that transformed it into a small pistol that could shoot six hundred rounds a minute with more reliability over longer distances.

Not that accuracy was needed in that situation. Savage snatched at the man's wrist to twist it up and away from his head. He gasped and cringed away from the heat from the muzzle as three rounds fired right beside his ear. The flash blinded him, and the sounds deafened his ears, but he struggled to bring himself back from it. His mind was stunned, but some deep instinctual drive forced himself to continue to raise his own weapon while he forced the gun in the man's hand away from him.

His assailant grunted suddenly, and his body jerked. It seemed his comrades weren't willing to wait for their man to move out of the way. They were there to kill the intruder and didn't seem to care enough about one another to stop them from shooting anyone to get to him. He wasn't sure if he should be flattered or horrified—or maybe some weird combination of both?

Pain seared in his right shoulder and he flinched instinctively. One of the team had managed to shoot around their dead comrade and actually hit him. It was a graze but damn, it was painful—painful enough to make him mad.

Savage realized that he'd fired his Glock at the man above him, and he had absolutely no idea how many bullets he still had in his weapon.

Then again, there was a way to find out. The body was still in place on top of him as a meat shield. It wouldn't last, of course, but that didn't mean he couldn't take advantage of the situation for as long as he could.

He adjusted his grip on his weapon, tried to aim around the heavy corpse, and pulled the trigger twice. One of the three men who pushed closer dropped with two bullets through the chest. His teammate behind tried to back away but lurched as one of the slugs exited his comrade and lodged in his stomach.

That was the end of the good news, the operative realized when his gun clicked empty.

The last man standing stared at him and actually seemed amused by the death of the men around them. Savage shoved aside his very dead human shield and scowled at his adversary as he scrambled to his feet.

"Empty?" the assassin asked mockingly, and his smile widened. He raised his weapon toward the ceiling and pulled the trigger a couple of times. The soft click went almost unheard over the way his ears were ringing. "Me too. In all honesty, I didn't anticipate that you would put up this much of a fight. I assumed you were one of those CIA boys trained in Langley to be great at infiltration and deceit but not that great in a gun battle. Oh, well, I stand corrected."

Savage narrowed his eyes. Most of the guns in the room were empty—or he assumed so, anyway, from the man's lack of effort to retrieve any of them. The one in the hands of his now-dead meat shield certainly was. He took a moment to study his opponent, who definitely looked odd. He was tall and lean with an angular, asymmetrical look to his features. His hair was blonde, as was a hint of scruff on his cheek. The British accent was the real puzzler, though.

"Let me guess," he said and held the man's gaze while he inched his hand into his jacket toward the comfortable weight of his knife. "Former SAS turned bodyguard to the incredibly rich?"

"Right on the first half," the man said. "My name is Linus, and for what it's worth, I really do believe in what Carlson is doing. I've seen the world and didn't much care for it. I think what the man is doing will work, mate. You should come aboard. Even if you don't like his style, you have to admit that saving the world and being paid well for it is something to consider, wouldn't you say?"

"Are we really having this conversation right now? With my ears still ringing from all the bullets that we've exchanged?" Savage slid his knife clear from the jacket with his right hand. He sighed. "Fine, if you really want my opinion, I'd say you're as batshit crazy as your boss. Happy?"

"Let me guess, then," Linus said with an easy smile. "Former…Navy SEAL, I think, brought in by an old friend in the military. You don't much care about morality or boast about saving the planet. You talk a big game, but you're not in it for the money, either. What you want out of this is a modicum of self-respect. You don't feel you've earned it, but your friend has. You trust him to know right from wrong and you merely follow the path he's laid out for you. All the while, you blindly hope it's the right one."

"Rangers, actually." He shrugged, his tone almost bored. "The rest of it sounds about right, actually. Now, will you let me and my doctor leave here alive, or do we have to go through you?"

"I'm afraid you'll have to try to go through me, mate." The man's smile didn't falter as he withdrew a Bowie knife from his jacket. "But I have to warn you, I'm as tough as a four-pound steak."

Well, that answered the question about whether that was actually a saying anywhere else but in the States. It wasn't like he would ever ask it or really care about the answer, but it was never too late to learn about foreign cultures.

His adversary attacked. He was impossibly fast and timed his momentum for maximum impact. They collided and Savage barely managed to push the Bowie aside to avoid a blade in his ribcage, aimed for his heart or lung. He shuddered as the cold steel slipped under his suit jacket and sliced easily through his shirt to find the yielding flesh of his arm.

"Fuck!" he roared and twisted his body to withdraw from the cutting edge of the weapon. He thrust his elbow into Linus' jaw to force him a step back and brought his knee into his groin to hopefully end the fight in an abrupt, if dirty, way.

The man backed away another step and blocked the blow with his hands. The operative took advantage of the change in position and stabbed his knife toward his opponent's neck. That blow was blocked too, but he grinned with a hint of satisfaction when the blade grazed his target's cheek and drew blood.

Linus powered his knife in a thrust toward Savage's gut and forced him to retreat and take another step to the side as the assassin pressed his advantage and tried to sweep his legs out from under him. The tactic was only partially successful, as Savage dropped away and stumbled into the bedroom. It was enough to give him space, though, and he rolled over his shoulder to push onto his feet again.

He grunted and the pain of the pressure on his battered ribcage made him roar in agony as he hauled himself upright. His lungs sucked air, and with each breath, they pushed against the aching bones. He needed to be careful. The pain distracted him, as did the impulse to keep his breathing light. His body needed the oxygen now more than ever. Blood seeped from the incision in his arm and the bullet wound in his shoulder. There were other cuts and scratches here and there, as well as a couple of bruises, but those would be the least of his concerns if he couldn't stop the bleeding.

"I'm really glad you're putting up a fight," Linus taunted and chuckled with perverse mirth as he rolled his neck and followed him into the bedroom. "You have been a pain in my boss' side for far too long, between you and me. I had hoped that you would live up to that kind of reputation and not merely be some lucky bloke with a gun. That would have been terrifying, really. It would undermine my abilities as a security specialist."

"And you know something? I hate to disappoint." Jeremiah steeled himself and dragged in a deep breath. He winced when his lungs pushed at his ribs. "I truly hate it. Honestly, I wouldn't be able to sleep. Do you want to rob me of sleep now, Linus? Because that would be mean."

"You're stalling," the man said equably. "That's good. You know that you're beat, and you know that you have to think of a good, unconventional way to get around the fact that you're about to die. Defiant until the end. I can respect that."

"I really couldn't give a shit about your respect," he said. Frankly, he didn't, but the man was right. He was stalling. Also, he wasn't sure if Coleman was still in the room. If she was, he hoped she would take the hint and make a run for it. Anja had to be working on a way for her to get out alive with all the documents. If she hadn't gone already, of course. Coleman was a smart woman—a doctor, no less.

In that moment, the smart move would be to get away from the man if he could or at least get him out of the room. The idea spurred him into action. He raised his hands and launched forward. His adversary smoothly dodged his attempt at a thrust and as he crashed into him, tilted his body away and grasped Savage's collar to drag him over his hip in an expertly executed judo flip.

The operative landed hard and the air pushed out of his lungs in an agonizing rush.

"Okay," he gasped. "Maybe offense wasn't the best defense in that particular scenario. Fuck..." He groaned and probed cautiously at his side.

"I'm afraid you're right." The Englishman seemed genuinely sad that the fight was coming to an end. Savage felt a little down about it himself. He gripped the knife he'd somehow managed to keep in his hand and tried to stand. His effort ceased when Linus put a boot on his chest and forced him down once again.

"If it's any consolation, it will be quick and relatively painless." He planted his knee firmly on Savage's chest as he lowered to press the sharp edge of Bowie knife into his neck.

"Not really." He fought instinctively against the attempt on his life. He'd tried to kill his opponent, of course, but he really didn't want to think about that. The sting of the blade grew sharper.

He fought the urge to close his eyes and fixed his gaze on his killer. Linus blinked and Savage frowned as he tried to make sense of it—as well as the fact that he was now covered in pottery. But as the man's weight lessened and he almost fell forward, Savage knew this was his chance. It was now or never. He grasped Linus' hips as the man toppled and heaved him off before he scrambled to straddle him. With his own knife in hand, he leaned over his back and slid the blade under the assassin's neck. He gritted his teeth and sliced in a single swift motion. A splash of warm liquid seeped over his hand before the red stream soaked into the carpet.

The silence that ensued was deafening. There had been no gunfire for a while now, of course. He no longer fought for his life and all he could hear was his breathing—as painful and ragged as it was—and his heart hammering in his chest like a runaway jackrabbit. Despite the agony, every breath felt so much sweeter.

He turned slowly. Coleman stood as if rooted to the spot and stared at them with a panicked look on her face.

"I...I thought you'd taken off already," he said and struggled for another breath. "That would have been the smart thing to do, between you and me."

"If I had, you would be dead right now, and I would have had a hard time getting my ass out of this hotel alive," Jessica retorted waspishly. "So...you're welcome."

"I only meant that it wasn't the smartest move," Savage replied and chuckled as she offered him her hand to help him to his feet. "Thank you, though. I appreciate you staying behind to help me."

"Come on." A blush appeared on her cheek as she wiped the blood that had transferred from his hand to hers on her dress. "You took care of six guys and only needed my help with the last one."

"That last one was tough. Those SAS bastards grow a tough breed of operatives. And you wouldn't think it with those posh accents they make them speak with, but there you go."

"If the two of you have finished scratching one another's backs..." Anja said in Savage's ear for the first time since the fighting had started. "Are you both all right? There aren't any cameras in there so I can't really tell."

"I'm a little banged up, but I think I'll survive." He

nodded, more for himself than for her given that she couldn't see him.

"I'm fine too," Jessica said.

"Good. Because all that gunfire is bringing every single cop in the city down on your heads. They should be there in the next five minutes, but I've managed to clear the service elevator with some creative use of the fire alarms. That should provide enough confusion that you can use it to escape. But the clock is ticking, so you need to leave now."

"Thanks for the help, Anja," Savage said.

"Anytime, Jer." Her voice was soft and might have held a slight tremor, but he couldn't be sure. "But get out of there alive. Oh, and the new motel is burned too, so I think that our comms are compromised. You might want to get rid of that earbud and I'll get you a new one later. I've texted you the address and room number of a motel I just paid reservations for."

CHAPTER TWENTY-EIGHT

They made their escape down the service elevator with no difficulty at all once Jeremiah had recovered his pistol and checked that they'd left no other evidence of their presence there. The hacker had triggered the sprinklers as soon as they left, which would hopefully degrade any DNA they might have left.

Thanks to Anja's use of the fire alarms, they moved unhindered through the employees-only section of the hotel on their way to the parking garage. His wounds hurt far more than he was willing to admit, and he had to rely on Jessica to help him more than he would have liked, both in the hotel and until they finally reached the garage. It took longer than it should have to reach where they'd parked the car.

"Here." He shoved the keys in her hands. "You need to drive. I don't think I'm in any condition to manage."

She nodded, took the keys, and help him to the passenger side of the car before she hurried around to slide behind the wheel. Once they were both buckled in, she started the car quickly and eased out of the parking spot to drive carefully through the maze of cars. The exit opened without any need to press a card to the RFID reader on the side.

Once they were out of the garage, he removed his earpiece. "Anja wants to talk to you really quickly. When you're finished, throw the earbud away."

He sounded like he was out of breath—much the way he'd sounded since they'd left the penthouse. Her couple of classes in medicine told her that he had trouble breathing not so much due to a problem with his lungs, but rather as a result of the blood he'd lost.

She took the earpiece but didn't insert it in her ear immediately as she heard sirens approaching rapidly. White, blue, and red flashing lights flooded the area. Savage made an effort to straighten in his seat and, despite how much blood he'd lost, he took the time to close his jacket over his torso to cover the blood as a police car rushed past them, the sirens shrill and clamorous.

Jessica put the bud in her ear as soon as they were clear of the chaos. "Anja, it's nice to be able to talk to you."

"And it's nice to hear that you two are alive too, Jess," the Russian replied cheerfully. "Look, I'm so sorry. I should have known better. I didn't pay attention and those goons arrived without any kind of warning. I should have been that warning."

"Don't beat yourself up, Anja." She laughed and a part of her wondered how she managed it. "You did the best you could. We wouldn't have gotten in there at all without you. And we got out of there—with the files and the photos, no less—which I'll call a qualified win, thank you very much."

"Have we forgotten the part where I was stabbed?" Jeremiah asked. He flashed her a quick glance and only partially looked like he was joking. "And shot? And judo-flipped onto my aching ribs? We've conveniently forgotten that part of the night, have we? Okay, my bad. Never mind."

"Oh, shush, you big baby." The hacker sounded as if she was holding back a laugh. "Don't tell him I said that."

"Anja is very concerned for your welfare," Jessica said and grinned disarmingly. "Do you think we should drop you off at the hospital?"

"And have the police come and ask why I'm the man who shows up with gunshot wounds, mild tinnitus, and a stab wound right after there's been a huge shootout in one of the most prestigious hotels in the city?" He raised an eyebrow. "I think I'll pass on that, thanks. I left a lot of DNA evidence behind in that room—which Anja's little sprinkler trick has hopefully compromised—but I could be one subpoena away from being locked up. And you too."

"Well, for what it's worth, I do think he needs medical attention," Anja said. "And not from a hospital. You took medical classes in your time in college, didn't you, Jessica? Maybe you could patch him up? Besides, I can probably work a little magic and make sure that if there is DNA evidence left behind that's actually usable, it's improperly stored or something."

"My studies were years and years ago," Jessica said. "Of course, I'll do it if no one else is available, but I can't promise I'll be any good at it."

"Is she asking you to patch me up?" Jeremiah looked horrified. There was a definite trace of doubt in his features, and she didn't blame him for that. She doubted herself too. After a moment, a look of acceptance preceded a shrug that seemed to say he might as well let her do her best. It was probably better than what his best would be anyway.

She took a deep breath and made sure to keep her eyes on the road. "I'll need medical equipment. Something out of a pharmacy—something clean to help stop the bleeding and to sew it up. I won't take any bullets out of you, though."

"We never took bullets out of a gunshot victim in the field," he said and frowned as if he tried to recall the facts. "Not unless the bullet threatened the patient's life. Otherwise, they simply patched them up with the bullet inside and let their body handle it until we could get them to a surgeon. You don't have to worry about that, though. It was a through and through. A graze, really."

"You sound like the kind of man who's walked outside of metal detectors for years now," Jessica said in an effort to keep his spirits up. It was a good thing that he was able to make jokes. It meant that shock hadn't settled in yet and she still had time to patch him up.

"Not really." He leaned back in his seat, but his eyes remained open and focused on the road. "Bullets aren't generally magnetic. They do come up in the full body scan, though. I have a paper from my doctor about that, actually... Uh, I had a paper from my doctor."

Jessica glanced at him. "Are you serious?"

"No," Jeremiah replied and shook his head.

She breathed deeply and stared at the road ahead as she steeled herself for what would come next. "Anja, I need a location for the nearest drugstore or pharmacy. Maybe something that's closed so I don't have people around to raise their eyebrows when I ask for prescription drugs."

"Two blocks south of your location." The hacker appeared to be one step ahead of her already. Jessica followed the woman's instructions and slowed when she saw the sign to a local store that had been closed for an hour. Then again, not many stores would be open at…fuck, was it only nine? How was it that early? It felt like she'd spent hours curled under that bed, half-expecting that one of the bullets would find her and hoping fervently it wouldn't.

She parked directly outside the store, turned the engine off, and left the keys in the ignition. Anja had told her to throw the earpiece out, which she would do as soon as it was practical to do so, but it also made sense to get rid of the car that might have been seen escaping from the hotel while first responders arrived on scene. The Russian had said that she would erase all trace of them having been there, but that only included digital records. She didn't doubt her skills, of course, but even the hacker couldn't help it if someone's phone was picked up, or a witness memorized the plates of a car that sped away from a shootout barely minutes after it happened.

"Why is this place closed this early?" Jessica asked.

"It's a family-owned establishment," Anja replied. "I saw a heads-up on it. It says on their social media account that the matriarch is in labor, and as the whole family has to be there for it, they closed and sent the employees home early."

"That's fortuitous."

"Considering that the only other option we would have on this side of town is an animal hospital closed for repairs, yes, it's very lucky. And it's about time some luck went our way, if you ask me."

She walked around and reached the passenger side, and Jeremiah smiled in a coy way that told her that he had figured out what she planned and seemed to approve.

"So, we'll leave the car behind now, will we?" he asked as she helped him out. She stayed close, but it seemed that he was able to move without too much trouble. He was slow, of course, but there weren't any cars nearby—or people, for that matter—which made the next part a whole lot easier.

"Well, yeah." She flashed him a look that was part irritation. "And don't ask me why since you already know why."

Savage responded with that little know-it-all smirk of his that could be so infuriating and tapped at his ear. It took her a second, but she finally nodded when she realized what he'd tried to say. She removed the earpiece, dropped it on the sidewalk, and crushed it under her heel.

"I doubt that Anja would appreciate you doubting her skills like that, but it is the smart move," he said and grinned as they reached the front door of the pharmacy.

"How will we get in?" Jessica looked around and wished she'd at least thought to ask the hacker before she destroyed their only point of communication.

Her companion smiled again. His cheerfulness made her wonder if he really had lost as much blood as she'd thought. Still, from the way his pale face reflected in the streetlight, she hadn't been wrong. He looked up at one of the cameras, not at her, and a second later, the electronic door slid open.

"Like I said." He preened, his expression smug. "Never doubt Anja's abilities. You may not always like her attitude, but you can trust her to come through every time."

"I actually quite like her attitude." She stepped hastily through the doors. A few lights were on, which allowed them to browse the pharmacy to their heart's content. Jessica assumed that the woman more than likely erased all digital files of them having been there at every step they took, which meant that while it was probably a good idea to hurry, they didn't necessarily have to rush and miss anything critical.

"Here." She placed a couple of packages of gauze in front of Jeremiah on a nearby counter. "I'll need to stitch that wound to stop the bleeding. The one on your arm, I mean. You'll have to find a way to slow it down."

He displayed none of his usual resistance to her ideas and merely raised his sleeve a little to reveal the wound from Linus' knife. It wasn't that deep, but it was into the tissue. Jessica made a face as she inspected it before she pressed an absorbent cloth to the wound.

"Hold that in place," she said softly and waited for him to press onto the wound himself. "Is it like this every day? Your life, I mean? All gunfights and violence and running around trying not to get killed?"

"Are you asking about my life in general or my time as a corporate spy?" he asked and shifted his pressure on the cloth as she began to wind gauze around his arm. "Although the answer to both would be yes. I took time off when my first three tours of service were over. I had some friction with my ex-wife, and I wanted to spend some time with my kid. She was growing up without me. As it turned out, the friction wasn't about my absence so much as about me.

"When things turned sour, I elected to do another couple of tours to get out of there. The US government put a lot of money into training me to be a killing machine, and they would have been very disappointed to discover that I'd been slacking in my responsibilities. So…aside from that little break, yeah, my life has been a mixture of gunfights and violence and recovering from the aforementioned gunfights and violence, only to be dropped into another round. It's not a great life, but it is one that I'm suited to."

"I don't think anyone can be suited to something like this," Jessica said softly and turned her scrutiny to where the bullet had injured his shoulder. "You don't get used to the violence, you merely become conditioned to it. While it's not something you enjoy, it's something you can tolerate."

"So long as other people don't have to tolerate it, that's fine by me," Jeremiah replied, his voice uncharacteristically soft.

Jessica looked at him and wondered if he meant that. Now wasn't the time to really ponder it, though. She told him to sit on a small bench placed conveniently to one side and entered the pharmaceutical area to rummage around for a few minutes. When she returned, he lay sleeping on the bench. Startled and half-afraid that he'd somehow died in the short time while she'd searched for the things she'd need to patch him up, she shook his shoulder.

He awoke with a start and gazed owlishly at her. "I have everything I need," she said and stepped back quickly to give him space to stand. "We should probably sew you up at the motel."

He nodded. "Probably."

CHAPTER TWENTY-NINE

Anja made sure that they were already checked into the motel when they arrived. Someone waited with keys for them at the front desk. Despite the nicer look of the place, the tall, blond man didn't ask for an ID or even raise an eyebrow at the blood-soaked suit Savage wore as he handed the keys over. A glint of recognition in his eyes suggested amusement, but they moved away from the front desk and toward the elevator without unnecessary questions.

Once they were in the elevator and alone, he looked at Jessica, who stared at him with an odd expression.

"Is this...one of those places?" she asked and tilted her head as she scrunched her face into an expression that might have suggested distaste along with real curiosity.

"One of what places?" he asked and kept his face as deadpan as possible.

"Well, one of those no-tell motels." She looked around once more and held tightly onto Savage's burlap bag that they had filled with all the medical materials she needed to treat him.

"Well, you would know, right?" He couldn't resist a grin —he had waited for the perfect opportunity to bring the topic up. "You were the one who had been in that motel before we stayed there. Your phone connected automatically to the wi-fi, remember."

"Come on. You won't make me tell that story, will you?" she demanded as the elevator dinged. The doors opened and they stepped onto the fifth floor of the building and proceeded through the carpeted hallways toward their room.

"I don't want to pry into your life, Dr. Coleman." He walked slowly and accepted help from her, his hand on her shoulder so he could lean a little when he needed to. "You work hard at a job you love—I assume, anyway—but everyone needs relaxation. I've done the same myself over the years, and while it would be hypocritical of me to judge you for it, you can't expect me not to tease, right?"

Jessica chuckled. "Remember the fact that I'm the one who'll clean you up and ensure that you don't die of sepsis before morning. So be respectful—at least until I'm finished."

"I'll keep that in mind." Jeremiah chuckled and pressed the keycard to the lock on the door. It clicked open immediately. For a motel, this place was surprisingly high-tech—which was why Anja had been able to make reservations for them, he supposed.

"Back to your original question, though," he said as he pushed the door wide and turned the light on. "I think this is one of those no-tell motels. I don't know…call it a hunch."

It was a good hunch. As they stepped into the room and the lights came on, his first clue was that most of the lights were shaded in red. They illuminated the room with romantic lighting that he knew would definitely not be the best thing for Jessica to work with while she treated him. Most of the room contained a plethora of heart shapes fashioned into the furniture, including a chair. The bed itself wasn't shaped like a heart, though, thank goodness. The problem, of course, was the fact that there was only one.

"Trust your instincts, Savage," Jessica said with a chuckle. "Do you think Anja's trying to tell us something? She's not the best at making personal suggestions, so do you think that she's perhaps sent us a message?"

"What kind of message?" He cleared his throat and avoided her gaze as he walked to the chair, sank onto it, and sighed gently.

She opened her mouth to respond but seemed to have trouble articulating the words. Thankfully, the red lighting in the room was enough to hide the blush that touched her cheeks. "Nothing. Never mind. Let's get that shirt off you."

"I wonder how many times that particular line has been used in this room," he commented as she moved to the bed, dropped the bag onto the silky red satin sheets, and pulled the zipper open. Jeremiah did as he was told, lifted his shirt clear of his torso, and after a moment's thought, tossed it aside. If the truth be told, he would probably have to burn the damn thing anyway. He wouldn't worry too much about keeping the room clean, all things considered.

Jessica turned one of the bedside lamps on—thankfully, it wasn't shaded in red—and pointed it directly at the canvas of bruises, blood, and scar tissue that comprised his chest. Some looked more recent than others, which made her wonder how many times he'd been in similar situations before. She checked the bandages to make that they were all still in place and none had soaked through before she moved to the minibar. Predictably, it contained only tiny little bottles. They were whiskey, though, and branded too, which told her that they would have a better experience than they'd had with the tiny bottles of vodka at the previous motel.

It was, for some vague reason, a little reassuring that they were in an establishment that at least held to a higher standard than the one they'd vacated earlier that day.

She didn't bother to pour the amber liquid into the glasses that the room provided. Instead, she simply handed Savage one of the bottles.

"I thought we picked something up from the pharmacy to clean the wounds." He looked the whiskey with a somewhat bewildered expression.

"We did." She chuckled and took a moment to crack another bottle open and raise it to him in a toast. "Cheers."

Jeremiah nodded. He acknowledged that they both needed to have calmer nerves for what lay ahead, so he readily followed her example. They clinked their bottles together and downed them quickly. The comfortable burn slid down his throat, but Jessica looked like she needed a moment as she exhaled a rough breath. She seemed flushed and her cheeks a little heated.

"Are you ready?" he asked and tilted his head at her he leaned back in his seat.

"As ready as I'll ever be." She nodded firmly and focused her attention on unpacking the materials from the bag. A pair of gloves emerged first, which she pulled on with the practiced efficiency that he recalled in himself when he was in the middle of a firefight. This was her job. Well, not technically, but something like it. She shifted closer, and Jeremiah helped by dragging his seat closer to the bed. He simply waited while she made a closer examination of his wounds while she removed his bandages.

"You'll probably want to take a shower after this," Jessica said with a nervous chuckle as she dabbed a soft cloth with antiseptic liquid. She turned back to him and realized that her hands were shaking. And, for some totally ridiculous reason, she couldn't stop them. She dragged in a deep breath, looked down at them, and pressed them together. The trembling stopped, but she knew that it would simply start again when she pulled them apart.

She closed her eyes and tried to focus on something more appealing than the harrowing experience she had recently endured. When he moved, she opened her eyes and his hands wrapped around hers to squeeze them gently. She wasn't sure if the unexpected tenderness came from the blood loss—which wasn't helped by the alcohol, of course. Whatever had caused it, though, her hands no longer shook, and her mind had lost focus on the memory of the gunfire from which her ears were still ringing. Something entirely different had crept in to replace these things.

And it wasn't the time for that, as tempting as it might

be. She doubted that it would ever be. Her mind simply wandered, and now that she no longer thought about what might have happened in the other hotel and how close she came to losing her life there, she needed to stop thinking about what might happen in this one.

Down girl, she told herself firmly and met his gaze with a smile.

"Are you good, Doc?" he asked and quirked an eyebrow at her.

She nodded. "Thanks, I am. Let's get this over with."

Jessica refocused and tried to ignore the calming warmth that radiated from his bare chest as she removed the last bandage from his upper arm. It was the deepest of his handful of wounds, and the man's knife had bit deeper than she was comfortable with. She didn't like how calm her patient was through this, either, or the way he toyed casually with the empty bottle in his fingers.

"How many times have you been through something like this?" she asked. Conversation might help her to keep her mind off the fact that his wound had opened again—not to mention the other things that still lingered behind the practical demands. "I can tell from the rest of your chest that this isn't the first time you've dealt with wounds of this nature, but how many times have you been treated out of hospital like this?"

Savage tilted his head from side to side as he considered his answer to the question. "This is not the first time, definitely. A couple of times, I've found myself in a situation where first aid was needed without access to a hospital. Black ops fireteams don't usually run with a medic on hand. Most of the guys know first aid, though, but not much else. You can tell from the weird shape of the stitching." He pointed out a couple of scars, one on his chest and one on his right arm. The former was round, with only a couple of stitches, while the latter looked long and jagged.

"That's a bullet wound. It was a through and through, so there's another matching scar on the back." He indicated the round one. "It wasn't really life-threatening, but we were stuck in a forest and needed to keep it from getting septic. This was shrapnel from an exploding car bomb. That was more life-threatening. My boys did a good job, but it looked as ugly as hell all the way through."

"What about this one?" Jessica asked and gestured to a two-inch scar over his stomach. Without thought, she let her fingers glide lightly over the unsurprisingly firm muscles there. The stitches were off balance and all four of them improperly placed.

"That one I did myself." He grinned sheepishly. "I managed to be gut-stabbed by a drunk guy in a bar on my first leave back in the US. We got into an argument about…uh, something, after my fifth round of tequila. Although I was all tough, military man and all and didn't back down, I didn't see the knife until it was already in me. Still, I beat the living shit out of the guy anyway."

"If you were in the States, how come you didn't go to a hospital?" she asked.

"Well, I was drunk, and therefore not in any condition to make the best decisions of my life. Besides, when you show up in a hospital with a stab wound, the doctors will ask questions, they'll involve the police, and that felt like a chickenshit thing to do. Even if the guy pulled a knife on me in an honest bar brawl, I still didn't want to get him in trouble."

"Or get yourself in trouble, considering that you had beaten a man unconscious," Jessica retorted as she cleaned the fresh and old blood from around the new wound.

"Again, drunk, not making the smartest decisions—fuck!" he snapped when she got a little too enthusiastic with her efforts.

"Pipe down, you big baby." She smiled to soften the admonishment. The wound was now clean enough and the blood flow had stopped, so she drew a small contraption from inside the bag. It looked like a stapler, but it was plastic and disposable.

"This will probably hurt," she said softly, focused her attention on the wound, and held it closed with one hand as the other pressed the surgical stapler to the injury. She hadn't expected to find one in a family-owned pharmacy but had pounced on it the moment she'd seen it. The store apparently supplied smaller clinics with certain lines of medical equipment—a second income-stream which had been a real bonus for what she had to accomplish.

Jeremiah made surprisingly little noise as she applied ten staples to the wound that traced over his bicep. It seemed that he didn't really mind the pain she had warned him to expect. He grunted a couple of times, but other than that, remained perfectly and utterly still as she sealed the wound.

"You weren't kidding about that being painful," he said finally once she was finished. "I assume you want to use that thing on this graze on my shoulder too. If you do, I think I'll need more alcohol in my system."

"Actually, you don't." Jessica squinted and shifted closer to inspect the wound on his shoulder. "Alcohol—it's numbing effects aside—acts as a blood thinner that will keep you bleeding."

"Right." He sighed morosely and raised his arm a little so she could wind the bandage off his shoulder. "I think I wouldn't mind risking it unless you have something in the way of painkillers that might help me sleep another way."

"As a matter of fact, I did find something for the pain and to help you sleep." She dabbed a new piece of cloth into the antiseptic agent and attended to his wound with quick, deft strokes. "This one isn't half as deep as the other one, though. It's shallow and more of a graze. You don't need any stitches here."

"Many thanks to the big, bearded dude in the sky for that." He definitely looked relieved as she reapplied the bandage to his shoulder.

"Keep it clean and you should be fine."

"Excellent." He paused, his expression hesitant, before he said, "I don't suppose you could help me wrap my ribs a little? I think I might have bruised a couple."

"You think?" She flashed him a wry smile. "I hid under the bed and I could hear your moans when that man judo-flipped you. I didn't need a class in med school to tell me that had to hurt. So, I brought something else." She retrieved a roll of tape from the bag. "Anesthetic tape to bind your chest. It'll help to hold your ribs in place and let them heal and provide some tingly numbness at the same time. I read up on it when…someone I knew had a broken rib and wouldn't stop complaining about it. Come on, get up and put your hands up. I need to wind it around you."

Jeremiah did as he was told as she moved in closer—close enough, now, that she could feel his warm skin under her fingers. There were dozens of scars around the tattoos, she realized as he stood taller than her by about a foot. But they didn't detract from what she saw. He looked more like a canvas. All the bruising and the wounds, new and old, were merely experiences. They might be horrifying and painful, but they were living memories of what he'd gone through.

She stopped when she realized that she had completed the binding on his injured ribs. Her hands seemed to work automatically to sever the tape and toss the roll aside, but she couldn't pull away from his presence. Something about him drew her in, the compulsion strong and tempting. She ran her fingers over the tiny scar on his stomach, the one with the drunken stitching that he'd told her about. His reaction as he sucked a breath in told her that he was ticklish. She tried to pull her hand away, but his hand wound around hers to hold her fingers in place.

It was…something. In all honesty, she wasn't sure what it was, but to say that the shared touch didn't have its own unique brand of electricity would have been a lie. Her instincts nudged her irresistibly to lean closer.

"That someone you knew," he said, his voice almost a whisper. "Is he your boyfriend?"

"Ex, actually," Jessica murmured, almost entranced by the man in front of her. It was difficult to tear her eyes away and his body seemed to be drawn in by the pull of her gaze. "He was a nice enough guy, but he had a bit of temper. Not against me, but against men he thought were hitting on me. It reached the point where I couldn't have any male friends without him getting all worked up. He punched a friend when I hugged him, and the friend punched back, hence the whole research on that…tape…"

Her voice trailed off. His right hand remained on hers and dragged it up to pin it against his chest. He held her gaze as his left hand moved down over her hair, brushed it gently to the side, and tucked a few errant strands behind her ear. The touch sent tingles down her spine. Those immediately turned to shivers that compelled her to seek the sensation again. Her fingers splayed over his bare chest and felt the soft thud of his heartbeat. A reciprocal hammering resonated in her chest and increased its pace in anticipation when he removed her glasses gently and pressed his mouth against hers. His lips tasted fresh and warm at the same time. She leaned into the kiss and breathed in the magic of it.

Suddenly, he pulled away and dragged that delicious taste and feeling with him. He took a step back and set her glasses on the bedside table with a slow, careful movement.

"Look, this might be all a little new to you." Despite the disappointment, he sounded the perfect kind of breathless. "It's a common feeling to experience right after being in the middle of a gunfight, which makes it more—"

"Shut up." She placed a finger on his lips. He was hot and she wanted him, but damn, he had to lose the habit of talking at the wrong time. "Just shut up."

She threaded her fingers through his hair and yanked him down to her again. He was willing, at least, and leaned into her kiss. She felt hungry—almost literally enough to bite at him—but she would have to settle for a taste. With a soft moan against his lips, she took the initiative and pressed her body into his as she walked him back a couple of steps. He sat in the chair he'd used while she'd treated him, but she didn't want to think about that.

Although she did have to keep it in mind. He was battered and bruised, and she couldn't be too rough.

Her dress glided smoothly up her thighs as she hiked it up so she could straddle his hips. The motion eased him gently back into his seat as she pressed herself into him. They met in a delicious contrast of his hardness and the softness of her body so delicately accentuated by the thin dress that she wore.

She sighed softly, breathed him in, and ran her fingers through the thick, short curls of his hair. They seemed to trace their own path down to the firm, warm arch of his neck, over the muscular shoulders, his chest, and finally, his arms. In that moment, she needed to touch and feel and wanted the same in response. His calloused fingers tugged her dress higher and she shivered with a delighted moan as his hands caressed her bare skin.

"Fuck," he hissed against her lips.

"You know…" She straightened and look down at him as a smile played over her full lips. "That's exactly what I had in mind." Calm and deliberate, she accentuated her words by moving her hands to the belt that held his pants in place.

CHAPTER THIRTY

The first thing Jessica heard was the sound of the shower running. It wasn't an unpleasant sound, more like white noise on a television.

The bed was more comfortable than she would have thought, which further reinforced the idea that this place was somewhat higher-end than she would normally have been able to afford. Apparently, their benevolent overlords had a healthy budget that they didn't mind Anja splurging with when necessary. They needed a place to lie low, all things considered, and the hacker had selected a romantic motel near the outskirts of the city for them to do so. It wasn't like the police would look in a love nest for people involved in a shootout in another hotel.

Then again, maybe the woman was trying to tell them something. She recalled making a snide comment that the hacker had tried to send them a message by making sure that they were in a romantic room with only one bed. Knowing Savage, of course, he would have elected to sleep in the chair. Or on the floor. Army guys always tried to show that they were tough and gentlemanly like that, even if they had just been through the human equivalent of a meat grinder.

Except…he hadn't.

It took her a few seconds to realize that—or remember, rather. The heat, the connection, the way she'd pulled him in to kiss her after he'd tried to stop…it all flooded back. She'd wanted more. No, she'd needed more.

Her eyes opened and she looked around at the room. The red lighting had faded, thankfully, and light seeped in through the shades, which told her that it was already morning. It was odd how this was the second morning in a row that she woke in a room she had never been in before, but this time, she felt relaxed. Not quite safe, perhaps, but something like that.

She pushed up on her hands. The covers dropped and she realized that she was still naked. Quickly, she hauled them up with a flare of panic. She wasn't sure why she was so modest when she had felt more than a little aggressive the night before. That simple truth was confirmed by the way she'd dragged her own dress off and fought her frustration as he'd struggled with her bra.

Why did she feel like this, now? More importantly, why hadn't she felt that way the night before?

The shower stopped running and she wiggled to the side of the bed. Things were still blurry, but she remembered where he'd put her glasses and she put them on before she focused on the room. She recalled it being messier before, littered with dirty bandages they hadn't bothered to throw away, the burlap bag hurled off the bed as they took its place so that it strewed its contents, both medical and...well, decidedly not medical.

Yet everything was already clean. The bandages were gone, and the bags were neatly arranged in the corner. She doubted that anyone from housekeeping had been allowed inside, which meant that Savage had cleaned up himself.

It was odd. While military guys were supposed to be fanatical about cleaning, she hadn't really pictured him as the obsessively clean kind. More importantly, she didn't think of him as the kind who would keep it quiet so that she could sleep through it.

The bathroom door opened to spill a small cloud of steam and Jeremiah. He wore only a motel towel tastefully colored a rich wine-red. The bandages that covered his shoulder and side were obviously new, which confirmed to her that he'd at least had the sense to remove the old ones before the shower. He'd also applied the new ones more neatly than she would have given him credit for.

"Morning." He sounded way cooler and more collected than she felt at that moment. "I'm sorry if I woke you, but you said last night that I should probably shower, and... well, after we were distracted, I was too tired to follow your advice."

She didn't say anything but watched him closely as he moved deeper into the room. He'd hung her dress over the chair he'd sat on the night before and she wondered if he wanted her to get out of bed and give him one more show before she put it back on. She was tempted to oblige. A rush of conflicting feelings derailed her attempt to think clearly. Her body surged, too, but those sensations were less conflicting.

It soon became apparent, though, that a free show was the last thing on his mind. He scooped the dress up and tossed it to her with barely a glance at either her or the garment.

"I'm waiting for Anja to contact us. She'll want to know what's in the files we stole from Carlson's room, and I think that the sooner we get them to her, the better. But it would also be stupid to parade ourselves around town. Carlson will have to be more careful now that the police are looking for whoever destroyed his room—which, aside from his mercenaries who are all good and dead, means the two of us. I don't doubt that he still has connections who will be willing to gun us down in the street if they see us. That tells me that we should probably stay inside."

Jessica continued to watch him as she fumbled numbly for the dress he'd delivered to her in such a nonchalant manner.

"Oh," he said, still rambling as he crossed to the burlap bag, rummaged for another gray Polo shirt, and hung it on the counter beside the door. "If you want a shower, you might want to go in now. It took me five minutes to get hot water since the motel runs on one of those ancient boiler systems."

She could still think of absolutely nothing to say and instead, tried to make out what was going on in his mind. He seemed calm and much the same as he'd been the day before when she first met him. Which was odd. So much had happened in so little time that she struggled to grasp why he would act like nothing had happened.

"What?" He tilted his head and frowned, which made her realize that she was still staring.

"I'm just… I don't… What happened last night?" Jessica asked, dragged the dress over her head, and managed to put it on despite her awkward position on the bed. Once she was dressed, she pushed the covers aside and swung her legs off the edge.

"I take it you don't mean us breaking and entering Carlson's hotel room, trashing the place, and stealing a bunch of his documents, right?"

"You would be correct." She stood in front of him with her arms folded. He looked uncomfortable and seemed to try to avoid her looking at him by shifting back a few steps.

Finally, once he realized that he wouldn't escape without a conversation, he sighed. "Look, I've seen it a hundred times. People come out of a life-threatening experience in need of comfort. I'm not sure if there's an actual scientific name for it, but it's real."

"That's really not the point here, Savage," she grumbled. "Last night wasn't something that happens to me often, and I think we need to talk about it."

"Look, I can't do that, Coleman." Jeremiah stepped forward and put his hands on her shoulders. "As of right now, we're—well, I'm in the middle of a very dangerous fight. I need to be able to put myself in dangerous situations and make the right call fifteen times in a matter of seconds. No offense to you, but…doing something like talking about this is…distracting."

"What, so I'm only a distraction?" she asked, decidedly miffed.

"Well, you're distracting," he corrected and sounded a little less confident than he had a few seconds before. "Last night was fun—for both of us, right?"

"Well, that's a smidgeon of insecurity I didn't expect from you." Jessica laughed. "But yes. Very much so."

"Come on, give me a break." He smirked. "It's been a while. Anyway, in this kind of situation, I don't think that I can take the pressure of making all those decisions in the middle of a combat situation if my priorities are wrong. If we talk about it, that officially shifts my priorities one way or another, and that affects how the mission goes. Once we're done with all this, we can talk, but… I can't do that now. Not yet."

Jessica looked down. It wasn't what she wanted to hear, of course, but she could understand where he was coming from. She hadn't really met anyone like him before, but she assumed he was the type who would put his mission above all else—much like she had put her career before everything else in her own life—but it wasn't the response she had hoped for. His reaction didn't surprise her, quite honestly, but she couldn't help a tiny twinge of annoyance that wanted to smack him on the side of the head to force a straight answer from him.

Either way, he'd made his choice. He had put the mission first and would let the chips fall as they might. It was time for her to get with the program.

"Okay, fine." She breathed deeply and looked at him, careful to force the pained expression from her face. It very obviously made him uncomfortable, which wouldn't help either of them. "We can put this conversation off until we don't have anyone trying to kill us out there or until that's no longer such an emergency. But you should be warned that means it won't be a conversation that's touched with the post-coital bliss that I feel right now."

"I think that might actually be for that best," he responded with another irritating smirk. "Decisions should be made with a cool head and unimpeded by emotions and...uh, bliss, as you call it."

She smiled and stroked her hand over his, which was still on her shoulder. "Not all decisions," she murmured before she moved away. He nodded. She could tell that he tried to convince himself that he had made the right decision. *Let him mull over that for a while,* she thought with a secretive smile.

"I think I'll take that shower now." She turned toward the bathroom and hesitated when the room's phone rang shrilly.

"I'll get it, don't worry," Savage said, and she waved airily and closed the door behind her.

Jeremiah snatched the phone up. Tingles still climbed his arm from where her fingers had traced lightly over his hand.

"Hello, Mr. Smith, room five-oh-seven?" The man's voice sounded way too peppy than would be considered normal so early in the morning.

"Speaking." He tucked the phone between his shoulder and his ear as he shambled toward the bed.

"This is Michael from the front desk. You have a package waiting for you here, delivered by a Miss Artemis."

"Artemis? Really?"

"I'm only passing the message along, sir," the man replied and sounded like he was smiling politely. That was the only time that he'd ever heard someone using that voice—thick and cloying like molasses, and usually as messy.

Jeremiah shook his head. "I'll be right down to take it off your hands. I need to get some clothes on."

"I await in anticipation, sir."

He didn't bother to reply to that as the line was still open but did have a few choice words for the man when the call disconnected. His irritation was perhaps excessive, but he didn't feel quite in his right mind. She called it bliss and he called it confusing, but the fact remained that he needed to get his head back in the game. He donned a fresh set of clothes and stuck with the Polo shirt, jeans, boots and breezy attitude that would allow him to look normal to anyone who might notice him.

Hopefully, his ordinary appearance would safely obscure the fact that he had a combat knife in his pocket and a gun tucked in his belt. He really should have purchased an underarm holster from Max, he acknowledged as he stepped out of the room, locked the door, and made sure that the gun couldn't be seen before he made his way to the elevators.

"Mr. Smith—so kind of you to come down at this early hour," the clerk said. He was young with the slick look of a manager-in-the-making, and he withdrew a small manila package which he handed over without a word.

"Do I need to sign for it or anything?" Jeremiah asked as he took it from the man's hand. He had an idea what it contained, but after what had happened the day before, he didn't want to take any chances.

"No need for that, sir." The polite smile was enough to

make the operative grind his teeth. "The fact that it has been delivered into your hand is enough knowledge for me."

"Well, thanks for your help, Michael from the front desk." He pulled a twenty from his pocket and set it on the counter. The man stretched out a hand and the bill disappeared. Maybe he was a magician in the making but the possibility wasn't of sufficient interest to ask. He turned away and headed to the elevators.

By the time Jessica had completed her shower, he stood outside the bathroom door with a small earbud in his hand and proffered it to her.

"What's this?" she asked and squinted at the tiny piece of technology.

"Anja wants to hear from you." He grinned and sauntered toward the bed.

"Don't you think she would rather talk to you, considering that you're the one running this mission?" she asked but inserted the device, nevertheless.

"Well, she would like to hear from all members of the team." He nodded as if he'd said something impressive. "She's tired of hearing me bitch about the state of the mission and talking about killing people and wanted a fresh perspective from your side. I think she wants to know if I'm stable enough to keep on this team or something, but that's between us gals. And she managed to send us two earpieces this time."

Jessica tossed her loofah at him, which he dodged deftly. "Asshole."

Jeremiah didn't respond and spoke to Anja instead.

"Anja, Jessica is online now. Can we talk about what happened last night?"

"Nice to have you on this line, Jessica," the hacker said. "How are you doing? Is everything okay?"

"Everything's fine on this end," Jessica said cheerfully. "How's it going with you?"

"Well, night is starting to fall here, so I'm currently running on coffee and prayers at this point—not that I believe in the latter." A low chuckle punctuated a slight pause disturbed only by an odd squeaking sound. "I've kept an eye on the local authorities. I managed to clear any digital evidence that you two were in the hotel, which leaves the police a little confused. Thankfully, they're chasing their own tails as they make their way through most of your work. There weren't any survivors from the gunfight, though—thanks for that, Savage—and no one noticed anyone coming in or out of the location. So, as far as the police are concerned, you two appear to be in the clear."

"That is good news." Jeremiah didn't hide the surprise he felt. He wasn't used to hearing good news in this endeavor, and small miracles had a way of making him feel better about the situation they were in.

"There is some more news, although I'm not sure what to make of it," Anja continued. "As it turns out, Carlson was able to hire someone to piggy-back into our comms last night, which was how he knew there was a robbery in progress in his room and so knew to send his goons up armed and ready for a fight. I cleared it out, though."

"Are you sure these comms are secure?" He had to ask the question, even though it might offend her. "I don't mean to question your abilities or anything, but the guy in the lobby who handed them over to me was a little hinky."

"Who, Mike?" she asked. "No, he's a friend from college. He's a little weird, but I'd trust him with my life. He's solid, trust me on that."

"Fair enough." He dropped heavily onto the bed.

"Anyway, back on topic," the hacker said pointedly. "I managed to track the system they used to hack my comms, and from there, I was able to track a couple of communications to and from Carlson's men while he tried to figure out what was happening. If it makes you feel any better, it seems that we caught him by surprise, and he panicked somewhat when he realized that someone had broken into his room."

Jessica nodded and from the grin on her face, Savage felt confident in his ability to speak for both of them on the topic. "Thanks, it does make us feel much better."

"I thought it might." Anja laughed. "Anyway, after the dust settled and they discovered what had happened, I saw that Carlson actually sent word to the teams in the field. It doesn't seem that he's told them to keep an eye out for the two of you—which makes sense since he doesn't actually know what Savage looks like except for a quick sketch."

"Wait." Jeremiah pushed up from the bed and a troubled expression settled on his features. "We stole paperwork that could damage his efforts to keep his hands on his company, and he doesn't have people rushing to get it back? That doesn't strike you as the least bit suspicious?"

"Yes, actually," she said, and he could hear the now familiar creak of her rocking back in her chair. "He can't search the whole city for you, obviously, and he has to assume that you have gone to ground in an effort to avoid being located. That said, I didn't think he would abandon the chase so quickly. But it's there. They aren't looking for you."

"Call me crazy, but Carlson doesn't seem like the kind of man who would let something like this go, right?" Jessica interjected. "I never actually met him, but he didn't come across as the kind of person who would let the reality that he was robbed of incriminating documents go. He would want to find them, right?"

"Unless he's made the assumption that we aren't the ones in possession of the documents that were stolen." Savage rubbed absently at his jaw in the way he usually did when his mind worked hard. "Think about it. He has to assume that we would have sent these documents to Monroe and Anderson by now. That means he would play damage control."

"So...what if he's not simply pulled the people off the search for you two but has he's set his dogs on Anderson and Courtney instead?" Anja asked.

"Isn't the term 'sicced his dogs?'" he asked.

"Both terms work," Jessica replied irritably. "Anja, is there any way you could check? We shouldn't act on hunches at this point."

"I'm already on it." A few minutes of tense silence passed while she worked her magic. Jeremiah was well aware that it went way beyond magic or simple skill. There were technical aspects to everything the woman did that came with a lot of work and knowledge gathered the hard way. It was human nature to take the work of someone who sat behind a desk for granted, especially when they weren't actually visible to him.

It wasn't easy, but he tried to make sure that he never fell prey to that particular cliché.

"I don't know if this counts as evidence," the Russian said finally. "I wasn't able to break into their comms again, so I used something of a roundabout route—corporate records of the companies Carlson has used, to be precise. They checked out a group of SUVs and enough fuel to last them a while. There's also a record of them drawing a small arsenal out of their weapons inventories."

"Where could they be going?" Savage asked. "And what kind of situation would call for a small arsenal and a fleet of SUVs?"

"Well, I assume that the cars are because they can't actually check a...fifty caliber sniper rifle onto a commercial flight." Anja sounded nervous. "And from what I can tell, it's enough fuel to get them to and from Virginia."

"What's in Virginia?" Jessica asked.

"Anderson's house out in the country," she replied. "The house he went to visit last night because he wanted to check in on his family, who are staying there."

"Shit." Jeremiah tensed as his mind clicked into overdrive. "What about Monroe?"

"Well, I wouldn't worry about her," Anja replied. "She's staying in the penthouse of a veritable fortress building in Philly. Even if Carlson sent anyone after her, I would bet against them every day of the week. That woman was in the Zoo. She can handle herself."

"How about Anderson?" he asked. "He's...well, he was Special Forces too, right?"

"Yes, but he's in an isolated position and has his family to protect. With the amount of firepower that is apparently headed his way, all his training might not amount to much."

He wanted to argue that someone with special forces training shouldn't be underestimated either, but he was aware that they didn't have time to waste on his silly pride. They needed to stay focused.

"Look, this might be a wild goose chase, but it can't hurt to go over there and make sure he's in a secure location. And if he's not, to obviously get him and his family out to somewhere that's easier to defend, right?" Anja asked abruptly.

"Yes, but we still have to deliver the documents to Monroe. We haven't had time to scan them."

"I can do that," Jessica interjected. "If Carlson's goons aren't looking for us anymore, I could probably reach an airport and fly out to your location to hand all these documents over to you without too much trouble, right?"

"Right," the Russian said. "Although it needs to be said that I don't fully trust you yet, and I'll track your movements all the way through, understood?"

"I understand." She nodded, apparently unfazed by the other woman's bluntness.

"What?" Jeremiah protested. "Are you crazy? I'm responsible for your safety, and you're nuts if you think I'll let you take a plane on your own."

"It's the best plan, Savage, and you know it," Anja said firmly. "We need someone to cover all our bases, and while I think that your duty to protect Dr. Coleman is awesome, we need all hands on deck for this. There is no more time for hand-holding. I'll buy the tickets and make sure her way to the airport is secure. I'll sign off here."

He glared at Jessica. "If you think that—"

"I'll stop you right there." She moved closer, her posture calm and determined. "You were the one who said you needed to stay aloof to keep from making the wrong call in situations exactly like this one. You know that if there's any fighting where you're headed, you won't be able to cover me and help Anderson to protect his family. You know that it's the best move to send me with the documents while we have this opening in Carlson's security. It's the right move, like Anja said. You said you needed to be able to make the right decision with your priorities, right? Well, that still applies."

Jeremiah opened his mouth to argue but he realized that he had no moral high ground to stand on. She was right. Checking to make sure that Anderson didn't need his help was the right move to make, and he couldn't go there with Jessica. To leave her twiddling her thumbs wasn't the smart play either. It still felt wrong to leave her alone, and if he thought about it, the reason why was obvious. His priorities had already shifted.

The truth gave him pause, but he chose not to think about it too hard.

"Try not to get killed in Virginia," she said. After a second, she stood on her tiptoes to press a light kiss to his lips. "I still want to have that talk with you."

He nodded. "I can't make any promises, but I'll try."

CHAPTER THIRTY-ONE

Jeremiah made sure to drop Jessica off at the airport. It seemed like the smart tactic to make sure she had everything she needed. He doubted that Carlson would try to make a move in such a busy and open place, especially one so crowded with cameras and security. It would be a nightmare to conduct, which was the precise reason why most of the assassinations he'd run himself were always performed en route to the airport, and not inside. There was simply no way to get in and out without a hundred police officers and security people determined to be a hero.

It still felt wrong to both leave her and send her. And, he reasoned belligerently, it was wrong that it did. He didn't like the sensation that nagged at the back of his mind and told him constantly that he'd made the wrong decision. It made him doubt himself and his decisions, and he really couldn't afford to do that at this juncture. He needed to be focused.

It was annoying how she was in his thoughts now. All

he needed was to enter that state of mind in which he could be of use to Anderson if their adversaries did come and put his family in danger. It irked him that all he could think about was the fact that he'd had to leave Jessica at the airport. She'd told him to be safe and reminded him again that he needed to survive if they wanted to finish that talk of theirs.

For the first hour of his trip, he couldn't get that out of his head. Anja had told him that she'd boarded the plane safely, which assured him that at least she hadn't tried to screw them over. He wasn't the trusting type, but there was something in him that really wanted her to not be the kind of person who would betray them like that. With the hacker's eye on her, he was sure that any attempts to double-cross them would be caught and quickly corrected.

About halfway through the second hour of his four-hour drive to Virginia, he wasn't sure which mental attitude he would have preferred. He had a history of putting people out of his mind. Whether they were actually dead or simply dead to him, he was always good at keeping his mind compartmentalized and being able to deal with emotional problems when he was ready to deal with them. Sometimes, they took a little longer, which was why he had stayed away from his family for all this time.

Of course, he now had more reasons to avoid them, but that was another compartment that he would dig into another time.

For now, he needed to keep his mind on what was happening. Yet, despite his need to enter that detached, killing-machine separation, the novelty of his response to

Jessica presented an oddly tempting alternative. He sighed and refocused his thoughts on the mission.

Anja gave him regular updates of what was happening with the rest of their team. Monroe had sent a security contingent to meet Jessica at the airport and escort her all the way to the Pegasus building. After he and Anja had unwittingly exposed a horde of security flaws in the place, they had put a lot of effort into making it all but impenetrable, electronically or physically. Jeremiah wasn't sure what they'd achieved in the physical aspects, but he had to assume that with Anja's help, the electronic security would be top-of-the-line.

He gripped the steering wheel so tightly that his knuckles turned white. The driving didn't require much focus. The car that he'd rented had one of those self-driving features that you could turn on once you reached a highway. It allowed him to simply let the car cruise without much effort from his side. Of course, he had to remain seated in the vehicle, and occasionally, it would remind him to put his hands on the wheel to make sure that he was still awake. Other than that, all he had to do was stare out into the admittedly gorgeous landscape and think.

As it turned out, being stuck in a car with his own thoughts wasn't as pleasant as he thought it might be, even though he now drove a spanking new Cadillac Escalade. Turning the local radio on was a bust. A couple of films on the big, heads-up display allowed him to pass the time watching what looked like a fictionalized version of what was happening in the Zoo. They were already making films about it.

Some of the larger budget movies would take a couple more years to be released, but those with the smaller budgets, minor directors, and lesser-known cast members were already available around the world. Of course, the fact that they were already being publicly played on an open radio broadcast didn't augur well for their ratings on the more prestigious streaming platforms.

They offered only brainless action, terrible one-liners, and all the tropes that Savage usually needed in the films he watched when he wanted to turn his brain off. But he was too distracted to enjoy it. His mind already worked in overdrive as he watched the napalm-infused explosions and people firing massive guns without ear protection. Despite all that, the characters were able to grumble and growl through their lines a few seconds later, and he couldn't help but mentally dissect everything to the point where there was no enjoyment in the finish. He was almost glad for the silence that came to him once it was over. Almost. It wasn't exactly an improvement, but it also was no worse.

Jeremiah eased his fingers around the steering wheel and adjusted his grip a little.

"You should be coming up to the road that turns off to Anderson's home right about now," Anja said. "The GPS in that car of yours should show that. Let me know if you see anything in the area that tells you that an attack on Anderson is incoming."

"I assume you've at least warned him about it?" he asked as he approached a road that peeled away from the highway. He assumed that this was the one she meant, and he switched the car out of self-drive mode, took over himself, and eased into the right lane and off the highway.

"Well, yes, but as it turns out, getting your family out of a country estate isn't exactly easy. And he said that his home is actually a lot easier to defend than a car out in the middle of the road, especially since he has a Suburban. He doesn't like his chances against what will probably be four SUVs out in the open. Carlson has dropped the gloves by now, so I doubt that a carjacking is out of the question. I didn't agree, but he seemed adamant."

"You should have insisted," he said. "Being on the move makes you a lot harder to track and attack than if you stay in one place. I think he's made a mistake."

"I'll send the message along," she replied dryly.

"Well, it's a moot point right now," he said.

"What do you mean?"

"I think they're already here." Jeremiah tensed and slowed his approach. "That, or a bunch of guys decided to have a big hunting party only three miles away from Anderson's home and to bring all their SUVs with them."

"Shit."

"Yep, that about sums it up," he grumbled as he pulled his car over behind the other vehicles. He took a moment to scrutinize them while he considered the options. They wouldn't have left their vehicles unattended, especially out there in the boonies. He would have someone to deal with there.

All he needed to do was make sure that the men were actually headed toward Anderson's house while he waited in his car. He had to risk letting the ex-colonel take care of these men on his own and not charge in himself. If he had any chance to make it there, he needed to be cautious. Slow, and methodical would keep him and, hopefully, his boss alive. For now, there would be at least one man he could deal with.

Sure enough, the door of the SUV parked at the back opened and a man in fatigues stepped out, a hand on his weapon as he walked over to the SUV Jeremiah had rented. His face wore a look of confusion, but he was being cautious. The operative pulled his phone out and assumed an expression of frustration, although his hand clasped the suppressed Colt that he'd taken from the men who had tried to kidnap Jessica. He'd kept the weapons since the serial numbers had already been filed off and he could never have enough guns.

Anja, thankfully, had another contact who had met him at the first gas station and simply handed over the ammo he required for these, no questions asked on either side. One day, he'd have to ask her about those underground gun running contacts. Of course, if the police pulled him over at any point, he would have a lot of questions to answer, but in that moment, the problems he had to focus on didn't include the local police.

The man narrowed his eyes as he tapped the window with the butt of his pistol. Jeremiah nodded brusquely like he hadn't seen the weapon and fiddled with his phone. At another more insistent tap, he looked up with an annoyed expression and widened his eyes as any unsuspecting traveler would do when he saw the man's weapon. Quickly, he depressed the button that would open his window.

"Sir, this is a restricted area," the man said sternly.

"What?" He did his best to look confused. "No, I…my

GPS told me to come down this road. I'm meeting my friends for a hunting trip, and they weren't great with directions. They must have thought that it was funny to simply give me coordinates, but here I am, and I think I'm lost. Never trust technology, right?"

"Sir, you really have to leave," the gunman said, a note of frustration in his tone.

"I want to leave but I won't drive around these fucking boonies without any idea of where I'm going." He rolled his eyes and looked at his phone. "Can you at least tell me where the nearest gas station is? I think I'll find them there drinking beers and laughing at the idea of me being lost."

The instinct to not be a terrible person and help someone in need overrode the orders to not let anyone approach the Anderson country house. The lookout glanced at the highway as he ordered his thoughts to relay directions and took his eye off the operative for barely a second.

He had no chance to tell him where the nearest gas station was. Savage drew his pistol clear and the loud pop of the suppressed shot drove the slug through the man's right eye and out the other side with a spray of red.

With his weapon cradled in his right hand, he stepped out of the car and quickly inspected his target. He was dead, there was no doubt about that, but he crouched beside the body and searched beneath the man's jacket to reveal a body armor vest. After a quick moment of thought, he decided to strip the man of it and donned it himself. You never knew when you would need something like that in these situations, and why turn his nose up at free equipment? He took in a deep breath and rummaged further. An encrypted radio was attached to a clip on the man's hip.

"Anja, I have a radio here. Could you crack it and get me intel on what the people are up to?" He lost interest in the body and moved to open his burlap bag in the back of his car. At least he didn't have to haul it out. His ribs and other injuries would already be a handicap, and he'd take whatever he could to avoid making it worse unnecessarily.

"Will do. Keep it in range of your earpiece, and I'll be able to get a solid read on it," she replied.

He nodded and slid the radio into his pocket before he removed his weapons from the bag. With swift but considered actions, he discarded the pistol and replaced it with his Glock, which he tucked into the back of his pants. He slung his rifle over his shoulder and gripped the sawed-off shotgun in his hands. It had a strap too if he needed it, but he preferred to hold it if he could.

Satisfied that he had what he needed, he locked the vehicle and hiked into the woods that surrounded the road. It felt good to have real firepower with him this time around. Pistols were decent enough weapons. They were small, had enough stopping power to be dependable, and were all around versatile firearms, but they weren't the best at anything. They were Jacks of all trades that you could carry around easily.

But when the time came for a gunfight, he knew he would rather have a shotgun or a rifle in his hands. An assault rifle would have been better for the range, but unless he could get his hands on a weapon his enemies dropped, he wouldn't have access to one. A shotgun, a knife, and a hunting rifle would have to do, for now.

As he pushed deeper into the woods, Savage scanned for tracks. He'd been trained in hunting the enemy in wilderness almost like this. Boots were easy to identify in wet woodlands, which allowed him to follow their fairly direct route toward Anderson's house.

"How close are you to cracking that encryption, Anja?" he asked and pitched his voice low while he swiveled his head constantly as he slowed his approach.

"I have it…now. Patching you in," she replied. A touch of static crackled over his connection as a couple of men spoke.

"How's that approach looking, Overwatch? Over."

"Approach is clear, Ground Leader. I repeat, you are clear all the way to the house. Over." Both voices used hushed tones, but he was able to hear them clearly.

"Overwatch," Savage mumbled belligerently. "That means they have a sniper overlooking the house now. I need to find him. Anja, can you send me a topographical map of the area?"

"Come on, Savage," the hacker complained. "Your phone doesn't even have reception that deep in the woods. You're lucky the satellite connection has kept us live, but at this point, I don't have any visual aid on the area. You're on your own."

"Yeah, I was afraid that was the case." He studied the area around him while his mind raced. Anyone who would set up in an overwatch position would have to be uphill and most likely at an angle to cover as much of the house from one spot as possible. It was a long shot, but he had to take it. He wouldn't be able to assist Anderson if someone fired at him from behind. His first priority was definitely that sniper.

He slowed his approach even further, draped his shotgun over his shoulder, and retrieved the garotte from his pocket. The chances were that he wouldn't be able to find the man in time, but he could always set up where he could slow their assault down. That might hopefully put himself in a position to pick the sniper off that way.

The odds weren't great, of course. While he had decent enough skill in long-range shooting, he had never really qualified as a counter-sniper. His business was usually conducted up-close and personal.

"I have a signal," Anja said softly. "One of the radios near you is giving off a ready signal. It's roughly to your northeast. Keep heading that way."

It had to be his sniper, Savage mused. He could only hope that they hadn't brought enough people to merit a spotter for the man. They couldn't be more than five-hundred-yards away from the house, though. Why would they need a spotter?

"That's right, Savage," he grumbled under his breath. "Way to stay positive."

"What was that?"

"Nothing."

He pressed on, his eyes peeled for anything out of the ordinary. Ghillie suits these days could blend into almost any environment and he would have a hard time finding it. All he could really do was keep moving and hope he tripped over the man. He'd actually convinced himself that this was his only option when he spotted a small hump in the forest chaff. He froze and narrowed his eyes to scrutinize the shape, then grinned. A man lay prone with a big 50-cal sniper rifle.

Or, Savage thought with a small, ironic grin, *just come out right on top of him.* He inched closer, careful to watch where he placed his boots. The man wore no covering of any kind. He simply lay on a tarp on the ground and hugged his rifle close. The operative gritted his teeth at the implied insult. Anderson at least merited a proper hit. Did these guys really think so little of the man that they didn't bother to equip their sniper properly?

Time seemed to slow as he edged forward with elaborate caution. The man seemed relaxed and even careless. There was nothing in his posture or attitude that suggested real alertness or focus. He was clearly not a sniper by trade. Jeremiah prepared the piano wire and grasped the handles firmly as he scowled his disapproval. The attitude was definitely disrespectful toward Anderson. He had been Special Forces, for crying out loud. Did they really think that half-assing it like this was the proper way to kill an ex-Special Forces colonel?

Savage launched onto the man, who hadn't even noticed his approach. The sniper grunted in pain when his attacker's elbow jabbed into his back. He tried to cry out to alert the team that he was under attack, but the garrote was already around his throat. It was thin but not thin enough to cut into his airways or even draw blood.

The target grabbed at the wire as his assailant planted his knee in his lower back and used that as leverage to pull upward. Odd ticks pulsed against the garrote's wire as the man's carotids tried desperately to supply his brain with oxygen. At this point, all training was choked out of his mind and his only instinct was to try to breathe again as the deadly tension cut off his airways.

Savage applied more and more pressure and tried to make sure neither he nor his victim made a sound. The sniper made a desperate grab for the rifle to get a warning shot off, but his attacker moved quicker and shoved the weapon with his foot.

There was an almost tangible sensation when the man's brain ceased activity and he slumped forward. With no time to wait for him to die from the chokehold, the operative drew his knife and plunged it firmly into the broad back beneath him and twisted it roughly. He felt the man's spine snap, and the would-be killer exhaled one last, dying breath.

"I take it you found the sniper nest, then?" Anja asked.

"You could say that." He growled his response, a little out of breath as he rolled the man off the tarp and retrieved the cannon of a rifle he'd had to push away in the struggle. His grin wide, he cradled it into his shoulder.

"Well, hello, beautiful," he said softly and almost intimately as he traced his fingers over the hard steel lines of the weapon. "Where have you been all my life?"

"Do you two need a room?" the hacker snarked.

"Despite what you may have heard on the Internet, Anja, bigger is better—at least when it comes to guns," he retorted with a giddy laugh.

"Do you have an erection right now?" she asked. "Because...gross."

"Tell Anderson that his house is about to be breached and that he has someone covering him from afar with a big-ass rifle." Savage snapped back to reality. He made sure that there was a round chambered and that the safety was off before he aimed toward Anderson's house.

"Already done, Kilgore." Her chuckle definitely sounded sarcastic.

Savage ignored her. He wouldn't let the hacker ruin this moment for him. Yes, he liked making his kills up close, but there wasn't a man alive who couldn't appreciate the sheer majesty of the 50-cal sniper rifle. *Hell,* he thought with a grin, *with this thing, I could probably kill a building.*

It was overkill from this distance, which he gauged at a little over five hundred yards. He ran the quick calculations that he remembered from his time training with long-distance shooting to account for the wind and the drop. The rifle itself was already zeroed in perfectly, so he didn't need to add anything to that.

Satisfied, he settled in to wait but within a few seconds, a group of ten or so men broke from the foliage. Unlike the sniper, these were professionals. They moved smoothly in groups of three or four each, remained under cover, and never allowed their lines of fire to cross one of their comrades.

Their efficiency really was a pity. He'd hoped for the same shoddy attitude that had characterized the sniper. Savage took in a deep breath and released it slowly as he watched them proceed unerringly toward the house.

"Tell Anderson that his approach party is close," he said, his voice calm. The cold control settled in his stomach and adrenaline pumped through his body. He welcomed the calm realization that he was ready for a fight.

"Will do, Savage," Anja replied. He remained silent and tracked one of the men in the crosshairs of his rifle. He didn't need to actually hit anyone—only grab their attention and slow their movements—but he really wanted to make this first shot count. His selection was the one who seemed to lead the group. He could tell that from the way that he motioned for the two teams of three to break away and flank the building as he and three others pushed across the last patch of open ground.

He breathed deep, exhaled slowly, and reached the end of the air in his lungs as he squeezed the trigger.

Bullets from a gun this big wouldn't be stopped by the body armor these men wore, so he didn't bother to try for a headshot. The body shot was effective, and the slug powered through the man and out the other side in a wide crimson spray. The ammo didn't make much of a hole going in, but they were certainly showy on the way out.

The leader fell instantly, and from the blood that poured from the wound, his quarry wouldn't get up again.

The group of three remaining men froze and looked at their leader before they spun in an effort to make out where the shot had come from.

Jeremiah yanked the bolt back, ejected the spent casing, and slapped another one in.

"Overwatch, come in," one of the team yelled over the radio. "We have another sniper on our six. Repeat, we have another sniper on our six. Confirm!"

"No shit, dummies." He grinned and aimed at the man who was talking and squeezed the trigger again. A quarter of a second passed before his target's head exploded and Savage wondered if this was the shot that would alert the attackers that he was shooting at them from their now-dead sniper's nest.

CHAPTER THIRTY-TWO

It wasn't the perfect arrangement, but Anderson was aware of the fact that he couldn't have his family caught in the crossfire of what was about to happen. There had been a moment of doubt when Anja had first contacted him some hours before to inform him of a possibility that there might be a heavily armed group of men headed his way.

It hadn't been the right choice to stay there, in retrospect. It was actually one of the dumbest choices he'd ever made, and that wasn't a low bar to clear. He'd made any number of serious mistakes in his time and he really didn't want to have to repeat them, not with his family involved.

He wanted to be able to blame his PTSD, and the inherent desire to stay in a place that his mind had somehow assumed to be safe was the kind of thing his doctors had told him might be a problem. Of course, they hadn't really anticipated that he'd be in a combat situation again. Honestly, he hadn't thought it would be an issue either.

Besides, blaming what had happened to him in the past wouldn't help him save his family. He needed to act, and he needed to take precautions. The house had already been set up like a small fortress. The windows were all paned with bullet-proof material, the doors were all reinforced with steel bars, and he had weapons hidden throughout. He had been a fan of Kevin McCallister while growing up, and those had been the instincts that he'd drawn from when he'd designed this house. It had been as expensive as hell, especially on a government salary, but he'd managed to do most of the manual labor himself. It was a work in progress, though, and he could only hope that the effort he'd already put in was enough to help him hold these invaders at bay.

He gritted his teeth and listened for the click that told him his wife had locked her and their kid up in the basement from the inside. At least that way, they would be kept safe from any stray gunfire. For himself, a vest of ceramic body armor would have to do.

His hands shook when he heard the first gunshot. It was loud and echoed in the way that told him it had come from a long way out. Anderson drew in a ragged breath and tried to stop the tremors, but they seemed to have spread to his knees. While he hated the weakness, he couldn't allow it to interfere.

Resolute, he ignored it and strode over to the section of his foyer that opened to a small gun rack. He removed the Beretta M9A5 and slipped it into a hip holster before he dragged out the M1020 combat shotgun he'd used so many times before. Well, not this one, specifically, but it was the shotgun assigned to men who were likely to head into close-quarters situations. The thick spread in the buckshot rounds that came with it was enough to clear a room in two or three shots and it was easy to load.

Anderson knew that because he had spent the last few hours mechanically going through the motions of loading every weapon in the house. All the while, he'd continued to hope that he wouldn't need any of them.

We should have left, he told himself as a phantom tingle started in the burn scar on his arm. He closed his eyes and shook the sensation aside. Memories of his friends and comrades in arms devoured by the flames fed by the helicopter's fuel tanks could not be allowed to take center stage.

"Oh, God, I should have left," he said aloud and something akin to panic surged as the gunfire outside the house picked up momentum. Anja had told him that Savage had taken up a position beyond his house and would use a rifle to hinder their approach. That would definitely help, but with their sheer force of numbers, they would inevitably break in soon.

His heart thundered and he ducked behind the bar that had been reinforced with steel to provide proper cover. He drew in quick, shallow breaths, but the oxygen didn't seem to register in his brain. It was an odd thing to know that you were having a panic attack but couldn't do anything to stop it.

Time slowed and the room seemed to shift like he hovered above his body and watched himself go through the motions. That separated self hoped and prayed that he could get it together before the men broke in to kill him and his family. His fingers tingled and his mind drifted to all those times he'd walked out of dangerous situations alive. He made a list of all the places he'd gone into and escaped without so much as a scratch. They'd called him Old Ironsides in his battalion due to the fact that he almost never showed up with anything worse than a couple of scratches and bruises. He'd been lucky.

The realization slowed his heartbeat and he calmed enough for his mind to slip back into old patterns. People needed him to fight back. He needed to fight back and damned if he would die crouched behind a bar.

This driving need was new. It was never something he'd felt in the field and Anderson paused to consider it for a moment. These people attacked his home. They endangered not only his life but those of his family. There were certain lines you simply never crossed, and these men had already stepped way beyond what was acceptable or even explainable.

He wasn't calm, he finally realized, he was angry—full of white-hot fury that exploded through his body from the inside. The shotgun settled solidly into his grasp. A whomp was immediately followed by an explosion. They had launched a grenade at his door. Not the front door—Savage would cover that and the side entrances. The big boom of a long-distance rifle still cracked every few seconds. He wouldn't try to hit the men but rather, keep them away from the door, limit their options, and funnel them into the kill zone. That kill zone was what he had to use to protect himself.

A swift action pulled the bolt back to chamber the first of the ten buckshot rounds into the shotgun and he heaved himself up from behind the bar.

"Anderson, Savage tells me you have some hostiles approaching from behind the house," Anja said and used the speakers of his house smart appliances to talk to him.

"How many?" he asked and scanned the room. Thankfully, none had managed to break in while he gathered his courage before he stepped out from cover.

"He's not sure." She'd apparently heard him, but he had no idea how. "It can't be more than three or four, though. He says that he has four of the ten at the front dead, and the others are pinned down."

"Roger that." He kept low as he circled to the back door.

"Why do military people say, 'Roger that' over the radio anyway?" the hacker asked. It was odd to hear her talking as the house, but there were many things weirder than that in this situation that needed his attention.

"It's a replacement for 'okay' in a conversation over the radio," he explained, not sure why he had focused on that instead of the fighting outside. "It's to avoid confusion during combat situations—much the same reason why they use the NATO phonetic alphabet."

"Right." He wasn't sure if she said anything after that. She probably did, knowing her, but it was all drowned out by a loud explosion across the room. Anderson quickly regretted not having stashed any earplugs as he dropped hastily to the ground to avoid the splinters of shrapnel. What he assumed was a shaped charge entirely demolished the back door of his house.

The room instantly filled with thick, acrid smoke. He saw nothing but a thick, gray fog for a couple of seconds as he crawled prone and kept his shotgun pointed at the door, ready to respond the moment he caught sight of any movement.

A man stepped through the door and predictably, ran a sweep for anyone who might be standing up to face him. It was possible that the smoke was too thick to see someone crawling over the floorboards. Either way, he wouldn't give the man any comfortable options. He steadied the shotgun and pulled the trigger. The intruder froze at the telltale sound of the blast, but his reflexes were too slow. The buckshot impacted him like a sledgehammer before he could react, and he stumbled back a few steps. The force shoved him outside the door, where his head suddenly exploded into a red mist.

"Savage says that these guys have body armor, so you might want to shoot for the head," Anja said beyond his ringing ears.

She was telling him this now? Well, technically, the one telling him this now was Savage, but either way, it was good to know—better late than never. He couldn't exactly aim for the head with a shotgun, thanks to the spread, but it would be something to keep in mind if he had to use his pistol.

Anderson rolled to the side and behind cover as more men came into view. They were more cautious and wouldn't risk being shot like their comrade. Instead, they laid down suppressing fire without any methodical pattern. From the sound of the bullets, they used assault rifles—M24 carbines, most likely. They fired wildly and weren't likely to actually hit anything. He realized that they simply tried to fill the air with as many bullets as possible in the hope that something would find a target. The old spray and pray tactic could be very useful.

They maintained the steady barrage and a couple of men barreled in and used the cover fire to try to find their target inside the house as the smoke started to clear.

The ex-colonel found one of them first and smirked as the man's head snapped back when nine pellets of double-aught pounded into his face. He staggered and fired uncontrollably in a reflexive trigger pull. The kill caught the attention of his teammates, who turned to face the defender.

Instinctively, he fell back a couple of steps and sprayed the room with as many rounds as he could while he retreated in the direction from which he had come. His ears had numbed to the loud noises. One of the invaders fell back and three more pushed forward into the gap as his gun clicked empty. Obviously, some of those whom Savage had pinned down must have pushed through to join the breach team. He dropped the shotgun and it swung from the strap as he drew his pistol.

The men were reloading their weapons as they stepped inside, which gave Anderson enough time to stumble back behind the reinforced bar. He'd stashed shotgun rounds there that he could reload with and an MP5 submachine gun in case he didn't have the time. For now, though, he needed to dissuade them from a forward push. He jerked upright and fired his pistol in the direction of the men who clustered near the door. None of the bullets were kill-shots, which reminded him that he was still a little rusty, but his enemy fell back behind cover to regroup.

He used the time to good effect, located the case of shotgun rounds, and reloaded. It took ten rounds, which he fitted quickly, and he chambered the first. Thankfully, he didn't have time to really consider what would happen if he couldn't stop these men. The thought was ever-present and nagged at the back of his mind, a constant reminder that he needed to survive that fed the fire in his gut.

His jaw tensed and his fingers hoisted the shotgun with the ease of familiarity as he straightened behind the bar. He could no longer hear gunfire from outside and wasn't sure whether that meant Savage had been taken down or not. Hopefully not, but he couldn't focus on that either.

One of the intruders, dressed all in black, stepped out of cover and Anderson raised his shotgun. The explosive charge leaving the barrel accompanied by the heavy kick of the shotgun knocked him back a step. His target catapulted back with a soft grunt of pain, but he was able to drag himself behind a couch and out of sight.

The ex-colonel realized his mistake barely in time. A volley erupted and sprayed across the bottles of respectable beverages behind him. He ducked instinctively as glass and alcohol showered his back as he fell. Thankfully, they hadn't used the advantage of him caught out in the open to good effect.

That wouldn't happen again, he realized as he checked the number of rounds left in his shotgun. Seven. He hadn't thought that he'd fired three already, but you lost track in heated situations like that. It was so well-known that it was almost a cliché, by this point. He retrieved the submachine gun from where he'd tucked it under the ice bucket. It wasn't his preferred weapon, but when it came time to deliver as many bullets in as little time as possible, there weren't many others that could beat it.

A thump preceded an explosion that snapped him out of his reverie. It had come from the front and he knew immediately that someone knew about the super-fortified door. These people were very knowledgeable about the work he'd put into his country house.

The realization seeped in below his calm and triggered the paranoia that walked hand in hand with his condition. He acknowledged the truth that he'd already been invaded at a purely information level. Now, however, they broke into his house and tried to hurt his family. He told himself to snap out of the panic attack that loomed insidiously again and dug deep for the anger. It flared, white-hot and invincible, and empowered his roar of defiance.

"Semper fi, motherfuckers!" he bellowed as he cleared the bar and his finger worked the trigger as quickly as possible. His shoulder absorbed the repeated kicks without complaint. A couple of the men whom Savage had delayed in the front entered cautiously and looked around as if they were a little uncertain what they would find. He wondered why the team didn't use a comm system to stay in touch with each other but decided not to ask questions about that now. He pulled the sub out from under the bar, aimed it at the door as he cradled the stock against his shoulder, and fired.

The three-round burst pounded him like a mule's kick, and he staggered but managed to gather himself and gripped the sub with both hands. The invaders who were caught in the doorway tried to fall back. Two made it to safety but two others collapsed with almost simultaneous thuds. He grimaced as their blood stained the hardwood floor.

Anderson felt a moment of elation when his attackers backed away from him, but he regretted the impulse a second later. He'd been away from the game too long, and combat wasn't like riding a bike. Not by a long shot. He'd performed better against a team of killers than most, maybe, but that would be cold comfort if he were dead.

His mistake was to focus too long on the new intruders in his living room. For a brief instant, he'd forgotten those who'd entered from the back who simply waited for him to come out of cover. Something like a sting from the world's biggest wasp seared his shoulder. A second strike felt very different—like someone had gut-punched him with a fist the size of the average brick. He lurched back into the bar and glass shattered before he collapsed.

He couldn't breathe and this time, it wasn't a work of his tortured psyche. The armor had reacted to protect his chest and now clamped around his torso and prevented him from sucking oxygen in. He looked around and realized that when he fell, his weapons had slipped away from his numb fingers and clattered away. They lay only barely out of reach beyond the mess of broken glass and spilled bourbon.

"Fuck!" he finally managed to gasp. He scowled at the armor, touched his shoulder, and winced at the explosion of pain when his fingers found the bleeding hole beyond the protective area the vest. It seemed entirely logical to promise himself that he would invest in a suit that would protect his whole body when he got out of there. The kind that they used in the Zoo, he decided. It wasn't always effective against the creatures found in there, but against regular humans with guns, it was a lot more useful.

When he got out of there. *When, not if.* Anderson rolled those words around his brain as he focused on one of the black-clad men who circled the back of the bar that he had used as cover. The assassin held a carbine in his hands, and he looked briefly at Anderson before his gaze searched for a weapon. Satisfied that his quarry was helpless, he took a step forward and aimed his weapon at the ex-colonel's head.

When. Not if, Anderson reminded himself as he stared at the black barrel of the carbine aimed directly at the center of his forehead from not even two yards away. The man clearly didn't intend to miss.

The killer's attention was yanked away, and Anderson realized that he'd been about to lose his nerve. The reality of that scared him a little because he knew he needed to believe and follow it through. Distracted, it took a second before he focused on what had diverted the man's attention. A shotgun fired two shots in quick succession. The familiar *whoosh* was hard to miss, and he grinned with both relief and pleasure.

Savage was still around, that old bastard. Hope flared to drown out his momentary weakness. He had to make use of the advantage and the unexpected reprieve.

It was very clear that his would-be executioner had lost his focus. He swung his carbine to attack the new threat, which gave his erstwhile victim the opening he needed. Anderson lashed out with his right leg and caught his attacker on the knee hard enough that it overextended and with a painful pop, snapped out of joint. The man screamed in pain and stumbled onto the support of his remaining functional knee. He looked up and into the pistol that Anderson had kept in his underarm holster.

"When," Anderson gasped. "Not if."

"What the fu—" The question was cut off when the ex-colonel decided that he wasn't in the mood to explain and simply pulled the trigger. His adversary's head snapped back, and his body followed to slump in a motionless heap.

"Inside joke," he grumbled as he heaved himself to his feet and tried to hold onto his weapon while doing so. "You wouldn't get it."

He finally cleared the bar and paused to take stock of the five men who were still alive and had their hands full dealing with Savage. The man looked…monstrous. Anderson recalled the first time he'd met him while he'd still been in the hospital, recovering from his fight. He'd seemed a little off but nothing out of the ordinary. If the truth be told, he wasn't even that impressive a specimen. While he'd seen video of the man since, nothing was really quite like seeing it live and in the flesh.

The one thing that struck him was how calm Savage looked. His face revealed no expression at all, which was odd considering that it was splattered with blood. A pair of bodies sprawled outside on his porch. Those were the shotgun victims, he assumed. A third man could be seen inside, clutching at his slashed throat.

Savage still held the shotgun in his hand, but the target directly ahead of him was too close to bring it to bear on his head. Buckshot wouldn't penetrate the armor these men wore, and logic said the operative had to know that.

Whether he knew or not, he didn't care. He pulled the

trigger anyway. The ear-splitting blast made Anderson flinch and the enemy backed away, looking like he'd had the breath knocked out of his lungs. Hell, he looked like his lungs had been punched out of his chest as he fell and landed hard on the couch. Savage raised the shotgun to his opponent's head and fired. Both Anderson and the man in question flinched, equally surprised when all they heard was the click of an empty firearm.

The man's relief was short-lived, of course, as his attacker quickly gripped the shotgun with both hands and lurched forward. He pushed his shoulder into the blow and shoved the butt of the shotgun into his adversary's face. Death was instantaneous and the body slid off the cushions without so much as a grunt of pain.

Another man approached from behind but in a smooth, controlled swing, Savage gripped the barrel of his shortened, sawed-off shotgun and used the firearm viciously as a club. The gunman fell and tried to rise, but another blow was delivered with a resounding thwack, followed almost immediately by a third. He tried to push up off the ground, but his assailant already had a knife in his hand and quickly put it to use. The blade sank into the back of the unfortunate attacker's neck.

The fleshy sound of steel as it carved through meat and bone punctuated the end of the fight.

Savage grunted, straightened slowly, and scanned the room.

"Are you all right there, sir?" he asked and directed a concerned look at Anderson, who struggled to stay on his feet.

"I'm doing just fine, dog face," he replied with a chuckle.

He immediately regretted it, though, when his bruised ribs pressed painfully into the hardened ceramic plates. Savage hurried around the bar to support him and held him upright as they moved to the dining room, where he put the injured former colonel down on one of the seats.

"You have a through and through on your shoulder here," he noted as he snatched one of the cloth napkins from the table and pressed it firmly against the injury. "And a hard hit to your vest. It looks like it kept you from getting turned into a kebab, though, so it was worth it."

"It doesn't…feel like it right now," Anderson hissed through clenched teeth as the other man worked to undo the straps on his vest. "My wife will kill me if she sees you using the napkins she chose to treat a wound. I appreciate the effort, though. And…saving my life and all that."

Savage smirked. "Well, it wasn't the first time that I had to drag a man's ass out of the fire that he jumped into his own damned self, and I doubt it'll be the last."

"Come on, man, I just got shot," his boss retorted. "Twice."

"And I just saved your damn life," he replied with a smarmy grin. "And that of your family. So I get to take some shots too."

His family. Right. "Oh, shit, Anja, are you there?"

"I am here, yes," she replied through the house's speakers.

"Well, that's creepy." The operative looked around and actually shuddered.

She didn't answer him. "It's good to know that the two of you are alive and well, Anderson. You should know that the cops and paramedics are already on the way. It seemed like the kind of situation that you might like to have on record."

"Good call." He shook his head when he remembered why he'd contacted her in the first place. "Could you let my wife know that it's safe to come out again? It…is safe to come out again, right?"

"As far as I can tell," Savage confirmed.

"Will do, Anderson," she replied, and the speakers went quiet.

"Look," he said as he helped the older man out of his vest." I have someplace I need to be and some business I need to take care of in a very small and rapidly thinning window of opportunity. One that I'll miss if I have to make statements and possibly get written up for shooting a bunch of people on your property. Not to mention that technically, I'm supposed to be well and truly off the radar. Will you cover for me?"

Anderson nodded. "Get out of here. I'll handle the paperwork."

"Appreciate it." He almost patted the man on the shoulder but thought better of it. "Heal up, Colonel."

Jeremiah left the dining room and walked slowly toward the door. It had been tough to go through this fight with all his previous injuries still fresh and definitely tender. He would have to see a doctor about it soon and maybe have a nice long nap and a couple of days of rest and relaxation after this. Before that, though, he had to hike through the afternoon heat back to his car and start driving. Anja had given him a timeline. While he had time, he wanted to be prepared for what he hoped was the last confrontation of this little corporate civil war.

He froze when he caught movement out of the corner of his eye. There weren't any men left, he reminded himself. And this wasn't a man he now faced.

She was a taller woman, lean and beautiful in a modern and elegant kind of way. At the same time, she looked as hard as her husband, and her hands held the Glock in a perfect stance.

Well, almost perfect. He noted a young boy hiding behind her, his face pressed into her back to hold whimpers back.

Jeremiah's hands came up slowly. "I'm not here to hurt you. I helped your husband eliminate the home invaders, and now, I'm leaving. He's alive and well in the dining room. Alive, anyway."

"It's okay, Ivy," Anderson shouted from the window. "He needs to get out of here."

The woman hesitated. It was a good instinct, but her gun lowered slowly. The boy relaxed when she did so and immediately broke away from her to race toward his father's voice.

"Thank you," Ivy said softly. He responded with a nod and turned away to continue his retreat out the door.

CHAPTER THIRTY-THREE

Carlson took a large swallow of his drink and his lip snarled in displeasure. *This hasn't been one of my best weeks.*

There were moments in his life that he considered to be victories. Finally taking over the company after his father's death and after most of the board members had made it clear that they didn't believe in him enough to give him the top spot was one of those. Proving them wrong had been how he'd earned his laurels in the business world and had been the foundation that brought him the respect of the people he had worked with and against. He'd shown them that he had the kind of ruthlessness and political skill that was called for in the upper echelons of company control.

Earning the first non-government contract for the goop that had come from the sky in what felt like forever ago was another. The board hadn't wanted to share their finds and were determined to ensure that all the profits were strictly for the military. It had been him, though, who had strong-armed those assholes into sharing. Of course, that had eventually ended with the goop being sent to the Sahara and the whole clusterfuck it subsequently turned into. But he stood by his actions, especially in light of everything that they were learning and extracting from that place.

It had proven to be a tough gamble to stand by, but he had. He'd believed that what happened over there was the future of mankind and the little blue marble they called their home planet—and even the way humanity would actually reach beyond it. So much of the research he promoted went into keeping his company solvent despite massive expansions over recent years.

Of course, money was only there to keep the investors happy. Cash certainly helped to keep him in a relatively comfortable position, but what he really did all this for—his justification for using extreme measures to keep his place in the company—was the future of mankind.

Megalomania aside, he knew what he did was for his fellow man. He knew that if he actually told anyone about his plans, he would have to launch into a tirade like every other person who thought they could save the world with phrases like "greater good" and "bigger picture." In reality, that was exactly the kind of conversation that nobody liked to have. It sounded too grandiose to be true, and when people actually counted the cost of what he did, they would back away.

Well, he assumed so, anyway. He hadn't actually told anyone about his attempts to turn the goop extracted from the Zoo into fuel that could sustain the world's needs once the oil wells ran dry. Or, for that matter, about the scientists involved in the research who told him that the byproducts from the goop's usage went from negligible to beneficial to the environment. There were even tests that showed potential for fuel for rockets that could be sent into space which would weigh a quarter of what traditional fuel did and provide up to three times the burn rate. Everything was on the table with this stuff.

But now, he had to put a halt to it all because two people were small-minded regarding the sacrifices made. They would do their best to steal it all from him and use the equally small-minded policies of the men and women in government and their power against him. It wasn't fair, but it was life. He hadn't expected to change the world single-handedly without a couple of obstacles along the way.

Carlson leaned back in his seat and toyed with the glass of apple juice in his hand. He had told himself that he would stop drinking so much and he had done precisely that. Of course, he would have preferred tomato juice since it would have served as a replacement for the Bloody Mary he usually had in the morning when he did this kind of cold-turkey quitting. But, with Linus gone, he'd had to find a replacement who wasn't quite up to snuff.

He scowled at the glass as his limo pulled into the airport. Of course, he would have to put all his plans on hold as he would leave the country before the warrants and subpoenas started flooding in. Everything would have to wait until he finished his vacation. He would start in Switzerland, he decided—collect his resources and bring everyone up to speed on his situation. Maybe a couple of months in the Caymans would be beneficial too. That might make Monroe and Anderson think they had won before he returned with all the considerable might of his foreign allies behind him.

Since targeting them directly had failed so miserably, it was all he could do, really. In retrospect, his campaign had been a mistake, but he had reacted to their very aggressive business style that forced him into a situation he simply wasn't comfortable with. It was annoying to have to work around people like that.

As they moved onto the tarmac, Carlson smiled at the sight of the corporate jet all ready and set for takeoff. There had been a hint of petty revenge on his mind when he'd made sure that the plane that would spirit him away from all his troubles was a company plane. His sense of satisfaction had marginally improved when he'd secured his current position in Pegasus and filed all the paperwork that would keep him on the payroll. In essence, he remained untouchable until he returned from his time abroad. He didn't like having to accept small rewards like this, but they deserved it. That and much, much worse.

The vehicle eased to a stop and a few seconds later, his new driver stood outside and held the door open for him. Carlson sighed and really hoped the jet had a fully stocked bar. He didn't remember if his request had included the fact that he was on a cleanse. If it had, he would be miserable all the way to Bern.

He stepped out and buttoned the top of his jacket before he strolled casually to the plane. He wasn't sure he liked the fact that whoever had made the arrangements didn't think to add a security team to ensure that the short walk across an open area was made without any attempts on his life. While he knew he was in the right, people tended to react poorly when large numbers of armed men were sent to kill them.

His momentary concern proved unfounded and he made his way up the steps and paused to look around and enjoy the last touch of the morning breeze that drifted by before he stepped into the cabin.

No flight attendant greeted him. A quick glance confirmed that even the pilots seemed absent. Carlson couldn't help the alarm bells that now rang loudly in his head, all made worse by the fact that when he stepped onto the passenger deck, a stranger waited for him. The man sipped from a glass filled with an amber liquid and a couple of ice cubes.

Well, at least there was a stocked bar there. Unfortunately, his moment of relief was quickly dashed when he realized that there was a gun in the visitor's other hand.

The intruder didn't look like much, really. His brown hair was slicked back, and he wore a black suit with no tie that looked new and rather expensive. A cut on his eyebrow and another on his lip as well as some bruising on his knuckles was ample evidence that he wasn't there to talk. It seemed logical that he was most likely the man responsible for the lack of reception by security, stewardess, or pilots.

Carlson took a deep breath to calm the nerves that suddenly stirred as he walked over to sit across from the stranger. He had to admit, the man knew how to make an impression. The slick, clean-cut appearance and the all-black suit gave a sense of a civilized man that contrasted sharply with the bruises and cuts.

"I assume you're the one whom I have to thank for all

the misfortune that has crossed my path over the last week or so," the executive said with a pleasant smile.

He took a moment to pour himself a glass of scotch and dropped a couple of ice cubes in it before he leaned back in his seat. "Between you and me, I didn't think that Anderson and Monroe had the balls to come after me like that but damned if they didn't come through. My first time conducting an aggressive company takeover was actually very similar, believe it or not. For one thing, it was Pegasus that I took over after my father passed away. Of course, back then, I had the help of my friend Linus, the man who—"

"The man whom I killed in the hotel. I remember," the intruder in black replied and took another sip from his glass. Even his voice wasn't that impressive—not too thick, for one thing, and not the kind of gravel that most men tried to pass off as a growl. He wasn't there to talk to the man he had thwarted for the past week and a half. Instead, he gave the impression that he was simply there to have a chat over a drink. Linus had told him there wasn't anything about the man that stood out and that he wouldn't recognize him if he came across him on the street. Carlson hadn't believed him, but he did now.

Poor Linus. He would send his family a gift basket for the funeral since he wouldn't be able to attend in person.

"Well," he said after the silence hung between them for a little longer than he was comfortable with. "I don't suppose I could ask you for a name. I respect what Monroe and Anderson have been able to do, but you're the one who painted the canvas they're selling."

He shrugged in response. "Call me Savage."

Savage. Huh. He liked that. He tilted his head and smiled. It wasn't a real name, obviously, but rather a title the man had given himself. Normally, he wasn't a fan of people giving themselves mean or edgy names, but in this case, it fit. He'd seen the results of the man's work.

"Well, I'm afraid I'm on a tight schedule," he said when things went a little too quiet for his taste again. "Playing hardball isn't the kind of thing I would usually associate with moralists like Anderson and Monroe, but hey, I don't mind being wrong once in a while. It keeps me on my toes and fills me with hope that the world does indeed have the capacity to surprise me. So, what do you want? I assume Anderson and Monroe want my time at Pegasus to come to an end, and while they have no idea of the consequences of their actions, I won't put my life on the line to keep them from making the biggest mistakes of their lives."

Savage remained silent and simply stared at him while he sipped casually from his drink. Carlson couldn't help but feel annoyed. There was hardball and there was hardball, but you had to play for it to work, right?

"Look, what do they want, hmm?" he asked and made to take another sip from his drink before he realized there was nothing but ice left. "Do they want me to sign over my shares in the company? I'll expect to be generously compensated for them, of course, but that's nothing that a quick meeting with some numbers and checks won't solve."

His visitor remained silent and the executive let his frustration show as Savage calmly finished his drink and put the glass on the table beside him before he leaned forward.

"Well, you have one thing right, Carlson," he said with a small smile. The man's weapon was aimed directly at his stomach. "Your time at Pegasus is at an end, although probably not the kind of end you wanted."

"I don't understand," he mumbled and tried to shift out of the way of the gun in as subtle a way as possible. Did this man intend to kill him? More importantly, did he think he would get away with it?

"You see, Carlson..." The way he said the name sent chills up the executive's spine. "You made two mistakes. The first was to assassinate the people who worked for you—and after you'd already fired them, no less."

The grim expression darkened and triggered a responsive shiver that Carlson couldn't control. "The second was to go after a man's family. In normal circumstances, I would be here with papers and a check and tell you not to return to the country for a couple of years. But you crossed a line and made it personal.

"See, between you and me, I'm not that great when it comes to morals. Call it an abusive stepfather and an absentee mother or something, but either way, I've always needed to be around people who laid out what was expected of me by society when it comes to right and wrong. It doesn't always make sense, but honestly, it doesn't always have to. One thing I learned is that you don't go after the innocent or the families until you're ready to put everything on the line and you don't care about the consequences."

Carlson gulped, his mouth suddenly dry, and his gaze flickered to the decanter of scotch on the table. He really needed another drink.

"I can tell that you're like me in that way," Savage continued. "You don't really have your own set of morals, so you abide by those given to you by others. You don't care about your own family, so it wouldn't make sense for me to go after them either. So, to hurt you in a way that warns you to stay away from Monroe, Anderson, and their families if you are ever in the mood for revenge, I'll need to take something else away from you—something you really do care about. Like, for instance, the ability to walk without a cane for the rest of your life."

"What?" he asked but rather than answer, the man lowered the sights on the suppressed Colt in his hand and pulled the trigger. The pop was louder than Carlson had anticipated, and pain radiated through his leg as the bullet shattered his kneecap and sliced through the joint to tear the tendons inside.

"Fuck!" he screamed as he fell from his seat and clutched his right knee. He jolted and shrieked in agony as he tried to drag himself along the floor and away from the madman.

"They told me not to kill you," Savage said coldly. "But I felt that a warning was in order. You don't fuck my employers or those who can't fight back."

"It...was only business," Carlson hissed through clenched teeth. He'd never been shot before, and this was easily the worst pain that he'd ever felt in his life.

His attacker stood with casual ease and took the time to close the top button of his jacket before he towered over the wounded man.

"Of course. This is also only business. Here's what's gonna happen. The first thing you'll do is surrender your

Pegasus shares. The board will either buy them or sell them, but don't expect the best price. The value is bound to plummet when word gets out that the ex-CEO has been arrested."

"Arrested?" Despite the pain, Carlson managed to voice his scorn and indignation in equal measure. "You have no proof—at least nothing that can be used in court."

Savage laughed, and the sound burrowed a cold coil of dread in the executive's stomach. "You forgot the file," he responded. "You know—the one you inadvertently left in your office?"

"Fuck."

"Don't ever underestimate me, Carlson. I know everything there is to know about you—like how your fireteams were destroyed when you sent them against Anderson and how no one out there is willing to sign on to replace them. I know who they were and where they came from. Oh yes, we tracked every last one of those sonsofbitches so I could be sure they paid for what they did. Now, it's your turn."

Savage crouched beside him and despite his suffering and his fear, he could do nothing but stare at the calm, unassuming green eyes of the man who held his life in his hands.

"The FBI has all they need to prosecute you and put you away for a long time. But don't think I'll forget about you. If you want me to stay away, you'll forget everything about me when they question you. And, should you ever be tempted to make a comeback against me or my employers, remember this." His attacker patted his cheek, then made a face when he felt the cold sweat that now sheened his skin. "Remember me. And remember the lengths that I will go to and that I can reach you wherever you are, even in jail. Do not push me."

He straightened and tucked the pistol into the holster under his arm, then retrieved the glass he'd used, shook the last few drops out, and slipped it in his pocket. "Your escorts should arrive soon. Enjoy your extended jailcation."

Without a backward glance, he strolled out of the plane.

"Fuck," Carlson snapped. He'd been outplayed. He had no doubt that his assailant had covered his tracks. Even if he'd left the gun, it wouldn't have traced back to him. How the hell had he been so blindsided?

He would have time to think about the answer, Carlson realized, as the shrill wail of sirens intruded through his rampant thoughts. Too much time, given what that fucking file had contained.

CHAPTER THIRTY-FOUR

Jeremiah sighed and shifted as unobtrusively as he could to ease his stiffness. He had been running and gunning during the past two weeks and had risked his life and put himself in the middle of a corporate battle that he really had no place being involved in. He had lived a dangerous life ever since he'd started his so-called new beginning as Jeremiah Savage.

Which made it all the more annoying that he would probably die of boredom in a conference room while a group of lawyers went over all the legal ramifications that resulted when one of the former CEOs resigned their shares from a company due to, quote, "personal issues."

He'd smirked when they'd said that. Anja had told him that an FBI team had been brought onto the plane to stabilize Carlson for transport, and he'd been moved directly to a high-security medical facility. His condition was reported to be stable, which meant he'd be able to stand trial. He knew that he'd enjoyed his meeting with the executive a little too much, but the results were what mattered, right? He was off their backs for good—hopefully, anyway—and now, they continue to run the operation of…well, of whatever it was that Monroe and Anderson wanted for Pegasus, without anyone to interfere.

He hadn't shared the specifics of what happened on that jet. All they knew was that he'd threatened and intimidated the man enough that he'd surrendered all his shares in the company for sale. He would be paid for them based on their sale value, which was currently an ongoing process.

The details on that weren't exactly clear, at least not to him. They talked numbers and percentages that mostly went over his head if he was completely honest. He was only there for the part of the meeting that would follow after the lawyers left the room. While the legal team was bound by all kinds of attorney-client privileges, that didn't change the fact that the fewer people who knew about his role in all this, the better. For the record, he was merely a security consultant who was there to help restructure the personnel who would join them in the building.

He liked that—security consultant. He could start a business and be a private eye with a drinking problem and an obsession with fedoras. He'd always been a fan of Humphrey Bogart and his hunt for the Maltese Falcon. Of course, what was displayed wasn't the reality of the private eye business, especially these days, but that didn't alter the fact that it was an interesting line of work.

Plus, he knew he looked good in a fedora.

He leaned back in his seat as most of the people left, engrossed in conversation. The day was winding down in Philly, and most of those involved would head home to enjoy the weekend with their families. A couple of folks would burn the midnight oil in the building, but for the most part, they had the place to themselves.

Jeremiah, Jessica, Anderson, and Monroe sat around the table and Anja joined them over the speakers.

"Well," Monroe said as the room fell silent for the first time in what felt like forever. "This has been a long couple of weeks for everyone here. We're under no illusions that it's over. What we want to do with this company won't be accomplished without a lot of obstacles. However, I do think we can safely say that this has been a successful first step on a very long road."

He could agree with that, although he didn't know what it was about this woman that made him curious. A PhD suffix at the end of her name explained why everyone called her Doctor Monroe and told him that much of her life had been spent in the sacred halls of academia. Then, she became the specialist who had survived the most hours in the Zoo of all time. There had to be something wrong with her by that standard alone.

Jeremiah shifted uncomfortably in his seat. It had been only three days since he'd walked away from Anderson's country house. His ribs still bothered him, and the stitches in his arm itched the way they did when the wound was on the way toward healing. He had to resist the urge to scratch, though. It wouldn't do to open anything and stain the expensive suit Pegasus had shelled out for him so that he wouldn't stand out in this meeting.

That meant any more than he already did, of course. He didn't look like any of the law and economy buffs who had been in the room before. Anyone with even a smidgeon of observational skill could tell that he looked a lot more like Anderson than any of them.

"Do you have anything you'd like to add to this conversation, Savage?" Monroe asked and focused on him.

The operative blinked and realized that he'd let his concentration slip. He peered at the other three people in the room with him. "How does Dr. Coleman's situation look at the moment?" he asked and raised the topic that had been on his mind up to cover the fact that he hadn't paid attention.

"Well, we'll have her make her deposition on what Carlson was up to in that facility of his," she said and adjusted her glasses to look at the papers on the table in front of her. "But it doesn't seem like the Pentagon will push for an investigation until he has completed his recovery. Until then, all we can do is make sure that all our ducks are in a row and keep an eye on what he's doing while he's incarcerated."

He nodded. "In that case, I have nothing else to add."

"Excellent." She smiled and fixed him with a frank and open gaze. "Your work with us has been invaluable in the success we've enjoyed thus far, but I don't think it's over yet. We would like to keep you on retainer for future work."

"I don't have anywhere else to be. Literally." He shrugged to make that truth seem unimportant.

"Well, your check will be mailed to your apartment." Monroe packed the papers into a file. "As well as a little extra to secure your retainer. If there's nothing else?"

He shook his head and eased himself out of his seat with a soft grunt.

"Then this meeting is adjourned," she said.

"Yeah, yeah, I have places to be on this end," Anja added before she signed off. Jeremiah couldn't help a small smile as he moved away from the table and made sure to shake Anderson and Monroe's hands before he left the conference room.

It still seemed odd that he had broken into this place ten or so days before and now, he walked around like he actually worked here.

He did work there now, right? That was what he understood being on retainer to mean. They wouldn't give him an office or a cubicle or anything, but he did report to his bosses—or benevolent overlords—in this building, and that meant he worked there.

That apartment of his was a nice little place and certainly better than the motel rooms he'd had to endure since he'd left the hospital. Still, the one-room, one-bathroom unit didn't really feel like home. It was a place to crash and store his things but not much else.

Jessica joined him as the elevator dinged to announce its arrival. They stepped in without saying a word and spent most of the ride to the ground floor in silence.

"What do you think of Dr. Monroe?" she asked as the numbers on the display wound down to single digits.

"Anderson gave me her file before the meeting today," he replied honestly, careful with his words. "Apparently, she's something of a force to be reckoned with whom Carlson has been after for a while. But I don't know… There's something about her that's a little…"

"Familiar?" Jessica asked with a grin as his voice trailed off.

He tilted his head from side to side as the doors opened at the ground floor and the two of them made their way through the lobby. "Yeah, I suppose familiar works. It doesn't sound quite right, but it'll do until I think of something better."

She nodded as they stepped outside into the rapidly cooling evening air of the city of Philadelphia. "Well, I'm glad that you made it out of everything alive and…more or less in one piece."

His chuckle was a little dark. "I don't really feel like I'm in one piece, but I'll take it."

They stood outside the Pegasus building for a moment, the silence comfortable between them.

"So," he said and broke it before it became awkward. "Do you feel like having that conversation now?"

"Here?" She looked around at the very public place where they stood. "Definitely not. And certainly not sober. Would you care to join me for a drink?"

Jeremiah smirked and raised his hand to hail a taxi. "Sure, I can go for a drink."

AUTHOR NOTES - MICHAEL ANDERLE

OCTOBER 8, 2019

ARRRRGGGGGHHHHH!

(Before I explain my screaming, THANK YOU for reading this book!)

So, the book you have right now is the ORIGINAL book 01 of the Savage Series. It was released as a two-book, book 01 originally (it was supposed to be 3 book, book 1 but book 03 was taking too long so we released only the first two in the first book.)

Confused yet?

You see, normally we release books 01, 02 and then 03 before we wait a bit and then release the omnibus (many of the books together.)

For Savages, we published books 01 and 02 together as book 01, then book 03 as book 02.

It was, shall we say, *a bit of a mess.*

So, it came time to split them up into their original books, but now we had yet another problem...

Book 03 was too short.

<SIGH!>

So, add another 40,000 words (almost another whole 'novel' by SFWA standards) into (new) book 03) and Bob's your uncle, right?

Well, we hope so!

Additional covers, new author notes, new words in the story and new releases to get these books back out there. Never say that publishing is a clean profession – it sometimes gets really, really messy as we try to navigate this new publishing paradigm.

Also, there are many readers (perhaps you) who do not WANT large (180,000+) word books and will appreciate them back at their shorter size.

I am assuming this is your first time to read this book, if so WOOT and WAHOO and YIPPEE! (Ok, that last one was a mistake.)

I appreciate you taking the time to read our stories and hope you delve deeper into the ZOO Universe.

There's nothing there to kill you...

Or is there?

Could the nations of the world be doing something in the Sahara we aren't aware of... yet?

Ad Aeternitatem,

Michael Anderle

OTHER ZOO BOOKS

BIRTH OF HEAVY METAL

He Was Not Prepared (1)

She Is His Witness (2)

Backstabbing Little Assets (3)

Blood Of My Enemies (4)

APOCALYPSE PAUSED

Fight for Life and Death (1)

Get Rich or Die Trying (2)

Big Assed Global Kegger (3)

Ambassadors and Scorpions (4)

Nightmares From Hell (5)

Calm Before The Storm (6)

One Crazy Pilot (7)

One Crazy Rescue (8)

One Crazy Machine (9)

SOLDIERS OF FAME AND FORTUNE

Nobody's Fool (1)

Nobody Lives Forever (2)

Nobody Drinks That Much (3)

Nobody Remembers But Us (4)

Ghost Walking (5)

Ghost Talking (6)

Ghost Brawling (7)

Ghost Stalking (8)

Ghost Resurrection (9)

Ghost Adaptation (10)

Ghost Redemption (11)

Ghost Revolution (12)

TEAM SAVAGE

Kill or Be Killed (1)

Dead or Alive (2)

Vengeance or Death (3)

THE BOHICA CHRONICLES

Reprobates (1)

Degenerates (2)

Redeemables (3)

Thor (4)

BOOKS WRITTEN AS MICHAEL ANDERLE

For a complete list of books by Michael Anderle, please visit:

www.lmbpn.com/ma-books/

www.ingramcontent.com/pod-product-compliance
Lightning Source LLC
Chambersburg PA
CBHW020236110726
47898CB00004B/1279

9781642024982